William E. Kirchhoff

Heavy Air

ISBN: 061546226X
ISBN-13: 9780615462264

Table of Contents

CHAPTER ONE 1
CHAPTER TWO 13
CHAPTER THREE 21
CHAPTER FOUR 27
CHAPTER FIVE 33
CHAPTER SIX 41
CHAPTER SEVEN 49
CHAPTER EIGHT 63
CHAPTER NINE 77
CHAPTER TEN 89
CHAPTER ELEVEN 95
CHAPTER TWELVE 105
CHAPTER THIRTEEN 111
CHAPTER FOURTEERN 117
CHAPTER FIFTEEN 121
CHAPTER SIXTEEN 125
CHAPTER SEVENTEEN 129
CHAPTER EIGHTEEN 137
CHAPTER NINETEEN 147
CHAPTER TWENTY 153
CHAPTER TWENTY-ONE 155
CHAPTER TWENTY-TWO 161
CHAPTER TWENTY-THREE 173
CHAPTER TWENTY-FOUR 181
CHAPTER TWENTY-FIVE 185
CHAPTER TWENTY-SIX 189
CHAPTER TWENTY-SEVEN 197
CHAPTER TWENTY-EIGHT 205
CHAPTER TWENTY-NINE 217
CHAPTER THIRTY 229
CHAPTER THIRTY-ONE 239

Heavy Air

CHAPTER THIRTY-TWO 249
CHAPTER THIRTY-THREE 261
CHAPTER THIRTY-FOUR 267
CHAPTER THIRTY-FIVE 275
CHAPTER THIRTY-SIX 283
CHAPTER THIRTY-SEVEN 289
CHAPTER THIRTY-EIGHT 297
CHAPTER THIRTY-NINE 303
CHAPTER FORTY 311
CHAPTER FORTY-ONE 325

CHAPTER ONE

BOGOTA, COLOMBIA 2000

The hot wind stream eddied as Jack bumblebee'd the private helicopter across the airfield located on the western outskirts of Bogota. After resigning his military commission, he used the flying skills the Army gave him. Now he was a contract pilot for a helicopter service in Bogota. "*Help me, Rhonda. Help, help me, Rhonda,*" the thumping song of the Beach Boys' drifted in and out of his thoughts, competing with the scores of details a helicopter pilot must do to safely land the machine.

Whisperin' Jack Dalton swung the tail of the mechanical bird around hard and let it settle gently down. Other pilots, air traffic controllers and anyone dialed to his radio frequency could easily recognize his distinctive rasping voice; the consequence of a throat wound. Harry, the Blue-Headed parrot clamped to a make-shift perch suspended from the cabin ceiling squawked, "*Beer! Beer!*" as soon as he reached over and shut the helicopter's engine down. The parrot excitedly jumped off the perch and settled on the pilot's shoulder, looking around with regal arrogance. He was a gift to Jack by one of the founders of the United Self-Defense Forces of Colombia, after flying the paramilitary leader's injured young son to a Venezuelan surgeon. The bird had been hand-fed and raised by an old farmer who cared for the militia commander's prize parrots. The rich blue coloration of its head was that of a mature cock. Devoted to Jack like a faithful guard dog, Harry was a bird with a lot of attitude. He accompanied Jack on every flight.

Swinging down from the hot cockpit after the flight over the green swarm of jungle and mountains from Quipama with an ease of an experienced aviator, Jack wiped his faded denim sleeve across his forehead. He pulled off his thin flight gloves, exposing the splotchy white and pink flesh on the back of his left

1

hand. Under his shirt a trail of scars ran up to the biceps like a miniature lava flow. The pale white scars contrasted with the rest of Jack's deeply tanned skin. Tender reminders of his accident in the Gulf War.

A dusty late model Ford 150 with a camper cover bounced across the dirt road from the hangar area. The driver, a mule of a man with a sunburned face and wing nuts for ears stopped the truck. Jack gave the mechanic a thumbs up to signal the chopper was mechanically okay. The man in coveralls countered with a raised index finger. Jack flashed two fingers toward the sky. The meet-you-for-a-drink sign.

An imposing, mustached emerald dealer with a stainless steel Glock in his hand, and a guard armed with a nasty looking automatic rifle, stepped down cautiously from the helicopter on to the tarmac. Jack had flown the dealer and his muscled assistant in from an emerald processing plant in the hills. Without a word his passengers awaited a heavy Mercedes with tinted windows as it left the shade of a faded pink building that housed electrical generating equipment. It cruised up slowly to the dealer and his guard. Jack watched as his passenger got in the car and drove away. Hairs on his neck prickled and not just from sunburn. Heat waves boogied in the heavy Colombian air, diesel exhaust and oily dust slammed his senses.

"Harry," said Jack in the soft raspy voice of a battlefield tracheotomy survivor, "let's g…o get a…"

"Beer! Beer!" squawked Harry as he playfully tugged at Jack's sunglasses with his dangerous curved beak. The subtle hues and iridescence of the parrot's plumage shimmered in the setting tropical sun like one of Elvis' rhinestone capes.

He waved at a cab driver who sat on the ground, shaded from the sun by his ancient vehicle, which had began life as a Chevy sedan; now a hulk with wired up doors and a nasty smell. The cabby stood and opened the rear door with some difficulty.

A frail little girl of six years, appeared as she always did when Jack landed. She carried a small yellow flower in her tiny hand; his good luck girl. She lived in poverty with a dozen other brothers and sisters, in a tiny shack with a tin roof. For reasons Jack didn't understand, she had one day showed up with her flower offering. She melted his heart and tormented his sense of good. He worried about her and gave her a silver dollar every day she met him. He knew she turned it over to her mother but so what. He tried.

He stroked the top of her head, bent down and held out five silver dollar pieces between his thumb and index finger.

"Adios niña," he rasped, trying to smile. The child reached out for the money with her two tiny hands. She separated four of the dollars and thrust them back at him. Still kneeling, he shook his head "no," and clamped his hand around her tiny fist.

"You keep," he lectured softly. With a tightening in his throat, he kissed her gritty forehead, stood up and turned toward the cab with wet eyes. He thought of all the kids who would succumb to the tragedy of Bogota's wretched underbelly of life. Flying for so many years in the lower Americas caused him to develop a special concern for the little ones destined to a hellish existence amid crime, greed, corruption, damned by the accident of birth.

Jack wasn't much for talk. But, to the little ones, the frail children of the Third World shit holes he always seemed to be working in, Jack was a magnet. They seemed to sense the natural compassion of the tall American pilot who always gave them something with a smile and often a thin tear in the corner of his eye. His silver dollars sometimes made the difference between living and dying.

Parrot on his shoulder, Jack bent his lean upper body and crawled inside the ugly-smelling cab. The floor was littered with soft drink cans, a yellowing newspaper and a rag that was once a hotel towel. It had a warm, fetid smell, like the inside of a tin doghouse in the Texas sun. He settled his worn brown Wellington boots on the floorboard, pushing aside the debris. Harry jumped from Jack's shoulder to the top of the front seat back, fluttering his wings to gain balance as he dug his claws through the seat cover.

"A good flight, Señor Jack?"

"It was an *okay* flight." he replied, the constant rasping burr in his voice. It was his last flight. Filled with a tinge of melancholy, he found it difficult to articulate his thoughts.

"Es bueno?" questioned the cabbie in the tired-sounding voice. He drove as he spoke, slowly with the caution of an old man.

"Every flight you walk away from is okay," Jack said with a hearty laugh. Then his mind flicked back to the flaming accident that left his arm and hand scarred. Harry stared out the window as the driver threaded the car down the narrow streets. The heat dissipated slightly through the open windows of the cab. The sweat on Jack's face dried slowly as he leaned his head back and focused on the near fatal incident in the Gulf that gnawed at his gut every time he lifted a helicopter into the air.

It was his sixty-third combat mission. Sometimes he flew three in a single day. Jack began his career as an infantry officer. Eventually selected for flight school, he qualified as a helicopter pilot and was recently promoted to the rank of major. A West Pointer, everybody knew Dalton had the makings of a combat leader. He had the right stuff, the calm I'm-in-charge demeanor required to get things done under combat stress. But the desert crash changed everything for Jack and sent him on a course of life with a separate reality, out of sync with the rest of the world.

The hot, thin air of the hard sand dunes provided for less than normal lift. Jack and his copilot, a thin, younger gun, had slammed the vibrating medivac Huey down on a postage-size clearing to rescue a squad of shot-up special operations troops that were cut off from their mother unit. The copilot in the right side seat had been flying with him for just over three months. Already they were close friends. It was the strong kind of I'll-risk-my-life-for-you friendship that bonded warriors together since the world's first battle of disciplined armies. The moment Jack feathered the bird down on the blowing sand, the landing zone filled with a tangle of fear, cursing, web gear, blood and the racket of men shooting off complete clips of ammo. Two soldiers dragged a gut-shot trooper by the arms into the right door as enemy rounds shattered the Plexiglas windshield and punched neat holes in the walls of the overloaded helicopter.

"I've got it!" yelled the normally reticent Major Dalton, jerking the controls free from the copilot. Fear made the copilot automatically squeeze on his set of the dual controls. Jack made one attempt to get over the rocky outcrop in front of him, but the overloaded ship wouldn't lift. He spun the lugging machine around. The din in the back of the copter was maddening. The copilot started to unstrap his harness to get out of the overloaded aircraft. A wounded special ops soldier screamed insanely, others fired their automatic weapons out the side doors. The chopper swung and crawled in a weak hover.

Sweat soaked his dirty flight suit as Jack fought to get the overloaded machine in the air. Getting some low-ground-effect hover, he began to circle the chopper which flayed about like a giant out-of-control scythe. The panicked copilot thought Jack had been shot and reflexively grabbed at the controls.

"I've got it!" shouted Jack as he jerked at the control sticks and twisted the wounded steel bird into a tight accelerating circle that gave him transitional lift. He pointed the nose of the copter toward a gap between the trees and punched the overloaded machine out with sheer will. Suddenly the copilot flopped forward with bone matter and grey stuff splattered against the inside of his helmet's face shield. He had taken a .50 caliber round as large as a big man's thumb, upwards through the cheek.

Jack never heard the explosion. After nursing the crippled aircraft back to the base with his torn and moaning cargo, he yelled into the helmet mike for the medics, and set the Huey down on the sandy pad soaked with motor oil. A long buried mortar round exploded under the weight of the heavy bird. The helicopter's avgas ignited with a soft whump and turned the helicopter into a steel coffin covered with liquid fire. The blast picked him up, blew off his helmet and tossed him out of the cockpit, twenty feet against the corner of a sand-bagged revetment. Blood and dirty sand covered his face and chest. He felt himself bleeding out where a piece of shrapnel had pierced his neck. The burning avgas that splashed on his sleeve, cooked through the Nomex and seared the skin. The raging fire dissolved the mortally wounded copilot's face into something that looked like boiling soup. The screaming stopped as the aircraft became a hellish cauldron.

Mindless panic swept through the desert compound as crews dove into bunkers, believing they were under heavy ground attack. The air was ripe with smoke, fear and avgas. But the explosion came from a round that had been lobbed into the compound in an earlier attack. It laid buried in a grave of soft earth like a time bomb and exploded when the helicopter's landing gear touched hard on it.

Strong arms lifted Jack off the ground and onto a faded-green, canvas field stretcher. A medic with a pushed-in face and a pasty complexion pinched the spurting carotid artery shut and jabbed a plasma bottle in his arm. Jack sucked in air, making a tinny sound, like cold wind rattling against a screen.

Another medic, a black kid with a do-rag wrapped around his head, crawled up to Jack and rolled him from his side to his back. His face was going blue from cyanosis and he jerked his head from one side to the other in a frantic, wild-eyed search for air. The medic probed for the thyroid cartilage, then slid his hand down to the cricoids cartilage and inserted the point of his K-bar knife between the cartilage rings. The heavy knife punctured Jack's windpipe vertically with a mushy crunch as his head jerked and thrashed. The poorly placed blade ruptured the cricoids cartilage and nicked the pleura. The medic fumbled and dug into his shirt pocket until he found the cutoff shell casing he carried for this purpose. Jamming the shell casing into the slit in Jack's neck caused the blood to gush out of his neck, propelled by the air trapped in his lungs. The foaming blood spewed with a force that splattered across the face and chest of the exhausted medic. Sweet air was sucked across his powder-burned skin into his searing lungs. Jack's thrashing calmed as he faded in and out of consciousness. His skin was clammy and his respiration bad. A morphine shot cloaked him in nothingness.

Four men picked up the stretcher and, in a jolting run, carried Major Dalton to the medical evacuation helicopter that had finally arrived. At the in-country evacuation hospital, the air thick with stink; triage surgeons and nurses hovered over him. They cut away the remaining scraps of his green Nomex flight suit and sandblasted boots turned crusty brown from blood. The deep sleep of the anesthesia began to ripple through him, erasing the terrible pain.

6

The MASH team stabilized his wounds. Then they loaded him on an Air Force plane that transported him to a military hospital in Texas where an inelegant red mass of a building would be his home for the next six months, while his burn wounds were treated.

Ten minutes later the cab stopped in front of the White Rhino, Bogota's combination hotel, exotic bar and specialty brothel. A wide, three-story building with a large veranda, the teakwood building had been built sometime in the 1930s. It catered to a strange array of people: arms dealers, con artists, mercenaries, Eurasian whores, cartel soldiers, drug-runners and pilots. It was a "take-it-or-leave-it" place with no apologies. When Jack signed on to ferry machinery with a contract air service he was sent to Bogota where helicopters were needed in the Colombian jungle.

Jack paid the driver with U.S. dollars and walked up the de-caying stone steps into the hotel. As he picked up his mail at the desk, the albino dwarf who stood on a box, winked a nod at him and challenged, "You are not really leaving us tomorrow, my friend, are you?"

Smiling at the little man whom he had befriended, Jack laughed. "You bet I am. But I'll probably be back. This place grows on you." Saying goodbye to people he liked had always been hard for Jack. In his business, many of those to whom you said your goodbyes would shortly disappear into some crevice in the Third World. "I truly hope so," said the miniature human with a French accent. He liked the tall friendly American pilot who treated him with the respect and dignity few short people received.

Jack walked up the two flights of steps to his third floor suite. The kitchen, bar and dining room occupied the first floor. The brothel took up the second level, and the third floor consisted of hotel rooms for people like Jack. Third World people. Not tour-ists. His suite was just two sleeping rooms connected by a door. In one room was his bed. The other room he used to store his gear and house Harry's perch. Like most contract pilots flying in foreign countries he paid rent by the week, expecting to move to another base with a couple of days notice, or be dead. The White Rhino had been his place of residence for nearly a year now.

Out of habit he surveyed his surroundings before stepping out of his leather boots and placed them upside down over the chair back. There were too many crawling creatures not be cautious, a scorpion bite in the morning was a bad way to start the day. A man of few possessions, his two room suite contained a desk with a laptop, a disc player and his collection of sixties music, a bird perch made of polished driftwood, some books and two large, battered metal trunks. On the bed the maid had placed a pair of freshly laundered cotton pants, a checkered cotton shirt and a change of underwear. On the desk was a letter from a publishing house.

After the rigid life as a West Point Cadet, he was able to let out his inhibitions as a combat soldier. In this free-wheeling environment the lid came off his personality and libido. He was like a grenade with its pin missing. No painful self-analysis, and he didn't auger in with self-reproach. He just did what he wanted to do, discovering that he got a thrill balancing on life's fault-line. The war scene was his milieu; the pungent smell of singed oil, hot gun ships chucking and bucking in the sky, roaring armored personnel carriers and tanks on the dust belching roads, water that tasted like piss, hooch maids and whores who giggled and laughed with him. He was fascinated by the action and consequences of war in Sudan, the Gulf and the other far away lands the Army sent him. He was a war lover and action junkie, simple as that. An ardent student of the ancient Chinese general-philosopher, Sun Tzu, Jack believed in the coldness of complete objectivity, always including himself in its cutting assessment of the real situation.

War was wild and dangerous, full of death and decay. Its choreography was strange yet fascinating. A grand game where the winners got to live. Now, flying in places like Colombia for private parties, was as close he could get to real action. Medically discharged from the Army after his wounds had healed he signed on to work for the Army as a civilian pilot. He heeded the gnawing feeling that a routine job wouldn't work for him. That's when he began to realize that he had a deepening dark place in his soldier's mind.

"Sounds to me like you might have what we medical types call the Counter Phobic Syndrome." The words still echoed in his memory. He could still remember the distinguished gray-haired female psychiatrist and the stale air of her office that gripped him. Sure, he told the shrink, that before the crash, the unrelenting pressure of flying felt like a heavy weight. That he was having hallucinations and couldn't sleep. That he had been strung tight during the day, feeling guilty because there were times he couldn't land the helicopter and extract the grunts. People had died because he couldn't get his steel bird down through the machine gun fire. But nobody told him that with the war winding down and the need for chopper pilots fading that the Army was discharging pilots for CPS. Pilots exhibiting the Counter Phobic Syndrome, the psychological drive that causes them to seek the edge; the thing that made them fly their machines through a wall of enemy fire, what made them so good at their jobs, were no longer needed. The last thing he remembered was the woman psychiatrist telling him was that he was running on fumes. And a week later he was discharged after the Army had stripped his emotional gears.

He was not completely abandoned, the Army placed him in a job teaching pilot recruits. They sent him to Fort Wolters, Texas as a civilian Instructor Pilot. There, in the hot, windy wastelands south of Fort Worth he taught young men to fly in the training helicopters. He took the job seriously. When he was hovering in the aircraft, really floating, he felt free of life's burdens. He approached the job with an almost religious commitment. He had to do everything he could to train his students for the day when they would be flying overloaded choppers with a cargo of wounded grunts screaming, and hydraulic fluid spewing from the thick rubber lines that connected the controls to the whirling blades of the aircraft. Their final graduation would be on the battlefield just as his had been. This was a pass and no-fail grade.

After his first class graduated, whatever was holding him together vanished, and he lost interest in what he was doing. Sleep escaped him and he drank to make the darkness cover his memories. Then, when he went out to the flight line in the early morning after heavy drinking, his head would feel as though feverish snakes had crawled through his ears. He was depressed and experienced hyperventilation at times when he would demonstrate certain flying techniques to his students. Showing a student how to hover low to the ground in a strong wind he forgot where he was, and started to feel the terror of a combat pilot waiting for his ship to load on a hot LZ.

In his mind he was always there, *really there*, in the helicopter, exposed to the large caliber rounds as he sat in the aircraft's cockpit surrounded by fragile plastic. You couldn't do anything except wait as your gut tightened and your bowels turned to loose jelly. You were a fucking pop-up target in a shooting gallery, where you escaped the enemy's bullets based on landing a foot one way or the other in either direction, accidentally turning your head a millimeter, or what kind of eyesight shooters had when they pulled the triggers of their rifles. It was then Jack started to believe that what made difference between pilots who died and pilots who survived; between living, wounded horribly or just getting nicked, was not training, but dumb fucking luck.

That was years ago. Now, like the compulsive gambler who finally understands he can never win, Jack knew he had to quit contract flying. He had to get out of the ever-so-risky business. A letter from his publisher had changed the course of his destiny, his book would be published. His book, *Jungle Nights*, was a short account of his father's life as a company commander in Vietnam. Using a collection of photos taken by his father during his tour in Vietnam, and the letters he had so dutifully penned to Jack's mother, Jack was able to overlay his combat experience on that of his father. On a chance, he had mailed it to a military publishing house and it was accepted.

The deal required Jack to agree to a book signing tour. Blown away with the possibility of doing something other that flying, Jack jumped at the opportunity. He had already outlined his thoughts for a second book.

An hour later, after a shower in tepid water, he packed his few pairs of chino pants, cotton shirts, his CDs, books and flip-flops. He was ready to leave Bogota for New Orleans in the morning. All that remained for him to do was to pick up his final paycheck.

CHAPTER TWO

BOGOTA, COLOMBIA 2000

With Harry marching behind him like a small green defiant soldier, Jack entered the large room that served as the dining room, bar and stage. It smelled of tobacco, cooked rice and the musky odor of sex. The new mirror that ran the length of the wall behind the bar was polished brass, not the usual glass. The mirror was Jack's contribution to the White Rhino's decor. Jack had a deep, hard guy temper which he tried to control by walking away from potential fights with a smile that masked a fury few could understand. But sometimes his temper could slip its leash like an attack dog.

One day after standing down from a flying job shortly after he arrived in Bogota, Jack found himself looking into the then glass mirror at Harry. In front of Harry was the brass thimble that he always drank from. Harry was pecking away at the golden liquid with preened up feathers. Back and forth his beaked head would pivot, spritzing beer in a small arch. Some of the beer fell on the silk shirt of a man sitting on a stool away from the bird. Irritated with the beer on his sleeve, and trying to impress the Eurasian whore he was entertaining, the man reached out and swatted Harry off his stool. As the bird flopped and fluttered on the floor, something hot pierced Jack's brain. Spilling his drink as he stood, his teeth clenched, Jack hammered the man three times in the face with a right, followed by two jolting lefts. Before he could get control of himself, Jack twisted the man's wrist hard, jerking his arm up behind him. The whore screamed and bounced off the stool looking for a way out of danger. No stranger to bar fights, she was willing to lose a customer if she could save her make-up and trolling clothes. Jack fast-walked the puking face into the contorted reflection in the mirror. Red shards clattered to the floor. A chunk of facial meat seemed glued to the broken mirror as Jack slammed the melon-like head into the jagged surface. He stopped when Big Jules jerked him away from the bleeding man who was crying in a squeaky voice.

"Beer, Beer!" yelped Harry.

"You broke my mirror, fuck your mother," laughed Big Jules.

"This broke your mirror." Jack pointed to the bloodied man being loaded into a dirty cab. The whore was long gone.

"How much?" asked Jack, breathing hard.

Big Jules was thoughtful, this was not the first time the mirror had succumbed to a bar fight.

"Get the best. I'm buying." He hoisted Harry to his shoulder and stood for a round at the bar, the patrons still stunned by the action.

A huge brass mirror arrived some weeks later. It was Jack's monument and Jules was proud of his own genius. Those who drank at the bar came to know that the parrot that drank beer from a thimble was not to be toyed with. The story quickly became a legend.

The sepia toned image in the brass mirror served to deepen Jack's tanned, not-quite-handsome face, soft grey eyes flecked with blue and worry lines that ran like tiny streams across his forehead. He sat down at an empty table and watched the room fill up with mainly male patrons for the traditional Friday evening show. Out of the pocket of his shirt he took the small, bronze thimble he had bought for Harry in Bangkok and set it on the table. The bird fluttered up and balanced on the back of a chair. As the barmaid approached he squawked, "Beer! Beer!" Jack flirted with the fat woman as he always did when she served him. She wiped the table clean as she took his order.

The hotel was run by Big Jules, whom he could call friend, an alcoholic French National who claimed he had deserted the Foreign Legion. Jules was well over six feet, exceptionally jolly with a tight gut; he boasted of having only one testicle. He claimed the other one had been shot off in Ethiopia but his performance was in no way diminished. Instead of being some sort of handicap, the one-nut Jules became a challenge for women who knew

of his condition. There was always a lady who wanted the experience. His knobby head, that seemed to be an extension of his
thick shoulders, stayed flecked with razor nicks from a daily inept
shave by one of his whores. A handlebar moustache and thick
monocle in his empty left eye socket gave him a fearsome look.

At any time of the day or night, clientele could be found loung-
ing in the eclectic assortment of heavy wooden chairs, drinking or
smoking marijuana. Upstairs, on the second floor, was the brothel
that the flyers called the Runway. Operated by Madame Margo,
a beautiful, fortyish Frenchwoman with billowing red hair and a
lush body just shortly past her prime. The specialty of the house
was world class fellatio.

At the White Rhino a blow job was an art form; always a work
in progress. Lacking any inhibitions, and completely proud of her
talented stable, Madame Margo would be putting on a performance contest in a few minutes using the patrons as contestants.
The crowd was always hooting and pounding on the ancient
wooden tables. The tables in the area where Jack and Harry sat
were off limits to the girls. Serious business, anything from making arms delivery payments to planning an execution took place
in the confines of these corner tables where the whores were
required to keep their distance.

"Well, how was your flight, Whisperin' Jack?" inquired a tall
man sporting a straw cowboy hat and a half-smoked Camel. Hal
Fawcett, Jack's flying boss was one of the few men who called
Jack, by his nick name, Whisperin'. He jerked back a heavy chair
and sat his big ass down. He pulled off his hat, revealing a streak of
white hair down the middle of his head that made him resemble
an aging cartoon skunk smoking a cigarette. "Still whispering; It's
my last one," said Jack with a smile acknowledging his throat with
the universal neck slicing gesture. He pulled on a cold bottle of
Mamba beer the waitress had set in front of him. He quit drinking hard stuff months ago, after an excruciating hangover caused
him to drop a chopper on the deck so hard a skid rail split. More
gin than tonics, cooled with thick chips of ice, washed away the
flaming nightmares, but delivered the snakes and shakes in the

morning. His enemies, the hard stuff, were starting to affect his reflexes so he put the brakes on sucking up the high-octane stuff. Now he, like Harry, stuck to beer; Mamba was their favorite.

"Any problems?"

"No," said Jack with a wry smile. Fawcett was one of those guys who always worried, it was his mission. Colombia's emerald trade, where emeralds were sometimes worth fifty times as much as cocaine, was cause for worry for a man whose helicopter was used to move the stones from the mining town of Quipama.

Harry drank his beer from the thimble. Like the Mafioso lords, Harry insisted on "wetting his beak" each time there was an opportunity to do so at someone else's expense.

"Why quit now. It's the best paying one you've ever had for doing legal work," chided Fawcett. The hot ash on his cigarette fell as he pulled an envelope from his pants pocket and handed it to Jack saying, "Here's your bonus pay." His monthly pay was ten thousand dollars. The fifteen percent bonus he received was for lasting on the job one full year. Jack counted the money, put it in his shirt pocket and buttoned the flap.

"Thanks. Find a replacement for me yet?"

"Yeah. A guy who was flying for an oil company. Larry Brecker. Know him?"

"No. But this is an easy job so long as nobody starts a firefight while the bird is on the pad in Q town."

"Did you ever think you'd make ten thousand a month hauling greenies out of the jungle?" asked Fawcett, referencing the emeralds that kept them all in business.

Jack pulled hard on the cold beer. "Most of my flying jobs didn't make sense to me. I did it for the money, and I'm just damn glad to be getting out of here alive. My theory is that a year of flying anywhere is pushing your luck."

"You'll be back," chuckled Fawcett, cleaving to the notion that pilots like Dalton flew somewhere other than stateside until they were too old to fly or died in the cockpit. Once a China Soldier, (the old-hands that worked as semi-mercenaries in Southeast

Asia and the Orient) always a China Soldier was Fawcett's opinion. Whisperin' Jack would be back. No question about it.

Fawcett waved to the little brown waitress who stood at attention by the bar. He ordered bloots. Fawcett had a thing for the unhatched baby chickens eaten raw In a bloody pulp, chased by a drink of beer with a spoonful of small clams. It pleased him that observers paled at his performance.

Fawcett looked at Jack with a wide grin and asked, "What kind of flying job are you going back to? Ferrying a bunch of fuck-faced tourists over the Grand Canyon? Isn't that pretty tame for an ex-Army Major and contract cowboy?"

Jack set his empty bottle on the table and Harry cackled, "Beer! Beer!" Then he turned his empty thimble over, signaling he wanted a refill.

"I'm done flying for now. Going to New Orleans," responded Jack with a thin smile.

"What for?"

"Can't tell." Jack could but just didn't want to explain to Fawcett that he was going there to do a book signing. If he did, then he'd have to talk about his book with Fawcett.

"Spook shit?" Fawcett believed Jack was going back to work for the Company.

"Could be," was Jack's lazy response. Pretending to be an author was spooky enough. At least he wouldn't get shot at in a bookstore. How dangerous would life as an author be?

Beaten back by Jack's noncommittal answers Fawcett ended the conversation saying, "You leave tomorrow, don't you?"

"Yep. That's why I needed my final payout today." The wailing of a Colombian violin interrupted their conversation, Madame Margo setting the mood. Her girls had been moving through the crowd selecting participants from the screaming and whooping men, bringing them willingly to the stage.

Trying to ignore the performance they had seen many times, Fawcett said, "You are one hell of a pilot. I hate to see you leave the business. Pilots like you are hard to come by. All the old hands are fading away. The young bucks never flew combat. Makes a big difference. You know how to reach me. Hear?"

Jack nodded in response as he studied the burn scars on the back of his hand. He'd seen too many ex-pilots with similar scars on their faces. Ugly men with melted skin that caused people to stare, or quickly look the other way. Maybe so, he thought in reaction to Fawcett's offer, but if I don't get out of the business I'll either be dead, a candidate for a horror show or become someone like Fawcett, an old-hand guy trying to eke out a living before the world retires him.

"Just remember, Jack, every time there is a fuckin' war the same crazy people always show up, don't we?"

"This is my last war."

"Want to sell the bird?" Harry whipped his head around, centering one of his blinkless eyes on Jack's as though he understood Fawcett's offer.

"No. Can't do it. Harry goes with me. Besides, you don't even know what brand of beer he likes," replied Jack with a wry smile. The parrot cut his tiny eyes back around to Fawcett and yammered, "Beer! Beer!" Jack filled up the thimble with Mamba beer and watched the show.

"How you going to get him through Customs?"

"I'll feed him a half a downer and stuff him in a carry-on bag."

"Sell him to me. I'll take good care of him," persisted Fawcett.

"We're family."

"Bullshit," laughed Fawcett.

Jack smiled as he poured some Mamba beer in the thimble for Harry.

Deep in thought he didn't notice his mechanic and friend approach. Boomer Smythe was a big block of a man. Ears like sails and a smile with teeth he could wedge a small cigar through, he was an ex-pat like Jack. He was thicker in the middle than when he first joined the Army during the Nam days. Calorie-laden mess hall food, beer and no exercise had added to his girth. But there was nothing flabby about his bulky body and the deceptive power of his arms and chest. Boomer was tough. A seasoned man with a very low threshold for bullshit. He could make most men wear their balls for earrings if provoked. Older and wiser with most of his whoring and some of his fighting behind him, Boomer ended up working for the same air outfit, back when Jack was flying the hard-to-maintain Bell 212 equipped with Pratt & Whitney twin-engines airlift in Angola via Zaire.

When the waitress served the men, Boomer growled, 'You'll be back."

Laughing, Jack said, "That's what Fawcett said."

"He's right."

"Not this time," predicted Jack. Then he asked, "How 'bout you? How much longer can you keep up with the pace?"

"I'm out in a year. I'm gettin' too old to fight. Hell, I can't even fuck without paying some whore a bonus."

"Here's to the next life," offered Jack as he lifted his glass of beer. Boomer toasted and Harry squawked, "Beer, Beer!"

CHAPTER THREE

NEW ORLEANS, 2001

After Bogota she lived with him until he convinced her he wasn't capable of loving her. She was a stunning Creole woman with deep roots in the plantation south. French blood flowing in her veins. She had a lavishly exotic and sensuous bearing. Bittersweet memories of her crowded his thoughts; her thick, coal-black hair. The champagne-soft smile, and eyes lit from a constant sexual fire.

Her name was Mariana. They met by chance when he was signing the book at The Big Easy book store, just off of Chartrus near the French Quarter. His book, not really the first novel he'd hoped for, was his compilation of his father's letters and photos sent to Jack's mother while he served in Vietnam. Jack sold the book rights too low and agreed to showing up at book stores to drum up sales. The book signing appointment in New Orleans was intended to be a two-day deal. A librarian, one street person and an out-of-work mime were the only browsers who showed any interest, until she showed up and asked him to sign her book.

Mariana, a Tulane University journalism graduate, was working as a newspaper editor from across the street and had seen the book in the window with his smiling, slightly puzzled face on the jacket.

They spent the evening watching people stumble down the "Nawlins" sidewalks with go-cups. It was a massive congestion of expensive cars, blue-black kids chewing pure sugar pralines, sweating pedestrians, blazing wet headlights and drunks lying on the park benches. Black teenagers danced in the street; in a bar, naked women humped and moaned in a pile of kinky pubic hair and fleshy breasts, while the audience from Iowa and Illinois screamed. A funeral for a dead musician was accompanied by sorrowful dirges and the shuffle and clap of the "second liners."

They sipped liquor coffee at Café' du Monde, across from Jackson Square, where centuries old mossy buildings dripped with fancy ironwork. They spoke of the bad war; the death of her father, and growing up alone; her own fight for personhood in a cruel world. Then the night at her place. It was a fancy shotgun rental overlooking the fish ponds, trails and gazebos of Audubon Park. It was the hungry coupling of a passionate woman and a driving man. Both held each other tightly in arms that ached until the early morning hours.

They ate in the ramshackle shrimp houses built from decayed cypress wood along Lake Pontchartrain and in the upscale restaurants that served the red-hot Creole cuisine, jambalaya, etoufee shrimp, and boiled crawfish that looked like bugs and tasted like heaven. Haitian art on Royal Street, and the soothing music at the Palm Court Jazz Café, drew them close. Zydeco spots, and the mixed music scene in the French Quarter were the noisy places they haunted in the smokey night. They listened to blues saxophonist Gary Brown at the 544 Club and hung around the Old Absinthe Bar. They listened to hotshot guitarist Byran Lee make sweet music that playfully contrasted with the younger brass bands of the Dirty Dozen, Rebirth and the Chosen Few.

Two weeks later they rented the cottage in Key West so he could work on his next book without the distractions of New Orleans. Mariana quit her job and happily followed him to the Keys. A year later, after too much whiskey, late night falling down drunks and no book, she left, cutting him hard and storming out of the cottage. The note on the aging refrigerator said it all. "Face up to it, Jack Dalton, you aren't a real writer. Your only book was about making war on a bunch of little yellow people in the jungle. It was your father's book about his experiences, you don't have another book in you! There's no love in you either."

Mariana had dug deep into his emotional wounds and came to understand the dark side of a troubled mind. One time she screamed at him with the energy of nuclear fission, "You have an unconscious death wish. There's an evil in you, a devil man who won't let you write anything good. He won't let you go."

In a quick spate of packing, recriminations, and door slam-ming she moved to San Diego and found a job writing for another newspaper.

His rent was paid for a month in advance, and that's how long he stayed lavishly, uncompromisingly drunk. His first real binge since quitting the hard stuff, when he almost crash landed in Bogota. He was a frequent visitor to the bars up and down the hot, humid streets of the Keys, which served the tourists and gay hookers. He would take Harry the parrot with him and pour blast-head boilermakers of raw, stinging whiskey and foaming glasses of cold draft beer that gave his gut juices a jump start to a volcano of acid. His all-day drinking would reduce his brain to the level of a mindless, nickel-and-dime boost artist. Once, he woke up in a small town drunk tank. The seatless toilet with crusted shit cling-ing to its side offered him a crooked smile; snoring drunks, cof-fee that tasted like bug juice and a floor stained with vomit, urine, cigarette butts and blood the color of iodine. His T-shirt and chino pants were flecked with blood from an unknown source. There were times he forgot to feed Harry.

Buzzing like a tuning fork in the mornings after, the lights flashed in his mind. Great apocalyptic neon signs singing with the voice of Mariana, "You got a devil-man in you." Dark phantom shadows would crawl across his whiskey-soaked brain. A crush-ing headache would stay with him most of the day. After each drinking bout, a steel hat-band cinched by an unknown force with the strength of a trucker's come-along chain would tighten and squeeze his brain. A hard pull on the bottle would chase the spi-ders back in their nests and lubricate the raw spots in his throat and where the drinking had roughed up his insides.

The deep, melodious voice rolled across the desk of AirContract Florida's owner and chief pilot. "You were one hell of a pilot but I can see your head isn't screwed on as tight as it used to be." After a brief reminiscence in Miami with one of his former flying bosses, Jack was forced to listen to the hard facts. The man continued on, "Jack, I can't give you a job. Something happened and you got the Jim Beam bite. Somewhere along the line you quit wanting to be a top pilot and started drinking too much. Everything I have is in those two choppers sitting out there on the pad. So I got to have dependable pilots. Sorry, Jack. I can't use you but I can make some calls. A police department out in La La Land is advertising for a pilot." He tossed Jack a week old *Rotary Wing Magazine*.

The door clicked shut as Jack left the small office carrying the magazine. He felt like a dog that had chewed through its leash and strayed off. His anger, like dry heat, scorched his throat.

Squinting against the harsh glare of the Miami sunlight he spotted the dead neon sign of a cocktail lounge on a building that belonged in a cubist painting. Inside, a heavyset bartender with broken capillaries road mapping his heavy jowls guarded the bottles of Jack Daniel's, Early Times, Canadian Club, some Bushmills, Jameson and two boxes of Garcia y Vega cigars. Old Waylon Jennings sang from a hyped-up juke box that held singles from everyone from Aerosmith to Los Lobos.

"Beam and beer," ordered Jack in a gravely voice. Anticipating the malt-like taste to cleanse the wooly feeling from his mouth, he reached into his pocket for some bills. The smell of vodka sweat from a bald guy wearing a snap brim hat and a red T-shirt competed with the stale beer smell.

"Kinda beer?" The bartender had fleshy ears big as bath towels, they were hung just below a mangy scalp. His thinning brown hair was swept backward making him look like a faded out Elvis. He wiped his fingers on a damp towel as he waited for the response.

"Any kind. So long as it's cold and another one behind it." The first slug fired up some heat in his belly and the beer feathered a chill up his backbone.

In a soft you-all accent a woman sitting on a bar stool at the end of the bar nodded toward the *Rotary Wing Magazine* Jack had deposited on the narrow bar. "You a pilot?"

Lifting the cold bottle with ice flakes still clinging to it he said with a tight smile, "I used to be one. Now I'm looking for a job."

The woman fired a starchy stare through him. The skin on her face was so tight a cat couldn't scratch it and her eyes had that off-center look of the deep craziness. Leaving him to his own thoughts, her zombie like attention reverted to the glowing square of the TV hung from the ceiling. Then she stood up and Jack's male interests went flaccid. Moving like a duck, she adjusted her fat lumps of breasts, and marched out the door, a pair of faded Levi's vulcanized to her ass. Jack studied the potato chips hanging like tobacco from a bent wire, the pickled floating pigs feet and a jar of old boiled eggs with a greenish hue. Hoisting another drink he drifted into a welcome void with no beginning or end.

On the last day of the month he sobered up, packed his gear, collection of sixties records, books, and Harry for the trip to California. The old car, a 1973 Mercedes four door, had been finely tuned by its former owner who sold it to Jack for three thousand. They headed north on the overseas Highway, the only direction of the road, through the Marathon, Duck Key, Plantation and Key Largo up to Miami in search of a flying job. The only way he could support his writing habit. Jack drove as fast as he could up the 120-mile chain of two-lane bridges and causeways that linked the forty-odd pieces of land with scenery that is pretty much the same: tangles of dense mangroves, sunburned snorklers, snowbirds towing campers, miniature Key deer the size of dogs, charter boats with names like Captain Kidd and Margaretville. Hemingway's "Saint-Tropez of the Poor" was nothing more than little scraps of land that invaders from the hungry megalopolis of Miami/Fort Lauderdale had ravaged with strip malls, combustible housing and endless miles of narrow concrete streets.

CHAPTER FOUR

SOUTHERN CALIFORNIA, 2002

Forty-two-year-old Jack Dalton sat alone on his couch, watching an over excited TV talk show host fire up a barely responsive audience. The hand that thumbed across the remote was strong and weathered. Fine hair, like corn silk spread from the back of the hands up the lean forearms. At first glance, he was just another middle aged guy, but one with a bunch of secrets and a mind that troubled him. It was Saturday, everybody's day off. Next to the couch, on a wrought iron stand, there was a large saltwater aquarium filled with small, brilliant-colored fish. Watching the small TV screen flicker, and as he changed it, he unconsciously rubbed the keloid scar on his throat that was evidence of his field tracheotomy and the source of his Whisperin' Jack nickname. His hand went there when he needed a reminder of how precious life was. The shiny scar tissue contrasted with his handsomely weathered face. He rubbed the tension out of his hands by pressing them on the knees of his chino pants. He pushed his fingers back through his thick, dark-blonde, hair with his left hand, the wrist circled by his old stainless steel Rolex. His good luck flying piece. Like most pilots he was more than a little superstitious. Once, he cancelled a flight because he forgot the Rolex when he left his room in a hurry.

He combed his hair straight back in the push-back style of a young Kirk Douglas. Not bad, he often thought for a guy who had been shot at, burned, crashed and back from the dead. He felt lucky his hair wasn't pure white. Dalton was groping for a new life as the recognition of a maturity slowly closed around him. A one-time overachiever who breezed through the tough academics and hazing at West Point, his military career was destroyed by a hidden mortar shell during the Gulf War. The mishap nagged him into his struggle with the bottle. Flames would flicker in his nightmares, and if he didn't drink himself into a stupor before try-ing to sleep at night, then the searing reddish-yellow globules of burning avgas bubbled in his nighttime brain.

For a short time the sale of the book about his father's expe-riences in Vietnam was enough to let him quit his flying job in Bogota; to write the second book. When he ran out of money he returned to flying the fragile hummingbird machines, avoiding the stifling world of a regular job. The growing fear of middle age joined his recurring nightmares.

So now he was flying again against desires and better judge-ment. It was the only way he could make enough money to live on and have the time to work on his second book. He felt trapped while he worked in the tired, nondescript municipality of Border City, California as a pilot for the police department. He hoped the new book would uncage him.

His hope to write for a living did not evolve from a belief he was a real creative artist. Years of flying dangerous vibrating machines that dropped from the air like heavy safes did it. So did age. The gambling blood of a young aviator had been choked out of him. Too many bad landings. Too many close calls. Too much flying in palm-sweating, ulcer-causing, fear-producing heavy air. The words from Dion's "Runaround Sue" drifted from the speakers as he looked out of the windows into the dense, condominium neighborhood.

After landing the job with the Border City Police Department he used the money he had saved from his flying gigs to buy a comfortable house in Baja, California Mexico. Aside from his col-lection of books, his father's records from the sixties, the ancient Mercedes he drove and Harry, the Baja house was his only posses-sion. Owning it gave him the first point of reference he had since he left home for West Point.

Following the New Orleans debacle he leased one of those places in Border City where the singles crowd lived, and he hated it; loud, smelly, a pool full of horn dogs looking for mates. He went to the aquarium and tested the water for acidity and alkalinity. Searching for the Red Top Zebra he purchased earlier in the week.

He found it behind a bunch of *lagenandra*, where it was sparring with a Banjo Catfish. He turned off the aquarium light, satisfied his newest family member was adjusting to its new surroundings and roommate, Harry. The parrot sauntered in from the kitchen and fluttered up to the top of the aquarium where he bent low watching the action through the glass with benign interest.

Leaving Harry with some food and a taste of beer, Jack left the condo for a workout. He quickly pulled the Mercedes out of the parking lot, past the sliver of fairway from the golf course bordering the condo property, the sun blinking off the car's chrome. Down H Street and then over to Highway 5, heading for Balboa Park.

Despite the Saturday afternoon nightmare of traffic and heat, the sea air smelled clean and comfortable as he drove north on Highway 5. The 280 SE black Mercedes sedan he bought in the Keys for the trip to California was a real piece of running road iron. Some of the last of its kind he thought as he gently pressed down on the gas. The big 4.5 liter engine growled with a liquid smooth response even though it was over twenty years old. The three-pointed metal star proudly gracing the hood shone in the bright afternoon sunlight.

He passed erratically stacked, one-room apartments like molding wedding cakes, Madame So and So's Dance Academy, wholesale jewelry stores, used car lots, and liquor stores. The grimy urban effluvia passed quickly as he put the big six-seater car in the fast lane and fed fuel to the massive engine. The speedometer registered at 160 miles per hour and Jack knew from experience the boxy, yet nimble, car would run almost that fast on its touring Michelins. It would pass anything except a gas station, he thought. He maneuvered around a Nissan Xterra with a full compliment of bolt-ons and a huge my-logo-is-better-than-your-logo and watched brake lights glimmer and blink in front of him. It reminded him of tracers and his mouth went dry.

With the sunroof half-way back, he was warm and sunlight bounced off of the classic's steering wheel and instrument panel. Jack took in the vigorous, deep blue sky and then pushed a tape into the deck. The sounds of the Coasters' "Yackety Yak" bounced gently off the rich leather interior. Two ripe young girls, young enough to be his daughters, in a daddy-bought-and-paid-for Miata, gave the stately black car a complimentary glance. He cut the speed and dropped behind them to catch the Park Boulevard exit he came close to overshooting. They blew him some unchaste kisses and he caught himself smiling. He parked the car in Balboa Park at the curb on President's Way. The Shirelles' song "Will You Love Me Tomorrow," faded as he shut the engine down. After changing into his running clothes in the restroom, Jack pushed at the front fender to loosen his muscles. Hard at first. Then with all his extended strength. A popping sound jumped off his right knee, warning him of age.

Running hard, sweat started to soak his shirt. Leaving the sidewalk, Jack accelerated his pace through Balboa Park and its usual gaggle of outer fringe humanity. Overhead, a white and orange Coast Guard helicopter clattered disruptively in the clean blue sky. Its noise jerked Jack's thoughts back to his first conversation with Assistant Police Chief Lee Dykes Hart.

Hart smelled of talcum and Old Spice while Jack sat across from him during the job interview. His eyes looked like oysters oozing out of the half shell. The broken capillaries testifying to his lifestyle, were a contrast to his pale white skin. On the desk, opened to the section devoted to videos, lay the Xandrin Gold Collection Edition Catalog, with its guarantees to supercharge one's sex life. A kinky cop. Just what I need for a boss, thought Jack.

"Major," purred Hart, emphasizing his former military rank, "you got one hell of an interesting record if everything on this application is accurate." Hart looked directly at the tall, well-constructed man in a madras shirt, khaki trousers and polished, well worn brown Wellington boots. The age on his application indicated he was forty-two, but he looked to be no older than the mid-thirties. The man Assistant Chief Hart was talking to, leaned forward, high energy coming right off his skin. His eyes said "don't fuck with me" and Hart felt

more uneasy about what he planned for this guy. Nevertheless, he needed a certified pilot damn quick.

"It's all accurate," was Jack's polite response. He was anxious and ready. The job would give him the time and money he needed to write. His crash-and-burn dreams had faded away. He would fly long enough to finish the book.

"You haven't been flying for some time now. Why so?" said Hart, smiling diplomatically.

"I took time off to write a book."

"Did you?" was Hart's challenge.

"That's one reason I'm interested in the job. I hope to eventually write for a living."

"If your resume is copacetic I'd say you can handle this job. Is it?" he asked again.

"Yes." Jack thought, did anyone say copacetic anymore?

"Got any problems with flying into Mexico?" inquired Hart with raised eyebrows.

"No. So long as it's legal."

Hart gave him kind of a lopsided grin, his facial muscles tightened as he pronounced, "It's legal. We work with the Ensenada Police Department in what we call the Border Cities Police Program. It's an information exchange program of sorts. No big deal, but the Chief or I fly down, once a week, for a briefing by the Ensenada PD. You know, tourist stuff. Fact is, we fly down to the Big E every Monday morning. The police brass treat us real well when we come."

"No problem," commented Jack casually. He had no reason to believe the Border City Police would be doing anything but legal flying, despite his instinctive distrust of the man interviewing him. He still had a nagging notion he might be swimming in the wrong pond.

Hart shot him a stiff look and challenged Jack. "You never flew any illegal missions? Come on. What do you take me for? You're resume has 'wrong side of the line pilot' stamped all over it."

"Maybe that's what it seems like to you but it's not so."

Hart rose, eyeing Jack studiously. The police official was smaller than he looked behind the desk. Extending a soft hand with polished fingernails, the police official announced, "Mr. Dalton, it's been a *pleasure. You are hired. The helicopter is out at Brown Field. I suggest that you go over there in the morning and check it out. Be sure you can fly to Ensenada in a week from next Monday." The meeting was over.*

A week later Jack went to work flying a Bell 206 helicopter for the Border City Police Department. He was able to hire Boomer Smythe, who after leaving Bogota, relocated to Chula Vista, California. Boomer jumped at the chance to make some steady money and Jack was pleased to be working with an old hand. Now, he and Boomer flew the rig down to Ensenada once a week, always on Monday morning.

CHAPTER FIVE

Cracking the throttle as he gently hauled up on the collective, Jack lifted the seven-place Bell LongRanger off the helipad at Brown Field in a low ground effect hover. A stretch version of the popular JetRanger, it flew at a maximum speed with a range of 325 nautical miles. For a micro second he experienced the sweaty terror that comes before a combat flight. The moment when fright would hit him like a cocaine rush; a body orgasm. Pulled by a powerful Allison engine, the helicopter rose and flew gracefully away.

The wind stiffened a bit and the mechanical bird started twisting in the polished sky. Jack glanced at the Electronic Flight Instrumentation System. Satisfied the bird's avionics were accurate he spoke into the radio mouthpiece. After getting clearance from the tower he climbed to three thousand feet with unhurried deliberation. Moments later he took the machine out over the harbor with the ratcheting sound of the helicopter bouncing off the choppy air. He cut through the sharp shadows of clouds and caught a single probing beam of the sun on the canopy. Above he could see the crimson underbelly of the low clouds. Below, toy ships tied up at the docks and the ones steaming through the harbor looked like models in a young boy's room. The harbor was under siege by an armada of vessels with the sun turning the Pacific a molten metal texture. Sea gulls shrieked, wheeled in the air and dove into the blue-green water.

Jack's gloved fingers flew over the LongRanger's switches and controls. He flicked on his navigation lights and made a final check before he squeezed the in-cabin mike. Static burst in the earphones of Crew Chief Boomer Smythe and the passenger, Assistant Police Chief Lee Dykes Hart. Boomer's tongue toyed with the plug of Redman tucked between his front teeth and lower lip.

"We'll follow the coast," Jack announced. Nobody answered. He pushed the rudder pedal down and shoved the cyclic control over, maneuvering the craft into a smooth, gentle turn as he lined up on the rugged coast line for the seventy some mile flight. The day was heating up fast, catching the tail of a hot Santa Ana wind. It would have been faster to follow the toll road down the Baja peninsula but Jack wanted to see his beach house in Mexico from the air.

Skirting the west side of raucous Tijuana with its fly blown glitter, it reminded him of Calcutta. He flew in a southerly direction; below, the new bullfighting arena grew in size. Puffy clouds, held the sun in an artist's sequence, a perfect seascape by the Creator. Whoever it was. In the trash covered parking lot the verdigris copper statue of a matador and charging bull took shape as the helicopter pushed through the sky. Tamarisk trees and potted pink and white hibiscus were scattered about. A single Mexican fan palm swayed in the parking lot. A second statue, a rider herding seven bulls, stood apart from the matador, frozen in time.

Banking to the west, he moved out to sea into the small wet wind that had traveled across the Pacific. He knew it well, flying with the mechanical boredom of a long-haul truck driver. Avoiding the belching smokestacks of the electric power generating plants that poked their smoking obelisks into the air; where they were joined with the noxious emissions from a Pemex Refinery in Rosarito. He flew off to the right of a rock ridge and high backs loped cliff. Hang gliders riding the wind under colorful canopies bobbed like brilliantly colored flowers in the wind. Fishing boats bounced in water, blotched with waves, and swells four feet from trough to peak. To the west, gigantic clouds rambled landward. Sea lions vamped on the wet rocks in the blinding sun under an exquisite deep blue sky. A pod of whales mingled with their dolphin escorts in the azure water below. Expensive cliff side haciendas and dreary fishing shanties shared space and hung over the ocean from small cliffs at the Puerto Nuevo lobster village. Satellite dishes were scattered about. If the locals had

WilliamE.Kirchhoff

(clearing)

little else, they would have the dish for the novellas and soccer games, thought Jack.

A macadamized road with yellow shoulders, turned abruptly from the ocean at a drunken angle. Every so often it degenerated into dusty gravel. Below, dust billowed from a plain of sparse vegetation like the balding scalp of an old man. Diesel buses puked oily smoke, cars with bad tires hip-hopped over pot holes on what was the road. Long haul trucks with blaring horns sped north and south along Ensenada Cuota over what was once occupied land, farms, orchards and homes moved to open the door to a much needed commerce. A few cars moved slower down the free road, Ensenada Libre, the drivers wary of its twisting vicious meet-your-ass curves and falling rocks. Small "descansos" or homages to the dead, dotted the curves where loved ones crashed and burned.

Blinking his eyes from the sun's glare Jack focused on the road below as he held the aircraft steady. Tired from last night's jarring, fitful sleep his mind felt like a piece of tough steak being tenderized with a meat pounder. The pain was always inside from invisible wounds he couldn't treat.

"That's some mean goddam real estate between the fertilizer factory and here," griped Boomer as he watched an ancient truck navigate one of the narrow, dust-blowing roads. "Those rocks would sure bend my bird if we lost power."

Jack swung the chopper landward at Rosarito Beach, dropped it down, and flew over vast expanses of beaches, observing the rusting carapaces of wrecked cars that had plunged to the rocks. He lined the nose of the aircraft up on the Playa La Mision beach-front colony. In minutes, his house jutted out from the side of a small rocky escarpment. The colony below was a collection of brick, stone and stucco houses running parallel along the beach in two tiers. A Mediterranean look and feel, the enclave was an example of what Mexican skilled labor and U.S. dollars can accomplish. Unlike the old world where castles and towns chose the highest ground for fortification and built from the top down, the builders of Playa la Mision chose the best beach lots where the only fears were high waves and incompetent legal help. To get to the beach from Jack's house there was a steep stone staircase, crossing a flat terraced area and then, the walkways between the houses built directly on the beach.

The two-mile long beach was virtually isolated. It was enclosed at the north end by sharp cliffs and fallen rocks that formed jagged barriers. The isolation of the beach caused those who walked on it, especially at night, to experience the feeling of aloneness.

Through his sunglasses Jack watched a spinning dust devil bounce up from the side of the narrow road leading to the beach. A thin, milky haze was developing. The enclave looked like a toy village from the air; Spanish cupolas, tile roofs, eucalyptus trees, palms, bright flowers, and here and there Moorish geometric designs which seemed superfluous and out of place. A single stick person commanded the empty gray beach. A car crept up the narrow macadam road that linked the houses like a tangled rope. On a slab of concrete, a gang of Mexican laborers bent wire and reinforcing rods for the walls of the house they were building.

Boomer peered out through the Plexiglas windshield and spoke into the aircraft's intercom. "Which is yours?" Jack put the helicopter into a soft circle and crossed over the house. Below, a long white brick house with a front courtyard guarded by a high wall, became centered as the helicopter circled. He pointed out the window as he held the collective stick with one hand and said, "That one." As the small grouping of houses slid under the helicopter the intercom barked, "Fly over the Love Boat." Jack responded to Assistant Chief Hart's abrupt command by pushing down on the rudder pedal and shoving the cyclic control toward the stop.

Jack banked the vibrating machine over on its side and snapped its tail around. This caused his passengers to strain against their chest harnesses as he made a run over the luxury liner steaming toward the Port of Ensenada. Flying perpendicular to the coast line where the highway cut paths between low mountains and the high ocean side cliffs, Jack banked and continued south.

Flying over a deserted stretch of Highway One, guarded by a toll-gate, Jack watched the dust-booming construction projects that dotted the outskirts of Ensenada. He flew over the small fishing community of San Miguel. The land was bleak with undistinguished buildings and a bad smell. Sportfishing boats, a few luxury yachts and purse seiners crowded the anchorage with cargo ships and a floating seafood processing plant.

Approaching the lowlands that sloped down from the scrub-covered hills to the north, Jack flew out of the crescent shaped Bahia de los Todos Santos. Flying over the blinking waters of Puerto Ensenada, the high Chapultepec hills off to the starboard, he headed toward the Naval base and air field. Scattering a squadron of dirty white seagulls as he descended toward the Cuartel located on Avenida Reforma between City Hall and the monument to Benito Juarez. He slowed the aircraft. Below, the harbor was a turgid mix of luxury boats, floating fisheries, slums, warehousing and busy eateries, some nearly ready to slide into the brackish waters.

Orbiting the chain link fence parking lot littered with rubble and bird-droppings behind the Caseta de Policia, Jack waited for the wave of the landing signal. A Mexican policeman, raised both arms and waved his hands in the universal "come" motion. Jack clamped his fingers tight around the cyclic and collective control and went into a large circle and brought the Bell in for a flashy landing, dropping down so fast that the skids brushed the tarmac before he pulled the nose up hard and flared to stop the engine. The downdraft of the rotor tore at the man's shirt. The big Allison engine whined to a stop, making a noise like a sow with a bit tit as it shut down. The uniformed policeman opened the right side door of the aircraft. With the beery breath of a recent lunch he welcomed the chopper's passengers. His yellow Chiclets teeth broke into a mean, fuck you Gringo grin. The beat of the engine calmed to a stillness when the spinning rotors stilled. Pungent fumes assaulted Jack's lungs. He slipped off his headset and left it inside the cabin. Hart debarked and shuffled across the weed strewn hardpan toward the Police Building.

The moment Hart left the helicopter Boomer climbed out of the copilot's seat. He automatically started to do a walk-around inspection of the idled bird, more out of habit than need. Touching the hot aluminum skin of the stilled aircraft he fiddled with the control knobs and wiped off the canopy.

At the rear of the building Hart entered a side door guarded by a reddish-brown dog. Peeling yellow tile glistened momentarily as he opened the door. Familiar with the layout, he walked down a narrow hallway laced with clunking water pipes. A stream of greenish black effluent dripped from a rusting four-inch sewer pipe that hung from the ceiling by tin strips. A dank odor rose up to meet him. He entered the office with the words *Commandante Gomez* on the glass pane of the old fashioned door.

Jack glanced at his crew chief after Hart left them. Boomer liked to give you the impression that he was a Georgia Cracker. But beneath the facade of gruffness, peckerwood lingo, and a course appearance was a smart and well-read man. Boomer's mind was honed as sharp as a razor. He had a tough, flinty stance about life. And, he had hands that could fix anything from an altimeter to a transmission. After retiring from the military, Boomer worked for Air America as a chief mechanic at the air operations base in Bogota. He was part of the flying circus that let you live in a clean spacious apartment, fly some sphincter tightening missions during the day and then return home for steaks and a couple of beers or a dry martini served by one of the beautiful young Eurasian women who seemed to always be in the world of the flying mercs.

Jack's last near death crash drove him toward a saner occupation. He dug out his dad's letters and journals and wrote a book. And the goddamn thing sold. He was aware that he might be just a one trick pony, capable only of a one time rambling account of his father's Vietnam war experiences. *Jungle Nights* sold modestly and he enjoyed the small success of being in the public eye, however briefly; a little publicity, a magazine spread, glowing letters from old timers and action lovers who relish a safe but gripping visit back to their futile war. He had done the tribute book with such a passion that the publisher overlooked his writing deficiencies in favor of the blood and guts, you-are-there experiences. He had touched the deep recesses of memory in guys who knew the war his father fought in was a shitty one and probably would be their last. They read, absorbed the nastiness they endured, nodded in their recliners and had another beer.

Boomer's only one fulfilling outlet, was the Sons of Liberty, where membership was restricted to ex-Army NCO's who had seen combat. He was bored. When Whisperin' Jack offered him a mechanic's job he jumped at the chance to do something other than rust away in the old age of civilian life.

"OK, 'rotorhead', now what do we do?" Jack smiled involuntarily when called a 'rotorhead'. The old hands before Jack in the Air America outfit were fixed wing pilots. They flew C-46s, C-47s, Caribous, and the aging C-123 in and out of the laterite and red clay strips all over Asia. They believed that pilots like Jack had scrambled brains because they spent their time hanging below the swinging propellers. Jack was briefly with the Southeast Asia flying bums, but long after the threat of communism was over, the Berlin Wall chopped up for tourist trinkets, and Washington mounted a new and futile war on drugs. Hellraisers, spoiling for action generally did not give a shit about anything but the psychic value of flying vibrating windmills in lands with limited navigational aids and ill-tempered weather for a modest monthly paycheck These tin jockey, aerial cowboys and alcoholic airplane drivers didn't fit in elsewhere. Dangerous flying, some whoring, a little bit of friendly brawling and a constant search for adventure were the dues you paid to belong to the club. Now Jack was no longer a member.

Jack unfolded his lanky frame from the cockpit and finger combed matted hair from the headset. In the distance he could hear the grumbling of the powerful diesels in the shipyards. The smell of *carne asada* caused him to look up into a set of brown eyes yellowed with age. He shook his head in a 'no' at the ancient vendor, but gave him a handful of peso change. The old man's hand was wrapped in a towel crusted with blood. A beggar with no feet sat down in the shade of the helicopter and gutted a freshly caught fish.

"Hussong's?" asked Boomer, wanting to know if Jack wanted to go to the well-known tourist bar at the west end of Ensenada.

"Nope." Jack did not want to tempt himself with a cold beer. He still had enough control over his drinking not to fly when he was drinking. Long ago he rejected the twelve hour 'bottle-to-throttle' rule that pilots followed; no drinking with less than twelve hours to takeoff. "Besides, we don't have enough time. 'Shit for brains' told me to be ready to take off in exactly one hour," he said referring to Hart.

Boomer acknowledged Jack with a quick salute, turned and strolled down the boulevard toward the harbor.

CHAPTER SIX

An hour later Boomer returned from the harbor docks, riding in the cab of a Mercedes truck which arrived in a flourish of noise and stopped next to the helicopter. A rangy Mexican with a grease rag wrapped around his neck, slid from the cab and dropped to the tarmac. He gestured to Boomer and they wrestled two fifty-five-gallon drums into the back of the helicopter where Boomer secured them with a nylon tie-down.

Hart hustled to the LongRanger a few minutes later, sweating and puffing, escorted by a single policeman. Hart clambered into the back of the helicopter and sat next to the two strapped down drums.

"CALMEX PETROLEUM PRODUCTS," announced Hart. "Why all the fuckin' oil?"

"Same grade, but cheaper if you buy it down here, should make those yuppie assholes happy we're so e-co-nom-i-cal," said Boomer as he strapped his safety harness. Looking out through the thick window Plexiglas, Hart bitched about the heat, the smell and the Mexicans. Boomer settled in, keeping his silence.

"Let's get the fuck out of Dodge," was Hart's response.

Jack, lifting off with effort, pulled for extra power against the hot afternoon air. Against the plastic canopy he caught a glimpse of strain on his reflected face. The vibrating excitement mixed with a feeling of fear he still felt when he lifted off, sucked his nuts up, almost burying them in the hollow of his gut. A rubbery feeling gripped his bones and the unquenchable fear filled his consciousness. He pushed the memory-jolting blast of the burning crash out of his mind so he could concentrate on flying.

Overcoming his thoughts, Jack adjusted the trim to compensate for the extra weight in the rear, and then followed the toll way north up the peninsula. He fought off boredom with instinctive flying. Smiling, he was grateful that no one was shooting at him. Boomer dozed, snoring and grunting as his head slid forward and then snapped backwards as the machine jolted and bucked. A wandering, sooty cloud drifted through the herringbone clouds that gave depth to the sapphire-blue sky. The angled rays of the sun break-danced off the Plexiglas windshield. As they approached Tijuana from the south, a laconic voice came over the radio. "Border City cop chopper, this is the Brown tower and we've got a report there is fire in the ditch. Copy?"

"Roger," said Jack. "We'll be over it in about fifteen."

A few minutes later, Boomer sniffed and muttered, "Smoke," pointing a thick index finger toward the Plexiglas windshield.

Jack squinted to get a better vision. Boomer, wide awake, studied the black mushroom in the distant sky.

"Where's the fire?" Hart was on the intercom, and squirmed in his seat.

"Looks like another dump fire in TJ."

Leaning back from adjusting the radio knobs, Jack said, "The tower at Brown field says it's in the canyons."

It was a no-man's-land, host to desperate people between Tijuana and San Diego. A nasty gash of hard scrabble land of stinging cactus and flinty rock. An inferno of a few square miles of inhabitable acreage with a savage mood. The way of illegal border crossers with all their worldly possessions hanging from their backs, willingly trying to pass to the U.S.

During the day, hundreds of men, women and children mobilized on the mesas waiting for the sun to set. It looked like the gathering of a raggedly-ass invasion force. Benign lumps of people carrying "pollo" bags, huddled around cook fires that sputtered and spit smoke from wood scraps and trash. The "migra," the dreaded immigration services, patrolled. Runaway camp fires in the canyons were common and dangerous because of the speed with which the flames moved through dry grass and dead cactus with a wind tunnel effect.

"Look," exclaimed Boomer pointing down. Below, a person was trapped in a ring of swirling flames. Reacting automatically, Jack dropped the vibrating machine through the patchy acrid smoke and intense yellow flame and rolled it around for a tree top run. Tense, his heart pounding he felt the adrenaline rush and pressed on. Boomer was silent, but cut him a wary glance. He unstrapped his safety harness knowing what was expected of him.

"What the fuck are you doing?" Hart yelled as he watched below. The machine veered to its left, props flickering like a windmill as it dropped in a violent way.

"Checking to see if we can help." Jack caressed the LongRanger into a turn. He could hear Hart's dentures make a clicking sound in his headphone.

The ground-flames ran like liquid orange down the hillside and then tore into the canyon break like a flash flood of white, curling heat. The propeller of the helicopter beat the rising smoke back, creating an orange and black haze, a closer view of Hell, with deceitful rays of sunshine. Ashes swirled in the air as flames crested, then flowed down the canyon side like rivers of molten lava. Suddenly Jack planted the skids on the burning ground. Something made a loud pop, like a gunshot. The inferno noise of the fire drowned out other sounds. An electric tingle danced across the burn scars on his left hand and arm. For a millisecond he was landing on the mortar shell that sapped his soul for so many years. Sweat soaked his clothes.

"You crazy bastard!" screamed Hart in genuine fear as he watched Boomer snap open the seat straps and struggle with the Plexiglas door. His face looked desperate and bile surged in his gut as he watched Boomer disappear into a wall of swirling smoke. Hart, furious and confused, yelled, "Take off! Take off!" Gasping, he had worked himself into a lather with sweat and soot mixing on his face. "This fucker will blow!" he screamed pounding Jack on the shoulder.

Jack ignored him as he held the rumbling machine in place with stiff shoulders and angry eyes. Despite the intense heat, chilled sweat rolled down the middle of his back as he fought off the urge to pull pitch. Too much heat and the avgas would explode. It was *the crash* all over again. He bent forward to suck in some air. Smoke hissed out of the small crevices in the rock. Billowing smoke, then leaping tongues of fire raced off to the sides of the machine. Harry the parrot, sensing the danger, snapped his head back and forth causing his plumage to stand up.

The down draft from the whirling blades held the hot gases at bay momentarily. Suddenly, a running man burst through the wall of smoke, burning particles and orange tongues of flame. Small explosions trailed him. The slightly bowlegged Boomer carried a frail old Mexican man who clung to his back in a death grip. Even with a load, Boomer had a bulldog balance. No wobble or bounce. Panting and grunting, Boomer pushed the brown body through the rear door and climbed in. Jack lifted the bucking machine out of the electric red haze with precision. Boomer unzipped the grayish-green, fire resistant flight coveralls and wiped soot from his face.

Minutes later, the bird was down on the pad at Brown Field. Hart shakily climbed down from the rear door. Clamped in his hand was the aluminum brief case. He walked out from under the whirling prop and waited defiantly. When Jack came around from the other side of the helicopter, Hart commanded in his best cop voice, "What were you trying to prove, landing in that goddamn inferno!"

Jack let Hart have his rant. He pushed his scarred left hand through his sweaty hair before he said anything. Color flooded his face and tension rippled in the air before he responded slowly in a mere whisper. "The old man was going to die for Christ's sake. If we hadn't scooped him out he'd be fajitas." Rage blooming up from his neck, a sheen of sweat beaded his forehead. The angry blood came under the skin of his face. The scar on his throat pulsed. He was inches away from pinching Hart's head off.

"Listen Hero, when I'm on board you take orders from me!" flailed Hart. Boomer had deplaned with the old Mexican who was having a coughing fit and begging for water. Hearing Hart start to rant Boomer thought if Hart's brain were dynamite, it wouldn't blow the nose off a hummingbird.

"No. That's not how it works when I'm in the left-hand seat. I'll take you where you want to go and bring you back, but in between, I'm available to do what I can to help. Aren't you guys supposed to protect and serve? You can always get yourself another pilot," said Jack, shaking his head slowly, in a hard flat voice which flung the statement in Hart's face. A light plane landed, its ripping engine noise and prop wash drowned out the explosive response from Hart as it rolled by on the runway. Jack looked at Hart and tried to think of something good about the guy. Nothing came, a coward, an empty suit.

Hart turned abruptly and walked to this car which was parked by the small hanger that functioned as the office and maintenance shed for the Police Department helicopter.

Boomer, looking at Jack, shrugged with a wide grin and said, "Forget it. He's just another asshole we gotta put up with if we want to get paid. Been doin' it all our lives. He ain't got the stones to do nothin'. I wouldn't give him the steam off my piss on a cold day if he was dyin' of thirst."

Jack said nothing as he watched the assistant police chief drive away, his wheels squealing on the black tarmac. Boomer unlocked the office shed and dragged a dolly back to the helicopter. With Jack's help they wrestled one of the barrels out of the aircraft onto the dolly. Boomer pushed the load back to the shed. The old Mexican limped over to help him. Boomer laughed and gently told him, no. Returning to the helicopter for the second barrel, he stopped where Jack was working on his dog-eared flight log.

Jack knew Boomer had a little scam of his own. Whenever they flew down to Ensenada he brought one or two barrels of aviation oil back and sold it to the local airfield supplier. It was the time honored way of NCOs in the military. A two-bit deal by most standards, Boomer only made about a hundred bucks for both barrels, but he wasn't paid that much by the Border City Police Department to crew their helicopter. Jack didn't care. Guys like Boomer always had to have some little side business. Besides, he was a skilled mechanic, an old warrior and a hard worker with dog-like loyalty.

Boomer rattled on, "What do you think we should do with our old señor here?" He nodded toward the old Mexican now squatting in the shade.

"Immigration folks, I guess. Better take him to the offices in Otay unless you want him living with you for the rest of your life."

"I still think we're making runs into Mexico and bringing back dope. You get your hands on that shiny suitcase Hart is always clutching like a monkey with the last banana and you're going to find some high grade coke."

Boomer rolled his upper lip up and sucked air through the space between his front teeth as he listened to Jack. Out of habit, he jerked the zipper on his flight suit up and down a couple of times. Coughing up a plug of phlegm, he looked at Jack out of the corner of his eye, spat and listened. "Who is going to stop a helicopter with Border City Police Department banner on both sides of the top?"

"I don't think we're muling for the Police Department. I think Hart goes down for some strange pussy and some kinky sex. That's all it is and that, my friend, is how the cow ate the cabbage. Besides, who cares what the B.C. cops are doing. I don't and you shouldn't either so long as you got enough time to haul your ass down to your Meskin hidey hole house. Where else you and me gonna get a job working three days a week and sometimes it ain't even that? You want to go and get shot up in one of those A-rab countries?"

Jack made a casual noncommittal shrug but his mind raced with thoughts of federal prison.

"Cover your ass or lose it. That's the way it's always been. And that's the way it will always be," pontificated Boomer as his tongue toyed with a flake of old tobacco. The plug of Redman, tucked between his front teeth and lower lip, made his face look distorted, like an aging squirrel. Boomer pulled a bag of sunflower seeds from the pocket of his shirt. Harry looked at the seeds expectantly as Boomer tried to bribe him to repeat his name.

"Boo-mer," said the man slowly, holding out the sunflower seeds. Harry snatched some from the palm of Boomer's hand and squawked, *"Beer! Beer!"*

"The only word he knows is beer," said Jack with a half laugh. "You've tried to get him to say your name a thousand times and all he is going to do is take your food." He watched Boomer continue to beg the bird to repeat his name.

"Boomer, I've got to get going." He punched the crew chief lightly on the shoulder and ambled, laptop computer in hand, to the Mercedes parked next to the shed. Harry jumped and fluttered, half flying and half walking as he trailed after him.

On the way home he parked his ride at the liquor store a short distance from the airfield and bought a pint of gin and a plastic bottle of tonic water. Later, at the condo he mixed himself a drink and tried to flush from his mind the burning helicopter that took his friend's life in the Gulf War years ago. Landing in the brush fire in Tijuana took him back to the tragic accident in the desert. Later that night, after he finished the long cold drinks he had made, he drifted into a tortured sleep where apocalyptic dreams revisited as his face melted into a horrible, red-black lump like the young copilot left in the flaming seat of the metal bird destroyed by an errant mortar round.

CHAPTER SEVEN

The overpowering smell of urine, feces and fear smacked him in the face with the ripping force of a punch as he opened the door to the Humane Society's animal shelter. No stranger to the smell he nevertheless gagged back the coffee and bucket fried chicken from the Colonel to fortify himself before stopping at the building painted a faded mustard color.

"Here's your newest pet, Punch," exclaimed the gotch-eyed fat female night guard at the animal shelter with a leering smile. A backdrop for a gold front tooth. She spoke to a heavy, roast beef body of the man. She handed him a big, mangy-looking Tom cat with cataracts covering its dull green, veiny eyes. A kinder person would have seen the torment in the old boy. "Enjoy," she said, deliberately failing to disguise the sneer, she flicked the wet tip of her tongue over a trio of lip sores.

"You need to choke your motor before I do," he threatened.

"You're our only regular cat buyer. Can't you get some pussy without buying it?" she teased.

"Fuck you, and the rest of the pukes who work in this snuff house," snarled the red-faced man as he thrust a ten dollar bill forward. He snatched the massive pile of fur from the plump arms of the woman. Coyly she stuffed the money in the front pocket of her two-sizes-too-small jeans. Levi's that looked like they were steam-ironed to her ass.

The disgusted glare she gave him was a look that was hot enough to fry bacon. But, ten bucks was ten bucks, and he bought three cats a week that should have been either adopted out or put to sleep. This old Tom was waiting for the needle anyway.

His eyes narrowed into a web of lines as he bitched, "Fuckwad, this raggedy piece of fur better be something special after that dead piece of meat I got from you last week. My Bastard needs some action."

"I could give a ferret's fuck." The hot zoo smell in the building fogged up his mirrored sunglasses. He strung together a bunch of street oaths as he struggled to get the squirming cat through the paint-peeled, wooden door that screeched against the broken sidewalk. He stuffed the objecting cat into an old duffle bag and wedged himself behind the cracked steering wheel wrapped with duct tape.

The door to his sun-faded blue Buick opened and shut with the metallic groan and pop sound that old car doors are heir to. The tailpipe was almost rusted off and the whitewalls were the old-fashioned wide kind, curb-scratched and peeling. On the seat of the old Buick, lay his tools, a pair of sweat-bleached sap gloves and a scarred and chipped, heavy baton.

Turning the ignition on, the starter motor clicked and whirred and finally caught. "Pain in the ass," he thought as he drove down a mean street in unincorporated San Ysidro, California; a nasty collection of wrecked houses and lonely businesses that quit at the U.S. and Mexican border. Not the Ray Ban, butt-floss swim-suit, great tanning machine of Southern California. It was the home of Dairy Queen, taquerias, above ground pools, Chevys and K-Mart. Passing a botanica and an outlet supermarket, he braked for a cadaverous, scabby dog with loose moving skin that loped in front of his worn tires. His car, the collection of mechanical groans and rattles continued to shake and stall at the stop sign.

Out of a concrete block, windowless bar tiptoed a young *maricón* wearing gold platforms and matching body suit. He groped and made lewd sucking sounds at the teen-aged, wide-eyed *pollita* as they met in the crosswalk. A fat cholo, in a gimme cap and Yosemite Sam mustache, pulled up next to Punch, his speakers pumping Latin rap. The Mexican spat phlegm on the glass-littered sidewalk and haughtily drove off in his Mercury Cyclone 390 with a peeling Tijuana one-day paint job. The bright red, electric Tijuana Trolley rumbled by on the trestle, competing with the blare of radio music jumping from the vibrating boom box of a passenger. Rapid fire slang, bebop and Spanglish jive floated heavily on an almost indiscernible breeze filled with the unmistakable odor of burning trash.

Twenty minutes later he parked the car on the oil-spattered, broken ribbon of concrete that was once a driveway to his garage. His South County neighborhood spoke loudly of decay; last stop, a place for a man who'd nearly run out of options. Breathing tightly he hauled the duffle bag up the steps. Kicking aside a pile of soiled clothes, he crossed the peeling tile floor littered with empty beer cans and burger wrappers, carrying the bristling cat to the basement door. The reek of dog shit and urine oozed out.

Alvin "Punch" Packer, one of Border City Police Department's finest, opened the slightly warped, cheap wooden door by twisting the loose, black doorknob. The house was a sweatbox. Beads like glycerin sprung from his forehead. A thick, rumbling howl billowed up from the bowels of the wet-smelling basement. Walking down the stairs in a stiff gait, like a man with a fused knee, he breathed in the stink. He grinned at Bastard the big, ugly dog; a fighting pit bull, lunging against a sheepskin collar yoke that fastened him to a treadmill. The dog and treadmill were enclosed in a cage made of chain link fencing and heavy lumber. Eight by eight in size, the floor was littered with dried bones, feces, tufts of fur and a congealment of rotting flesh and shredded organs. Hanging in front of the dog, as an enticement, was a small cage with a terrified white rat with bloody paws clawing insanely at the bars. Packer was proud of the indoor training facility he had built. His dog, leashed to the treadmill loved the taste of fresh animal blood and would run until he dropped from exhaustion.

The feline in Packer's arms started to squirm violently and the ugly dog could smell the cat's fear. It snarled and saliva foam dripped from its fangs as it ran and pressed like crazy against the sheepskin collar that held it on the treadmill. With one hand, Packer opened the door to the cage and shoveled the big cat inside. In a panic, the squealing cat clawed its way to the wire mesh ceiling of the cage. The dog stopped running on the treadmill and tugged savagely against the collar, slinging wet drool around the cage.

Packer reached behind the dog's neck and jerked the slip collar off. The pit bull wheeled and stood up on its hind quarters. Its powerful fanged jaws clamped around the squealing cat's tail. The hysterical cat dove off the cage ceiling, leaving hair attached to the big dog's yellow teeth and purplish red gums. The dog lunged after the shrieking cat and scooped it up in powerful jaws and quickly cracked its spine before it became a mist of red viscera. The dog attended its prey and Packer laughed like a meth head.

Retreating up the stairs, Packer dressed in his Border City police uniform and collected his High Standard, Model Ten twelve gauge, equipped with a flashlight and short barrel. Around his sprawling gut he hung his badly worn pistol belt, complete with a wooden baton and can of Mace. Sweating and blowing cat hair he picked up his mirrored sunglasses and opened the refrigerator. Carefully stuffing six cold cans of Budweiser in a cheap plastic briefcase, he snapped the lid shut and left. Intense heat boiled on the street and the car's engine rattled, thumped and complained. He had an hour before roll-call at the Border City Police Department. He would use his free time to building what he called his "backup retirement fund."

The pear-shaped man swished lightly through the door and onto the deck where the high-tech spa pool was. He wore an expensive silk kimono. His face was chalk-white from heavy make-up causing his red lips to look like a slit throat. A gold chain circled his neck. The pool was on a concrete shelf that hung precariously over the mini-canyon. The canyon was nothing more than a drainage sluice when it rained and a dry gulch the rest of the time. Six people could perform a variety of acts in the pool that was shielded from the one neighboring house by a tall block wall.

The draping sleeve of the silk robe touched the warm water in the tub when the dopey-eyed man poured a scented liquid from a delicate crystal bottle. The outside temperature was cooling as a breeze mounted, rustling the branches of the eucalyptus trees. The evening sky was bright in the direction of San Diego. Satisfied that the water was sufficiently warm, heated to induce a relaxed drowsiness, he flicked drops from his soft girlish hands and wiped them delicately on a soft pastel colored hand towel.

With intense desire Lee Dykes Hart watched her as she stood timidly in the doorway separating the master bedroom and the spa. He drew a breath as the atmosphere became highly charged with expectation and pleasure. His penis moved under his silk robe like an eager rabbit. Smiling at her beauty he watched her nibble tentatively at her lower lip with brilliant pearl white teeth that contrasted her dark skin. He was almost breathless and his pulse rapid. He fumbled out of his robe and lubricated his erection with the warm spa water. Shivering like a smackhead on rosebud dust, his thin, pasty-white legs quivered with expectation. He leaned over and placed a freshly cut rose in the band that held her coal black hair. His soft belly flushed with color as he stroked the ten-year-old's face. The child had deep eyes and high cheeks with a beautiful mouth.

The barrel-chested Mexican with an ancient burnt-black welder's face shield sitting on his head like an open knight's helmet struggled to open the warehouse door. The late afternoon strings of rain made plopping noises when they hit his faceplate. He spit through a jaw full of yellow nubby teeth. The door of the warehouse, constructed from old lumber and corrugated metal, grudgingly opened. Behind the warehouse was a string of tin-roofed shanties. Ensenada *trabajadores* who worked on the boats in the harbor kept their tools and supplies in the shacks. Near the warehouse, separated by an overgrown weed patch, was a long concrete dock. Smaller ships from the port tied up against the barnacle-covered concrete. Next to the dock stood a series of decrepit jetties built on wooden stilts and poles that looked like tree trunks in a swamp. A breeze ruffled the greasy water and pressed against the welder's back as he forced open the stubborn door to the warehouse. The wind had booted up during the early afternoon, slapping the tin rooftops with rain. Clots of lumpy black clouds churned in the sky, with the throaty grumble of thunder.

Inside, he rolled the fifty-five gallon drums painted green with the words "CALMEX PETROLEUM PRODUCTS" wrapped around their middles. The empty barrels were easy to move. On the top of each barrel was the heavy screw cap. But the bottom had been carefully cut out with an acetylene torch. Next to the two barrels were smaller aluminum cylinders with airtight seals. The welder lifted a drum without a bottom and placed it over the top of one of the cylinders. Approximately an inch of space separated the cylinder and the walls of the barrel. There were nine inches to spare between the top of the aluminum cylinder and the petroleum barrel lid.

The welder turned the barrels over on end, with the screw cap down. A strong man, he was able to lift the heavy, silvery cylinders high enough to insert them into the repository of the barrels. *Jijole*, he exclaimed. He'd never understood those crazy gringos, what could these things be? Better not to ask, this job meant meat for dinner, and a little something for the old woman to make her smile.

The aluminum containers held twenty separate heavy-polyethylene bags. He flipped down his helmet and concentrated on his task, ignoring sweat dripping in his eyes. He sealed each barrel by welding the cut out bottom back in its original place. Red sparks jumped from the welding rod and bit at the legs of his tattered pants as he carefully laid a thick bead around the bottom edge. After using a nubbed down brush with black paint, he covered the new welds. Satisfied with his artistry, he turned each barrel over, unscrewed the screw cap and poured in a thick, black heavy oil. The rich oil slid effortlessly between the walls of the two barrels. It covered the aluminum, six or so inches at the top of the drum. When the oil reached the top, he set down the jerry can and sealed the drum by tapping the screw-cap shut tight with a small hammer.

The welder walked out onto the concrete dock. He lit a smoke and wondered if the thunderstorms were lighting the sky in his beloved Oaxaca, so far away. Tomorrow he would go to church and pray. Monday, the American with the money would come and pay him to deliver the barrels to the aircraft. Dirty rain dribbled on his once-mahogany skin that had aged the color of warm tar. Staccato thunder rattled in the hills above the City of Ensenada, reminding him of home.

Security Officer Tracy Ann Combs worked for the Neutron Security Corporation of San Diego. She was an unarmed security guard with a lower level I.Q. Only a generation out of the trailer park, she had tried to get into law enforcement without success. Her chunky body looked its best in uniforms. A size 20 with a size 6 mind. Tonight she was working a beat in Border City, driving a white sedan with a yellow flasher on the top. After she ran a red light, a police cruiser parked at the Swifty Mart store pulled out of the dark and followed her. The officer behind the wheel of the patrol car did not use his siren emergency lights. He just pulled up and motioned Tracy to pull over.

"Did you know you ran a red light?" The Border City Police Officer asked the fleshy woman packed in a dark uniform.

Tracy shook her head no and smiled at the rail-thin, hard-looking cop who had pushed his hat back on his flat forehead. She pushed her hat back on top of a bale of bleached blonde hair that tumbled out, and flashed a smile at him.

"Wanna go for a ride?" said the bluecoat with a bit of authority in his voice. He squeezed a lifted eyebrow out of his angular face, nodding to the passenger seat.

"Ten-four, I'm out the door," laughed cop-groupie Tracy. She opened the door of her car and climbed out. The police officer watched her stand up, adjust her giant tits and get into the front seat of the police cruiser. Her laugh made a hard ripple. She thought she sounded sexy, like in the movies.

Radioing in with a Signal Forty, the cop went off duty with approval from the dispatch center. He turned the beat-up Holstein, with over a hundred thousand on the odometer, and drove a short distance to a Montessori School located in his district. Tracy rattled on with the jargon of a police wannabe.

Overlooking a small man-made lake, the Montessori School was well protected from the street. A narrow private road led to its entry. As he drove, he dropped his left hand on one of Tracy's jodhpur thighs, a not-so-casual act since he had to reach across the mobile digital terminal that was mounted between the front seats. Encouraged because he got no resistance, the cop got right to the point.

"I want you to suck my dick. I bet you're good."

Tracy Ann smiled at the police officer who appeared to have flames flickering in his loins and said dryly, "Why don't you just lay your cock on the seat and I'll hammer the sap out of it with my flashlight." Before he could find out if she was pissed, or seriously ready to go down on him, headlights from a car entering the private road to the school danced across the hood of the car. Both of them blinked at the brightness.

"What the fuck!" The cop's chest jumped like an over-amped doper and his blood pump missed a few strokes.

"It's another cop car," exclaimed Tracy Ann, pleasant surprise lilting in her voice.

"Sit tight," he ordered as he snapped open the car door and walked over to the other car. Slowly, the electric window of the other car rolled down. Behind the wheel, grinning like he had won on a game show was a fellow cop known as Big Gil. The twenty-nine year old black wiggled his lips like a goat chomping on a can and said, chuckling deeply, "Whassup, bro? You doin' a little inter-ro-gat-ing?" He drew out the word in the best black comic style. "The old breathalyzer test?"

The cop put both hands on the front door of Big Gil's car and showed off a narrow smile that was accompanied with a long, Kentucky horse laugh. He spit and said, "I was just about to find out what this chick likes about cops."

"I know she'll like you, pardner," drawled Big Gil, with a knowing smile. He started to speak when the radio crackled, "Three Ten."

"Shit," exclaimed the cop as he opened his car door and unsnapped the radio receiver from the clip on the dash. He thought, just when I get a chance to get a little R&R I gotta go into service on some pissant call. He answered, "This is Three Ten."

"Accident with injuries at Brown and Center. You are the first unit," the radio crackled.

"Three Ten responding," he grunted, getting in the car. He jammed on the accelerator and blew the bouncing car up the road in the best NASCAR tradition and Tracy could feel her juices zipping, just like in the movies. The car leaped forward with the wind thrumming on her half-closed window.

"Is this legal? I mean, is it okay for me to go on a run?" she asked, her eyes wide with excitement. The policeman didn't answer, but dumb cunt came to mind.

Flicking on light bar, the officer instructed, "Just say you're in the citizen ride-along program. Just keep your mouth shut, but don't worry, nobody will ask." His lips split into a smile of anticipation. He knew what kind of jump start lights and a squealing siren gave a cop groupie inside the tight, cramped front seat of a bouncing squad car.

The cops called it the "Union Hall," a dark cavernous room in an out building attached to the City Yard. A sizzling streak of lighting followed a boom of thunder as the summer storm passed quickly out to the ocean. Giggling from the post excitement of all the flashing lights, crackling radios, sweat and gruff masculine voices that surrounded the accident scene they had just worked for the past two hours, Tracy said, "Are you sure it's okay to go in?"

"Hell yes, little lady. I'm officially on a 10-30. Off duty," sang out the cop as he twisted his key in the lock. As he flipped on the light switch, Tracy observed the splayed, soiled furniture, pool table and general disorder.

"What is this? Some kinda club?" she asked in her false, watery voice she thought sexy. Torrents of rain flung themselves against the window panes and plowed furrows in the built up grime on the glass.

"Yeah. It's the Police Association Hall."

"Police Association?

"It's like a union hall. This is where we meet. Sometimes we take care of serious business, but it's mostly a place for some R&R. Gil will be coming over. Should have been here by now."

"Gil? Who is Gil?"

"The black dude who pulled up on us at the school just before I had to go into service with the accident. He's having trouble with his old lady, so I 'spect he'll stop by for a few brews," he explained in the fake hipness and insularity found only around cops. Raindrops hammered a wet tattoo on the flat roof.

"It's cold in here. Air conditioning is too high," said Tracy Ann as she pulled at her wet uniform blouse.

"Peel that top off. Ain't nobody going to care in here," suggested the cop as he shucked of his wet uniform shirt." Shirtless, he crossed the room, returning with a Budweiser in each hand.

"Besides, you don't want to get beer on it." He returned with a Budweiser in each hand and watched Tracy Ann shed her blouse and line up a shot on the pool table.

"My brothers learned me to shoot pool."

"Anything else they learned you to do with a stick?" teased the cop with anticipation in his face.

She smiled slyly and protruded the tip of her tongue between her small front teeth in response. About fifteen pounds overweight with an inch or so of stomach flesh bulging over her uniform belt, Tracy's pool shooting form was wildly erotic. A broad shooting pool with her tits encased in a wide-strapped, sports bra gave him a prodigious hard on. Beer in each hand he walked up behind the bent-over Tracy Ann and leaned against her. He placed both cans of beer on the edge of the pool table, gripped the edge of the table with his hands and ground his throbbing groin into Tracy's uniform-encased ass. Dropping the cue on the table, Tracy tightened her cheeks and ground back. He gripped the felt edge tighter and pushed his pelvis hard against her ready ass. Tracy pushed back with her hips. Then, in a quick motion, he pushed her pants down around her ankles, exposing a ripe set of bare, quivering cellulite-pitted buttocks. Both were breathing hard and fast like a couple of overheated dogs about to have a stroke. They heard the key in the lock but neither missed a grinding beat.

"Good lovin', that's what I like to see," said Big Gil as he shut the door behind. Tracy Ann's eyes locked on Gil's as her head followed him across the room. He stopped directly across the pool table and proceeded to unbutton his uniform shirt.

Breaking contact with Tracy Ann's grinding ass, the other cop took a half step back and unbuckled his gun belt. He pulled the long barreled pistol from the holster before he dropped his web gear and shoved the snout of the gun between Tracy's legs. Flinching from the cold blue steel, Tracy bent her knees slightly as she felt the upward pressure of the gun barrel against her lubricated skin.

"Do it," she said in a hurried voice.

"Do what?"

"Gun fuck me. Hurry!" she pleaded as she leaned forward over the pool table pressing back against the gun barrel. In front of her, Big Gil pulled his 9mm Beretta from its holster and moved it within an inch of her wet lips.

"Gun suck," he declared as he unzipped his uniform trousers. She looked at his eyes and watched them light up like a flare in his chocolate face. Then Tracy's pink tongue flickered like a mamba snake going after a bird as it tried to wrap around the gun barrel.

Armand Box, PhD, a marine research scientist was returning from a short trip into the Baja peninsula where he spent three days in Guerrero Negro studying a rare crustacean that inhabited the Scammon's Lagoon salt flats. The drive north on Mexico Highway 1 was familiar and tiring. He passed small villages clinging to the dusty hills and escarpments, with a quick look. The road climbed and twisted around a primordial cliff; then it dropped into dry creeks and eroded earth as it bore tourists and Mexican commerce north from points south. Entering the pungent seaport of Ensenada from the Mexicali Valley, he passed the wharf, the giant cruise ships, the Port Captain's Office and the Customs and Immigration Office. Professor Box passed the stink of the fertilizer factories on the north side of the city. What a strange place to build condos, he observed.

Ninety minutes later the professor arrived at the border. The wait for passage through an inspection lane was noisy and long. For close to an uncomfortable hour he sat in the hot afternoon sun, breathing diesel fumes and dirty particles. Finally, waved through by the guard, there were no questions asked. The painful pressure building in his bladder caused him to stop a few minutes later in front of the first roadside restroom on the U.S. side of the Border. He left the Eighteenth Street exit and stopped his car in front of the small brick building. Getting out, he noticed a nondescript car at the far end of the littered parking lot. A heavy man, wearing blue pants and a T-shirt hanging over his bulbous gut, washed his hands at the sink. Nodding with polite reserve to the ominous man with fading arm tattoos, Professor Box went to the farthest urinal. His bladder relief was interrupted by a hard hand on his shoulder. Still urinating, Box turned into the face of the heavy gutted man.

Curiosity turned to penetrating fear that shrouded him in a pissy-smelling fog. "You are under arrest for public lewdness," growled the man as he stuck a police badge in front of Box. Color flooded from the professor's face as his life and academic career spun in front of his wet eyes. He forced himself to resist fainting, and a snuffling, crying sound left his throat as his pulse jumped like the downbeat of a kettle drum.

Minutes later Punch Packer had what he wanted; all of his victim's money. One hundred and three dollars. His little shakedown scam had worked perfectly once again. It was pretty simple graft. He'd pick out some "wimpy little mousefucker" and threaten to haul his ass in as a pervert. He'd let the vic sweat things out for a few minutes and then he'd cut the deal, their freedom for all the cash they were carrying. Picking the right person was the key to his success. It had to be a straight wearing a wedding ring. A guy who didn't look like he'd go to the cops. A guy who would bug out, just glad to be gone.

The breeze and rain off Bahia de los Todos Santos cooled the night as the Mexican commander with Asian looking eyes impatiently sat in the back seat of his chauffeured Ford LTD. Still as a snake, but ready to strike, Commander Gomez rubbed at his slightly pock-marked jowls. Driven from his expensive home in the outskirts of Ensenada, he waited patiently for the plane to land. A cautious and nervous man, he always carefully checked the area before its arrival. One could not be too careful in Baja with the Attorney General sniffing around for corruption. *Chinga tu madre*, the only thing that Mexican police work was good for was the opportunity for acceptable graft. Earlier, a cannonade of thunder passed across the city. Now the rain muffled the sounds of the night, making a noise like the tinking and pinking of cooling gun-barrels as it hit the hot runway.

The landing lights of the Convair 440 blinked red in contrast to the sky that was spilling down rain. The inbound plane from the Cayman Islands via Miami and Houston swooped down to meet the steaming tarmac. The big plane lumbered to a halt on the slick runway while streaks of bouncing headlights flickered from cars on the highway like a shivering string of Christmas lights.

As the plane taxied to a stop, a good-looking young Mexican with heavy scar tissue on his left cheek looked at Commander Gomez alert in the back seat of the LTD. At the command of "mueve el carro!" the young police chauffeur fired up the big Ford motor and drove across the runway. As his car approached the Convair, both Gomez and his driver watched the plane's door drop open. Leaving the LTD, Commander Gomez walked purposefully across the wet tarmac and handed a heavy metal briefcase to the copilot who reached down from the flight deck. No words were spoken. By the time he returned to his car, the plane had taxied back to the runway. Seconds later, it lifted off in the wet night with water spraying off the spinning tires being pulled by a mechanical force into the belly of the plane.

Tension drained now that the briefcase and its contents were the responsibility of someone else. Even though he participated in this drama every week and was heavily armed, he was always wired tight when he took the briefcase to the airfield. Its contents if known could result in his death. He would relax tonight with his mistress before going home to his overfed wife with cow's hips. Another week would pass before the payments from the shop-keepers would be due. Never a religious man, he crossed himself and wondered if the Virgin was interested in the prayers of a thief.

CHAPTER EIGHT

Skimming along the long, dry ribbon of concrete called Eighteenth Street, with a thick stogie jammed in his teeth, Officer Alvin Packer, badge number 103, looked for some action. Turning the steering wheel with his hands encased with cowhide sap gloves loaded with powdered iron, he drove south on Highland. It was close to midnight. A red-neck racist who was proud of his neo-Nazi views, Punch loved hassling "smokes and spics." The master of the mean street, he was proud of his reputation as a rank ole' boy who went after "jive-ass, trash-talking niggers and Mexicans," with a vengeance. He rolled into a neighborhood where the thudding beat of strip joints competed with each other's electric bounce. Taking a deep drag on the half-smoked cigar, he flicked on his red lights because he had found himself some action.

A lavender-finned Fleetwood, pimpmobile with a gaping hole in the muffler, suddenly swung over the line in front of his cruiser. It wandered, then jerked back to its lane as the oscillating lights bounced and shimmied off stark brick walls and ugly construction rubbish that filled a vacant lot. Busted springs on the right side caused the car to wallow. Packer's red lights assaulted the rearview mirror and pulled the car over. The big cop with a beer-belly brought his car to a halting stop. He opened the door and removed the heavy baton from the makeshift holster in the door panel. He moved toward the stopped car with surprising speed. A mean looking black, with a face like heated rubber, stared at him with hot eyes. The misty beams from the street lights overhead cast a grey sheen to his face.

"Stay put!" Packer commanded. Through a hard glare, the muscular male with a scabrous face grudgingly obeyed the order.

Stopping some ten feet from the car, Packer lit up a fresh cigar with a wooden match. His eyes never left the driver who stared straight ahead with swollen, bruised eyelids, vapor-locked in anger.

"What say, Twinkie?" challenged Packer in sharp voice as he moved closer to the car. He was met with angry silence as the man's eyes were glued to Packer's fists of iron.

Then the driver of the long heavy Cadillac, vintage 1970s, slowly said, "See-gar, watcha doin' stopping me for? I ain't boost-ing or heisting tonight. Jus' lookin' for some warm pussy." Odor from the man's reddish nappy hair covered with pomade, poured out of the car.

Packer laughed harshly, secretly proud of his street name, "Big Cigar." He stuck his head inside the car and sniffed the inside. The heavy aroma of marijuana hung in the air. "Taking a little mota?" More hard silence. The man knew better than to talk back to Packer.

Packer said abruptly, "Give me your buy money and get your black ass off my turf." The man reluctantly lifted a thin, worn billfold out of his shirt pocket and deposited all the money in Packer's outstretched hand. The starter motor on the finned car caught with a hacking cough as it pulled away, pistons clang-ing hard. Needs rings, thought Punch. Tonight luck was with the pussy hunter in the rusting Coupe de Ville. Busting the really bad dudes was the only way Packer kept score so he let the driver of the Cadillac go. But he still practiced the dictum of the hardened street cop; stop anyone who looks like you can bust. Officer Alvin Packer, aka "Punch" or "the Big Cigar," liked nothin' more than to slap potential perps with his thud gloves. The martial arts stuff was for pussy cops. Long past his prime, Packer could still drop just about anyone with a hard punch to the throat with his thud gloves.

Flicking on the dash light he counted out his "pension money" and jammed it in his pocket with a smile. Twisting the ignition, he swung his snuff-juice stained cruiser south. He watched a tomcat lick its nuts under a streetlight. The thick iron bars on the windows and doors of liquor stores blinked back at him when his headlights flickered across them. Ramshackle houses yielded to run-down flop houses, and boarded-up fore-closures lined the street. Some vato low-riders rumbled past his car.

The beat he covered was thickly populated by midnight cowboys, sailors, ex-cons and homosexual bikers hanging out in windowless saloons that were loud, dark and dangerous. The eerie glow of the flickering, mercury vapor street lights and neon rippled over the Apache Girls Go-Go, the Cabrillo skin-flick theater, watery-eyed drunks and gang graffiti, washing his car with psychedelic rainbows. A band of wildly indignant Mexican youths, looking lethal and unpredictable as nitro, wearing hair-nets, Dago undershirts and shiny black pants, jived to the music of their boom boxes. As he drove by, they stared at La Policia, the barrio name for the police. A limping Native American Indian, with a tattoo on his arm of a blue snake speckled with black dots to cover puncture marks by a hypodermic needle, moved down the crusty sidewalk. The words, "MI VIDA LOCA," colloquial Spanish for the drug life, were cursively inscribed under the snake tattoo.

Moving deeper into his turf and into the barrio, he spotted a crowd of about twenty home boys rapping and openly smoking dope. The macabre sound of a thumping radio blared as a pair of low-riders, sporting lots of gold rope and earrings, glided by. Red bandanas wrapped around their heads, each gave him his best hard-ass look. Packer stared back in a moment of quiet triumph from the general sanctum of his police cruiser. Then he coughed up a plug of phlegm that could stop up a drain and spit it out the window. The glob landed in the street, where it lay like a lone oyster.

Leaving the barrio, he steered the patrol car out of the main artery running parallel with US 5. In the distance, headlights floated as an oncoming car drifted from one lane to the next.

Then, in an instant, the car picked up speed and zeroed in on the yellow lane marker. The car, an ancient Olds, lurched forward and slammed into the fender of Packer's car. The Olds careened off the police car, hit a garbage can, and blasted its way down an alley, scattering trash barrels in its path.

The impact nearly threw him into the passenger seat. Stunned, Packer recovered fast and crawled back to the driver's side. Grabbing the wheel, he bounced the machine off the concrete apron pan, whipped the wheel around and went thundering down the alley in pursuit. Wet dust and gravel spewed in the night. His blood pressure up, his face turning purple he raced after the car, following it across a grade school playground as it headed into a dead-end corner. Trapped, the driver slammed on the brakes, jumped out of the car and slipped on the pea gravel as he tried to get away on foot. After taking less than a dozen steps, he stopped. Vomit frothed from his mouth. He stood there, heaving what was left in his guts in the glare of high beam lights that bounced across the schoolyard.

Packer, his adrenaline pumping to the max, slammed on the brakes of his black and white. Gravel flew, making pinging sounds as it scattered across the Oldsmobile. He jammed the gearshift into neutral, jerked his High Standard, short barreled shotgun from the dash clamp, flipped off the safety and pumped a load into the chamber. CLACK! CLACK! The sound was unmistakable. The man ran in a panic.

Packer raced after the runner just ahead of him, yelling into the night, "Stop, you mutha!" as he stumbled head-long into a piece of playground equipment. He jerked the curved trigger reflexively. The chaw of tobacco dislodged from his jaw. The gun jumped from his grip. The explosion deafened him. Pellets from the shell hit the man in the back of his head from a distance of less than fifty feet, tearing off the left side of his cranium. What was left of his splattered face was nothing but red gore with white bone fragments sticking out like pieces of broken glass. One shoulder hung like a limp chicken wing. The force of the double aught shot propelled him five feet with his face bouncing and scraping along the surface of the playground. Dead as he hit the dirt, a deep red trickled among the gravel.

Packer approached the downed man cautiously, his heart pounding crazily in his chest. Adrenaline screamed through his veins making him hot and sick all at once. Sweating and out of breath he tried to control himself. He bent down and groped for his victim's pulse. He couldn't feel one. The shock power had turned the body into a bloody stew of viscera. Fear clutched at Packer's stomach as he began to realize the enormity of his fuck-up.

His breath came in gulps. Panic, deep panic, began to set in. That god-damn Murphy thing again, everything went wrong. He'd become involved in a high-speed chase without notifying dispatch, and shot someone in the back who didn't have a gun, or any kind of weapon for that matter. Sweat drenched the back of his shirt. The crotch of his pants was soaked with the rancid perspiration that seeped from his pores. His mind raced, he had to do something quick.

Packer went to his car, pulled out the jacket he wore when it was cold. He walked over to the still warm body and pulled his illegal "throw-away" gun from his ankle holster. Then he stuck the grip of the gun in the dead man's hand. Packer's own hand shook so violently he had difficulty getting the dead man's finger through the trigger guard. He wrapped the jacket around the pistol, pointed the gun at the side of the police car and fired two muffled shots. One lodged in the trunk with a thunk, the other missed the car completely and whined off into the night.

Leaving the untraceable gun in the dead man's hand, Packer went back to the car, keyed the radio mike and called in for assistance. The dispatcher responded. Moments later, a police siren screamed and moved in close and braked hard. Packer lit a cigarette, his lips wetting the paper. Blowing smoke he prepared himself for the questioning that would come. His nerves felt strung like catgut on an old violin, as a crowd of rowdy blacks and Mexicans converged on him. The mangled body on the ground was still. Breathing hard, like a wounded moose with wolves at bay, he faced the growing menacing crowd. It raged around him until he jacked a round in the shotgun – clack, clack – and pointed the gun at the group, yelling, "Stay back!" One man, with a dirty rag wrapped around his skull started yowling at the top of his lungs. A squad car, and finally an ambulance, arrived. Within minutes the situation started to get out of hand. Three more cars, one of them ferrying a K-9 officer, arrived. A salivating, growling German shepherd on a short leash kept the jostling crowd back as investigators poured over the car, measured the distance from the body and picked up evidence. Nervous patrolmen wearing body armor braced against their cars with shotguns jammed on their hips and watched, as grim-looking supervisors in civilian clothes talked to each other in hushed tones.

Two bozo cycle jocks in custom-tailored uniforms, dumb and full of themselves, arrived. Wearing oversized black Gestapo boots, helmets with huge chin straps they came to the scene in great dramatic style. They roared up with beacons of red lights. They shut off the Kawasaki KZ100s yipping in unison and peeled off their black leather gloves. One of them knew Packer. "Making your contribution to society, Punch?" He said with a knowing smirk.

"Yep. Just standing 'round, rappin' with a bunch of fuckin' assholes," laughed Packer, nervously, as he waved his shotgun in the direction of the crowd. He pulled a snot-dried handkerchief from his pocket and scrubbed the sweat off his forehead. In the umbrella glow of the street light, a "no wants" metallic response crackled over the radios from central communications. The ballooning tension in the crowd faded as Punch Packer left, riding in the passenger seat of a white, unmarked investigator's car.

He thought, no wants, no warrants, no weapon, I'm fucked.

The parking lot of the NevadaLine Card Club was a car show crammed with gleaming, new, high-priced models as well as banged-up pick-ups with gun racks and Rottweilers guarding the tools. The huge car moved almost cautiously, its heavy tires revolving so slow you could read the raised rubber marquee. The flashing neon sign lit up the parking lot, flashing like heat lightning. Silva Buno parked his black Lincoln Town Car between a Mercedes and an old Chevy. Sucking at the raw juice from a blister on the inside of his cheek he got out of the car, exuding menace like a bad odor. Silva Buno was the Chief of Police of Border City. A cadet-sized Napoleon with shady connections in Mexico. It was a good thing to never mention small or short in his presence.

Crossing the pitted concrete parking lot, he entered the one-story building that occupied the most valuable property in Border City. Inside, hundreds of people sat at cramped poker tables. Space in front of him instantly opened up in the room thick with people, smoke and noise, as he walked smartly through the crowd. The NevadaLine Card Club was one of many legal card clubs in California. It was the most prosperous and only one located between San Diego and the Mexican border.

The click of poker chips rattled lightly against the background of multilingual voices. Smoke clouds hung above the tables as scantily attired bar girls worked their way expertly between players. It was close to midnight and the place hummed and vibrated with a Saturday night kind of energy found only in casinos. Pai Gow and Super Pan-9 were played by Asians and Filipinos who shook and slammed the brass bowls holding the game dice. A cigarette pusher, with the vacant eyes of a working girl, smiled automatically at him. He waved her away and walked on.

He passed a row of cheap chandeliers to the short passageway that led to a small office complex. Signs designating the accounting, marketing and security offices were posted on the office doors. The sign on the office door farthest from the passageway simply read, "Private." Outside the door sat a large, angular man dressed in a poorly-fitting, three-piece suit, barely covering his shoulder holster. Reading the Racing Form with eyes surrounded with layers of scar tissue revealing his occupation, he beat a tattoo on the soft carpet with dull black loafers as he read. Cheap shoes, cheap guy thought Buno. The mastodon-size guard nodded without enthusiasm and tapped lightly on the thick door. Buno knew him well. Ike "Crazy Ike" Dellagallo had done time for skillfully removing the eyes out of a man with a small fish gaff, and worked as Forbes' enforcer. A buzzer sounded briefly and Ike pushed the door open for Buno who stepped inside the richly appointed office and nodded to the red-faced man who yelled and gestured into a cell phone.

"You think I'm easy? A cunt? Listen you jerkoff motherfucker, I got wise guys that will chew the fucking ears off your fucking head. They live for that stuff. All I got to do is tell them to load up, be ready when I call, and they'll blast the shit out of you." Pausing for breath, he swirled the glass of Courvoisier in his other hand, smiled crookedly at the visitor, and revved up. "Don't get it in your dopey fucking head that just because you're a doctor you can welsh on your payments. To me you are just another zip-fuck behind on his gambling loan."

There was a moment of silence as the man seemed to grind the phone into his florid ear. He roared, "Cops! Don't even think of goin' to the cops. My guys will rip your welshing heart out before the cops get their dicks out of their hands..." He pushed the off button on the phone, as if to kill it, and looked at the man who had entered the office. Buno asked with a smile, "Loan collection problems, Laz?" He knew what was going on. Laz Forbes, in addition to owning the NevadaLine Card Club, was a money lender and apparently, a doctor, who had borrowed gambling money, was behind on his payments. Way behind.

"These fucking doctors can make you rich when they start gambling 'cause they ain't any better at gambling than they are at doctorin'. But just because everyone else in the world kisses their ass they think they can call the shots when it comes to paying off a loan. You know the kind."

A stunning blonde woman, with the good looks of a world-class call girl, sat across from the channel switcher. She wore an expensive business suit of mauve raw silk and across her lap was an open alligator-skin brief case. Long, dangling stone earrings accented her high cheekbones and beautiful mouth – a woman pushing the hard side of forty, with the lushness of a much younger woman. She looked at the world through cool, cool eyes, like half-wet sand glistening with a water sheen. She was writing something on a yellow legal pad. Strong elegance, the kind that most males reacted to with a tingle in their crotch but are fearful for their manhood, surrounded her.

Swaggering around the room in tough-guy style, Buno nodded to the woman who blinked back acknowledgment; eyes that said no interest, beat it, Shorty.

"It's behind the desk," said Forbes. He had just hung up the phone with a phlegmy voice like someone had squeezed his throat. There was nothing attractive about Laz Forbes besides his money and power. A homely Mediterranean mutt with a face peppered with acne scars and an ugly fat body that he cursed everyday in the mirror.

Curling smoke wafted toward the vaulted ceiling from the Cohiba cigar he waved. His private room was decorated with heavy gold, white and brown furniture that pressed sharply against a huge wall mounted TV. He wore a pair of cream-colored slacks with a spandex waist to accommodate his ever increasing bulk. A blue silk shirt with bright flowers on it, a little too small, was stuffed into his pants. On his feet he wore handmade alligator loafers with twin tassels. The kind that said, "Hey! Lookahere! These cost a grand." Forbes sighed heavily through thick lips as he lifted the cut glass tumbler full of Courvoisier to his mouth. He was a man who took care of himself, showering at least twice a day. But an hour after he had showered, powdered his balls and put on a clean shirt, he started to decay. Sweat drove the clean from his shirt and the beard on his face grew like sprouted devil grass.

A "made man," Forbes was more than the owner of a card club. The boss of a small offshoot of one of the twenty-five or so remaining Italian families, Forbes belonged to a *Famiglia* that held pervasive power in the southwest.

It was in the San Diego fishing industry and on the waterfront that Forbes made his name as the enforcer for the *Famiglia*. His excellent work record earned him the underworld franchise of Border City. If you resisted Laz Forbes you had better have an asbestos asshole. His specialty was to have two of his thugs hold you down while he applied the orange-blue flame of a blow torch to the brown-rose anus flower. Within seconds, a man's testicles began to melt like ice cubes on a griddle, and shit would stream out of a cauterized colon. Not a pretty sight but highly effective.

The card club in Border City was his own genius. With the immigration of the gambling-hungry Asians to the San Diego area, he captured a market where a hundred thousand dollar bet was not uncommon. But most of his money was made in loan-sharking. He charged 10% interest every five days and never even had to worry about reporting it to the IRS. His clients were glad to pay. Buno retrieved the Haliburton aluminum briefcase. Raised it with one hand and thumped it with the knuckles of his empty hand. Full. It made a noise like an unripe melon.

Snapping shut her expensive leather briefcase and rising from the plush chair, the woman said, "Gentlemen, I'm going to leave unless you need some additional information." She paused as both men locked their eyes on her and then continued, this time with advice. "Laz, I'd watch the dealers a little more closely. I can't tell from the receipts if they are skimming but they probably are. The problem is we don't have any overhead one-way cameras so all we can do is watch them from the floor. Next week, I'll run the take at each table and we'll change the dealer's routine. Be sure you get an accurate count of the players."

"Good enough," said the man. "You're the expert."

She laid a folder on his desk. "The deposits from our bank check out okay. I've been receiving weekly verifications over the wire on the delivery date and it corresponds to the shipments."

Pausing, she looked directly at the card club owner. He said nothing but nodded affirmatively like a fat puppet.

"Goodnight," she said with a smile on her Norma Jean lips as she stood, her silk blouse stretched across her full breasts, a small diamond hung in the V around her neck. She left a trace of Ombre Rose perfume scenting the room as she walked out the door on a pair of long legs encased in black nylons. The exit walk, slow and confident, had a hypnotic effect on Buno.

Pointing to the closing door Laz said casually, "Sometimes she can be a paranoid pain in the ass but that's the smartest thing I ever did with this operation."

Sensing Forbes was in a good mood, Buno asked, "You boning her?"

Wincing he gave Silva Buno a cold, hard look. "No way. She ain't just another head of hair you use to clean your pipes. This is one of the help I don't fuck around with, not that I wouldn't like to try some of what she's got. Hiring her away from Caesar's in Vegas was a stroke of genius. She knows gambling operations better than any pit boss and she's greedy enough not to worry about what's legal and what ain't. We couldn't have put together the deal down south without her. Those fuckin' beaners would be cheatin' us blind if we didn't have her working the books." Forbes paused, swirled his drink with slow circular motion and went on, "Things still sweet with Commandante Gomez?"

"Yeah, but we may have to up his take some 'cause he's catching on to how well we're doing."

"Yeah, I expected that. Too bad we can't take him out like we do whenever a middle guy gets greedy," Forbes chuckled, twisting his lips in contempt.

"Gomez has an airfield we don't have and the contacts with the distributors. He's related to most of them. We don't have a choice, Laz."

Winking, Forbes snapped back his thick head with an icy smile. "We need to talk about something. Listen my good friend," said Forbes, "I'm getting a feeling in my bones that something ain't right with the Ensenada scam."

"Yeah?" questioned Buno with an affirmative heavy breath, letting the question hang in the room. Then he reminded Forbes, "Getting that chopper across the border is the easiest way for us to move stuff. You need to fly down there sometime with us and you'll see how smooth it works."

"No way. I hate flying in those fuckin' windmills." Forbes scowled hard through a clump of cigar smoke. A slick film of sweat spread across his face. The thought of it made him want to pee.

Buno interrupted to assure him. "We're okay, Laz. Nobody suspects anything. Don't forget, we got first-rate police protection on this deal. Besides, who knows anything about this except you, me and the cunt. And since we are all equal partners, nobody is going to drop the dime are they?"

"What about Hart?" challenged Forbes. "He must have some idea of what the fuck is going on."

"Hart doesn't know anything for sure. He's just a gofer with a briefcase. For all he knows it's full of fuck videos to sell to the tourists. Besides, he's scared shitless of me and I've got too much on his sorry ass."

"Better be right, understand?"

The grey beeper hanging from Buno's belt chirped like a tiny bird. He picked up a phone and jabbed at each button.

"Chief Buno here," he said contemptuously. Listening for a moment, he said abruptly, "Where?" He waited silently, then demanded, "Name?" Anger flushed his dark complexion a deep red and his cool-dude persona slipped away. "Fuck no! I'll come down and take care of it myself." Jamming the phone in his pocket, he finally inhaled. He stood up, instinctively rising up on his toes as small men do.

"One of my men shot a Mex." He picked up the aluminum briefcase and started toward the door.

Forbes chuckled with a learned meanness. "This isn't the first time a wetback got snuffed by one of your boys. What's the big deal?"

"This Mex was shot in the back running from the scene."

"What did he do? Steal a six pack?"

"Hell, no," came the angry reply. "It was a no-account traffic chase and one of my dumb fucks unloaded a shotgun on him. Now I've got to take care of a shitstorm of things before they get out of hand. This is the kind of thing that the fuckin' newspapers and TV get off on. There are media jerks and the ACLU crawling all over the police department. Always happens when we shoot a goddamn civilian."

"That's why you're the Chief of Police, shit storms are your specialty," laughed Forbes as he watched Buno slam through the rear door leading to the private parking lot at the rear of the building. The night wind came before the rain and the sky started to spit down lightly on the hot asphalt. Buno breathed heavily as he walked to his car. Firing up the engine of his Lincoln Town Car, he sped out the alley seething with anger that went straight to his stomach where it stayed with a growing ulcer.

CHAPTER NINE

The dull, tightening in his dry throat was painful reminder of the bad gin he had pounded down the night before. Furry tongue, sticky eyes, yes, all his old friends had dropped in. Rescuing the old Mexican from the Tijuana fire the day before played back the scene of the horrible fiery death of his friend. While it drove the need for alcohol in order to sleep, he couldn't stop the tape that replayed in his head. Harry was busy pulling the sheets off his body and hopped around on the bed like the nervous ringmaster of a small circus. Jack dragged the sheets back up to his face and tried to escape the marching band in his cerebrum. Harry tugged back, his feathers still scented from the smoke. Drinking himself into a stupor was the way to fight off the flaming dreams.

He got up, fed Harry and then showered longer than necessary in an attempt to clean the booze from his body. He tried to think through the rest of the day. Last night he had promised himself he would go to the federal authorities with his suspicions. After dressing, he loaded Harry in the car and they had a leisurely breakfast in one of those small diners that had six stools and a cook who doubled as the waitress. After a large orange juice, eggs and bacon, which he shared with the bird, Jack drove into San Diego. The Federal Building was located in downtown in the Civic Center area.

He parked in the massive underground parking garage of the Double Tree Hotel located at Front and E Streets. He walked across E Street to the building's entrance on Broadway, ducking down into the ground-level arcade of offices that surrounded a faux rock garden. The quiet noise of the water's gentle cascading motion was making him slightly nauseous. He checked his Rolex. It was almost noon. The building was done in the federal non-style with ATMs, snack machines, and well dressed clones stepping smartly on the marble. Locating the Drug Enforcement Agency suite on the building directory, he punched a button and rode the elevator to the third floor, dreading an encounter but wanting to get it over with.

He gave his name to the receptionist with unfriendly eyes and a fifty dollar manicure and asked to speak with an agent. He sat impatiently in the waiting room, reading warning pamphlets designed in three languages. When he told her he had no appointment she skewered him with a glare, before she punched up someone on the intercom, fingernails clicking like rat feet. A few minutes later, a young agent, with anchorman teeth and an acrylic glaze of hair spray, came out of his office. He extended his hand saying, "Mr. Dalton, I'm Agent George Rixton." Then, in the tone of an I'm-the-in-control bureaucrat, he asked, "What can I do for you?"

"Mr. Rixton, "I'm a pilot for the BCPD."

"Border City PD?"

"Yes."

"Is this a delivery?"

"No."

Rixton pointed to his office and motioned for Jack to follow him. Once they were inside he closed the office door.

"Are you a cop?" inquired the agent while flicking invisible lint off his Brooks Brothers wool suit.

"No. I'm a contract pilot."

"You just do the flying. That right?" interrupted Rixton as he leaned back in his swivel chair and put his feet up on the desk, pinning Jack his best agent-school stare. His richly polished loafers with twin tassels showed almost no wear or tear. Not a street operator, thought Jack as he watched the man's face for clues. He had a heady vision of sticking those ding dongs up the agent's haughty nose.

"I've flown with you guys. Are you an American citizen?" was the agent's combined response and inquiry as he fiddled with some papers on his desk.

Looking hard at him, grey eyes etched in permanent squint lines, he didn't like what he saw.

"Yes, I'm an American citizen and no I don't just fly the aircraft. I fly it according to instructions and FAA requirements." He felt his face flush with anger.

Agent Dickhead cleared his throat. "So just what is the problem, Mr. Dalton?"

Taken back with the line of questioning, doubt began to nag, and he thought carefully about his response.

"Look, the flying I do is for the Border City Police Department. Didn't I just say that? We fly down to Mexico on a regular basis."

"We?"

"Me, my crew chief and police brass."

"How high up in the chain of command?"

"Either the chief or assistant chief."

"How regular?"

"Once a week. Every Monday," rasped Jack.

"Where to?"

"Ensenada. Baja, California."

"Where did you learn to fly?" said Rixton abruptly

"In the service. I was an Army pilot. I left the service at the rank of major."

"Really," inquired Rixton. He knew that the rank of major was fairly high. "Any time in country?" His tone sharp, authoritative, and phony.

A faint smile crossed Jack's face in response to the punk agent's attempt to sound like a vet who did a hard tour somewhere. "Which 'in-country' do you mean? Why do you ask?"

Ignoring the question, Rixton proceeded with his line of questioning by saying, "What have you been doing between your Army days and now?"

Jack picked a spot on the agent's heroic jaw but cracked his knuckles instead, "Mostly flying."

"For whom?"

"Companies, individuals, mining and oil interests. I've been flying for a long time."

Agent Rixton opened his desk and pulled out a pack of cigarettes. "Care for one?" he asked as he extended his hand across the polished desk with a single phone on it. The hand had a slight tremor and the gaze was less direct.

"No, thanks."

"Mr. Jack Dalton, did you ever do any covert work for the government?" asked Rixton, emphasizing Dalton's first name. Then he continued with another question before Dalton could answer the first, a habit that Dalton found irritating. "You know, any murky crap for anyone?"

"No. In the Army I flew the usual helicopter missions. Mostly troop transport and medivac stuff. You have access to my flight logs if you need them." Jack paused, then continued, "Mr. Rixton, the reason I'm here, is that I believe the Border City Police Department may be ferrying something illegal across the border in the police helicopter I fly. I don't have any proof, but if we are, then I don't want to get caught up in whatever comes down."

"No proof?" was the agent's response as his right hand rose in question.

"None. Just a feeling."

"Who is *we*?"

"Myself, a crew chief and the Assistant Chief of Police."

"Well, Mr. Dalton we just can't act on a feeling, we'd be working day and night on tips from old ladies mad at their neighbors."

Jack felt his nag factor going up. "I know that," he shot back, "but I want to be dead sure that if there is anything going on that my crew chief and I aren't a part of it. The assistant chief is a guy named Lee Hart."

"What makes you so suspicious of your trips to Ensenada?"

"We go down there under the auspices of what's called the Border Cities Police Project."

"Never heard of it," said the DEA agent impatiently, in a voice edged with sarcasm, "but no big deal." He was checking his watch now. "The last people the DEA should worry about is another law enforcement agency. My job," he said pompously, "is to go after the bad guys, not some local cops who are flying into Mexico for a little tequila and tight T-shirts. What did you call that project or program?"

Jack remained silent for a few moments. Sparking stares leaped between them. "Border Cities Police Project."

"Well," commented Rixton as he stood, smoothing his immaculate cuffs. Moving around from behind the desk he stepped across the small open area to the office door. He twisted the brass handle; opened it to the receptionist area; a chorus line of chirping phones. Then he said to Jack with an imperious tone, "Your information is much appreciated, Mr. Dalton. I suggest you not fret about flying for the Border City Police Department. When we have time I'll check it out. But, if you are uncomfortable with it, perhaps you should find another job."

Holding back his anger, Jack tried to explain. "Look, Mr. Rixton, what I'm trying to do is work a steady job and write another book. That's why I pilot for the Border City Police Department. It's part-time easy work. Maybe I'm paranoid. I don't want to quit a job that pays me well but I don't want to be involved in some illegal stuff." He paused, looking Rixton directly in the eyes and continued, "I've been flying for so long that the only thing I can do that will pay me well is to pilot choppers. I can't quit."

"Oh, you're an author too, I'm impressed. Gathering material are you? Good guys, bad guys, shoot em up?" The agent looked at Jack like he was a first class yarn spinner.

Rixton looked at his watch again and said, "My guess is you're a little sensitive, and you're not in any trouble. A police department would be pretty stupid using its helicopter for anything illegal, especially in Mexico."

"Or pretty smart."

"Why do you say that?" challenged Rixton.

"Because no one would believe it was happening."

"Never heard of a police department dirty enough to use a helicopter illegally, even the BCPD City Department," said the agent with authority.

"Are you going to check this out?"

Dickhead smiled tightly, shrugged his narrow shoulders, and patted his expensive tie. "When and if necessary," came the officious reply. "Good day, Mr. Dalton." "Let me know about that book."

Jack left the chilled, air-conditioned office and walked unsteadily into the crystalline-bright early morning that would soon turn into another crappy summer day. He wondered what the penalty was for taking a federal employee apart.

Moments later, Agent Rixton dictated a brief memo for the file. He gave it to the overly blonde typist, her hair set in lacquered stone. "Type this and put it in the cover-your-ass file," was his flip instruction to the woman. The memo authorized a background check on Dalton and Hart if the agency had the manpower to do it; low priority stuff that would never get done, slipping through the cracks of an already ponderous bureaucracy which moved with the speed of a melting glacier.

While Agent Rixton was doing his duty as he saw it, Jack walked to his black Mercedes and tossed his sunglasses onto the front seat. Harry excitedly hopped down from his perch, bent his head in an odd angle and chirped *"Beer! Beer!"* Jack thought he would never get his clinched teeth apart. He got in, turned on the ignition and backed out of the narrow space. He left the San Diego DEA office knowing the well tailored suit was simply not interested. Somebody needed to do a full-tilt boogie on Rixton's head, he thought angrily. Driving away, he selected a tape from the console and inserted it in the deck, but he didn't hear the words as the Beach Boys cranked up on "Little Deuce Coupe." He needed some gin. Now.

The woman with a G-6 classification was on the very wrong side of forty. She wore very blue tinted contact lenses, a tight girdle, and a warped outlook on her life. She finished typing the confidential report dictated by Agent Rixton. Finished, she carefully rubbed her neck. Today it had more kinks than a preacher's conscience. That little schmoe she worked for was prancing around like a stud horse today and she was tired. Later that afternoon, after she had made a phone call from her office, she would share happy hour drinks with Lee Dykes Hart in the solitude of a pool side table at the Riverview Motor Inn in San Ysidro. There was no river or view and it had never been more than a cheap motel on the tourist route.

After meeting Hart at the motel for an after work drink she told him about the pilot's visit to DEA office and Hart said, "Sweet Thing, can you get me a copy of that report?"

Sweet Thing's real name was Norma Lee Lentz. Her stage name was Dicee and she once worked as a popular glitzy stripper in Houston clubs like the Crystal Pistol, the Copa and the Bayou; high tits, narrow waist, "them were the days," she often said. From Titus, Tennessee, she was the fourth daughter of a scary mother hogtied to Christian values. She began her career as an eighteen-year-old with a fake ID, full of awe for the neon twinkle and glow of the dance hall. At one time she thought she was a few kick steps away from Vegas. A favorite of the wild-eyed conventioneers, she easily gained star-stripper status by twirling her 44-inch boobs in opposite directions while shooting blank pistols at the noisy audience in fart-filled rooms where the cheap booze tasted like high grade turpentine. Diet pills, speed and too much drinking, provided her with a stocky body and a bad liver that forced her out of her high-kick career into a real job. Mean as a boxed rattlesnake and tougher than nails, she was one of many disappointed women who migrated to California. There, she ended up with a respectable civil service job in the regional Drug

Enforcement Administration office. She met fellow Southerner Lee Dykes Hart during a very boozy happy hour at the River View Motor Inn. For the past two years she shared inside DEA information with him. Not because she had a mad-on for anyone in the DEA; sharing the information with Hart just made her feel useful and important to someone. Besides, Hart was an Assistant Police Chief. A white-hat guy.

"I can't get you a copy, but if you are nice to me I might tell you what's in it," she said cocking her left eyebrow. "Everything we type with the word "confidential" on it is controlled. The DEA doesn't want anything walking away from the office. Especially info from a pilot who thinks his employer is doing bad boy things in the Baja."

Assistant Chief Lee Dykes Hart flashed his gold cigarette lighter and smiled at the woman. She caught the scent of his cologne, Old Spice, and just an old smell, like his plaid sport coat. On the marble table in front of him was a glass of Wild Turkey, poured neat. Hart's grey-flecked, coal-black hair, his vintage sport coat, gold neck chain and open neck shirt gave him the appearance of a restaurateur or a mid-level pimp. Winking, he coaxed the woman with a smooth oily voice, he thought sexy. "Honey Chile, y'all just try to remember what went in the report. I think I can sort out what's important." Sometimes her head was as vacant as a Houston high-rise, he thought. But, this was a serious matter. The pilot he hired was suspicious enough to go to the feds. Hell, he didn't think the guy was interested in doing anything except pecking away on his damn laptop when he wasn't flying. The arrogant prick.

Nodding when she lifted a frosted glass off the table, and pulling a drink through her lips that looked like old leather, she said, "Well, one thing's for damn sure. The guy you got flying your helicopter ain't just the ordinary, run-of-the-mill pilot."

"Well, sugar, what do you mean?" the thick accent rolled off of Hart's tongue like gooey honey as he made a come-on gesture with his hands.

"He was a helicopter pilot in the Gulf War," she announced.

"Big deal," said Hart, grinning darkly. "Every chopper pilot over forty must have learned how to fly in Arabia. That's why there are so many of them. What else has he been doing? What makes you think he is gonna be a problem for me?"

"Well hon," she said, letting the words roll off her tongue like a cat licking whiskers, "Your pilot strikes me as the kind of guy who won't quit once he gets a hair up his airborne ass."

Sensing a real threat, Hart leaned forward, put on his would-you-please-do-me-a-big-favor face and said, "Why do you think our flyboy is gonna be a problem?"

"Come on, Lee," she said coyly, "I know you got a little some-thing going. How else could you afford that pretty little car you drive?" There went that goofy eyebrow again.

Hart flashed a tight smile and lit a menthol cigarette at the same time before he said, "Listen, babydoll, every cop shop has some little scams. Pays for the nice truck, the bass boat. Makes the life a little sweeter when you can deal with the douche bags. This deal in Mexico ain't no big fuckin' deal, but I'd sure enough like to know what kind of people we got on the payroll, especially when they don't carry a badge. Anything else you remember about this guy?"

"You know Mr. Smart Ass, he mostly wrote him off. At least that's what the report I typed says. He's just a name settin' in the file for now but if his name pops up again, you boys might have a little problem."

"Sweet Thing, in the cop business we always got problems even though we're the good guys."

She thought for a moment, looking at Hart through boozy eyes, slightly off-center, "Well, maybe you ought to get rid of him."

"Can't figure him out. When I've flown with him, which is just about every week, he's real quiet, distant-like. Works on a book whenever we're in Ensenada. For sure, he ain't about to let anyone get to know him, but he don't seem like a guy who cares what kind of load he has to fly. That's why I hired him."

The woman shrugged her shoulders and said, "That's all I know, Lee. Come on," she said standing. She reached out for his hand and said, "I only got a half hour. Think you're up to it?"

"Up to what?" he laughed.

"Up to where I might have a better memory 'bout my boss's memo in the file." Winking at Hart she asked, "Now, is that being too faw-wahd of me?"

Lee Dykes Hart stood and put his arm around the generous hips, as her nylon skirt clung tight to her body like plastic wrap. He headed to the room the motel comped him, his pricey shoes crunched on the walkway with each heavy step. Inside, he kissed her, and she pulled a small, green cylinder from her purse, spraying her mouth with a strong peppermint mist.

"How bout a little Binaca blast," she said as she thumped Hart's bulging crotch with her index finger.

After his visit to the DEA, Jack drove out to the airfield. Boomer wasn't working on the helicopter and the maintenance shed was locked up, so he drove to his house. Boomer lived in the country on a small ten-acre farm he rented from a developer who was just waiting for an upswing in housing market. It wasn't much to look at, but it served his simple life. Jack parked, pulled off his sunglasses and put them in the pocket of his blue denim shirt. Harry balanced on his shoulder, he kicked through the devil grass and sticker weed landscape. The bird blinked in the bright sunlight. He knocked on the screen door and yelled, "Boomer!" No answer. He must be out back in his small barn, he thought. Jack found himself surrounded by four Sicilian donkeys. Clattering around like excited children, the affectionate little animals poked and nuzzled him. Harry shrieked jealously and flapped his wings, announcing the hairy intruders.

"Hey, Boss Man," hailed Boomer, his crooked grin dotted with gold teeth. Like a shepherd, Boomer pushed the 300-pound donkeys away like playful dogs.

"Donk!" yelled Boomer in a drill sergeant's voice. Immediately they ignored the visitor, went to Boomer, nuzzling at one of the zippered pockets in the overalls he wore, searching for sugar lumps.

"Wait here," he instructed. "I'll put these little feisty furballs out back." Boomer laughed as he led the herd of pet Sicilian donkeys, with dark stripes on their backs that formed a cross at their shoulders, to a small corral. He returned through the front door. Holding it open he invited, "Come on in."

Jack, with Harry on his shoulder, followed Boomer into a room with cheap smoked glass mirrors running along the wall. Jammed with military memorabilia; pictures of young men in battle gear; unit flags and ashtrays made from brass shell casings. A sign over the bar read WAR ROOM. Boomer pulled two beers out of a small refrigerator. Harry saw the beers and began his "*Beer! Beer!*" chant. The mirrors, installed against a warped wall, made the two men and the bird look almost grotesque. Jack pulled the small brass thimble from his shirt pocket and set it on the counter top. Ripping the caps off of the two Coors bottles Boomer banged them down on the bar. Droplets of water flooded off the sides of the bottles, forming small wet circles on the bar top. Drinking slowly from the bottle after he had poured Harry a drink, Jack commented, "I went to the DEA today."

Boomer gulped his beer, and said hurriedly, "What fer?"

Surprised at Boomer's reaction Jack said, "I told you. I'm suspicious about what we're doing. Wanted to at least go on record that we're just chopper drivers, not drug mules."

"How'd they react?"

"Not interested."

"Why not?"

"Don't know."

Both men were silent for while. Boomer drained his beer and wiped the froth off his mouth with the back of his hand and questioned, "Think they'll do anything?"

"I don't know. The little jerk of an agent I talked to wasn't interested. I'll give them some time and go back for an answer. If they haven't checked into it by then maybe I'll go to the FBI."

"You're really up tight about this," observed Boomer.

Jack looked at him and said, "Just covering our backsides. I'm too old to get caught up in some kind of drug deal. And so are you for that matter. Neither of us has enough years left to do time in a federal pen."

"Quit," said Boomer.

"Quit?" asked Jack raising his eyebrow and smiling.

"Yeah. That way you're off the hook. Me, I ain't got diddly for a pension so I can't. I'll starve."

"Quitting won't work for me either," said Jack. "I need this job as bad as you. Just for different reasons."

"Pardner, I know the feeling. Losing my Army pension has put my ass against the wall and I don't want to join the homeless in my old age. Seems to me that you got a similar problem. I mean, you want to quit jockeying windmills but you got to hang on to the job until you can sell your book. Am I right?"

"Right," responded Jack as he clamped hard on the empty beer bottle.

Pushing his gimme cap back on his head, exposing a white sun line and sparse red hair cut in an old fashion flattop, Boomer said, "Look. You went to the DEA. So what if they don't do anything? Your ass is covered. My advice is just keep flying and we'll be doing fine."

Jack countered with a question. "What do you mean, fine?"

"That I can save enough for retirement and you can get your book written. That's what I mean by fine," he said puffing up his cheeks until his reddish skin was stretched white.

After a moment of silence Jack started to walk back to his car saying, "Thanks for the beer. Gotta go." Harry flutter- hopped behind Jack as he opened the door to his car, got in, fired up the Mercedes and drove away. Boomer watched him as concern swept the furrows of his forehead. The heavy car made a crunching noise as its wheels rolled over the limestone driveway.

The something-is-wrong feeling crawled up Jack's spine. He'd been operating in the world on the marginal side of life too long not to pick up the early sniff of trouble with this flying job. On the other hand, maybe Boomer was right. Maybe he had been jockeying choppers for so long in the bizarre and strange world of South America where there wasn't any difference between the good guys and the bad guys, he was paranoid. The pesky rat of doubt nibbled away at his self-confidence.

CHAPTER TEN

Lee Dykes Hart pushed the buzzer on the outside wall of the large concrete block building covered with pinkish stucco. It had a vague Spanish style favored by Taco Bell architects. In the day time it looked more like a dental office than a fancy casino. A DO NOT DISTURB sign was riveted into the rear wall next to the private parking space protected by a TOW AWAY ZONE sign. Hart's ulcers ground furiously against each other causing a lingering pain in his gut.

Damn. He hated having to tell them what he found out. But he didn't have a choice. If the DEA came down on them he knew he would swing. Not Forbes nor Buno. They had the kind of clout that comes with lots of money, muscle and expensive lawyers.

He bled out a trombone fart as he waited for the door to open. The closed-circuit television camera, sealed in the wall behind a pane of Plexiglas observed him. With a click the bolt in the door jumped back as it was hit with an electronic signal. Hart stepped inside to the hallway leading to the office of Forbes' NevadaLine card club. Police Chief Silva Buno sat at the rear of the office where the private entry door was located. Hart hated coming to this place. It was like a meeting with the Inquisition. He could hear the screaming of the damned. He and the Chief never discussed anything but legit business in their police department offices. Buno was excessively paranoid ever since he discovered one of his cops wearing a wire under his body armor. Laz Forbes sat in an over-sized leather chair, his face tight as a balled fist. They had been waiting for him, and Hart knew they were pissed at just having to meet with him. Didn't really matter what the reason was. He knew he was just their goddamn gofer.

Silva Buno's cocoa-dark face cracked with the bone-chilling smile he was famous for. He motioned Hart to a chair with a short, abrupt nod and the CZ-75 Compact pistol. Buno ran the street action in Border City for Laz Forbes. Ten years ago, Military Police Sergeant Silva Buno was hired by the Mayor of Border City to appease the swelling ranks of Hispanic voters. A fluent Spanish language speaker he was heavy handed, with the instincts of a cobra. Buno slowly got a choke hold on the petty crime in Border City. Instead of getting rid of it, he carved out a piece of it. He dispatched the petty criminals and reached a business agreement with Laz Forbes, the made man with plenty of money and muscle. They were partners. Hart just worked for them. The street rumor, that Buno stuffed a bookie who owed him money into an Asphlund brush chipper was true. The recyclables people found shreds of flesh in the compost. But, Buno had mercifully killed him first. He handcuffed his hands behind his back and staked the bookie's legs to the asphalt street by driving a foot long steel stake through the cuffs of his expensive suit pants. The man died shortly after the heavy tire of Buno's big Lincoln Town Car crushed his pelvis and balls; popping his kidneys and pushing his guts up into his chest cavity. Silva Buno gained respect after that story made its rounds.

Hart knew how to deal with Buno, so he said quickly, "I blew it, Sil. Our pilot suspects something." Hart studied Buno and watched Forbes out of the corner of his eye.

"Are you shitting me? Is that what you wanted to meet with us about?" blanched Buno as he got up and paced to the side of the room.

Hart nodded.

"You picked him out of the litter, didn't you?" grumbled Buno.

Hart scratched his sweaty head before he answered. He was nervous. "Dalton was one of the three we interviewed. He looked to me like the best pilot of the bunch. From where I sit..."

Buno cut Hart off by saying, "From where I sit you don't know shit." He paused, glaring at the man standing in front of him. "Think he has any idea of the operation?"

"I dunno," drawled Hart. "He don't say much. He just flys where we tell him. Personally, I don't think he gives a shit. He told me he was writing a book, but other than that I don't know anything about him."

"What about the big, red headed ape who handles the maintenance on the helicopter? Bimmer, Bloomer."

"His name is Boomer Smythe and he's just a old dumb-ass sergeant who's working 'cause he cain't live on his retirement pay," said Hart.

"According to Norma, my informant, he didn't have anything specific for the DEA. Just an idea that things ain't right. Dalton is suspicious of what we got goin'," Hart revealed lamely.

"What's the DEA going to do?" demanded Buno, his hard eyes made him twitch.

"Nothing, according to Norma. Dalton was a walk-in, and the agent who took the beef was covering his ass by dictating a memo to the file. Norma says they do that every time they get a complaint. The agent figured Dalton was full of shit 'cause no police department would be muling dope in a city helicopter."

Forbes kept silent, snake-eyes watching these two comedians. The dressed up greaseball and the peckerwood could easily bring him down. Firing the pilot would cost big bucks, hiring a new guy would take time he couldn't afford, he had obligations.

He adjusted his bulk and gave them his best death stare. He was a past master of it.

"If the boy doesn't back off we'll be left with our dicks in our hands, comprende, am-ee-gos?"

"What about that briefcase, what made him suspicious? What made him think drugs? Mr. Hart, you want to tell me?" His big head pressed forward on a thick muscled neck.

Hart could hear the headsman's axe being sharpened and rack firing up. He had the crazy notion that they wouldn't kill him here, not on this expensive rug, so close to opening time. Buno saved him as he held open his hands in a benign gesture.

"The guy is probably covering his ass. Maybe he needs to wake up with a couple of ribs sticking through his chest," suggested Forbes. "You ought to be able to arrange that, Señor Buno."

Forbes began to pace, mulling things over he didn't want to put into words. The cords on his neck twitched, and the deep scowl signaled foul weather coming up. His eyes developed a hard shiny look, *el lobo*, the wolf, they used to call him in his younger days. Buno was the Chief of Police, but Forbes was a boss with strength of the family behind him, a made man, had deep, deep control over him. He was bought and paid for. Buno's main task now was to keep the cops away from his card club action and move the money down to Mexico in the police department helicopter.

Buno cleared the thickness from his throat. "We need to decide what to do with the pilot," he said dismissing Lee Dykes Hart with a wave and nod toward the office door. Then he stopped Hart with an order referring to Norma Lentz, "Have that cunt of yours keep tabs on him. If he goes back to the Feds we need to know. Got me?" Hart left on wobbly legs, he couldn't get to a bar fast enough.

"That dickhead's going to get us in trouble," said Forbes, referring to Hart. "I can feel it in my bones. We gotta get rid of his ass."

Buno nodded affirmatively. "He can't stay away from the pussy and he don't care what kind. But this time he gave us something good. No telling if the DEA is working him. No telling what he says when he's gettin' a blowjob from that bitch who works for the DEA."

"Is he still fuckin' little girls?"

"So far as I know. He gets 'em down in Tijuana. I don't ask."

"Kinky son-of-a-bitch."

"That's why we own the sorry cocksuck. His ass is ours. That's the only reason we can trust him with the stuff we're moving back and forth to Ensenada."

Forbes bobbed his thick head up and down and then went over to the stereo system built into the paneled wall. He turned it on. He cranked the volume up as loud as it would go. The Latin rap made the walls vibrate, and the room hummed. Forbes never took chances that his conversation could be heard by any listening device, even though his office was electronically swept every day. He wrapped a thick arm around Buno's shoulder and spoke into his ear. Buno's brow wrinkled but he nodded. Forbes pulled away from Buno and turned down the mind-shattering noise.

"Understand?"

"Yeah. I don't like it, but you're right. If we don't stop it, it's our ass."

"You can't trust a cockhound, especially if he's a cop with a hard on for little girls." Forbes laughed aloud, and the sound still echoed long after Buno left. The police chief felt like he needed a shower. Maybe two.

CHAPTER ELEVEN

The Border City Police Headquarters building was an undistinguished modern structure of tan brick. The locals called it Casa de Caca and it was high up on the City's list for remodeling. Inside, white fluorescent lights flickered and cast an eerie glow on the faces of the Second Watch officers as they prepared for the briefing that preceded every shift. Within the consecrated temple of macho cop, the squad room, the men shrugged off their jeans and T-shirts for familiar blue uniforms. Rifle racks with stacked shotguns and .357 Magnums lined the pea green walls, the floor thick with cigarette butts and trash. Tacked crookedly on the wall a bulletin board announced a variety of handwritten ads for boats, cars, tools; a few business cards and an occasional thank you note from a grateful citizen who obviously felt tax dollars were being spent appropriately.

The briefing officer was a stooped, solemn-faced lieutenant of forty-five. His blue, unblinking eyes with droopy lids, honed in on the officers in front of him. His tie was tucked smartly inside the front of his shirt, three buttons down. His black plastic-coated shoes, the kind that never need a shine, gleamed in the flickering light.

"OK, listen up troops," we got a suspected rapist. He is six feet tall or shorter, black or Latino driving a red or green Honda or Saturn." They all laughed and starting pitching brick-hard doughnuts into the wastebasket.

"That ought to be an easy one, just pick up anyone don't look like you," laughed an older officer with jug ears.

"Be on the lookout for a skin-head biker, wearing body armor, and there's a report that the topless lady on Fern Street is catching some rays in the backyard again, the neighbors are complaining." He completed his OPs report and read off a list of admin instructions.

"Juarez, report to the training officer ASAP. Packer you have an appointment with Chief Buno tomorrow at 1600 hours." As he droned on the officers glanced at poor Packer and they were glad they weren't in his sorry shoes. Nobody met with the chief unless it was serious ass-kicking business.

Every once in a while a dirty cop would get his tit in a wringer for getting too greedy or just fuckin' up. Most of the cops serving on the BCPD had something in their file that could get them charged, prosecuted and ultimately serving time. Those who didn't want to play in the deadly game, retired or high tailed to venues in fly-over states before their lives and reputations were ruined. A keep-your-fuckin'-mouth-shut culture, the BCPD's code of silence covered all the criminal action from fixing tickets to receiving stolen merchandise and delivering it to connections at flea markets up and down the coast. Chief Buno held their very lives in a delicate balance; he owned them.

Most recently a brave reporter left town after accusing the BCPD of a variety of misconduct and called it a "rancid heap of garbage." His quick exit was preceded with death threats and serious damage to his wife's car and his kid's play equipment. After another spate of unfavorable publicity and mysterious reprisals, the press and citizenry gave the department a wide berth. Chief Buno rebutted the charges most eloquently in English and Spanish on the local television station.

What the community at large perceived were the good looking uniformed officers who taught the anti-drug programs for kids, posed for photos at school fairs and shut down loud parties. Most citizens loved them; criminals and all people of color feared them. Driving, bicycling, or walking while black or Latino could be life threatening.

Flies buzzed lazily in the hot room and zoomed in on Packer's nose. He scraped the back of his meaty hand across a stubble of beard and shooed them away. He was wrapped in a sweaty sheet and the bedclothes swirled in a tangled mess from his pain-ful crawls to the toilet. Last night he was dogshit sick and begged to die. The clock radio at his side blinked close to noon and in a fog of near wakefulness he guessed it was Friday. He rubbed his neck and tried to avoid movement that would unleash the sledge-hammer pounding of a hangover. The death delivering kind that only a real drunk with a sick liver can get. Mouth sour, his tongue stuck to the roof of his mouth. Full of self-pity he stared at the yellow spot on the ceiling; paint had dripped down like stalactites. It seemed to take forever to remember where he had been the night before, but it was only a brief moment. He heard something slamming around in the basement. Fuckin' dog. It needed to be fed, he thought.

He was quickly reminded of the shooting incident as the sledgehammer nailed his brain. Shooting that wetback kid wasn't his fault. The beaner sideswiped him. That's what started the whole god-damn mess. Now there was a good chance he would get suspended or maybe even fired. Christ. He could lose his pen-sion over this. Need to call the union lawyer, now. So far the day sucked.

Cracking his eyelids, he sat up on the edge of his bed with effort. His head felt the size of a blue ribbon hog.

Thank God it was his day off, he thought. With eyes that refused to focus he looked closely at his Mexican Rolex. Twelve noon. Christ, he thought, I've been out like a light all morning and I got to be in the Chief's office at four o'clock.

Lifting his body out of the bed, he shuffled past a pile of dirty clothes on the floor on his way to the bathroom. He stared at the mirror; a sorry shit, an aging cop who had completely fucked up looked back at him. What his two divorces hadn't siphoned off his paycheck, he had squandered himself. Motorcycles and trick trucks at first, then bass boats and bad football picks. Living pay-check to paycheck he pissed it away on booze. He had to fight off the wooly shakes every morning, a couple of Buds, aspirin, and if it was really bad, some speed when he could get it out of the evidence locker.

He sat on the toilet stool with his pounding head in his hands; his hemorrhoids were on fire and rolling nausea made his mouth water. He got up, shuffled into the kitchen and opened his noisy refrigerator, searching for a beer. As he tilted his head back and drank deeply his head pounded with gruesome regularity. Shakily he gathered up a syringe and the vitamin B-12 vial. He needed to medicate his dog before the wounds got worse; had to get another couple of fights out of him. Between fights, he would shoot his dog full of penicillin and vitamins to help in the healing process, and rub his coat down with motor oil to make hair grow back. Fucker's gettin' the mange.

Packer had taken his dog to a fight three days earlier. Bastard, had survived his fight, but his right ear had been mangled, his muzzle ripped, and lost a chunk from his nose. Two weeks earlier he had fought in Bakersville; a fight that lasted two hours before his adversary croaked. Even in Packer's present rotten state, he took pleasure in owning a pit bull; he had to be careful around him. Son-of-a-bitch had tried to bite him more than once.

The pain in his side this morning was worse than ever. His liver was fatty and close to shutting down; he was a walking dead man. He'd long lost the ability to get an erection and the last whore he visited told him not to come back until he got rid of the dog stink.

He opened the door leading to the under-sized two car garage and picked up a dirty bucket. Returning to the kitchen, he filled the bucket with canned meat, and a couple of eggs. He slowly, painfully carried it down the basement stairs. Bastard, tethered with a heavy chain, looked like a buff-colored chunk of oily muscle and stared at him with glazed eyes. Sullen energy radiated off the animal's tight skin as Packer carefully set the bucket down and then unsnapped the heavy swivel attached to the chain anchored into the concrete floor. The dog was getting old and not worth a shit anymore, decided Packer. Its wounds hadn't healed as fast as they used to. It would last one, maybe two more fights decided Packer, as he ran some water for the animal as it furiously attacked the meat.

His thoughts rewound to the shooting. The fact that Chief Buno showed up at the shooting scene was still puzzling. Buno must be planning to put the arm on him or get rid of him. He would be an over-the-hill, out-of-work cop with no pension if Buno didn't trash the report. His job prospects would be zero, he could even face jail time. Even selling used cars on commission or working somewhere as a security guard would be out of the question if Buno decided to go against him.

He finished tending the dog, and his gut signaled he needed something to eat before meeting with Buno. He really needed a drink but that was out of the question.

It was four o'clock exactly. Packer, tapped lightly on the door, stood uncomfortably and inquired tentatively, "You sent for me, Chief?"

"Come in. Pull up a chair. We need to have a talk," Buno ordered. The chief did not stand, nor did he extend his hand. He was skilled at the art of power relationships and this was his turf. He knew being in his presence scared the hell out of Packer. It did everybody else, his control was absolute.

The small, expensively dressed man sitting at the ostentatious desk, loomed large and intimidating. Two flags, topped with golden replicas of the bald eagle, flanked Buno like cloth sentries. Packer felt like he was in the United Nations as he glanced at the Wall of Ego lined with autographed photographs of Chief Buno shaking hands with the world's dignitaries. There he was, in full uniform regalia, with Congressmen, a former Lieutenant Governor, A Mexican President and a long-gone U.S. Attorney General who had served time for letting some corporate outlaws slip by.

Silva Buno was the most powerful official in Border City. The Police Commission rubber-stamped anything he asked. Nobody could sit in the Mayor's seat without his backing. He had power and the trappings of power - his own luxury sedan, driver, a department top heavy with brass, and now the LongRanger helicopter, courtesy of Laz Forbes, his silent business partner.

On the slick surface of his green writing pad lay a manila file with the words "SHOOT TEAM INVESTIGATION" stamped across it. Packer darted glance and knew why he was standing before the chief; the file contained the report of the shooting and the Shoot Team's recommendation.

"How you feeling?" inquired the chief.

"Fine," lied Packer. The chief's tone made his butt pucker and his mouth go dry.

"We go back a long way, don't we, Punch," said the interrogator in a slow, friendly drawl. Not in character for a man whose speech was elegant and well thought out.

"Yes, sir." Packer's mind danced, trying to figure out what Buno wanted. He knew the man and was well aware of his reputation. Buno needed less jostling than nitro to explode, and he was much too quiet.

"You know I don't usually get involved with shooting investigations, don't you?"

"Yes, sir," responded a worried Packer. Buno had him on the point of a pin.

"Still raising pit bulls?"

"Yeah. But I don't fight them," he lied automatically. Why does he want to know, thought Packer as sweat began to roll off the insides of his thighs.

Buno lit up a cigarette, blew smoke toward Packer and chuckled, "Do you know what you get when you cross a pit bull with a prostitute?"

Packer knew this was a joke but said nothing, his sweating hands clasping knees like they would get away if he let loose.

Buno waited a moment and delivered the punch line slowly, "Your last blow job." Packer tried to smile and failed. Buno laughed uproariously.

"Got a lawyer?" The master interrogator quickly changed the tone of the meeting from joviality to cruel reality.

"No. Why?"

Buno got up and closed the door. Sitting down heavily in his big leather chair, he swiveled around and placed his feet on top of the desk. "Unbutton your shirt."

"What?" asked Packer, thoroughly confused and panicky.

"I want to see if you're wired. Kee-rist, Packer, do you think I am some fuckin' dummy?"

Packer, shaking his head, and straining at the neck button tight against his skin, opened his shirt to the navel. His fish white flesh spilled out over his belt buckle.

"You're clean, no body mike. Now we can hold a conversation just between us girls. You really fucked up, Punch." The chief turned from slick dude to the street thug he really was. "This time we ain't dealing with your drinking problem and we ain't bringing up charges for getting a wee bit over aggressive like you've been known to do. What we got here is a full on in-crim-i-nating report from the Shoot Investigation Team." Pausing for breath and effect, Buno continued, "Yo' goddamn ass is grass, and I is the lawnmower. You had no fucking business chasing that Mexican kid with a shotgun."

"I was working a suspected burglary. He fired at me first," interrupted Packer, trying to defend himself.

"Bullshit!" exploded Buno. Banging his desk with his small fist, he stood for effect, and he pointed a finger down at Packer and hissed, "I can hang your ass this time, Punch. Wouldn't take much to convince me that the bullets we dug out of your car were fired from your throwaway. Everyone in the department knows you carry one."

Buno pressed on, like rapid fire, "Where was your throwaway that night? Huh? Huh? The Shoot Team couldn't find one on you. Your ankle holster was empty." Before Packer could respond, Buno whacked his hand down on the folder and said, "There is enough in this fuckin' file to kick your ass out of here on criminal charges and take away your retirement pay just for good measure! The only thing between tossing your sorry ass out and saving you is me. Me!" he said louder. "The goddamn chief of police who had to come out on the streets 'cause you shot some wetback in the head with a shotgun. A damn good thing there weren't any witnesses. And I'm the one who has to deal with those *cabróns* in the media."

Packer remained quiet, drained by the reality of the situation. He had fucked up. Bad. Real bad. He got caught dead ass wrong and Buno was coming at him like a steamroller. He needed a drink and a lawyer, in that order. Sweat soaked his thick neck, Packer began breathing hard. This was going to hurt more than catching your dick in a zipper.

Buno's lips started to make small sucking sounds as he drew smoke from his wet cigar. "Maybe," he paused, "just maybe I can save your worthless ass, Punch," he said as he blew smoke through his pursed lips.

Packer, a cop for too many years, instinctively knew the offer he couldn't refuse was coming. "How?"

"Shee-it, Punch, it's simple. Real simple. I can file the Shoot Team's Report away forever. For fuckin' ever," he emphasized. "No eye witnesses. Nothing here but circumstantial evidence." Laughing, he said, "I'm the chief. I can do what I damn well please." Pausing, he cranked the fear factor up a couple of notches. "There's enough in this report," thumping it for effect, "to bury your ass in the yard with some of those guys you sent there. I can toss this report in the shitcan or on the D.A.'s desk."

"What do I have to do?" Packer asked calmly, knowing he would sell his soul to get off the hook.

"This ain't goin' to be as hard as you think it is, Punch. Matter of fact, you'll probably grow to like it."

Packer raised a puffy eyebrow as he listened inquisitively. Goddamn, he thought. Buno was serious. The shooting had all but flushed his pension down the sewer. Now he was being offered a way out, but it couldn't be good.

It took Buno ten minutes to outline the plan. Then he threatened, "You're only going to get one chance to do this right. Fuck it up and you'll be out with a criminal charge tagged to your ass and no pension. Once the job gets done, then this file disappears and I'll protect you. My guys will do the investigating," he said. Tapping his knuckles hard on the folder for emphasis, he went on, "Any questions?"

"No," said Packer, anxiously rising from the chair to leave. Premeditated murder wasn't something he wanted to be part of, but if he could do it right, it wouldn't be worse than what he would face in the joint.

After Packer left, Buno pressed the intercom connecting him to his secretary. "Send in Belenda," he ordered.

Belenda loved it when the chief called her in from the secretarial pool to help him with special assignments. Sitting across from him she pulled her tight thin dress up for the desired effect. Buno looked at her and with what could only be called leer and said, "How's my little nurse today?" Belenda could hardly type, but she was carried on the payroll as an administrative assistant. In recent months she received two raises for her special skills; skills that qualified her for a higher pay grade.

"Another headache?" she inquired, knowing what the response would be.

"Yeah, a real bad one," he said as he licked the side of his mouth. She knew what this meant and how to take care of it. Belenda's sole purpose was to relax the chief. Buno picked up the phone with his right hand and began drumming his fingers on the thick desk pad with the fingers on his left hand. Scooting his chair forward so his stomach was against the desk, he got ready. Belenda pulled a handful of Kleenex from her purse and dropped to her knees, disappearing under the desk. Buno was fond of making phone calls to other women while he was being treated for a headache by Belenda. Belenda went to work and Buno began pressing redial on his phone.

CHAPTER TWELVE

Packer's tortured Buick swerved into his driveway in a cloud of white smoke. He turned off the engine, pulled on a Bud and reviewed his meeting with Chief Buno. The worst had happened, he surely pissed away his pension by shooting that Mexican kid, not the first time he fucked up but now the markers of his transgressions were being called in. He didn't know if he was cut out for this shit. He was depressed and angry, the thought of going inside his shitty little house that smelled like dog piss and old clothes made him sick. He remembered the days when the house was clean, pretty curtains fluttered in the windows and there was a woman there who loved him. It was gone, all gone.

Inside, the red beacon on his answering machine blinked. He listened intently to the message. Fuck. No snoozing for him and this meeting wasn't going to be any fun.

Gulping a Vodka and Maalox, he belched hard and crawled back behind the wheel. The engine fired up with a back rap and cloud of smoke as he headed for the Another Place for the meet.

Twenty minutes later Packer sat alone watching the action on the dance floor, drinking ice cold beer with shots of tequila. The BCPD cop bar, open to law enforcement and closed to most civilians unless they were willing females was dark and rancid with the overpowering smell of stale beer and new vomit. The music thumped and twanged as three couples, young slick-sleeve cops and their groupie partners, shuffled and groped on the dance floor, the center of a familiar universe. Two old retired puss bags he knew vaguely sat across from each telling war stories. Smoke filled and noisy, Packer liked the winking lights and the stench of booze, sweat and sex that filled the place. A high level of flux-ing energy floated among the females looking for a good time with a young cop. Heavy perfume, wafting marijuana and the smoke from an open kitchen grill where an ancient Chinese cook labored, filled the gloomy room. Unconsciously, he reached down to his ankle. Shit, he remembered, the small leather holster and the throwaway gun were gone. He'd have to get another one. It was the only reliable insurance a good cop had.

"Punch, you want another drink?" yelled Wink Murphy, the bartender, trying to be heard over the blaring George Strait song. Wink had a face that looked like it had been weaned on a pickle. Saliva always pooled on his weak lower lip.

"Yeah, make it a double this time," answered Packer hoarsely. Pursing his lips as he belched and stared at his reflection in the mirror behind the bar. Sadly, he looked at the last vestiges of the once handsome cop, a magnet for pretty women, sworn to pro-tect and serve. Soon, very soon he could retire and draw a fat pen-sion. If not, he could always eat his gun.

Wink slopped the drink down. Packer pushed his money across the bar. "Keep the change," he said flatly as he started to back away from the wooden rail. Before he could turn around, he felt a hand on his shoulder and smelled the cheap perfume that brought back a bad memory.

"Hellooo, Officer Packer. Like to boogie?" a sexy female voice cooed. A memory-jolting blast. Without turning, Packer knew it was Doris McIntyre, a real lake of lard, who wanted more than a boogie. Dildo Doris worked as a radio dispatcher for the San Diego Sheriff's Department. She hung out at Another Place for the same reasons the cops did, booze, companionship, and the promise of raw sex. Like a bitch dog in heat, her generous lips were always ready to rapidly devour any man, so long as he was wearing a uniform or packing a gun. Even crossing guards and store security officers weren't safe.

Three weeks earlier she zeroed in on him at the bar. She had rubbed up against him, breathed in his ear and rattled on, "I bet I know why they call you Punch."

The old itch was still there and he laughed at the ego-boosting comment. "How 'bout I show you."

Almost before he got the words out of his mouth, she had grabbed his hand and led him out the door. So drunk he couldn't drive, they got into her '79 beat-up Chevy and ended up at his place. He remembered their pawing each other on the ride over, and trading spit on the porch while he grappled for his door key. Everything went down hill after that.

Punch had too much to drink and his bombed out body couldn't respond. Hers didn't help either. She spilled out of her jumpsuit, exposing a whale size stomach and pendulous breasts. All he could think of as he stared at the spinning ceiling was the flapping acres of flab on Doris' body. She shrieked something about him being a third-rate "yoonick" and a limp dick cop. She could suck start a leaf blower and the Mexican with it. Her blowjobs were legend. That night nothing but a miracle could fire Packer's used-up engine. Through booze fogged eyes he watched her kneeling on the bed pulling up panties that reminded him of a clown suit. She grabbed her clothes and stomped out screaming profanities as he laughed 'til tears spilled from his eyes.

Punch turned, nodded, and said, "Hi ya."

"I haven't seen you for a while, what's been happening?" she questioned with a let's-get-it-on grin. Her girth was now packed tightly in uniform pants.

What he didn't was want another clown show. "Doris, honey, I've got to meet somebody and have a private conversation about some official stuff. Know what I mean?" said Packer, raising his eyebrows. He noticed her eyebrows were shaved and applied higher on her forehead so she had the look of constant surprise.

"Wink, give this lady a drink down there where there's a vacant bar stool," said Punch as he nodded toward the end of the bar.

She slunk away showing him rumbling buttocks and a nasty glare. Packer was mad that he had to invest in a drink to get rid of her. Better than tangling with a man eating giant. He watched as she latched on to a cadaverous old hairbag sergeant who needed to fall in love that night. Punch wondered if she'd spit out the bones.

Two drinks later, and painfully aware of his aching gut, he spotted Detective Larry Mielke as he came through the door, he nodded at Punch. Mielke wore a poorly-fitting sharkskin suit with trousers that fell cuff less over his scuffed shoes, an unmade bed came to mind. Packer watched him as he slowly sauntered over. Larry didn't just walk, he slipped and slid turning this way and that, avoiding the sweaty bodies in his path. Smoke from the cigarette locked between his lips floated toward the ceiling.

They greeted each other with the nods and grunts of the police fraternity. They took a small table near a couple of cops tossing down boiler makers. One waved, came over and acknowledged Packer.

"You did good, shooting that greaser."

Packer, guffawed and replied, "One less wetback for society to pay for. Just call me the beaner blaster."

"You ought to run for governor, Punch."

"Any fallout from shooting that Mexican?" inquired Mielke staring through the smoke in the direction of one of the female vultures. He sucked the cigarette smoke deep in his lungs, like he was taking a hit on a joint.

Packer responded with a trace of sarcasm, careful not to telegraph his anxiety, "You've never seen a pile of shit I can't shovel my way out of, boy. Why the fuck do you care?" He paused and looked around. Dildo Doris smiled crookedly at him through a fog of smoke as grease from the grill fire sizzled and flamed. Mielke raised his drink in mock salute. He had called Packer for the meet. He wanted something sure as shit.

"Thanks to me, the streets are one beaner cleaner," bragged Packer, gulping down his drink. Never far from his conscious mind was the marker being called in by Chief Buno. Mielke was the messenger. The pension he was sure to lose was a big problem, but bigger still was the thought he might go to jail. The fucking newspapers were already making civil rights violation noises. Whatever the Chief wanted him to, he would do it, no questions asked.

"You're pretty close to retirement, ain't you?" questioned Mielke in a hoarse whisper. Packer's rocks tightened. Mielke wasn't trying to be sociable. The prick had something on his mind and it wasn't pretty.

"Yeah. Why?"

Before Mielke could answer, Packer got up, walked to the jukebox and punched in a selection. A burnt-out, redhead working behind the bar with Wink, cracking jokes with a couple of motor jocks, came over and took her time refilling Packer's drink. Mielke pushed a grin over his doughy white face and said slyly, "Hey baby, this department has got too much action going for you to be thinkin' about retirement. Your shit is way too ragged for that. 'Sides, you know we take care of our own." He paused.

"So long, as our own do what's right by us."

Packer's watery eyes drifted away from Mielke and froze on a short, plump, blonde groupie wearing heavy war paint and purple lipstick. Wired, her metallic-green eyes were pinpoints as she jigged to the music. Focusing his attention back on Mielke, he said nothing as he tried to figure out what the fuck Mielke was driving at.

Mielke pulled a crumpled pack of Camels from his pocket, lit one and blew smoke out of his nostrils. Shrugging, he absently wiped the Formica covered table with the sleeve of his sharkskin suit. "I know the dicks have been busting your chops, but word came down to me from the top to give the shooting a 'drive by'."

"Drive by?"

"You got friends in high places. Know what I mean? The man himself. Chief Buno. Got it?"

Packer nodded as Mielke rambled on like he was lecturing a rookie cop on how to get free burritos. "We're just taking a quick look at it. I guarantee you, the chief will be able to call it a justifiable homicide if he wants to."

"If he wants to?"

"Yeah, you know how these things can go. Either way, depending on what the investigators turn up." His knowing smile made Punch's stomach turn.

At the table next to them the skinny blonde with pink-lipsticked lips and a split tooth smile, closed her eyes as if she was in heavy pain or ecstasy. Her thin, hard-looking escort, a county vice cop, fueled his adolescent ego from the clouds of thick perfume that wafted up from her sweating cleavage. He poked around in it like he'd lost his keys. Packer considered what he knew his options were, clearly he didn't have any. Detective Mielke pointed out that Buno was covering for him, so long as he delivered. He began to feel like he was going to puke. Pay-back time was coming. Comin' real fuckin' fast.

Dropping some bills on the bar, Mielke checked his watch and announced, "I'm leaving. Got some things I gotta do for the chief." He was a rat, but he was the Chief's rat.

"Need help getting home? Doris can drive," Wink inquired in a flat voice. Packer left the Another Place infuriated. He felt like tearing Mielke's face off. Still smarting, he hurried out and fired up the Buick. He had to do something about this car, but who needed a ring job when you were going to jail, or be dead.

CHAPTER THIRTEEN

Boomer felt incarcerated like a prisoner in a cell full of hi-tech instruments as he sat in the co-pilot seat of the Bell LongRanger. The mid-morning sun whisked last night's moisture from the tarmac, veils of steam rose. He was basted in a sweaty lather under his well-worn coveralls as he waited for the bird to go airborne.

As much as he hated to actually fly in one of the machines he took care of, he *had* to work. Given the choice, he'd rather sandpaper a lion's ass than ride in a chopper. No other choice except welfare. The pension he had counted on evaporated with his court martial. Ferrying the oil drums from Ensenada helped him make up for lost ground.

The silence of the day was destroyed when the whining ignition engine activated. Jack nudged the responsive controls as he built up air pressure under the whirling rotor blades. He could feel the rhythms of the cockpit. With enough air cushion forming under the disk of the rotor blades, he pushed the pedals causing the tail to wag back and forth.

Looking at Boomer, he nodded, indicating he was ready to lift the machine off the ground for the short test flight. Boomer wiggled his shoulders against the crash belts. He adjusted his big frame against the canvas and aluminum seat and simply nodded back affirmatively. Jack pushed the cyclic slightly forward and added a little power by pulling up on the collective, twisting the throttle sufficiently to maintain RPM.

"Border City PD Helo One for takeoff," he spoke from his headset mike.

The Brown Airfield tower responded, "You are cleared for take-off BCPD Helo One."

The helicopter accelerated, skimming across the ground, reaching the point of transitional lift and jumping into a climb. Jack quickly powered the craft up to an altitude of three thousand feet, leveled off and flew almost directly north toward the Sweetwater Reservoir. Below, the clumps of Spanish dagger, acacia and stands of smoke trees looked like a low scrub jungle from the air.

Jack keyed his mike. Over the intercom, as the helicopter bounced against an air pocket, he said, "What do you think?"

"Don't know. Can't tell yet. It just don't seem right," was Boomer's terse response. Jack smiled. Boomer always gave him the same answer to his first question each time they went for a check ride. Jack's interest in the mechanics of flight was marginal, so he relied on Boomer's judgement. If Boomer said it would fly, then it would fly. A veteran pilot, he finessed the machine with delicate, practiced movements. Wisps of clouds marred the china blue sky as the chopper skimmed, then turned its belly into the sun. Sun streaming through the canopy warmed the cockpit.

"Take it on down for a run," said Boomer. Jack banked the helicopter sharply and swooped it down like a bird of prey. At one hundred feet off the deck Jack flared the responsive machine into a hover while Boomer studied the instrument panel and listened to the engine noise. Shaking the helicopter back and forth, then bucking it up and down, he flung it skyward. Leveling off he glanced at Boomer. "She's okay. We can take her on in." Boomer studied the instrument panel, watching the RPM, oil and manifold pressure gauges flicker.

Swinging the helicopter west, Jack pushed it against a slight Pacific breeze as he flew north of Border City, across the harbor. Crossing the concrete sliver of Strand Boulevard to the ocean, he banked left, holding the turn until it started landward, following Highway 905 to Brown Field. After receiving clearance from the tower he flared the Bell into a smooth landing and crab-crawled it as close as he could get to the airfield avgas truck.

Jack shut the engine down and Boomer began to top off the tank with avgas. Then Boomer walked toward the small, cluttered office that he and Jack used as their airfield headquarters. Meticulous when it came to his helicopter, Boomer's maintenance shed looked like a homeless camp. Oil smudged papers with flecks of grease littered the folding table that served as his desk; a stuffed iguana stood guard. Cigar butts were piled high in the coffee can he used as an ashtray and a two year old BEST TOOL calendar was tacked on the wall. Miss Monkey Wrench, smiled sexily holding up her enormous after-market breasts, adorned the wall.

"Hotter than the hubs of hell, ain't it," muttered Boomer. "Let's go get a drink. It's so dry the trees out here are huntin' the dogs," he bitched. The round-bottom clouds scudding overhead did little to dissipate the heat. Only the rains could sluice away the heat layers that mixed with the grime on the airfield's hardstand.

"Can't."

"Why?

"Just need to do some work on my book."

"Still seeing your old girlfriend?" questioned Boomer.

"Mariana?"

"Yeah, the black-haired lady."

"Off and on. We're just friends."

"I'll bet you're *on* a hell of a lot more than you are *off,* arncha' there cowboy."

Jack shook his head in semi-disgust. Boomer's peckerwood attitude about women got under his skin, especially when it was about Mariana. Once lovers, they were now a comfortable couple who liked each other's company. The fact that they slept together was incidental to the relationship.

Boomer cracked a warm beer and announced, "That's it for me. See you tomorrow, partner."

After packing up their gear and locking the maintenance shed, each drove away separately; Jack in his old, elegant Mercedes, Boomer in his sand scraped van that looked like it belonged to a Mexican lawn crew.

Jack and Mariana arrived at his condo at the same time. She stepped from her car as he pulled up, careful not to hook her delicate, expensive wraparound dress.

113

"Tough day?" he asked with a smile. He was glad to see her.

"No. Not really. But my job is not as exciting as yours." She was editing a popular weekly newspaper run by aging hippies and rabid ecologists.

He opened the door for her. Inside Harry squawked, *"Beer! Beer!"* and flew off his perch for a snack. "Meet you upstairs after I water the plants and feed the fish. Hey, I have a new Red-Top Zebra."

Mariana smiled at his genuine pleasure in a new fish. They now had what was called an adult relationship - they enjoyed each other's company, including sex, it was uncomplicated. Old friends, a relationship of dueling wits and good times. It was ironic that they both ended up in the San Diego area without planning to do so. Lovers who parted on bad terms in New Orleans, here, they were just good buddies who enjoyed things together and sometimes made love when the need arose. Neither had time for other emotional involvements. Jack was trying to write another book and she was pursuing a successful career as an editor. When they had separated over a year ago in Florida, Jack was sure he would never see Mariana again. She went smokin' out of his life and took a job with the alternative newspaper in San Diego. Jack tracked her down after she wrote to him, apologizing for leaving him in the Keys. She made it clear, under certain circumstances they could be friends. As lovers the sex was familiar, comforting and he seldom had the burning dreams when they were together. There was no longer the spark and flame, and he missed it. She dated a few well-dressed slugs, and he hadn't felt the need to be on the prowl. Tonight they were going to a movie she wanted him to see. He hoped it wasn't one of those chick films with lots of pointless dialogue.

Minutes later, wearing freshly pressed Chino pants and an off white polo shirt, Jack pawed around the refrigerator as she appeared in a silk running suit. He removed a half empty beer bottle. Harry watched with hard, dot-like eyes, waiting for the thimble to be filled. While Jack tended to Harry, Mariana climbed the stairs to the second story that was used as a library and wandered aimlessly among his books. Montesquieu's *Persian Letters,* de Tocqueville's *Democracy in America,* Rousseau's *Emile* and Nietzsche's *Thus Spake Zarathustra* shared space with *The Choirboys, Table Money* and *Iacocca.* She was amazed at the depth of this man who couldn't keep his feet on the ground.

The Beach Boys' "Surfin' U.S.A." spun on the compact disc player. A helicopter pilot who hopped around some of South America's most dangerous places, contented himself with old philosophers' books and 60s rock and roll. A parrot as his most constant companion. An interesting man, but there was always that danger sign, the touch of an outlaw. Glancing down at her watch she said, "Let's go. The movie starts in thirty minutes."

When he didn't answer she knew he was making notes in that little book he always carried. She left him with his thoughts.

Cops?

Cocaine?

Money*?*

He snapped the book shut, gave Harry some sunflower seeds and they walked into the warm tropical San Diego night that the tourism guys wished they could bottle up and sell.

CHAPTER FOURTEEN

The Black Cat Lounge was a bar you'd want to avoid unless you wanted to get shit-faced, a cheap blow job from a grateful whore, drugs, or an extralegal deal on a variety of merchandise. Two Sons of Odin bikers rumbled out of the parking lot flashing Viking colors, Dixie belt-buckles and black Prussian helmets. Their Harleys were the raked low rider models with chrome on everything but the tires.

The man parked next to a familiar-looking four-wheel drive truck. Inside his van were four heavy television boxes containing handguns. Checking to be sure the doors were locked, he headed for the bar door. He squinted against the harsh glare of the overhead light. Inside, he blinked to adjust to the darkness. Animal heads with horns and antlers were mounted against the scarred walls. The fifty year old dive, with peeling posters of female mud wrestling, was across from a metal finishing plant, and a string of body shops. The chunky barman, a heavy drinker and consumer of fast food, skillfully tossed a thin cocktail napkin in front of the man.

"What kind of beer you got?"

"We got Bud on tap."

"So gimme a Bud and a shot of Turkey."

The bartender poured him a shot and he downed it like it was his last day on earth. The television blared with some obese women fighting over a skinny dude with a cowboy shirt and a bad haircut. As the female sluggers sparred among screams and bleeps, a mountain of a man in a nylon running suit stepped into the bar from the restroom. He crooked a finger at the bartender who rushed to serve him as fast as his aching feet could carry him.

"Vodka," said the mountain, voice as cold as a Siberian summer, a cruel smile flickered across a cruel mouth; he took a table and motioned the man with the shot and beer to join him.

Vasi Ivanov, AKA, Victor the Constricter; a Chechen from Gagestan, raised in a Moscow brothel, former black marketeer, killer for hire, now connected to the local Russian gangs, a wholesaler of cheap Chinese guns assembled in Mexico.

The bartender hurried over with a bottle of vodka and backed away with the grace of a butler in a formal dining room.

"How many?"

"I got a hundred for all your pistols. Four boxes."

"The usual?" He was only interested in the cheap .22 and .25 caliber Saturday night pistols. There was no local market for the better guns like Magnums, Colt Pythons or Berettas. What the Russian wanted was the cheap pistols that his dealers could sell for rock bottom prices out of their car trunks at swap meets. The cheap, untraceable Chinese guns, packaged in Mexico, sold for two hundred a pop. Desperate people wanting a weapon quick; especially those who wanted one that couldn't be traced. His market was eclectic, gang bangers, crack dealers, petty criminals, bikers and every so often a stand-up homeowner living near the barrio or other bad neighborhoods who just wanted some cheap protection.

"Yeah. The usual," said the man as he nervously finished off the beer.

The Russian handed him an envelope with two thousand bucks in it. He took it without counting and unzipped a pocket in his overalls. He got fifty dollars for each pistol he was able to mule across the border. The boxes in the van would be gone, when he left the bar

Vasi paid the *máquiladora* forty dollars for each cheap weapon that was assembled in Ensenada. His mule charged him fifty dollars apiece to get them across the border. The Russian's profit margin was over a hundred percent. He'd make ten thousand off this shipment. Ten grand hard currency in a week wasn't bad.

The man took a long gulp from his beer glass and announced, "This is gonna be the last shipment for a while."

Making a tentative, jerking movement, the Russian smiled thinly. "What do you mean, my friend?" He grasped the man's wrist in a vice grip enough to make him wince.

"We got heat," the man responded, his face curling up in pain.

"Heat? What means heat?"

"Yeah. The authorities. The cops. The police."

"Explain to me," demanded the Russian as he fished for the right words, releasing the man's wrist now numb from blood loss.

"My driver is getting squirrelly about the deal. We got to back off for a while."

"A while?"

"A month. Maybe two. Let's see what happens."

The Russian downed two quick shots and calculated what it would cost him. Then he rudely reminded the man, "You, my American friend and business partner, will lose close to four thousand in your currency every week we are not in business. I and my associates will lose maybe eight or ten thousand. But that is nothing. It is the market we lose. Others will come in like jackals. If we can't supply, then others will. It is the law of your country's supply and demand. No. I don't think you will stop making shipments."

"Don't be a fool," argued the man.

Angered, the Russian clinched his teeth. The skin on his Slavic face was tight. "It is you who acts the fool. We have the perfect plan. Are you not receiving police protection?"

"Look, we need to just give this a rest. If we don't, we can lose the whole operation and some of us will be doing time."

"Time?" questioned the Russian.

"Jail," explained the man.

"Kill the squirrel."

"We will get us another, what you call them," he said as he searched for the correct word, "A driver. Kill him!"

"That's crazy."

"Then you will be killed by either I or one of my business associates." He stood and nailed the man with a glare. He smiled, exposing a mouth full of bad teeth that needed some work by a capitalist dentist. Then he left, taking the vodka and stiffing the bartender.

Finishing his drink, the man zipped up his coveralls and pushed back his chair. His hands shook. Jesus, he thought. A few years ago we were gonna nuke these fuckers. Now I'm taking orders from them to kill people. Gotta be another way, he thought, as a hooker sitting at the bar turned and eye-fucked him. He gave her a little salute waved her over. She was young. Probably under twenty-five. A strawberry.

"Do you do pictures?"

"Pictures, yeah, I do that kind of work. But no animals and no rough stuff. What do you have in mind?" she asked, running her fingers over the rim of her drink glass.

CHAPTER FIFTEEN

The shooter's CZ 527 Kevlar Varmint, fitted with a 24 inch.223 heavy barrel was equipped with a night vision scope. Hollowed out, long rifle bullets for maximum killing power, a silencer equipped model. Using the rifle was risky, but he didn't want to be doing this job close in. He figured he stood a better chance of getting away if something went wrong, by putting as much distance between the target and himself. After attaching the silencer, he sighted the rifle by looking through the scope a couple of times.

Lee Dykes Hart stopped after work for a couple of drinks at the Motor Inn bar. No action there, just a couple of fat Mexican tourists. Fuckers, he thought, shouldn't be speaking Spanish he couldn't understand. He ate his usual solo dinner at Denny's and it was dark by the time he left the restaurant. The shooter followed him into the industrial district where, minutes later, he parked his car in the trash strewn lot behind the 24 Hour Adult Entertainment Center. An old grey mama dog wandered aimlessly across the lot, teats hanging on the ground. Hart entered through the rear entrance, it always smelled like cheap perfume and Pine-Sol. He paid the untidy male attendant and was handed a cheap Polaroid camera. "Three shots," instructed the attendant. "It's a buck apiece if you take more. Ten minutes to set up your poses." Hart went through a door with a sign that said photo session. Inside, the bored model gave him her regular I-got-something-special customer smile as she hopped off her stool and tossed aside the fashion magazine she was reading. Hanging from the walls of the booth was a variety of special fantasy costumes, mostly the worst for wear.

"So, how you been?" she said inspecting her faux nails, and blowing gum bubbles. He was a regular who tipped. A rarity.

Most of her customers were cheapskate assholes with scabby hands and bad breath.

"Been okay little lady," answered Hart.

"The usual or something different and exotic?" teased the woman as she moved closer to him, letting the robe slip off her body. She reached for Hart's zipper with the practiced hand of an oral sex specialist.

Across the street, in an abandoned lot covered with the skeletons of wrecked cars, the shooter positioned himself. Leaning over the engine cover of an old milk delivery truck with a faded sign, his face tense, serious and contorted. He sighted his weapon with a Burris 3.5-10x50 mm scope with a Ballistic Plex reticule and flip-open lens cover. In the dull yellow light of the doorway it would be an easy shot. He just needed to be sure that once he fired, and it was over that he would pick up the shell casing. With the Gemtech suppressor there would be no noise, it would probably be hours before the body would be discovered. In this neglected part of town where refuse was part of the landscape, nobody would notice another pile of junk. The people who inhibited this place would be unwilling to call the cops. This was a safe killing ground. Time passed slowly, he tried to think about what it would be like when it was over, he'd be free. He thought about backing out, but the consequences were not acceptable. Sooner or later the target would get his rocks off and come out of the porno shop with a smile on his face. A head shot would adjust that smile and solve his problems.

The photo session went well and Hart remained inside, browsing through the slick sex magazines before he walked toward the rear exit. Pushing the door open, came face to face with a woman, obviously a hooker, entering the building. She flashed him an inviting smile. Hart's face was a blank mask as he turned his body parallel to the building to let the woman pass into the narrow doorway. As she pushed past him he felt a sharp breeze close to his face. The woman lurched forward, sprawled on the dirty floor. A doped up whore who can't stand up, thought Hart as he closed the door and walked to his car, eager to get away. He didn't want to be there if the shop called a black and white to run off a street-walker.

Astonished, the shooter watched his target turn abruptly as the bullet hit the other person, driving her through the doorway. His target kept walking in a casual manner. He had pulled the trigger a muscle twitch too late. The shooter froze. This couldn't be happening. His target was moving toward him. Christ. He had missed. The target had no idea he had been shot at; he was in too much of a hurry to leave. It was too dark and dangerous to get off another shot, so he quickly picked up the shell casing and slipped the rifle in the rolled-up rug remnant he brought along. Then he walked slowly and carefully across the debris-covered lot, down an alley to his car. He waited a few minutes before getting in. He poured sweat and prayed that no one had seen him.

CHAPTER SIXTEEN

"You hardly said anything about the movie. Is there anything wrong?" Mariana was familiar with Jack's moods, he was nervous and edgy.

The story line and cranked up sound of the war movie had Jack strung tight. Sometimes movies about war did that to him. For some reason, watching this painful movie engulfed him like the sensation of being lost in the dark. They drove in silence to his house. Mariana let the subject drop, not wanting to push Jack into one of his silent moods, so deep in his thoughts he couldn't be reached. When they arrived, she got out and waited for him to walk to the front of the car. Reaching up with both hands, she held his face and kissed him long and tenderly.

Jack opened the door to the house. "The spa is on, he said. "Let's get a bottle of wine and get in." That signaled to Mariana he was back from the wars he fought in his head. There was something more than a long lost war on his mind.

"Whatever you think. If you are really too tired, I'd just as soon go on to bed or would you rather I left?"

"Not a chance. My neck is stiff. I know some hydrotherapy will help," he said, referring to the jets pulsing in the spa.

"Sounds perfect. You get the wine," she said feeling better because he was feeling better.

He went into the kitchen and took two wine glasses out of the cabinet. Harry dozed quietly on his perch. He opened an eye, blinked and shut it. From the refrigerator Jack took a bottle of her favorite Zinfandel, removed the cork and filled the glasses. She had taken off her clothes and stood by the spa in the small room adjacent to the master bedroom. As always, he was struck by her exotic features and dark skin. Her rich black hair hung down across her perfect breasts, the soft tuft of hair below her flat belly always directed his eyes to her long shapely legs.

"Take one of these," she said, holding a small capsule in her hand.

"I don't do drugs," he laughed. "Booze, yes, but no drugs."

"Take this. Do it for me," she pleaded with real concern. "Dalmane. It's a sleeping pill my doctor prescribes. It will make the movie go away."

He held his hand out as she dropped the thirty milligram capsule in his hand, swallowing it with a sip of wine. He leaned his head back against the edge and stretched out his legs. He pushed the activator for the jets on high and positioned himself so that his throbbing neck received the most benefit. He became drowsy in the hot, 105-degree water and she left him with his thoughts, not wanting to interrupt any opportunity for him to sleep.

Mariana knew how hard it was for Jack to admit his attempts to write another book had failed. In his library he had researched the art of war from Attila to Zapata and, the outcome was the same. A series of short essays highly popular with war lovers; mostly academics, from around the world. But no great novel, no great pathos of Count Tolstoy, no front-line blood and thunder of Hemingway, just skillful examinations of war games and strategists. But there was something more going on in his head this time, more deadly, more real.

After a while he awakened and they both took in the silent skies above the open spa. He said, "Let's get out."

She rose from the water with sensual grace. Quietly walking through the sliding door she picked up a towel and began to dry off. She tossed the towel on the tile floor, pulled back the covers of the bed, and slid under the cool sheets. He watched as she pulled the sheet up to her chin: an act that transformed her from a sensual grown-up woman to a child needing warmth and security. Jack lifted himself out of the spa, toweled off, and climbed in next to her. Wrapping himself around her body, familiar territory for both, he found great emotional pleasure in simply lying with her in the warm nest of the bed. A trickle charge that did not require orgasmic coupling, just body contact, their bodies locked in a sensory weld.

Within minutes Mariana was in a deep slumber. Jack tossed and turned. The movie had been too real. It had jerked him back to the terrible explosion in the Gulf where he almost lost his life. Like the flickering frames of an old film, it all flashed through his memory again and again. He broke out in a damp sweat. Sleep escaped him; a common affliction.

Careful not to disturb Mariana, he got out of bed. The urge for a drink was powerful. If she hadn't been there, the alcohol would have won out. He padded barefoot to the kitchen table where her purse lay; digging through it, he found the brown plastic container with the Dalmane capsules. Ignoring the warning label, he took his second 30 milligram capsule in less than an hour. He needed that sleep. He needed to escape the war dreams and nagging suspicion about the BCPD. Intending to read until he could sleep he thought. He grabbed the first book within reach. He tried to concentrate, and made it through one paragraph. The drug coursing through his veins, took immediate effect and he nodded off. The book fell from his hands and he slumped in a comfortable chair; his drugged sleep free from the fire at last.

CHAPTER SEVENTEEN

Equipped with stolen license plates and a police band radio, the car slipped into a vacant space of the golf club parking lot. He quickly turned off the lights that washed across the buildings. Checking his watch, he turned to the prostitute and looked at her as she lightly bounced in the seat. The woman's low cut satin dress, slit high on the legs, shone in the faint light. A money hungry dingbat, she was thin enough to slide through a mail slot, but she had big tits and no conscience. His heart pounded against his chest like an out of control piston.

Her name was Autumn and she came from the San Diego outlands where she had attended one of those sprawling, dangerous, high school campuses, jerry-built of tilt up concrete with flat roofs, suitable for the animals they contained. She was twenty-six and a veteran hooker since she was nineteen. Before that, she gave it away to second generation trailer trash. Now, blonde and depressed, she had a deep scar on her chin where a drunk john had slammed her face on a bathroom sink during a frenzied anal fuck. On a good night she made a couple of bills. Tonight all she had to do was get in bed with a john who her partner would knock silly and pretend she was shooting him up with a needle. He would take pictures and she would get paid four hundred dollars for this mini-drama. He told her he was a private investigator and it was a divorce deal he was working on the wife's side. She believed him when hours earlier, at the Black Cat Lounge, he peeled out two one hundred dollar bills and paid her.

"Let's go. Be damn careful you don't walk under the lights," he said to Autumn, motioning with his hand toward a pool of yellow light on the blacktop.

"Gotcha, Chief." She was getting a little rush from the danger.

"Yeah. Yeah. We need to go through the drill again," he insisted.

"I take my dress off and climb in bed with the john."

"That's after I knock him out with my sap. Got it?"

"I got it."

They entered a line of pine trees after crossing a darkened corner of the parking lot. A puff of air carried the scent of warm night as the woman followed him. For a few minutes they tramped across the wet grass of the golf course. She slipped and cursed as she regained her balance. Leaving the fairway, they moved into the rough, tall grass that separated fairways eight and six. He moved surprisingly fast. The prostitute hurried and caught up with him. The dampness of the night cranked up her nicotine-filled lungs and she began to hack a soft, phlegmy cough.

"Jesus Christ, can't you keep quiet?" growled the man.

"Who's going to hear us out here?"

"Anybody within a hundred feet."

The woman did not respond. He was riding the adrenalin crest, and she was just scared.

They walked across the fairway closest to the street and stopped at the tree line, four rows of mature Ficus. The man stopped abruptly, causing the woman to bump into him as darkness swallowed them.

"Goddamn it, back off." He was getting edgy. They crossed the street, in the middle of the block of detached condos, to avoid the pooling street lights, and then huddled in the small alleyway. A nervous tic jumped across the man's cheek as he looked at the prostitute with regret. From his portable police radio, rigged with an earpiece, he could tell if anyone dispatched a squad car to the neighborhood. A surprise, he thought, was the last thing he needed tonight.

"Put these on," hissed the man as he held out a pair of green rubber gloves he had bought from a Handy Dan Hardware store.

"What are they?"

"Rubbers for a five pecker billy goat, you dumb cunt." The woman giggled and put her hands over her mouth.

I'll rap him on the head with my piece. He'll be out like a light. Then you strip off your dress and get in the rack with him. Put the syringe in his hand and start sucking his dick. I'll take the pictures and we'll blow out of there so fast he won't remember anything when he wakes up," directed the man with heavy authority.

The hasp on the fence door lifted and the door squeaked open. They entered the yard through a side yard. He motioned her to follow. The backyard was empty and the air conditioner hummed noisily.

Walking slowly across a brick patio with the woman behind him, he stopped at the sliding glass door at the rear of the house. From his pocket, he took a rubber suction cup, the kind used to hang things on the tile of a shower wall. He spit on it and pressed it against the glass at a point just above the locking device; he circled the cup until it gained suction. He tested it by pulling on it. It held. He removed a commercial glass cutter from his pocket and made four deep grooves shaped like a box around the cup. Wrapping a handkerchief around the blunt end of the glass cutter, he gave the section of glass a muffled tap. The glass square popped inward. He twisted it diagonally and pulled it through the hole. Stepping to the side, he reached in and unlocked the door, gently sliding it open. The house was dark; the furniture seemed to absorb the sound of the man's breath.

"Wait here. I gotta knock him out first. Then you get in bed with him," he whispered. "You got the needle?" She nodded. He could see nervous sweat forming on her upper lip. When this was over he would have pictures of Dalton doing drugs with a street whore. Moving like a robot down the walkway he stepped up and nudged the handle and the door slid easily. He pushed it open just enough to slide his body through and found himself standing in the living room of the house. Inside he let his eyes adjust. Nervous sweat ran down his left cheek. Dumb shit, should have brought a flashlight.

"*Bong! Bong! Bong!*" The sound exploded next to his head! He almost ran out of the house, his gut doing a fast flip-flop. On the wall, inches from his head, he saw the clock, its loud chimes sounding the hour. He tried to suppress his panic; hot sweat burned his eyes, even though the room was cool, his breathing sounded like a vacuum cleaner. A knot the size of a grapefruit swelled up in his throat.

He touched the .38 caliber gun jammed in his hip holster. It was an old five-shot top-break Harrington & Richardson he found at the bottom of a box of tools he bought at a garage sale years ago. Untraceable. He stood still for a moment longer and, hearing no movement, started toward the bedroom. The door stood half open. He stopped before pushing it wider. He could make out the body of Dalton as he entered the bedroom and silently stepped across the carpet. Dark shadows draped the bed. He moved jerkily to the side of the bed, fearful that Dalton would wake. Couldn't see his face. The sheets were pulled over his head. From the other room the bird squawked *"Beer! Beer!"* and then Dalton started to raise up from the bed with the sheet still covering his face. Adrenaline rocketed through the intruder's veins. He pushed the sleep-drugged lump, shrouded in the sheets back, to the bed as a piercing scream filled the room. The awakened sleeper fought frantically to escape. The wailing shriek unnerved him. The mind-shattering clamor unleashed his fury as he jammed his hands across the sheet-covered head and face, trying to stop the animal-like noise.

"Ouch!" he yelled as teeth circled the thumb, and bit down. He pulled back in pain, causing the rubber glove's thin latex to peel off his thumb. In a frenzy, he jerked his hand free and swung the sap hard as he held the victim's neck in a choke hold with the other hand. It picked up momentum as it came down hard from an overhead arc, and it smacked into the target with a crunching sound. He swung it three more times, feeling bones crunch each time he connected.

Suddenly everything was still. His chest ballooned. No lights. No sound. Nothing. Fear flooded his body. The whore stood there, her heart slamming against her chest wall, ready to faint.

The man jerked back the sheets and stared at the mound of tangled black hair. His mind screamed as his eyes fixed on the once delicate face of a woman. It wasn't the pilot. Matted hair framed the ugly indentation of the crushed bones of her once beautiful forehead. Broken like a fragile piece of clay. Tension tightened like clamps on the man's calves and ass. Where the fuck was Dalton?

The bird exploded in the room, hopping around madly, cackling and squawking, *"Beer! Beer!"* It flew at his face, forcing him to duck and back away. He swiped it away roughly and dropped it to the floor, feathers flying. Then he heard someone yell in a tired, gravelly voice, "Mariana. Are you alright?" The pounding of feet erupted at the other end of the house. "Mariana!" Someone yelled again.

He froze at the man's voice, then he clawed for the gun jammed in his holster as the bedroom door blasted open. A noise jumped from his throat like steam escaping from a bleeder valve. He stumbled back as the charging body careened off the bed. He saw the man fall hard on the floor and roll once. He fired. The cracking metallic rap echoed off the walls as the bullet tore harmlessly through the bathroom door. The smell of cordite and death filled the air. Dalton stumbled to his feet, vaulted over the bed, and jumped on him like an enraged animal. The bird shrieked and jumped up and down, half flying and half lashing out with its claws. He fired again. This time the bullet tore a chunk out of the ceiling. Then he swung the weapon hard, catching Jack across the left temple, and watched him drop to his knees. He swung the pistol down hard, striking him across the forehead with the two-inch barrel. Blood gushed from Dalton's nose as he cartwheeled over, unconscious.

The attacker escaped through the living room, his shoulder crashing into the frame of the patio door as he tried to go through the narrow slot. He ran down the side yard as the shadows reached out and grabbed him in his panic. The woman followed him, heels clicking on the bricks. "Wait! Goddamn you! Wait!"

"Shut up!" he hissed. His mind reeled. They had to get out of here before the cops showed up.

Suddenly, the night was hot, firecracker hot. He'd killed the wrong person. The woman. Who was she? Dalton was supposed to be there alone. Was he dead too? Had Dalton seen him? The whore had witnessed everything.

He bolted after her. The fact she was a witness to the killing was dawning on him. The two of them trotted down the alleyway and through the gate like cattle stampeding from a barn fire.

"Slow down, goddamn it!" He grabbed the whore by her dress, just under her outstretched arm and jerked hard. "Stop," he commanded. "If anyone sees us running, the cops will be on our ass in minutes."

Holding to a fast walk, they stopped at the east side of the first fairway. Both were breathing hard by now. He looked at the sobbing whore. Even the cheap perfume couldn't mask her fear. His mind whirred. Did they leave any evidence?

He tried to collect his thoughts as they trudged silently across the golf course, slipping on the dew covered grass as they walked up an incline. Jesus, he thought, a strung-out whore for a murder partner. It didn't work the way he planned it. He needed her in bed with Dalton to confuse the cops after he killed him. He didn't need any pictures. He was going to kill her and leave her there with Dalton's body.

He stopped suddenly, jamming the earpiece deeper into his ear, listening to the police dispatch.

"What is it?" said the woman, twisting her ankle and yelping as she ran up to him.

"Shut up, goddamn it. The dispatcher's talking. I need to hear what they're saying!"

The police dispatcher voiced his message into the 800 mega-hertz system. "District three-two-five?"

"Three-two-five. Elm and Baylor streets," droned the mono-tone voice of the patrolling officer as he advised the dispatcher of his location.

"Have a report of a Signal Eighteen at 909 Brentwood," said the dispatcher.

"Ten Four." "My ETA to 909 Brentwood is approximately two minutes."

He knew the area would be swarming with black and whites. They had to get out of here.

"Wait here," he ordered the woman as the radio went silent. They stood at the edge of the parking lot. "I'll get the car and pick you up." The temptation to drive off and leave her was almost overwhelming. But the cops would get her sooner or later. A doper always needed to trade information for a plea bargain.

Running to the parked car, he opened the door and got in. Stomach pushing against the wheel, he backed the car out and drove over to the side of the parking lot where the woman hid in the shadows of the trees. As she approached the car to get in, the man jumped out of the car and leveled the dull metal handgun with brown plastic grips on the car roof. The woman stopped and her face went white with shock.

"No!" she pleaded hopelessly. She was supposed to get $400 for this trick. She raised her hands to cover her face.

He jerked the trigger until the hammer clicked on an empty shell casing in the revolver, and the woman's head disintegrated as the sound waves bounced off the car. Her face vaporized in a froth of blood, brain and bone mass as the momentum threw her backward. She dropped on the asphalt in spasms, wetting the parking lot with blood and brains. Blood stink and the warm tropical air closed around him like a jungle wall.

CHAPTER EIGHTEEN

The other members of the autopsy team had already arrived at the San Diego County Coroner's building when Dr. Donna Berkley navigated her Lexus through the fissured parking lot. She could see a city ambulance backed up to the loading dock. A female attendant wrestled with a stainless steel gurney and a blood-stained pile of sheets.

Inside, an assistant in a wrinkled smock greeted her. "Great way to start a Monday isn't it, Madame Doctor?" Irritated with his work habits and his always greasy glasses she gave young Dr. Plough her famous *death stare*.

"It could be worse. You could be a regular doctor and have to work their hours. Our patients don't mind waiting. What do we have? I see the police and the media are hovering."

"Looks to me like two homicides."

"Two?"

"Yep. One's a whore and the other one's a civilian. Maybe wrong place, wrong time. The Border City head cop is personally interested in the case, and the uniforms are here to chase off the media goons. Our two subjects are at work stations, ready to be examined by two of the finest death doctors in the world," joked the boyish Dr. Henry Plough.

"Speak for yourself, big shot. What did I draw?"

"What used to be a newswoman. The body is in Theater One. Chief Buno has asked us to brief him as soon as possible. I said noon or after when we're ready."

"Good job, you have a great career in death ahead of you," she relented as she rushed into the pathologists' dressing room. Over the door separating the dressing room from the examination theater, the sign proclaiming No Smoking, Eating or Drinking in the Autopsy Room always gave her a chuckle. The heavy reek of formaldehyde hit her as she pushed through the swinging doors. Refrigerated air pumped softly into the room as she began to dictate to the mike extended from the ceiling.

"This pathological examination is being conducted by Dr. Donna Berkley, Chief Pathologist for the San Diego County Office of the Coroner. Assisting me is Pathology Assistant Monroe Tucker," she droned as she pushed the overhead microphone back from her face. In a small room, on the other side of the hall that separated the examination rooms from the administrative offices, a typist recorded Dr. Berkley's results. In an adjacent office another typist performed a similar task for Dr. Plough. At a console, whirring quietly, both conversations were recorded electronically.

Removing the sheet from the corpse's face, Dr. Berkley looked at her assistant. Reacting instantly, Tucker removed the sheet, exposing the body of a beautifully proportioned female with lush black hair, the head encrusted with dried blood. "I am examining an unembalmed female with dark complexion, middle thirties. Caucasian or possibly of Mediterranean extraction. Height is approximately five feet five inches and according to the table scales she weighs one hundred nine pounds. Subject is completely nude. One her right ring finger is what appears to be an emerald surrounded with small diamonds. A herringbone weave, gold necklace surrounds her neck." Pausing, she looked at her assistant and said too brusquely, "adjust the glare off the face." Without signal, Tucker began to sponge the crusted blood off the cadaver's face. Jagged pieces of flesh and bone shards were exposed.

"There is the presence of lividity on the posterior aspect and petechial hemorrhage on the inner surface of the eyelids," noted Dr. Berkley. She examined each nostril with an otoscope. "No ulcerated mucous membranes." She cut off each nail and placed each into an evidence bag. Berkley examined the cold body with a large magnifying glass, noting scars, moles and identifying marks. She signed each envelope and noted the time and Tucker's name as the witness.

Dr. Berkley continued her technical litany. "There is evidence of hemorrhage and substantial post-mortem lividity in the thoracic." The motor whined as Tucker turned on the bone saw that would split the chest cavity. Dr. Berkley's thoraco- abdominal cut signaled Tucker to begin. Using a pair of heavy stainless steel rib cutters, he carved through the sternum cartilage. The exhaust fans worked hard to remove the ever present odor of decay from the cool air. Somebody was humming a Beatles tune and Dr. Berkley called for quiet.

She drew blood from the heart and removed the lungs, tongue and larynx for faster examination before she went into the gastrointestinal system. Then she took fluid samples from the gallbladder, spleen, pancreas and kidneys. Finally, she took the surgical crown saw and cut a circle around the head, just above the hairline. The Beatles tune interrupted her concentration, something about Jude and sadness. As she dictated her findings, this one did make her sad.

Chief Silva Buno crossed his arms as he listened to the pathologist give her preliminary report. Before she was through, he interrupted and said, "Run that by me again, Doc. That don't make any sense."

"Well, it may not make sense to you but there is no question in my mind that the deceased took a bite out of the killer's hand. We could match up the blood types if you've got a suspect, especially if it's a man with a cut hand."

"A man? How can you be sure?"

"The location of the bruises on her neck, the distance apart and the depth tells us it was a large, very strong man."

"How can you be so sure?" he challenged.

"Rather than boring you with pathological jargon, which I'm sure you will either ignore or fail to understand, let me just say that her larynx was crushed before sustained head trauma. She had no air in her lungs and she didn't lose enough blood to bleed to death."

"O.K., I'll buy what you're sayin'."

"You have to, unless you can get another forensic expert opinion," rebuffed Dr. Berkley. The pompous little ass-hole was starting to make her mad.

"Are you sure about the time of death?"

"Within an hour, give or take a few minutes."

Chewing on his lip Buno said, "Doctor, could the man living at the house have killed her?"

"Sure."

"He could have?"

"But didn't."

"Why do you say that?"

"Mr. Dalton's blood type is different than what was found in her mouth."

"How do you know?"

"We checked with Little Sisters Hospital. That's where Dalton is hospitalized."

"You're sure."

Dr. Berkley looked hard at the police official. "I'm sure. It's my business to be sure." Irritated by his condescending attitude, Dr. Berkley broke off the conversation. The discussion was over.

At the Border City Police Department, the beehive blond with upturned tits, caused by a bargain rate breast job, spoke into the intercom, "Chief, there is a man on the line who insists on talking to you."

"Name?" growled Buno, pissed off at having to spend the morning at the Coroner's Office. He still had the dead stink of formaldehyde in his nose.

"No sir. He just says you will want to talk to him. I think it's one of your informants," she said knowingly.

"Put it through on the snitch phone."

"Yes, sir."

The red scrambler phone on Buno's teakwood desk chirped three times. Buno punched the small button that would garble the words unintelligibly to any listening device.

"Yeah," snorted Buno into the speaker.

"I fucked up."

"You sure did."

"Now listen to me, Packer," said Buno slowly. I know you fucked up bad, but I'm goin' to take care of the problem. Know why?"

Packer's scrambled brains let him only mumble a, "Why?"

"Your shooting screw-up is not only going to cost you your pension, but, will fry your ass if you don't do what I need done. You only get one more Chance, a-mee-go. One more. Blow it and you'll be facing a murder one charge. I don't want to hear from you 'til I call you. You got that?" he said, exploding in frustration.

"What about the shooting. Can the dicks tie anything to me?"

Buno lashed out verbally, "I read their reports. You're okay." Packer interrupted, unable to wait for the finish. "You sure, boss?" Packer had slipped into complete submission. Buno could hear it in his voice.

"Yeah. Keep your mouth shut and stay sober. I'll take care of the rest."

Buno hung up and returned to the other reports scattered on his massive desk. The killing involving his pilot's girl friend was going to take some skill, some serious smoke and mirrors. Just the kind of work he did so well. Punching his intercom he said, "Get me Detective Mielke."

Boomer sat motionless in the straight back chair by the window and stared out at the expanse of lawn. Earlier he woke at home at the first hint of dawn. The newspaper headlines screamed "Woman Killed; BCPD Pilot Injured." He left immediately for the Little Sisters Hospital where Jack had been transported according to the article. Sprinklers sputtered as they gently tossed water across the lush grass surrounding a string of serene low buildings with tile roofs. Jack lay in a tilt up bed with an IV hanging over his right shoulder. A large bandage covered most of his face. When he woke he thought he had gone blind.

The half-closed door to the hospital room opened slowly. An undistinguished man with a sallow complexion dressed in a cheap business suit walked in. Boomer looked up as the man held out his badge which identified him as a Border City police detective.

"How is he doing?"

"As well as you can expect. He's been through a load in the last few hours. He'll make it. He's tough as wang leather," said Boomer defensively.

"Who are you?" the detective asked.

"Boomer Smythe. I'm his crew chief. I work for you guys."

Thawed by the information, the man stuck out his hand and introduced himself. "I'm Larry Mielke, the detective in charge of the investigation."

Boomer challenged, "You don't suspect Jack, do you?"

Mielke said, "So far, all I know is that he was the only person there besides the woman."

Scowling, Boomer rose from his chair and offered it to the detective with a wave of his thick hand. Jack, coming out of his drugged sleep, pushed his face into the starched stiff hospital pillow. The image of the murder scene would not leave his memory. He swallowed a sob, the kind that comes from an inconsolable child.

"Hang on, partner. You've been in a tough fight with a short stick," consoled Boomer. He reached out and touched Jack's shoulder with a leathery hand that was covered with an elastic bandage that extended up his wrist.

Mielke introduced himself to Jack and said, "I'm going to wait until you are in better shape before I interview you for the record. But if anything comes to mind, then call me. I'm in charge of the investigation." He left his business card on the bedside table, nodded to Boomer and left. Both men were silent; Jack tired, fuzzy headed and Boomer deep in thought. The post-op nurse walked into the room and cranked up the I-need-to-give-you-something-for-your-pain purse of her lips. Tiny drops of the clear liquid formed bubbles on the white skin of Jack's buttocks as she pushed the needle through his skin. A swipe with the wad of cotton in her hand took them away.

After she checked Jack's blood pressure and left, Boomer said, "I'll go over to your house and take care of things."

"Take care of things?" asked Jack through a throat that felt like sandpaper. The shot in his butt had untied his constricted muscles but bile assaulted his throat.

"The mess the cops left. You don't think they'd clean up after themselves or call ServiceMaster, do you?"

"Check on Harry. I guess he's okay."

"Yeah. I'll be sure he's got some food."

"What happened to your hand?" asked Jack in a slow, tired voice.

"I cut my wrist out in the barn. No big deal."

Jack's eyes closed as he drifted back into the warm depths of the painkillers the nurse had administered. Boomer left the hospital room quietly and walked down the wide hallway.

Less than an hour later Boomer opened the front door of the condo and was met by Harry who immediately squawked and ruffled his feathers. Boomer extended his arm as a perch. Harry ignored him with puffed up feathers and an attitude. Boomer couldn't get close to the bird, even when he poured it some beer in the tiny thimble.

The crime scene unit had left the house in a mess. Forensic technicians had stripped the sheets and pillow cases. Carbon-based fingerprint powder, yellow tape, and other residuals littered the bedroom. Boomer could smell ninhydrin, a chemical fingerprint technicians used to lift prints. The carpet had an ugly black bloodstain and a section had been removed by the investigators. There was a crater in the plastered wall where evidence technicians had gouged out a bullet. Boomer felt like an intruder in the silent house. He picked up the phone on the night stand, still covered with fingerprint dust, and called a commercial cleaning service. He promised to meet them later that afternoon. Then he began to search for some evidence.

Assistant Chief Hart sat at his desk in the Border City Police Department building reading the morning report. This was his main job when he wasn't flying back and forth to Ensenada. It pissed him off that he was actually nothing more than a gofer. He knew that behind his back his nickname was "The Gofer." Whenever there was something that needed "fixin" or the lid slammed on it, Hart put on his spurs and white hat. It was his specialty.

The report he just read scared the living bejesus out of him. A woman, a prostitute, was shot approximately the same time he was there. At first he worried that they'd find out he was at the porno shop when the shooting occurred. He could keep that out of any official report, but everyone in the department, would know about it. Like the time he was in the nude mud wrestling arena when it caught on fire, and the newspaper had a picture of him running out with a drink in his hand. For weeks after, little piles of mud would appear on his desk. It really pissed him off. When it finally dawned on him that he might have been the target, beads of sweat popped out on his forehead. There was no mention in the report, that anyone was in the porno shop when the women was shot except the guy behind the counter and the model. According to the report all the counter guy could recall was the woman falling through the doorway. He said he didn't pay much attention to that because she was a known drug user and this kind of behavior was standard for the neighborhood. She had been shot in the head as she walked through the rear door.

Hart picked up the phone and dialed a four digit number.

"Captain Hansen."

"Chief Hart here," and turned up the speaker phone.

"Yes sir," said Hansen formally even though he despised Hart.

"Anything I need to know about the shooting last night?"

"Which one?" asked Hansen. Hart had not read the entire log of incident reports so he responded, "The one at the porno shop. Was there another one?"

"The one you're asking about the drugged up whore, we got *nada*."

"In other words, this one goes to the bottom of the pile?"

Hansen coughed over the phone and said, "Affirmative. She was probably shot by her pimp. Eventually one of our snitches will give us something. May take a year, may take two, but we'll get something out of it. It's the other murder that we may take some heat for."

"Something unusual?" asked Hart as he flipped through the pages of the morning report.

"Yeah. Some broad was murdered in your pilot's bed." Like everyone in the department, Hansen knew that Hart's main job was to go down to Ensenada every week in the helicopter.

"Dalton. The pilot?" questioned Hart nervously, instinctively going on alert.

"Haven't you read the report? Should be on your desk by now. The guy who flies for the department. Somebody killed his girl friend in his house."

"Jesus," exclaimed Hart. "Is he a suspect?"

"Don't know."

"Does the chief know about this?"

"Yes. Larry Mielke is the primary investigator. He's reporting directly to the chief on this one. I'm out of the loop. Personally, I think it was some doper looking for some buy money. There was another whore shot about four blocks from the pilot's house if that means anything."

"Bad night for whores, I guess."

"We got enough of that shit up on the Boulevard, the only thing it means is less paperwork."

"Thanks," mumbled Hart slowly as he hung up and began trying to piece everything together. The idea that he may have been the target of the shooter at the porno shop vanished as he willingly believed Captain Hansen's theory that it was her pimp who did the shooting.

CHAPTER NINETEEN

Laz Forbes wheeled his gold-plated Cadillac into the crowded parking lot of the Kozy Kitchen where he was to meet the chief. Buno's early morning call was puzzling and it pissed him off. He pressed his massive body through the restaurant doorway temporarily pleased with the cool air and smell of bacon. What really angered him was that the helicopter run to Ensenada was canceled. Not good news at all.

"Howdy," said the blue-hair who sat behind the cashier's counter.

"Mornin'," Forbes nodded absently as he stuck coins in the news rack and extracted the paper. He jerked out the Metro section of the paper and tossed the rest in a pile on the glass counter. One glance at the page revealed why Buno wanted the meet. The story detailed three homicides, apparently unconnected. Two in an up scale neighborhood, the other in the run-down commercial section near the Barrio. Jesus, three women in one night, he thought, and an assault on Buno's pilot. He checked the details carefully to make sure the names weren't connected to any of his own businesses.

He spotted Silva Buno. Sliding his ample frame into the booth seat across from Buno, Forbes said in a grouchy tone, "This better be good. I scratched my regular golf game with my best mark."

"Laz, we got ourselves big problems," warned Buno.

"Yeah, I just read about it."

"I got me three shooting deaths and an assault on my helicopter pilot to deal with. The fuckin' newspapers and TV reporters are swarming all over the station looking for info."

Forbes had to chuckle at the picture of this little shithead dancing around the questions from the media sharks.

"What happened to Ensenada Monday?"

"I couldn't get us a backup pilot."

"O.K. Big Shot, you said you had a pro for this job."

"Yeah. They are all pros 'til they fuck up," Buno whispered as he looked around to be sure no one was in listening range.

"Can any of this be traced back to us? What a fuck up." Forbes demanded, "Just what in the hell happened?"

"My guy blew it and killed the broad instead," said Buno disgustedly.

Forbes skewered Buno with flinty eyes. "If they connect you and me to this, Amigo, the Feds will be in on this if anybody suspects anything."

Looking at Forbes, Buno breathed deeply and said, "We're okay. I got one of the dicks I own in charge of the investigation."

Forbes coughed a racking noise and interrupted with a sarcastic challenge. "Another one of your pros?"

Holding up his hands, Buno said, "I can cover up the investigation. It's a local matter. All mine. Could have taken Dalton out with this one, but his blood type don't match."

Forbes sneered, "I got close to a half million invested in that helicopter that we pretend is the Police Department's. We got big problems if we can't fly our stuff down to Ensenada in it. I don't want to lose it cause you can't deal with this. Know what I mean?" continued Forbes, taking a deep breath.

"Laz, I can stop my guys from going too far with this investigation. That's why I got Detective Mielke in charge of the investigation." Then Buno offered, "He's in my back pocket."

"You need to get your hands on your shooter," Forbes threatened. "Killing a woman we don't need killed and missing the target isn't what I call a professional job. At that moment, Laz knew he should have left the killing to guys who knew what they were doing, not this little Mexican dipshit.

Both men were silent as the waitress checked on them. A nervous Buno smoothing his cuffs and pulling at his shirt collar.

"We need to take our guy out right away. No fuckin' waiting. If you can't do it, Ill get it done myself, *capisce*?" said Forbes.

"More coffee?" she asked. Both men simply nodded. The four-blade ceiling fan stirred the greasy air as they waited for her to leave.

When the waitress left, Buno began his counter argument. "Man, let's wait 'til all of this cools down. Don't you think that's best?"

"Best? Best? Are you completely loco? No way." Forbes slid his bulk across the naugahyde booth seat. Picking at his teeth with a small flat toothpick he said flatly, "Let's talk about this outside. You pay." As Buno followed the big man out the door, head down like an errant schoolboy, he realized that his shirt was soaking wet.

The hospital corridor looked like a river full of green- bellied fish, as nurses, attendants, lab technicians and doctors in scrubs maneuvered in and out of doorways.

"You have to be wheeled to your car, Mr. Dalton. Sorry, but that's hospital policy," said the nurse's aide, pushing Jack's wheelchair through the clutter and glut of green people.

At the curbside, Boomer's van waited with the door open. Boomer, squinting in the glare of the bright early morning sunshine, gave Jack a quick salute, hopped out and reached down to help him.

"I'm okay. They made me ride out here in this golf cart."

"The size of that bandage tells me you ain't quite as fit as you'd like everyone to believe you are," chastised Boomer. He rattled on. "You look like you been dragged through a knot hole."

Despite a pounding headache, Jack smiled as he climbed in the front seat of the vehicle and said, "Jesus, I can't stand hospitals. Nice folk in there, but I can't deal with it."

"Here," said Boomer as he gave Jack the folded newspaper that was laying on the front seat. "You'll like what you read. I mean if there is anything you can like about going through what you did. Listen, I tried to bring the bird but he won't have nothing to do with me. I reckon the fight has got him all in a dither."

"That sounds about like Harry," was Jack's slow response. It hurt to talk. Opening the thin morning section, he glanced at the headlines which bounced off the front page of the Metro section, "Investigation Clears BCPD Chopper Pilot. Police Mum About Murder Suspects." After reading for a few minutes, he let the paper slide to the floor.

"Well, at least I'm not a suspect."

Breaking in Boomer asked, "Did the detective contact you?"

"Mielke?"

"Yeah. Skinny little shit with a bad complexion."

"He came back last night. Asked a lot of questions. Their theory is some druggie looking for buy money did it." Boomer babbled on about the world going to hell and bad guys with guns should shoot it out in the Sports Arena. Jack felt sick, his head spinning.

Neither man said anything for a few minutes. Then Jack admitted, "Boomer, I feel terrible. Get me home so I can call Mariana's family and help with the funeral arrangements." It's the least I can do, he thought.

At his condo, Jack looked out through the sliding glass door at the flowers barely drifting in the slight wind; he did not want to go in the bedroom where she had been killed. A yellow invoice from the Tidy-Clean house cleaning service lay on the glass table. It was marked "paid." He reminded himself to pay Boomer back. The house looked neat and clean. It held no signs of the bizarre killing. Harry was ecstatic to see him. The bird flew up on his shoulder and pushed his head against Jack's face, signaling he wanted to be stroked. Petting the bird, he moved tentatively across the tile floor of the living room to his bedroom, diverting his gaze from the backyard. He stopped at the door, blinked his eyes reflexively, and stepped through the threshold. There was no evidence of the struggle except the hole in the wall from the bullet. Yet, something felt wrong and guilt haunted him. Mariana would be alive if he could have gotten to her killer in time. It was something he needed to deal with, but at the moment was of little consequence. She was dead and apparently there was no suspect.

As he stood in the bedroom Harry said, *"Boomer! Boomer!"* twice. "What did you say?" He reached up to his shoulder and gave Harry a perch on his index finger. He stroked the bird on its blue head. *"Boomer! Boomer!"* repeated Harry. Damn, I'm gone two nights and the bird has sold out to Boomer. Funny, Boomer had told him Harry wouldn't have anything to do with him. The bird's either fickle as hell or traumatized, he thought.

Jack took a San Miguel out of the low-humming refrigerator. Taking the cap off the bottle he went out to the small back courtyard of his house. His two-day stay in the hospital left him feeling depressed. Sitting in an old fashion wooden porch rocker, with Harry perched on the chair's arm, he let his mind drift. A thin strand of guilt wove through his brain. He jerked awake with the dread of calling Mariana's family in Louisiana.

CHAPTER TWENTY

Mariana's body lay in the pewter casket with the lid closed; a single rose with a long stem lay across it. Jack watched the handshakes and embraces with a misty gaze as the chapel filled. He sat apart, alone. Her sudden death felt like an amputation without anesthetic. The modest chapel outside New Orleans was filled with mourners. A gauze curtain behind the raised casket was flooded with large displays of flowers. As the organ music swelled he heard muted whispers, silent tears as the sunlight played through the vaulted stained glass windows. Strained emotions and unrestrained sorrow gathered everywhere. The cloying scent of too many floral arrangements sickened him as he began to feel the suspicious stares of blame from friends and relatives burning through the back of his collar.

The family minister droned on, and finally the soloist sang, "How Great Thou Art." The service was over, those who had gathered at the chapel walked the crushed stone driveway leading to the freshly opened grave; the raw gash of brown in the manicured lawn. Mariana's parents avoided his look as he left the burial grounds in a rental car. Driving back to the New Orleans airport, he was burdened with the feeling that somehow Mariana's death was related to his flying job with the Border City Police Department. Nothing he could pin down but the notion the hit was meant for him. It was just a feeling that he was flying in heavy air.

CHAPTER TWENTY-ONE

The doorbell chimed softly. The screen of his Sony television set stared at him as a young blonde Latina anchorwoman with a sultry look wrapped up her story.

It sounded again, then once more. He ignored it making no effort to go to the door. The chiming was soon replaced by heavy fists pounding against the solid oak door. Jack, angered at the intruder, jerked opened the door to find it was Boomer.

"You okay? You look like hammered dog shit," said Boomer, a lopsided grin fixed on his face. "Don't be doing what I do when I get down."

"What's that?"

"Go to bed with my whiskey," he said.

"No. I'm okay."

Harry fluttered into the room and landed in his cocky, sauntering bird step. At the sight of Boomer, he flew into a screeching rage of ruffled feathers and pecking motions. Boomer moved toward him, offering him his arm. Harry climbed on his tree perch and hid among the leaves.

"Independent little shit," laughed Boomer as the doorbell rang again. Boomer went to the door and looked through the peephole. Over his shoulder he said, "It's a cop."

"See what he wants," said Jack.

"You sure?"

Boomer twisted the door handle with his big hand. Facing him was a young Border City Police Department officer with an envelope in his hand. "Sir, is Mr. Dalton here?"

"Yes."

"I have an envelope for him."

"I'll give it to him," said Boomer holding out his hand.

"Sorry, sir," said the young officer apologetically. "I'm required to deliver it to him personally."

"Jack, you are wanted at the door," growled Boomer. When he reached the door, the officer handed him the envelope, a pen and a receipt. Signing for it, Jack said automatically, "Thank you."

"Have a good day, sir," the young officer said politely as he turned and left.

Jack ripped opened the sealed envelope. The letter from Police Chief Silva Buno officially advised him, in legalese that he was cleared of all suspicion of the murder. That, thought Jack, was the fastest murder investigation in history.

The private investigator listened politely as Jack described Mariana's murder and laid out his suspicions. Ray Compton was a former San Diego Police detective sergeant. He was also an aspiring writer. They had met at a writer's conference at La Jolla. About the same age and military veterans, they developed a loose friendship.

Compton was partnered up with three other ex-cops in the business of skip tracing, alimony retrieval, office anti-bugging and finding missing persons. Not Sam Spade and Amos Walker types, they were basically information gatherers that used their contacts in police circles. But most of their information came from credit reports, public documents and access to the many data bases available to information retrieval experts. The office was equipped with high-powered computers and other sophisticated communications equipment. Compton was currently handling a snatched kid case and an investigation for a lawyer specializing in sexual harassment, a light case load that enabled him to interview Jack the same day he called him. He shifted his soft middle-age body in the chair and rubbed his balding pate. He looked like an insurance salesman or middle-aged bank teller dressed in slacks and a light sweater. His nondescript appearance made him look harmless and almost invisible; his primary asset for the kind of work he did.

Sipping coffee from a SDPD memento mug he paused for a few seconds and then went on to say, "We get a lot of nut cases. People who think someone is trying to kill them; or probe their organs in outer space. What we usually do is give them a few days of protection service. They end up satisfied no one is hiding in their closet and we pick up some money to cover our overhead. I don't think you fall in that category, but anyone who believes that some cops are trying to kill him is a bit strange, especially when he's working for them."

Jack held his ground. "It's happened before. Both of us know that. You're an ex-cop. You know better than anyone else it can happen."

"I can't argue with that," said Compton. "And the Border City Police was always a strange group. When I was working detective the SDPD didn't have much to do with them. Fact is, we didn't trust them. A dangerous bunch of cowboys."

"That's my point. And I've been around enough flying operations to know when something isn't right. All I do is fly their helicopter down to Ensenada and back once a week. It's good money. I really don't know what the uniforms are doing. The assistant chief, a weirdo bird named Hart, always goes down with us with a metal briefcase welded to his hand. We stay on the deck at the police grounds for no longer than a couple of hours."

"What do you bring back?"

"Hart and the metal security briefcase he always carries."

"Anything else?"

"No. Not unless you count a couple of barrels of Mexican oil."

"Why the oil?"

"I let my crew chief do it. He sells it for a discount at the airfield and picks up a few bucks. He's an old-Army NCO. Got to keep those types happy." Compton smiled at the comment, recalling his days in the Army.

He asked, "You really believe it was the cops who killed your friend?"

"Well," Jack hesitated, "I think they're dirty, and my house was broken into and Mariana was killed after I went to the DEA."

Compton was familiar with the case. He had followed it in the media. He riffled the newspaper clips on his desk.

"Come on," chided Compton. "You don't believe the DEA is involved in this. I like you, but this is more than just far-fetched, it's grassy knoll stuff!"

"Maybe it was someone else. Someone not connected with the department. Hell, the cops wrote it off as a random break-in. I just didn't happen to be in the bedroom. Otherwise I would have been the victim."

"Anyone know that the woman was spending the night with you? An ex-husband, office boyfriend, anything like that?"

"No. Both of us are private people. I doubt anyone knew about us."

Compton thought for a few seconds. "Seems strange to me the BCPD didn't get rid of you after the incident. Wouldn't they want you gone if they thought you suspected them of doing some dirty flying, especially if you went to the DEA? Did you ever hear from the DEA after you went to them?"

"No. Nothing," was Jack's short response.

"Did you go back?"

"No. It was clear they didn't think much of me or my stuff. A rookie agent dealt with me and made it clear I was wasting his time. According to him they were after big time operators. I didn't have any more real evidence then than I do now."

Compton leaned back in his chair and said, "Can't promise you much, but I can probably eliminate some concerns for you by getting information that will answer some of your questions. Let's go over everything that you can think of. I need to know who you work with on the job, how the PD informed you that you were not a suspect, anything that might help. You need to tell me everything about your working and personal life from the day you started flying for the Border City Police Department." He smiled and suggested, "Pretend I'm your shrink. This treatment is going to cost you $200 per hour. I'll need a retainer of $2,000 for ten hours of work."

Jack wrote out a check and proceeded to answer Compton's questions with detail. "When can I expect to hear from you?" he asked as he rose to leave.

"Four to five days. Incidentally, I need a key to your house." Jack looked at the investigator and raised his eyebrows in question. Compton explained. "I need to get a feel for what took place the night of the murder."

Jack nodded that he understood, pulled one out of his pocket and asked, "Do you need a diagram of the rooms and where everyone was the night of the killing?"

"I do, but I'll get it from the police department."

"You can get it?" questioned Jack.

"Sure. If the case is closed we can do it through the Freedom of Information Act. If it's not a closed case we'll just use our sources."

CHAPTER TWENTY-TWO

Jack jerked awake to the infuriating back rap of ancient trucks as their Mexican drivers geared down to climb and descend the La Mision grade. The small canvas and aluminum chair, the kind people take with them to the beach, creaked as he shifted his sleep cramped body. Fatigue had sandbagged him, but now, sitting on the bedroom patio of his Baja house, he felt refreshed. Both hands covered the polished-wood arm covers; the knuckles milky white like the burn scar against his deeply tanned skin. The back of his suntanned neck held droplets of sweat in his curling hair. The breeze made a wind chime ring softly and a petal from the bougainvillea floated past. The slow wind tickled and massaged his bare feet like an attentive lover as he drifted in and out of a sun induced doze. It had been nearly two months since the murder. He pushed it into the recesses of his mind.

The sun spread its dying rays, and dropped from the sky with amazing speed into the sun-seared Pacific Ocean as his thoughts dissipated. He looked for the green flash, but there was none today. An aging surfer, balding, with a dirty blond pigtail, trailed by a gaggle of sand covered dogs left wet tracks in the dry sand. A full-beam smile broke across his brown-hued face as he watched a woman who had used up most of her forties, promenade in the sand. Oil slathered over her shiny body, especially her bobbing chest that came with a perfect set of expensive rebuilt breasts. A lot of that going around he thought. She laughed heartily at the old moon-doggie who was struggling with his fiberglass surfboard. She worked hard at soaking up everything the sun had to offer, ultraviolet, gamma, alpha and infrared.

Peeling off a pair of aviator Ray Bans, he rubbed the corners of his eyes. A faint coolness in the breeze drifted across his shirtless body. The sound of the crashing surf was like white noise, he hardly noticed it. The cool Pacific waters lapped up on the half-mile stretch of beach of the irregular enclave identified on the highway map as Playa La Mision and scoured the sandy beach in front of the group of sixty houses. The houses were strung out like an irregular picket line on the slice of land that remained between the highway and the ocean; an eclectic neighborhood of people who didn't bother their neighbors. The somnolent atmosphere appealed to Jack's sense for distance between himself and over-amped humanity.

Above the houses, slashed into the sea-cliffs, running from Tijuana to the semi-tropics at the southern tip of the Baja, was the toll way, officially designated as Mexico Highway 1. At La Mision the old highway turns inland. Then it climbs onto a level plateau, curving gradually down the coast at San Miguel, where it joins the toll way leading into Ensenada.

Jack picked up the laptop computer with his free hand and slid open the glass door that separated the patio from the cool interior of the house. Stepping across the threshold, eyes blinking involuntarily to the dark room, he set the machine on the bedside table.

Jutting out from the side of the house, the windows of the bedroom provided a panoramic view of the sea that was flecked with dancing flashes as the dropping sun fenced with the white-caps. A light sea breeze flounced the open curtains on both sides of the glass doors.

Smelling her expensive perfume, he could hear her breathe softly as she slept in the late afternoon coolness of the house. His eyes drifted across her body to the pile of clothes on the floor beside the bed and one of the Manolo Blanik shoes she wore on the trip to La Mision. He stepped over a crumpled pile that was a designer dress tangled around an empty champagne bottle. A still life subject for the 21st Century, he mused. The slender leg of the woman, with a spiked eel skin shoe still attached, stuck out-side the sheets. Overhead, oscillating slowly, one of the blades of the ceiling fan waved a pair of bikini panties. Moving across the tile floor he flexed his muscles and rolled his shoulders to accommodate old pain.

"Feeling better?" she asked with a wide, sleepy smile.

"I feel great but I couldn't seem to get anywhere with my book," he responded, pointing at the laptop he had laid on the small wicker table by the bed. "Did I wake you?"

"No," she said with a light laugh, "but you certainly helped put me in a marvelous afternoon sleep."

"It was all that good champagne we drank on the way down."

They had purchased two bottles of Cristal before they crossed the border and iced them down in a Styrofoam cooler, intending to drink them during their stay in Mexico. By the time they crossed the border the temperature was perfect. By the time they drove into La Mision the bubbly was gone.

"Maybe so," she said with a deeper laugh. "But you're pretty addictive yourself."

He glimpsed at the woman who stretched like a cat on the rumpled bed. She was one of those leggy, California blondes who improved with age. Shadows and fractured rays of the dropping sun filled the beamed ceiling of the room, playing across Velda's long silky hair. Too much champagne and too much woman, he thought; a demanding, aggressive lover, the noisy kind in the throes of passion. She had insisted on wearing her expensive, high heel shoes during their love-making. He made no attempt to understand her fetish because he found it wildly erotic. Her desires for pleasure contrasted with her professional life.

They had met by chance two weeks ago at Brown Field, roughly a month after Mariana's death. Jack was coming out of the Flight Plans office in the small terminal when a strikingly attractive woman in a teal colored business suit asked him for directions to the PalmAir gate, the carrier that flew daily to Palm Springs. He pointed in the direction of the PalmAir gate as she asked with a smile, "Are you a pilot? You look like one."

"Yes. But not for PalmAir."

She was an easy conversationalist, so in a short time Jack learned she was a CPA and the controller for a small manufacturing company. She frequently flew to Palm Springs to meet with the company's absentee owner. That night, when she returned from Palm Springs, Jack and Velda Dean went to dinner. He talked a lot about his house in Mexico, and she told him she would like to see it. Two weeks later they traveled to La Mision. In between the time they met at the airport and the trip to La Mision they dated four times. Enough to become intimate partners.

Cool silence brushed off the white plaster walls of the beach house. The stillness was broken by the soft sound of falling water from the large fountain in the front courtyard. He walked across the tile floor and opened the door on the east side of the house, stepping out on the stone floor. Big, bright red geraniums, with gnarled stems the size of a large man's thumb, flooded stone planters. Flower heads drooped and begged for attention, showing his recent lack of interest in plant maintenance. Wrought iron, pointed and curved, anchored across the top of the foot thick high wall. The house was built like a small fort, largely impenetrable.

Returning to the bedroom, he was reflected in the glass panel of the door. Then a smile broke across his darkly tanned face as he caught and held the eyes of the woman. He remembered their semi-drunken romp in the bed and Velda's demands the minute he unlocked the house. They had made love in a crazy, violent way. His shoulders were raw from the scraping of her nails and sore from her pounding.

"Hungry?" he asked her.

"Starved."

"Shower up and we'll go to dinner."

"Great. Where?"

"The Emporia. It's down the road a mile or so."

"Good food?"

He laughed. "The atmosphere is better than the food. You'll like it."

It was early evening when they drove away from the house. A dark velvety night was developing; a smuggler's moon. Jack parked the Mercedes, got out and opened the door for Velda. He locked the car before escorting her across the cobblestone to the entrance of the noisy barroom of the Emporia *cantina* and hotel, a ramble of buildings cobbled together like the set of Casablanca. Men stared openly at the ripe, sexy woman who held onto his arm; casual but possessive. The two bartenders looked at each other lifting knowing eyebrows. The night air was hot and steamy, unusual for a desert land abutted by treacherous sea. An unplugged guitar pierced the humid purple darkness with a familiar Mexican love song.

The usual Emporia crowd milled around at the entrance. The mariachis in their black and white *charro* suits looking for patrons, mixed with the coming and going of customers. A thin woman, with a hiked-up Lycra miniskirt and a mouth like a searing red wound, tossed them a jealous stare, "rich gringos," she whispered. A cluster of Mexicans, in best disco mufti postured at the front door. They scattered defiantly as a screaming 550 Honda slid up. The noisy machine was straddled by a banana bonzo in Tijuana disco shoes and a redheaded female in biker's leathers. From the rear of the bike the woman expertly stomped the kick stand down and ripped the heavy zipper down to her bare navel. A basket vendor, with a transistor radio strapped to his belt, sat next to an hombre with drooping lids. He held a thin, flat box with an assortment of jewelry in his hands that flashed with cheap rings. The vibrating beat from a Tijuana radio station jumped from the security guard's parked VW. Fish tacos were being hawked by the pushcart vendors. As Jack and Velda approached the door a screeching cat fight broke out in the parking lot. It started when one jealous whore stepped up behind a competitor who stole her trick and planted a kick in the middle of her bouncing ass. The kicked woman stumbled, recovered, and then turned on the other whore with a vengeance. As the women screamed and grappled, the drunken trick, confused in his almost comatose state stumbled around on the cobblestones and the mariachis strolled over to watch. A couple of gringo surfers and dirty kids selling gum joined the crowd. The fight ended as fast as it started as the winning *puta* jeered, *"chinga tu madre."*

The Emporia was not your standard, nuevo Tex-Mex, semi-authentic Mexican restaurant. Far from the frozen-margarita machine *cantinas* of Southern California. Resting on a rocky bluff, it was a place where you could get shitfaced any time, and laid some of the time, with no judgements or moral indignation, Jack explained. Kind of a Baja White Rhino. The "no tell, hotel" was where you went without your wife, or husband, if you could pull it off. A decadent, good-time, neon oasis where adolescents and old farts in jeans and lizard cowboy boots were among the uniforms of the night. The Los Reyes band carried its instruments and equipment inside. A drunk surfer with peeling sunburn slinked through the sweaty scene looking for the *baños*. Two "madristas" with ostrich-skin cowboy boots swaggered out, one was talking intently on a cell phone, waving his wrist bound with a heavy gold watch.

Jack steered Velda through the open door and past the quirky doorman equipped with a pocket-size electric cattle prod. The bartender behind the long narrow bar had slicked-back, wet-looking hair. Scars and tattoos announced a body that had lost its fight with the world. He chuckled at something and slapped his hand on the white Formica bar top. He was wearing a tan *guayabera* shirt with epaulets, side vents and pockets. A religious medal of soft Mexican gold hung from a chain around his neck. When he smiled, oily sideburns climbed up into his Dr. Spock ears. Chugging a frothing beer, he acknowledged Jack's entrance through the fringe of the crowd with a little half smile that broke through a set of bad teeth. Wiping the foam off his lips with a backhanded motion, he pulled two seven ounce bottles of Chihuahua beer from the cooler behind the bamboo cane bar. He slid them across the wet surface to a customer. Like soldiers, both bottles came to attention next to the brown 12 ounce Carta Blanca bottle holding a single stem of day old gardenia.

A sign that said "Prices of Drinks Subject to Change With Attitude of Customers" was held to the wall with rusty nails. Clumps of garlic hung from the ceiling in a maze of unattended, viney plants and green bananas. Smoke, from cigarettes and the

166

cloying scent of marijuana, spiraled toward the ceiling. A thin, sallow skinned girl with stringy black hair stubbed out a cigarette in a cheap, black plastic ash tray. She signaled the bartender for another banana daiquiri as her partner shuffled across the small dance floor guarded by an aging, black Rhodes keyboard and a fat bandleader. The room was a cacophony, a mix of revelers, orange sun glasses, wired eyes and twitching noses. The newly divorced were dressed in gold lame' pants, sucking limes with tequila shooters, trying to drink themselves gorgeous; drug traffickers, San Diego dilettantes, jarheads, businessmen, bandits, and federales were among the assortment of humans who gravitated toward this real or imagined decadence. The buzz of drugs, liquor and sex bounced in the air like storm electricity.

A piano tinkled through the drone of the noise punctuated by cursing and a thin, high laughter. Dizzy and ready to dance, her libido encouraged by tequila shooters, a middle-aged woman stood and began a dirty dance without a partner. Pushing aside the clump of bananas hanging from a rusted spike in the ceiling, Jack squinted through the smoke at the green chalkboard menu. The choices were the same every day: fish, the Mexican plate, lamb shanks, lobster and thick Mexican beef steak.

A well-dressed woman with a pink gash of lipstick and mammoth tits tottered out of the baño tucking in her Lacroix blouse. More than tipsy she maneuvered through the crowd in full sail, to a table occupied by her diminutive partner with a crescent of wiry hair surrounding his shining pate, and a crooked smile of anticipation. He rose, grappled with the heavy high-backed chair as the woman sat down hard on the thinly padded seat.

A large, hard hand covered with course black hair clamped down firmly on Jack's left shoulder. He tensed involuntarily and bunched the muscles in his right bicep as he started to turn.

"No! No, amigo," mocked the big man dressed in a Mexican wedding shirt, as he backed away gesturing don't hit me with his calloused pink palms. Light from a 60 watt bulb covered by a straw basket blinked and bounced off the man's heavy gold necklace that was camouflaged by thick clouds of black wooly chest hair. A cigarette stuck out of the corner of his mouth and a glass of Chivas was clamped in his hand.

"Sit your beautiful selves anywhere," he invited with a sweep of his arms.

Jack and Velda pushed back heavy wooden chairs and seated themselves at the out-of-balance table covered with a red table cloth.

"You are tight as a frog's ass, amigo," said the proprietor of the Emporia in a thick East European accent that rolled ahead of his large, practiced smile that was infectious.

"Alex, *que tal pues*."

The burly man smiled at Jack, showing extensive gold crown work. "*Bien, Bien*. An amigo of yours was here." Jack quizzically looked at him and said nothing.

Velda, with jealous interest, said teasingly, "I guess you bring all your female companions here, don't you."

Shaking his head, a serious frown crept across Jack's face. "No," he said in a flat laconic reply. "In fact, I've never brought any-one here. I always come alone."

"Yes, but do you always leave alone?" she parried and grinned at him.

Bothered by Alex's news, he waited until the *cantina* owner had escorted another customer to a table by the huge brick fire-place that dominated the room.

"What did the guy look like?" he asked when Alex returned after seating a pair of "beautiful selves."

"Big *hombre*. Maybe a *federale*? Maybe a tourist? Gettin' fat. Hard fat on this man. Who knows," shrugged Alex. He lit up another cigarette with a heavy gold lighter and blew whole puffs of smoke out of his nostrils.

The area around the rectangular bar was crowded, and peo-ple pressed against each other whenever they tried to move. Jack could smell the jalapeno and Scotch on Alex's breath. He looked across the bar at the oceanscape. The high night winds had ripped the clouds into strips of vaporous gauze that floated in the light of the quarter moon. The crashing surf noise penetrated the din of the barroom.

"What did he want?"

Alex responded with a shrug and said, "You. He wanted to know where you were staying."

"Did you tell him?"

Alex's thick forehead nodded. "I believed him to be a friend of yours."

"American?"

"*Norte Americano*," responded Alex.

"What did he look like?"

The *cantina* owner thought for a minute before continuing. "Maybe six feet. Thick man, big man."

"Hair?"

"The man had a hat on."

"Hat or cap?"

"Uh?"

"Did he wear a hat or a cap. You know, with a bill?"

"It was a cap, I think."

Jack continued. "How old?"

Shrugging, Alex said, "Hard to tell. Probably over fifty. Hard life on his face. Like mine," he laughed as he blew smoke out of a wide set of nostrils.

Alex peeled off his stool to greet a regular whose gait spoke of being deep in booze. Jack nodded to the boy waiter dressed in a wrinkled white shirt with brown buttons. Taking Velda by the elbow, he escorted her to a table. She rippled across the floor in her toeless high heels like a jungle cat. Sensation stirred in Jack as she brushed back her electric blond mane once she had adjusted her chair. The heavy gold necklace around her thin, gracious neck and well-endowed bust gave her a lavish bearing. He thought of French queens.

"Drink, señor?" inquired the waiter as he unfolded the heavy brown napkins on their laps.

Jack nodded toward an empty Chihuahua bottle on the table next to them and said, "*Dos*."

"Señorita?"

Velda smiled at the waiter and said, "Tequila, Cuervo." Turning to Jack she laughed and said, "This isn't your typical Mexican restaurant, is it?" She paused thoughtfully and said, "The Emporia. That's a fine, old world name." She ran her sharp pink tongue over the edge of the thick Mexican water glass.

Watching Jack look out the wide window at the unimpeded view of the ocean, Velda studied his face before she asked, "What was that conversation all about? I can tell it upset you."

Nursing his beer, Jack said, "Other than a few locals who do some work on my place, I don't know of anyone who would be looking for me down here, or for that matter I don't know of anybody who even knows I come to this place. The only person I talk to is Alex and I'm damn careful what I say to anyone else."

"Why?"

"I'm not interested in telling anybody anymore about myself than I have to. But what you say to Alex stays with Alex. Let's order, the food is great," he said abruptly changing the subject.

"Your house is lovely," ventured Velda after a moment of quiet. She looked at him and said, "You're a lucky person to have such a private place on the ocean." He couldn't agree more, but how private was it now?

They ordered; he had lamb shanks and she ordered the fish. He looked across the table at the ocean. He wondered who was looking for him. He was sure no one stateside knew where his house was. Maybe the person who was looking for him was a local, one of the other Americans who lived in the little village and visited with him casually. Sometimes someone needed a tool or some help. Maybe that was it. But why didn't that person come by the house.

His thoughts were interrupted when Velda inquired, "How long have you been coming down here?"

Smiling, he said, "Since I've owned the place."

She laughed out loud, hard. "That's what I like about you Mr. Jack Dalton. You know how to give someone an honest answer that tells them absolutely nothing. You like the solitude, don't you?" she observed.

"Yeah. Yes, I do. Here's to solitude," he toasted her with his drink.

Two hours later, they left the Emporia with a bottle of local wine. Outside, the local policeman, with a Zapata moustache and thick arms roped with muscle, watched them leave. Velda held tightly to Jack's solid arm. She danced slightly to keep up with his long-gaited walk. Her fingers, running up and down his scarred arm, felt cool and sensual. Later, at the house, they luxuriated in the tile tub equipped with water jets. He marveled at her statuesque body. She gave him a genuine smile of pleasure before standing up with exaggerated slowness. Water cascaded down her body as she straddled him. Then she lowered herself slowly, the exploding sensation of pleasure signaled that she had him deboned and filleted.

CHAPTER TWENTY-THREE

With the barrel of his silencer-equipped pistol, he lifted the latch that held the heavy gate. A gust of warm ocean wind snatched lightly at his sweat. Heat lightning zippered the sky. The trigger of the Walther P-38 felt cold to his touch, an edgy uncertainty gripped him. He failed the first time he tried to kill Dalton. Tonight he *had* to succeed. His muscles were cramped from waiting hunched over behind the low stone and masonry fence that ran parallel with the service road. An hour ago he watched from a distance until Dalton's car returned to the house. The familiar profile of the big Mercedes told him his target was in for the night. The moon penetrated the rolling clouds and made his coveralls look chalky. The pale moonlight gave shape to house and entrance. Close by on the highway, the sound of an eighteen-wheeler downshifting rapped in the warm Mexican night.

The man pushed the gate, testing it for noise. It opened soundlessly. Attached to the Velcro loop on the right thigh of his coveralls was an ax-like tool with a long sharp point. Moving across the expansive patio, his uniform shoes, the kind that beat cops and warehousemen wear, silently touched the tile floor. The intruder felt grateful for the ten-foot high, twelve-inch thick adobe wall which surrounded three sides of the house. The wall protected it from the service road to the rear and the neighboring houses on each side. Returning the pistol to its holster, he crossed the walled patio to the window and listened for sounds from within the house. Tense, his breath came with difficulty as he pushed against the door. It was locked. He looked around for another entry.

At the front, where the wall met the corner of the house, the roof pitched low to the enclosed patio. With hands wearing black leather gloves he moved one of the wrought iron chairs over to the wall. Stepping up on the chair, he climbed to the top of the wall and cursed silently when he gouged his knee on the overhanging tile. He moved quickly. Balancing on the ledge of the wall, he stretched, reaching up to the top of the flat roof, a distance less than four feet higher than his wall-top perch. He teetered twice before regaining his balance as a gust of on-shore wind threatened his balance. Struggling, he pushed off of his toes, twisting his body as he lurched upwards so that he was seated on the edge of the roof. Exhausted from the exercise, he lay back on the tile roof letting his heartbeat slow down after shooting up to the max. Minutes later, after regaining his strength and composure, he moved quietly across the tile roof to where it dropped off to a small inside courtyard that connected to the master bedroom. He studied the room below him. Three windowless walls and a large glass door enclosed the bedroom. Looking over the edge, he squinted into the darkness of the open door separating the master bedroom from the tiny courtyard. A small spa was submerged in the tile floor. The door had been left open and the spa was bubbling up hot steam and vaporized on the cool glass door. He crawled closer to the roof edge and started to descend. Entry to the bedroom will be easy once I reach the atrium floor, he thought. Killing Dalton will be a snap.

Sweat drenched Jack's body, the sheets and bed covers twisted in a pile at the bottom of the bed. He felt exhausted and emotionally winded as he woke himself from the recurring nightmare fires of his Gulf War helicopter crash. He lay still, staring at the ceiling, rubbing the old scars on his left arm. Slowly, his consciousness returned. Velda was sitting up in bed looking at him. She had pulled the sheets up to her chin, her face frowning in dismay. He ran his splayed fingers through his tangled hair.

"Fuckin' dream, it never goes away," he mumbled. She gazed into his face, searching for his torment. She moved to hold him, traces of cooling sweat trailing off her chest. Her thick, erect nipples pressed against him as she kissed him. His sweating body had aroused her. He pushed her away gently, the dream still nagging his memory.

Laboriously rolling off the king-size bed and out of his troubled dreams, he shuffled slowly past the steamy door that lead to the atrium. In the bathroom, he flicked on the light and searched the cabinet for some aspirin. Finding some, he filled a glass with water, opened the door to the bedroom patio on the seaward side of the house and stepped out into the cooling breeze. Velda, with a blanket wrapped around her shoulders, joined him. Both were silent as they listened to the waves hammer the sand on the beach below.

"Let's walk on the beach. I'm wide awake now."

She replied, "We need to get dressed."

"No we don't. The blanket is plenty. Besides, there is no one on the beach at this hour."

The man was at the edge of the atrium, readying himself to descend when, without warning, the dark interior of the house exploded in light. He froze with one leg hanging over the side of the wall. He heard a woman's soft voice against the roar of the surf.

"Christ," he thought. Dalton was supposed to be alone. There was a goddamn woman in there with him. As quietly as he could, he pushed himself back from the edge of the courtyard wall, scraping his knuckles. Crawling backwards for about three yards, he got to his feet, in a crouching walk, he moved back to the front of the house where the roof dropped off to the patio wall. Sliding down off the roof to the wall, he planted his feet on the edge of the chair. As it tilted unexpectedly, he jerked his feet back and let the chair settle itself. Like a frozen statue in a park, he paused. His instincts told him to run while his brain screamed at him to stay put. The T-shirt warm Mexican night gripped and held him as he crouched on the courtyard wall, trying to figure out who turned the light on. His heartbeat tripped and was firing hard. Tensed, with his eyes riveted on the bedroom, he waited for the light to go off. Time passed. The light stayed on. He waited fifteen minutes. Fuck it, he said to himself. It had to be done tonight. If he didn't kill Dalton, he'd be dead, simple as that. So he had to go back in the house and do it the hard way.

He moved back across the roof to the opening that surrounded the spa. Then he put the pistol in his mouth sideways and clamped down hard with his teeth. A faint metallic taste mixed with gun oil spread across his tongue. With both hands free, he leaned forward, grasped the roof edge and dropped into the courtyard enclosure. Jerking the gun from his teeth he moved quickly through the doorway into the bedroom. He raised his right arm, pointing the gun at the bed and began to squeeze the trigger.

The bed was empty. He whirled toward the door leading to the main part of the house, ready to shoot. No movement. The only noise came from the surf. Where in the hell are they? A power load of adrenalin pumped through his blood stream. His pulse jumped. Dalton must have heard him on the roof. He was either waiting in one of the other rooms in the house or he went out the back door. Bone-rattling fear grabbed him. Dalton could be waiting for him outside or going for help. But where was the woman? He'd have to kill her too. Sucking in his breath to calm himself, he blinked rapidly to adjust to the darkness of the house. Then he heard voices outside on the beach side patio. Moving closer to that side of the house he could barely hear them talking over the crashing surf. The words..."careful, don't trip"..."take more of the blanket," told him Dalton was not laying in wait for him inside the house. He and the woman were going down to the beach. Hell, he thought, this will be even easier. I'll just wait until they return. After they've gone back to bed I'll walk through the open door and take them out with two head shots.

Unlocking, and pushing the handle on the sliding door that led to the courtyard he slid the door open slowly and stepped outside. Then he slid the door back so Dalton wouldn't notice it had been unlocked when he and the woman returned from the beach. The smell of eucalyptus sweet and medicine-like came through the door on the breeze. He moved through the opening, across the courtyard as lightly as his heavy body would allow, he sat down against the brick wall, by the wrought iron gate and waited for Dalton to return to the house, knowing it would be from the beach side.

Below on the empty beach, Jack and Velda walked with their arms entwined, their naked bodies covered by the blanket. They wobbled close to the water and turned landward when a splash of sea spray hit them.

"Do you have nightmares often?"

"Yeah. I do. They started years ago, after I crashed in my helicopter in the Gulf War. Nothing I do seems to shake them."

"Is that when your arm was burned?"

"Yes. Does that bother you? Maybe I should keep my shirt on."

"No Jack. That's not what I meant. What I meant was...," her voice trailed off.

Silence.

She looked at him with compassion. "Was it painful?"

"The recovery was. I don't remember the burning. I blacked out."

"I can understand that. No one wants to die in a plane crash," she said innocently.

"It's not dying in a crash I worry about. It's dying in a burning coffin. Have you ever seen someone burn to death?"

"No. Have you?"

"Yes. And more than once," he said in a harsh whisper.

Touching him delicately on the arm, she said, "Take me back and let me hold you. I'll keep the dream away."

As they climbed the stairs from the beach to the house Jack said, "Why don't you go on in? I'll walk around to the front to be sure everything is locked up."

"Is there something wrong?"

"No," he half laughed. I just want to be sure we're all locked up. I don't know if I locked the courtyard gate when we came back from the Emporia. I'll go around and check it," he said over the roar of the surf and the barking of a neighbor's dog.

She laughed as he walked out from under the blanket. "You don't have any clothes on. Take the blanket."

"There's no one out at this time of night," answered Jack, but he wrapped himself in the blanket as he walked toward the front of the house. The brick and mortar walkway between the side of his house and his neighbor's was hard on his feet. With the blanket wrapped around his naked body he felt like some kind of pervert prepared to expose himself. At the corner of the house he stepped off the sidewalk and onto the service road. Damn, he thought, wishing he had either his boots or at least his flip-flops. The road gravel bit at the soles of his feet. The gate *had* been left open. Stupid of me, he thought as he stepped through, turning to close and lock it.

Suddenly he tensed and his pulse quickened. He heard a *phiffft* sound as sharp wind assaulted his left ear. Then the fire of exquisite pain poured over him as he took a heavy blow to the head. He swung back hard with a clinched fist and could feel blood and snot explode from his assailant's nose. Then, the blood drained from his face, he dropped like a spine-shot deer. He vaguely heard the scruff of heavy shoes rasping through the eucalyptus. He could feel himself falling but it felt like it wasn't him. His attacker escaped through the gate as the open hasp grasped at his clothes, claiming the ax-like tool he carried as he charged out of the courtyard.

Jack's skull buzzed with pain, and luminous shapes danced in his eyes. The glow in his brain was a lurid orange. Small, multiple suns floated through the pinkish fog as he tried to rise. Struggling to his feet he was forced back to his knees as nausea roiled through his body. Panic clawed as his thoughts cleared. Velda. What had happened to her? He rose from his knees and moved like a struggling colt. Overcoming the feeling that he was being sucked into dark, murky water, he lurched through the patio door.

Velda's silhouette against the moonlit sky moved up and down gently. She had fallen asleep the minute she laid down. Even if she had been awake, there was no way she could have heard Jack's encounter with the attacker. Distance and the roaring surf took care of that. Still in a semi-stunned state, he limped to the bathroom at the other end of the house. The wound was starting to cauterize itself. He soaked a hand towel in cold water and winced as he washed at the cut on his scalp. After taping a piece of gauze over the wound, he checked and locked the doors. He pulled his .38 Smith & Wesson out of his duffel bag and laid down on the long couch in the living room. It was an hour before he drifted into an uneasy sleep.

Dalton had surprised him. Christ, he had them coming into the house from the beach. Maybe he had dozed off but the next thing he knew Dalton was coming through the front courtyard gate with a blanket wrapped around him. He was slow getting the silencer heavy Walther out of the stiff leather holster and got off a round but Dalton was on him like a clawing cat. One of Dalton's swings caught him in the face just as he clubbed him with the barrel of the pistol. When Dalton fell, he took off and ran down the service road for about a hundred yards and then hid behind a large propane tank. Surprised that Dalton didn't come lurching down the service road after him, he lay in the protection of the dry roadside grass until early morning when Mexicans seemed to rise out of the wet earth and trucks appeared out of the dawn fog. Joining them unnoticed on the service road, he walked down the slight decline to the Emporia where his car was parked along with the other cars, trucks and the odd camper left there over night. Getting back across the border wasn't going to be a problem. Facing the welcoming committee would be a bitch.

CHAPTER TWENTY-FOUR

The night vanished with the first blush of the morning sun. Waking early and parting the drapes of the window, Jack looked out over the ocean front. The crusted blood and the brownish streak that made a shadow across his face were evidence of the beating he took last night. Sunbeams penetrated the bedroom drapes as he stretched, acutely aware of a soreness in his shoulder and cut face. In the bathroom, the hot shower washed away the congealed blood. The steamy air trapped in the bathroom invigorated him. Ten minutes later he stepped out of the shower stall. Drying off quickly, the soreness in his shoulder almost forgotten, he wiped the condensation from the mirror and proceeded to bandage his face. Too late for stitches, he pressed the edges of the wound together with a butterfly. Wrapping a towel around his waist, he left the bathroom. Velda's soft snoring gave evidence that she was still sleeping. Leaving through the master bedroom, he walked across the cool tile in the living area of the house to the kitchen.

In the kitchen he made a pot of coffee. He poured a cup and took one large gulp, anticipating the revival with the hot, sharp liquid. He took the mug, unlocked the front door and stepped into the courtyard. A soft breeze made the eucalyptus trees sway like a dance of wood nymphs. It was morning when all should be right with the world, but it wasn't.

Goddamn it, who was after him? he wondered. There had to be a connection between his flying job and the assault last night. Mariana was murdered for a reason. No question about it. Taking his coffee with him, he went out to where he had been beaten. Approaching the gate to look for clues he saw what looked like a small pickax lying next to the gate, just outside the courtyard.

He bent over and picked up the tool by its black rubber-encased handle. The serrated edge felt sharp, like a hunter's knife. He rubbed his fingers over the spiked point of the pick and felt a prickling along his spine. He had seen these before. Cops carried them in their cars. It was a type of extraction tool used to help automobile accident victims. The sharp, pointed, spike end was used to shatter the tempered glass of a windshield and the serrated edge could cut through the toughest of seatbelts. He was careful not to touch the stainless steel face. His thoughts connected hard and fast, the guy at the Emporia. Someone had tried very hard to kill him.

Returning to the house, he laid the ax on the kitchen table. Rummaging around in the drawers, he found a brown paper sack and put the ax in it. He didn't want Velda to know what had happened. Thinking about what could have happened last night sent an involuntary shudder through his body. Pouring a carafe of coffee, he stepped down into his library. He needed to talk to the private investigator he hired, as soon as he got back. Inserting a Bobby Darin disc in his compact disc player, he pulled back a chair and fell deep into thought as Bobby Darin sang "Splish Splash."

Velda drifted silently by with the cool grace, barefoot with only a towel wrapped around her thick, wet hair that fell in tendrils against her face. The Mexican clock on the library wall chimed nine times, always ten minutes slow. People on Mexican time.

"Feeling better on this sunshiny morning?" she cheerily asked, as she walked across the cool floor tiles.

"Hey, no sneaking up," he said, feeling foolish as he flinched slightly at her voice. He kept his back to her.

"My, my, aren't *we* jumpy this morning. What's the matter? Too much action last night?" she teased.

Cracking a slow smile, Jack turned, looking into the inviting, smokey-eyed stare of an exotic animal. She noticed the cut on his face as she moved toward him. "What happened? Jack, how did you cut yourself?" she asked with obvious concern. Her face twisted as she gently touched the cut.

"Ouch!"

"Sorry. You need to get that stitched."

"Probably. I'll have a doctor look at it when we get back."

"But what happened?"

He shook his head trying to smile a bit. "The step leading up to the front of the house had a loose brick. I stepped on it and it popped out like a loose tooth. I fell forward and hit my head on the handrail. You were asleep by the time I locked the front gate. Didn't see any reason to wake you up because I couldn't walk straight." Velda looked at him like she doubted his story but she let the subject drop with the admonition, "Be sure you have a doctor look at it before it gets infected."

Picking up his coffee cup, Jack followed Velda through the house and back into the bathroom. He watched as she blow-dried her hair, rivulets of water running down her back and into the crevice of her buttocks.

CHAPTER TWENTY-FIVE

Velda had to be back in San Diego by early afternoon. Jack hated to leave the house. It was where he was able to tie off a small piece of space in his life for some anchorage. When he was in La Misión he felt hidden from the world, like lying at the calm bottom of a swift moving channel. Collecting his shaving gear, he tossed his beat-up leather flight bag on the bed. He had changed the bandage on his face. Bruising was starting to discolor his skin a mean yellow-ocher.

"What can I do?" inquired Velda as she came out of the bedroom with a small travel case in her hand.

"Be sure you have everything. I'm ready to roll."

"Do I get to come back?" She looked at his face with soft smile.

"You bet," he said, as he touched her lightly on the shoulder.

Backing the big Mercedes out of the attached garage, he pointed it north and drove slowly up the private road leading from La Misión to Old Highway 1. Looking down across the red tile roofs of the houses that seemed haphazardly sited along the beach, he watched the waves fracture and break into white froth. The tires of his aging car crunched as they scooted and slid on the cobblestone roadway. Sunlight flickered on the tinted windshield. He narrowly missed a dirty brown dog as it loped along, sniffing for the errant taco in the trash. The sounds of Little Richard's "Good Golly Miss Molly" spun out of the tape deck. Velda sat beside him, silent, her hand resting lightly on his thigh.

"Where did you get the taste for 60s music?"

"My dad played all of the 60s stuff when I was a kid. I vaguely remembered the music until I discovered a box of his records in some stuff I stored. I played them one rainy afternoon and got hooked. I transferred them to tape. Now I collect every record I can get my hands on from that era."

Up on the highway, a Baja California bus overtook the Mercedes and smoked by with its horn blaring. It surged along with an assortment of panel trucks, wobbly-wheeled Monte Carlos and tandem-wheeled trucks with flapping, yellow tarps. Jack tapped the accelerator and watched the speedometer needle rise as his tires bit into the warm pavement. A film of dust covered the highly-polished, deep black paint on the heavy machine. The car growled as Jack swung it around a white water truck that moved precariously along the narrow shoulder of the two lanes that twisted up the coast to Rosarito.

Brown, odd-shaped mesas dotted with smoke trees spread across the landscape. High on the outcropping to the east was a rocky buttress, incised like a staircase. On the sides of the highway, the landscape, nearly barren of vegetation, bloomed with wrecked cars, beer signs, taco stands and patient people waiting for the bus.

Incongruous as it seemed, a full on movie studio flourished south of Rosarito. It was marked by a huge arched sculpture the local gringos called Gumby On Acid.

The onshore wind spun twin dust devils across the road. A never-ending picket line of white concrete fence posts paralleled the road. They saw spotted goats, brick kilns and humped over people tending small garden spots in the sandy soil. Sunlight zapped through the clumps of palm trees like a laser, promising heat in the afternoon.

"Is something bothering you?" inquired Velda, breaking the deep silence in the humming car.

"No. Just deep in thought. Sometimes my mind takes an unauthorized trip. I catch myself working on ideas for my book," he lied.

"Where did you learn to fly?" she asked and then answered her own question, "In the service."

"Yeah," he grunted.

"You learned to fly in the service but you didn't make it a career." She leaned close to him and tapped him on the shoulder. "Tell me why."

"Medical discharge," he said in a steely voice, oblivious to the silent forces that always seemed to take over his body when the subject of his discharge came up.

"Because of your wounds?" Velda asked, thinking about the ribbed scars she had felt on his muscular arm.

He responded cryptically, "Yes, kind of, and the ones you can't see."

Sensing that he was unapproachable about the subject, she stopped talking. Minutes later, they bounced down the dusty main street of Rosarito in silence. Soft dust puffed up under the tires of Jack's car as he twisted and jerked the steering wheel to miss the potholes and craters.

She continued to probe as she bent forward and looked at him with her head bent slightly to the side. "Have you always been a pilot? I mean, after you were discharged?"

"Yes. After the Army was done using me I went to work as a contract pilot."

"Contract pilot. What's that?"

"Air jockeys that flew our tin boxes wherever the customer wanted to go."

"Customer?"

"Usually the CIA, but sometimes someone else."

"Like who?"

"Sometimes it was supplies and ammo. Sometimes it was grain and supplies for a village. I've flown loads of pigs, people, body bags with pieces of meat stuck in the zippers, and evacuees and their chickens." Memories flew through Jack's thoughts. Servicing oil rigs off the coast of Indonesia, fire-fighting, crop dusting in the United States and flying the desert ice in Alaska was pretty tame stuff compared to the addictive adventure of Indochina and Asia.

"Was it worth it?" she said, breaking his reverie.

"Was it worth what?"

"Spending your best years as a vagabond pilot," she asked thoughtfully.

"Yes. For me it was," he said quietly.

After crossing the Border they cruised north on Highway 5 through Border City. A big, glitzy electronic billboard advertising the NevadaLine Card Club as the Las Vegas of the border caught Jack's eye.

"You play?" asked Jack.

"No. Never. I've done my share of gambling in Vegas and Tahoe but these places never appealed to me. They look sleazy from the outside. Besides, I don't understand the Asian games, do you?"

Watching the busy highway and changing the subject, Jack said, "Don't let me miss the exit to your place."

"Promise me you will have someone look at your cut."

"I will."

"Jack, there are better places to go than one of those emergency first-aid offices," she said in a disapproving voice.

"You're probably right. I'll go over to the emergency room."

Jack double parked the car in front of Velda's Little Italy condominium. She pecked him on the cheek, an open, beautiful smile on her face. "I had a wonderful time," she said happily as she got out of the car.

Driving away he was contemplative. His weekend was part horror and part pure joy. The intruder had assaulted him with intent to kill. Velda had smothered him with creative sex and the comfort of intimacy with a beautiful woman. He wondered, however briefly, if this beautiful woman would meet the fate of the others he had loved.

CHAPTER TWENTY-SIX

Punch Packer was in a world of hurt. Fucked up again. Buno would fry his ass. Armed with Jim Beam courage, he was past the threshold of control. His body and clothes were filthy when he arrived home. In the kitchen, he opened the bottle with a shaky hand and filled a water glass. Moving to the living room, he switched on the TV, hardly noticing the rerun hammering away on the screen. An hour later, anesthetized by the half bottle of whiskey, he pushed himself out of the chair. Stumbling to the basement door, he tossed his dirty garments down the stairs. He pulled the door shut. The lock didn't catch. He practically crawled to the bathroom. Stripping his underwear from his body, he stepped into the shower, hoping to get rid of the stink of the crime; he allowed the hot water to wash the evidence of his evening experience from his body, and the cobwebs from his mind.

In the basement, Bastard shook his head and stood up, his hair bristling on his neck as his shoulder muscles twitched. A sharp stink rolled off his body as he trotted across the basement to the pile of clothes, the heavy swivel on his collar rattled. The slavering dog attacked the beer and sweat-drenched clothes on the basement stairs, the dirty rags with the stench of bad body odor increased his aggressiveness; agitated him like meat dangling at the end of his nose. Growling, the dog lunged up the basement stairs and hurled his sixty pounds against the unlatched door.

I'm drunk-sick, thought Packer, dizzy, having a hard time standing as the warm water flowed from the shower head. The snarling dog hurled itself against the mildewed shower curtain, ripping it from the rings and shower rod and wrapping the man in a plastic fury.

Bone and tendon crunched as Packer futilely tried to defend himself against the jaws of the raging animal. A gurgling sound escaped his throat as the impact of the dog knocked him backwards against the shower wall. His heels shot out from under him and the back of his head slammed against the bathtub. He lay semi-conscious, his spinal cord severed at the high point of the vertebral column as the dog tore at his face and jugular. Scraps of pink plastic, hair and flesh washed down the drain. Blood from Officer Alvin Packer's wounds, mixed with the water from the shower, made a rosy stream as it swirled in a bubbling mass down the drain hole.

"Come on in the conference room and let's take a look at what I have. But more importantly, try to figure out what it means," said Ray Compton, the private investigator. The conference room was nothing more than a small office with a round table in it rather than a desk. Jack walked in with Harry on his shoulder. The bird cautiously eyed his new surroundings.

"You're really attached to that bird aren't you," said Compton.

"He's a buddy. Right now my trusted friends are kinda limited. He's one, you're the other."

Compton shook his head with a genuine smile. Jack was beginning to grow on him. Then he noticed the man's cut scalp and forehead and asked pointedly, "What happened to your head?"

"Somebody jumped me at my house in Mexico. Now there is no damn doubt in my mind that somebody is trying to kill me."

A deep scowl broke across Compton's face. "Damn, I was hoping this thing was a series of coincidences but this pretty much eliminates that theory. What happened in Mexico?"

Jack related the incidents leading up to the attack.

"The owner of the *cantina* talked with the guy who you think jumped you, why didn't you corner him the next day and get a better description of the guy?"

William E. Kirchhoff

"Alex doesn't know me that well. I'm just another gringo customer at his bar. Christ, he'd have been shark meat long ago if he
got involved with his trade.

"Who do you think it was?"

"Know what this is?" He removed the pickax from the grocery
sack by its rubber handle. Compton looked at the ugly looking
tool with interest before saying, "Yes. It's an extraction tool that
cops sometimes carry in their cars. It's used to get accident victims out of cars. Where did you find it?"

"The guy who jumped me in Mexico dropped it."

"Did you touch the metal?"

"No."

"Good. We may want to dust it for prints although I doubt
that it will do us any good."

Compton went over to a white grease board on the wall
with the residual of black marker ink and wrote, PEOPLE WITH A
REASON TO KILL JACK DALTON. "Let's list them."

"Can't think of anybody except the cops connected with the
flying I do for them," mumbled Jack.

"Come on," pushed Compton. "You must have pissed off
some people in your past. You couldn't avoid it in your business,
when you were doing your banana republic flying. And by the
way, where did you get the Whisperin' Jack AKA?"

Jack had not discussed his past in detail with Compton so he
was taken back at the question. "How'd you know about that?"
Even though they had become friends Jack had not mentioned
much of what he did before coming to Border City other than the
fact that he was attempting to write another book.

"It's easy," said Compton as he pointed to his computer screen.
"We can pull up a ton of information out of the data bases available to us." Recognizing Jack's apprehension he said, "Remember,
you hired us for this job, didn't you? Hell, all we need is your Social
Security number and date of birth and we can construct your
entire life without having to leave our office. The Whisperin' Jack
moniker came up during an email interview with one of your old
clients. And buddy, it's apparent that you led a very unusual life."

"Yes, but I don't need to spend hard earned money to find out what I already know."

Compton tossed the challenge back. "Want another PI? I'll give you a refund if you don't like my approach. I need to know as much as I can about you. You aren't actually a fountain of information."

Rebuffed, Jack answered with a simple, "No." He had started to develop confidence in the laid-back balding investigator. He liked him, and he knew he had to share everything that might help Compton.

Compton went on, "As far as I'm concerned you were flying where bad things happen to people." Jack nodded in agreement with the PI.

"I need to know if there is anyone who would still like take you out."

Jack rubbed the squint lines in his face and said to Compton, "I can't think of anybody. All that kind of flying was done over three years ago. I didn't steal anything, kill anybody or run off with anyone's special cargo. I was in my share of fights but that's the way it is in my game. Flight personnel seldom hold grudges. You never know who you'll be flying with tomorrow."

"New Orleans?"

"No. The only people I had anything to do with during that time were Mariana and the folks from the publishing house. Mariana is dead and what interest would the publishing people have in me? In fact, I sent them some more material for the book I'm trying to write."

"What was the reaction of Mariana's family?"

"They were crushed...angry."

Compton pushed. "At you?"

"Hell yes, wouldn't you be? But these aren't the kind of people that carry a killing grudge. Both her parents are good folk, teachers. Besides, if you believe it was one of them who followed me to La Misión, then who killed Mariana?"

"Don't know yet."

"That's what you are hired to do."

illiam E. Kirchhoff

"Anybody else?" probed Compton as he ignored Jack's slight. "You sleeping with anyone's wife?"

"No."

"Ex-wife?" questioned Compton persistently.

"No."

"Let's go over the DEA thing again," instructed Compton. "You didn't have any hard evidence or even circumstantial evidence when you went to them. So they toss you out as a loony. They figure they don't have a problem unless you can produce some actual evidence. Right?"

"Yes."

"But we both agree there's not enough for the DEA to investigate a local police department with the transportation of contraband for sale." Compton stood, poured himself some coffee. He took a sip, twisted his face at the sharp taste and said, "Want some?" Jack shook his head no.

"Now, would you like to hear about Velda Perkins?"

"Who?"

Compton wrote the name VELDA PERKINS on the board and said, "You know her as Velda Dean."

Peeling paint jumped off the door at Detective Mielke. His pounding shattered the silence, he watched the windows. The shades didn't move. No noise. Nothing from inside the house. Identical houses up and down the street, quiet except for the muted noises of soap opera drama, and complaining babies. Waiting in the heat aggravated his feeling of apprehension. A typical tract neighborhood of neat blue collar houses. But Punch Packer's house stood out from the rest. Scarred plaster and the lawn was brown with deep divots. Dirty oil pooled in the driveway and yellowed newspapers lay scattered about on the front lawn. Mielke twisted the door knob and leaned his shoulder against the door. It held. Standing back he flexed his left knee and bent his back. Two houses down, a door slammed and two boys ran into the street with gloves and a baseball. Shit, thought

Mielke as he uncocked his kicking leg, I'm too damn old for this stuff.

Mielke returned to his unmarked car, pushed the front seat forward, lifted out a pry bar and carried it back to the house. He walked around the side of the house, searching for the back door. A gateless cyclone fence, four feet high, blocked him. Piles of fly-blown grey dog shit lay everywhere. He climbed the fence cautiously. Still straddling the fence, he whistled. Nothing happened. He whistled again. No dog. Dropping off the fence on to creaking knees, he walked through the debris; dog shit, and rusted cans strewn everywhere. A doghouse and tin storage shed sat in the bright sun, heat rippled on the shed's roof. Weeds had claimed the backyard, except for the empty dog run. In the middle of the yard rose a three-foot-high metal post. Attached to the top of the post was a heavy metal swivel connected to a thick rusting chain. A circle of bare ground gave testimony of a dog spending hours running in an endless circle. Small animal bones and chunks of fur littered the brown path.

Pulling back the ripped screen door that squeaked with resistance, Mielke knocked three times and put his ear against the door. Nothing. He jammed the pry bar between the door and frame and pulled out his Taurus .38. The "Protector" model was his favorite because the compact wheel gun was built with a snag-free hammer. He pushed his weight down and the door popped as the frame split from the force of the pry bar.

As he pushed the door open, animal smells and a low throaty growl exploded in his face. The roaring mass of airborne muscle and frothing spittle was deflected in mid-air as the dog's shoulder caught the edge of the door that Mielke jerked back reflexively. The blocking impact from the corner of the door dropped the dog to the floor. Bits of saliva splattered Mielke's face. The dog bunched its muscles to leap again. Reacting instinctively, Mielke swung his gun up into the buff-colored wad of gristle and jerked off six adrenalin aimed shots. The canine went limp as it fell. Two bullets hit the dog in the throat, one in the right leg. The noise from the exploding gun in the room was deafening. A fuckin' pit bull, thought Mielke as he stood there sucking hard, his gut heaving, sweat drenched, pulling air into his chest. Then there was nothing but the sound of water from somewhere in the house. The rank stench of feces and the coppery smell of fresh blood hung in the air.

Mielke shifted the empty .38 from his right hand to his left. With his right hand he pulled the small .22 caliber Detective Special from the Sidekick holster at the small of his back. Bits of brain matter and fluids fell on his shoe as he changed hands. He yelled, "Packer!" in a shaking voice. He could hear himself panting.

No response.

"Packer! You there? It's me, Mielke!" He glanced at the pile of fur mass on the floor and then stepped cautiously across the peeling tile floor toward the sound of spraying water. Mist from the shower stream hung over the tub like a fog.

Packer's ravaged body lay in the bottom of the tub, pelted by the water from the shower. The bleeding had stopped from the gaping wounds. The skin was fish white in the facial area. Lividity began to darken where gravity had pulled the blood to the low places in the corpse as it lay in a crumpled pile. He hadn't been dead very long. Lacerations on the chest revealed fractured ribs. Packer's face finally had a look of repose.

Mielke checked his automatic reflex to turn off the running water. Then he backed away, careful not to leave any evidence that could be linked to him.

Shifting his feet, the young detective watched the Chief read the report:

PACKER, John, AKA Punch
DOB 12-14-40, MW, 5-11", 210 lbs.
Subj. a BCPD police officer.
Cause of death, assault by dog.
No weapons. Autopsy requested.
Photo at CAS
Sgt. Willby

Buno hunched over the typed report and adjusted his reading glasses. His forehead glistened where the receding hairline gave way, grudgingly, to the scalp. He ignored the rookie detective. His eyes looked out the window at the line of patrol cars in the debris-littered parking lot.

"Any questions about this?" he asked abruptly as he looked directly at the man standing on the other side of the desk, and shoved the report in front of him.

"No, sir. The responding officers found the animal dead when they arrived. I handled the crime scene work. The dog killed officer Packer but we haven't been able to determine who killed the dog. Place was a real mess. Two bullets in the dog according to the crime scene investigators. That's what killed the dog."

"That's all I need. Assign the case to detective Mielke. We need his experience on this one," he said as he dismissed the detective by swiveling his heavy chair so his back was to the man. Must have been a hell of a dog bite, he thought.

Hearing the door close behind the departing officer, Buno removed his reading glasses from his thick nose. After he pinched its bridge to relieve a headache that was building, he dialed Laz Forbes' number on his scrambler phone.

In the middle of the third ring, Forbes answered with a "Yeah".

Without preamble, Buno said brusquely, "Our man is still alive but my shooter is dead."

Forbes said in an angry voice, "I thought this guy was a pro."

"He was. He was a cop who did some of this kind of work for me before. He got killed by a dog."

"A dog!" responded Forbes unbelievingly. "Must have been some fuckin' dog."

"His own goddamn pit bull."

"Jesus H. Christ," he yelled, "Your job, get rid of him!" yelled Forbes. Buno knew what that meant. Fear gripped him, he knew what Forbes was capable of. Tension ripped through his body like a magic mushroom high. He was fuckin' responsible and had counted on Packer to do it for him. Then the dumb fuck Packer ends up as dog food. *Jijole!*. What else could go wrong?

CHAPTER TWENTY-SEVEN

"The nice lady you have been dating is Velda *Perkins*, not Velda Dean as you know her. She's forty-two, never married, and works for some people connected with the local mob." Compton's expression revealed concern. "And, I can see why you date her, damn good looking lady, obviously smart."

Probing his memory, checking his mental files, "No way. "That can't be so. Velda Dean is a controller who works for a manufacturing company." Jack did admit to himself that Velda seemed elusive, with a mysterious presence. A elegant woman who wore clothes that shouted high fashion, she was just too sophisticated to fit Compton's gangster-moll description.

Compton's response was, "You're half right. *Your* Velda Dean, my Velda Perkins is a CPA. But she doesn't work for any manufacturing company."

"Who does she work for then?"

"Technically she works for a holding company called Cal Investments."

"So?"

"On paper, Cal Investments owns the NevadaLine Card Club. Know where that is?"

"Sure, it's the big casino-type operation right off the interstate." In the murky corridors of his memory he recalled the idle conversation he had with Velda when they returned from Mexico. It was about card clubs. She told him she had never played in a card club. Now, Compton was telling him she worked for one.

"Have you ever been there?"

"No. And neither has she."

"Really?" Compton's eyebrows raised in automatic disbelief.

Jack said, "Because when we passed the club coming back from La Misión I asked her. She said she liked to gamble in Vegas and Tahoe, but not at card clubs, that they were sleazy."

"Bullshit. Velda Dean works for the owners of the NevadaLine Club," said the PI as he looked straight at Jack.

"How can you be so sure? It was a coincidence that we even discussed the subject but I remember what she told me. Why would she lie to me?"

Ray Compton pushed back from the table where he sat reviewing his notes and printouts. He blew air through puffed cheeks and delivered, "Velda Perkins is an expert gaming man-ager. She was educated at UNLV in Nevada and worked for the Hilton Casino in Las Vegas. According to my contacts with the Las Vegas Gaming Commission and IRS, she specialized in tax shel-ters for gambling profits. This woman really understands casinos operations. Know why?"

"No."

"She was a dealer."

"Drugs?"

"Cards. Our Velda worked her way through the university as a dealer and was eventually promoted to pit boss." With his pencil he tapped a photo of a woman with the long legs, shapely hips and the well-endowed bust of a Valkyrie approaching a limo. In a simple dress of rainbow muted colors she exuded sexuality. Continuing he remarked, "She looks like a show girl or high class hooker."

Jack shook his head slowly as he tried to piece together what the PI revealed. What Velda told him didn't match up with his information. He wanted to believe her and there must be a rea-son why the stories didn't match up. She probably had a good reason for not telling him everything. "What's this got to do with somebody trying to kill me?"

"Ever hear of a man named Laz Forbes?"

"No. Should I?"

"Probably not. Forbes is the Mafia boss down this way. I know, because when I was on the San Diego PD he was into just about everything crooked. Charged but never convicted, another Teflon Don. He owns the NevadaLine Card Club."

"You're telling me Velda Dean works for the Mafia?"

"Well, there is no Velda Dean so far as I know," replied Compton. But a woman named Velda Perkins is listed as the corporation secretary of the NevadaLine Card Club so, at least indirectly, she's working for the Mafia. Maybe she doesn't know it but I seriously doubt that. With her experience in the gaming industry, she's got to know the players."

"You're sure of all this?" asked Jack, hoping for a different answer. Compton looked at him thoughtfully before he answered. "Yes. I've double-checked everything. You told me that she didn't know you when Mariana was killed, and she had no idea you were attacked in La Misión."

"That's right," said Jack emphatically. "In fact, she was surprised when she saw the cuts on me the next morning."

"Surprised? Or just a good actor?"

Silent for a few moments, Jack said slowly, "Surprised. The way it played out she couldn't have been involved. We went for a walk on the beach because I woke up in the middle of the night. It was my idea. She was asleep. And when we came back to the house I decided to walk around to the front to check on the gate. That's where I got jumped."

"She didn't hear the fight?"

"No. The surf noise made it impossible to hear what was going on outside." None of this makes any sense. Why would a Mafia boss want to kill me? And if he did, then why get Velda, someone so important to his operations. I mean, don't those guys just come up with a hit man and do you in? Why go through all this trouble, even if there was a reason to off me?"

Ray Compton opened a folder and pulled a photo of a the woman in the colorful dress walking between some gambling tables. Around her thin gracious neck was a heavy gold necklace. Circled with a marking pen was the NevadaLine Casino's logo on a gaming table in the photo.

"Is that your Velda Dean? Our Velda Perkins?"

"Yes. How'd you get the pictures?"

Compton flushed two grainy photocopies out of his file. One was a Department of Motor Vehicles driver's license with Velda's picture on it. The other was a business license to own and operate a card club in California. Even in these unremarkable photos the woman looked good. She was listed as the corporation's secretary on a form that contained her photo.

Jack's defensiveness vaporized. He felt heavy, disappointed. "I still don't get it. I've got nothing to do with the NevadaLine club. I mean, there can't be a connection with the club and whoever is trying to kill me. But this doesn't make any sense either. Why would the NevadaLine Casino be involved? There is absolutely no connection between them and me. None."

Grinning like a man who was winning a chess game, Compton said, "If we can make the connection, maybe we can figure out who is trying to kill you and why."

"You think I've been set up. Don't you?"

"Everything points to that, but I'm like you. Why? She's too valuable to their business interests to be doing this stuff," said Compton. Then he continued, "Look, there is more going on here. Your dating a Mafia queen is not the way to insure longevity. My suggestion is that you go to the authorities. I'm an investigator, not a bodyguard."

"No way," said Jack. "I don't trust the BCPD anymore than you do. All my troubles started after I went to the DEA. Christ, maybe it's involved in this mess someway."

"I don't mean the local cops. Try the FBI," suggested Compton. Jack shook his head and said, "No. I've got no luck with federal agencies. It won't be any different than when I went to the DEA. I want you to check a couple of things out for me if you will."

"It's two hundred bucks an hour," said Compton reminding him of his hourly rate.

"I can handle a few more hours. Follow Velda and see where she goes. Who she talks to."

"Fine," responded Compton. "You have any other names that I ought to be taking a look at?"

"We've been through this before. The answer is no. That's what is so confusing about this. I have no idea why I'm important enough to be dead. I hardly know anybody out here. I fly the BCPD's helicopter so that I can work on my novel and that's about it." He stood to leave when Compton said, "One other thing. Here's your house key back. Got any idea what this is?" He held up a small plastic bag with a piece of balloon."

"No. If I had to guess, it's the end of a balloon that has been ripped off. Why? Where did you find it?"

"I found it in your house when I took a look around. It was in your birdcage. I had a hell of a time getting it away from your parrot. He's a beautiful bird, but meaner than hell. I guess he only knows one word. He kept yelling something like bemmer, bemmer, at me when I was trying to pick this out of his nest."

"Beer."

"What?"

"The only word my parrot knows is, beer."

He smiled to himself as he visualized the investigator trying to get something away from Harry. He studied the contents of the bag and said, "I don't think it's from anything I had, but no telling where Harry picked it up. What do you think it is?"

"The finger of a rubber glove. Mind if I send it to a private lab for prints? It will cost about two hundred to see if they can lift one."

"Will that do us any good?"

"It's a long-shot but I'd do it if it was me. I read Mariana's autopsy report and bits of latex rubber were found in her teeth. I doubt it but there may be a connection. Or it just may be something left by the crew that cleaned up the house after Mariana was murdered. If you kept the face of the extraction tool clean you found, I'll have it dusted too."

"I did. How much?"

"Each print job is two hundred."

"Okay, You're the expert. Let me know when you find out something." Jack thought about the cats having nine lives and he started counting how many he had left.

The man unzipped the breast pocket of his coveralls and pulled out a cigar. Lighting it, he sucked the smoke deep down into his gut and looked through the windshield of his van. Shit like this made him nervous. The Ruskie wasn't going to be happy with his story. Fuck him. What could he do about it?

Five minutes later, the Russian's car pulled up. Dressed in a black windbreaker, the Russian had the height and breadth of a bear. He departed the car and moved with surprising speed to the passenger seat. Inside the van, he immediately challenged the driver.

"So. Is our man dead?"

"He's still alive," responded the man grudgingly, "but I haven't missed a shipment of guns yet, have I?"

"No argument," said the Russian in his stilted English. "But you were ordered to kill him."

The man argued back, "I admit I fucked up, but this ain't Mother Russia. When you kill someone here, you can't just cover'em with snow, you got to have a plan. We got cops who know all about that shit. Fact is, we don't need to kill our driver. He ain't done anything squirrelly since the one time he went to the Feds and no one gave him the time of day. Without him we can't move. Besides, I'm with him all the time, each time we haul the stuff."

"There are always others who will do what is needed to be done for money."

"Maybe so, but this is a sweet deal for all of us. Let's leave it alone. The pilot and I are friendly. He won't go to the authorities again. Trust me. If he tries, I'll kill him then. I'll kill him immediately."

"If not, we will kill you, my friend," the Russian warned as he left.

Boomer Smythe slumped his shoulders and sucked deep on the cigar. Money made the world go around. He got fucked once, and the only other way out was to take up robbing banks. Whisperin' Jack was his friend. But despite the strong and unusual bonds, forged from many hours together in the air, it was either him or Dalton. The Russian made that clear. He needed some anger to kill. Some hate. He slapped at the tiny insect that was crawling inside his cap at the sweat line on his head. It was damn hard to hate a friend who treated you right. Life's lessons led Boomer to the conclusion that the world held no mercy for any man and his only hope for survival was self-reliance.

Maybe growing up in Slick, Georgia, below the skeeter line, did have an advantage. Raised in a ramshackle house on a road that was so rough the floorboard of a car would start thumping when you put in second gear. The man he called daddy worked in the Texas oil patch and was gone most of the time. His mother was a mean woman who was always yowling at the top of her lungs until they turned into jelly. When Boomer was eight years old the tuberculosis sent her to a sanitarium and then to her grave. By the time he was released from the orphanage he was a tough piece of meat with bulging biceps, wide shoulders and jaw that jutted out like an anvil. He enlisted in the Army at seventeen where the code of combat furthered his instincts for self-preservation.

CHAPTER TWENTY-EIGHT

"I'll be there," said Lee Dykes Hart lamely as he responded to Silva Buno's directions. Fear wrapped him like a tight shirt as he hung up the phone. He didn't like meeting with Buno this way but it wasn't the first time the chief wouldn't talk at the police station about something that was bothering him.

An hour later, with anxiety mounting, Hart drove his Porsche 911 Targa along the narrow macadam road that lead to the reservoir. He drove hard, whipping around curves and downshifting when he didn't need to. Lost in his thoughts, he failed to notice the big Lincoln pull up behind him. The startling sound of the car's horn broke his thoughts. It pulled around him and the driver motioned him to pull over. Wrenching the steering wheel to the right, Buno's brake lights shone in the dusk. Hart hit the brakes and jerked the little car to a halt. Damn. Buno must be really pissed at him. Buno vaulted quickly out of his car and jerked open the door on the driver's side of Hart's car, eyes glistened with absolute maniacal fury.

Hart began to open his mouth when Buno slapped his face with one hand and began to crush his windpipe with the other. He could feel his pulse jump and run, the tightening tension in his gut, the bitter taste of bile flooded his mouth. Buno whispered in a thick, dry voice, "You fuck. You chickenshit motherfucker."

Hart gagged as he jerked back, the enraged Buno dragged him from the Porsche. He took a kick to the stomach. Buno fired a mule kick into Hart's kneecaps and then hit him on the head. Hart fell to his knees and tried to protect his head with his hands. The blow did not come. Hart parted his hands and looked up. Buno raised his hands over his head as Hart's eyes focused on the metal, milliseconds before his brain exploded. Hart let out a heart-stopping scream as the thin steel tore membrane and tissue from his life-less eyeball and Buno jerked the pick from the bloody orb. Trying to stab him in the other eye, Buno missed, as Hart jerked his head back in terror. The ice pick sliced through his cheek, splintered the bone and snapped. Screaming insanely, Hart rolled over on his back, holding his face; his legs jerking reflexively. He died as the .22 caliber bullet slammed into his brain.

In the dwindling grey light that signaled the coming of dark-ness, Silva Buno pulled a pair of long-handled bolt cutters from the trunk of his car. Taking a deep breath to control his anger, he approached the body and began snipping Hart's fingers from his hands. The edges of the scissor-like clippers popped though the digital skin, then through the bone with a sickening crunch. Forbes was right. They needed to get rid of Hart. He was a weak, pussy-hunting dickhead who drank too much. Hart had served his purpose. The only downside to killing him was that he would have to go down to Ensenada until he could suck another courier out of the department. Buno did not like to fly.

Ray Compton and Jack sat at a table where the game was Texas Hold'Em. It was on the far side of the NevadaLine Casino, a vast room at street level. Mirrored pillars and the high mirrored ceiling made it look even bigger than it was. Around them, the noise of cards being shuffled for games like Pai-Gow, lowball and jackpot poker could be heard over the raucous talk, brags and complaints from the dealers and players. The games were fast and the house dealers shuffled low, skimming the cards across the felt. At the table where they played, some of the players had meals on small metal carts beside them. The Asians ate noodles with chopsticks but the gringos mostly ate hamburgers. Floormen put the names of would-be betters up on a chalkboard, and from time to time loudspeaker announcements signaled table openings for the waiting gamblers. The gamblers pounced on the cards dealt to them like monkeys grabbing for peanuts.

Compton was up about fifty dollars. Jack bounced above and below the line. It was the first time since he was a pilot trainee that he felt intimidated playing poker. The game moved so fast that there was a constant click of the cards and chips, and dealers shot the slow players looks of disdain.

While the dealer was shuffling, Jack said quietly to Compton, "Ray, I think your source gave you a bad lead. We've been here almost two hours and Buno hasn't shown. I thought your guy said he's here every Sunday night at 8 pm. It's almost 10 o'clock now."

"Your girlfriend's here, isn't she?" countered Compton with a subtle challenge. Jack nodded sadly. They had watched her come in earlier. So had a lot of other men. She turned heads no matter where she went. It was only after he saw her walk back to the off-limits area of the casino that he would concede Velda was connected. He just wasn't sure what to believe now. He had hoped she was just the NevadaLine's finance expert. But why would she show up on a Sunday night the same time as Buno? Why did she lie to him about never having gambled in a card club when she worked for one? The reason he and Compton were staked out, playing cards using his money, was because of some information Compton had dug up. Through a source, Ray had tracked down a dealer who informed them that every Sunday night Police Chief Silva Buno showed up at the casino at the same time, and went directly to the manager's office. It was just assumed by the informant that Buno was being paid off for providing the casino with some kind of protection. Compton convinced Jack that they should personally verify the information, so they just mingled with the crowd, playing cards. Velda's appearance on the scene at five minutes before 8 o'clock was no surprise to Compton. She was dressed in business attire and carried a matching leather purse and briefcase. Jack was struggling to piece things together, still hoping there was another explanation.

Compton was betting up when Jack nudged his arm. He looked up and Jack nodded toward the entrance of the smoke-filled room, where Silva Buno was heading toward the back.

"That's him."

"Okay. Let's play out this hand and leave. I'm up thirty bucks of your money. We'll split the winnings." Compton drew to five, six, seven and eight and lost the hand. He tossed in his cards and gave Jack a ten-dollar bill as he stood up.

"I gave you fifty to start with."

"You lose," laughed Compton. "Let's get out of here and try to figure out what to do about the fix you're in." A cocktail waitress approached them, and each man took the coke he had ordered. Walking through the smokey room, they drank them as they pushed through the crowd.

Ike, the hard man, who always seemed to be sitting in front of the door to Forbe's office, nodded at Buno, stood up, and said, "Evening." The mountain of flesh, jammed into an expensive blue double-breasted suit, tapped on the door. The sharp buzz from the electronic lock signaled it was unlocked, so he turned the handle and pushed it open. Buno entered without breaking stride. Inside the room sat Velda, dressed in a green silk pantsuit. Her long hair was piled high on her head and then twisted in a knot. Around her neck was a single-strand gold necklace.

"Boss," acknowledged Buno looking toward Forbes. He looked at Velda with a sly grin and said, "How you doing Miss Perkins?"

Forbes more or less grunted a response and Velda answered with a formal but obviously forced, "Good evening, Mr. Buno." She couldn't stand Buno. Whenever he looked at her he was fucking her with his eyes. "I'll be the one going down to Ensenada in the morning," Buno announced, grinning like a cat.

"Hart's gone?" asked Forbes.

Buno sat a small brown paper sack on Forbe's desk and pulled out a pickle jar. Inside were the bloody stumps of four fingers and a thumb. It took Velda a few seconds to realize what was in the jar. Dizzy, she quickly walked to Forbes' private bathroom.

They could hear her gag as she flushed the toilet.

Forbes smiled. "You did it?"

Buno nodded without saying anything. The noise of water in the bathroom filled the otherwise still office.

Velda returned. Her face was ashen and small beads of sweat had popped out along her neck line.

"What's a matter? Haven't you ever seen pickled fingers before?" Forbes asked meanly. She stared back at him blankly.

"We're all partners, aren't we?" said Forbes, giving her a hard look. Velda said nothing.

"You're thinking this is more than you bargained for. Aren't you?" He grinned at Velda. Buno watched with interest.

Velda's face flushed. "Laz, you hired me to make sure everything on the financial end works out right. I'm in for that ride, but nothing more. Besides, it wasn't my job to spy on the pilot. You have other people who are in that line of work."

Buno smiled and she jumped him hard, surprising both men with her anger. "What the hell are you laughing at. I didn't buy into this to be involved in a murder."

Buno started to say something in response but Forbes waved him off saying to Velda, "Honey, you need to think all of this through. If, and I mean *if* Chief Buno here did kill someone, and we now know about it, we are all partners, *capisce*?"

Interrupting, Buno said, "The law calls it an accessory. That's what you are now honey, an ac-ces-sory. Your choice is simple. You accept what you see as just part of doing business, or you talk to somebody. If you talk to anybody about this, even yourself, you'll be dead. But it won't be any easy kind of dying. Come here."

She hesitated.

"Come here!" he demanded. She moved toward him with apprehension. He grabbed her delicate left hand and pressed it down on the bottom of the metal bar sink. "Your little bitty hands are perfect candidates for the garbage disposal." For effect, he flipped on the switch of the disposal built into the wet bar. Velda jumped like a deer hit with a hot-shot. Forbes, watching Velda's face, said in a fatherly voice, "Let's talk about your new boyfriend, our fearless pilot."

Wrestling with her composure after Buno's threat, Velda said, "He doesn't know anything."

Buno challenge, "Then why did he go to the DEA?"

"I don't know anything about that."

"Why did you think we had you cozy up to him?" Laughing, Buno said, "It's not because we don't think you're getting enough action Miss-I'm-too-good-to-date-cops." Buno was still mad that Velda wouldn't go out with him.

Velda stood her ground, anger showing in her cheeks. "I've dated him to the point where he invited me down to Mexico with him. He's a nice guy, so I went."

"Mexico," exclaimed Forbes who wrongly drew the conclusion that there was some kind of a connection between their flying to Ensenada and Velda spending time in Mexico with their pilot.

"He owns a beach house south of Rosarito," responded Velda. "It's got nothing to do with our arrangement in Ensenada."

"You sure?" demanded Forbes.

"Yes."

"You sleeping with him?" butted in Buno.

Ignoring Buno's question, Velda said to Forbes, "He's just a pilot who wants to be left alone. My guess is that because he's been around some dirty deals he's a lot more sensitive. He isn't looking to be a hero or play detective. He won't go back to the DEA again."

"You sound pretty sure of yourself," challenged Buno.

"Look. I've got as much to lose as you do. I just don't think he is a threat, but if you do, then hire another pilot."

"No fuckin' way do we just give Dalton notice and get us another pilot. We either keep him so we can control him or kill the cocksucker," said Forbes, watching Velda for her reaction. Then he said, "You ain't getting emotional with this guy, are you?"

"The only thing I'm emotional about is money. That's why I'm in this deal. You don't have to worry about me," said Velda. Forbes wasn't worried. He knew Velda's passion was money, not men. Besides, she was in too deep with them to get out.

"Maybe we have to get ourselves a new pilot. I don't like to toss shit on a good thing but I got a feeling in my bones." Forbes looked at the man and woman as he made his proclamation. Buno frowned. He was starting to think through the problems associated with Forbes' order. They'd have to kill Dalton and then find another pilot. Killing was always chancy. Finding the right kind of pilot wasn't easy either. Velda's face was expressionless. Reading Buno's mind, Forbes said, "Get the job done in Mexico."

"Mexico?" questioned Buno.

"Yeah. Get your man Gomez to take care of the problem for us down there. Have Dalton fly you down to Ensenada on a regular flight and leave him with Gomez. Gomez' people can off him down there. They can feed him to the fishes in the harbor. That way no one will find him. And if they do, so what? The Mexican cops could give a shit about another dead American." He laughed at his own joke.

They left the NevadaLine Casino parking lot in Ray Compton's car, a nondescript Volvo. In the side mirror the building looked like a bad representation of the Alamo. As they pulled out of the parking lot, Compton turned onto a commercial street and started talking as he drove Jack back to his condo.

"Want my assessment?" he asked coolly.

"That's what I'm paying you for."

"This is some kind of money laundering deal. I don't think it's got anything to do with muling dope. Velda Perkin's background and Buno's connection with Forbes tells me you are probably flying dirty money. Your hunch that Buno is behind the attempts to kill you is probably right but some how the deal is wrapped around laundering money, not hauling drugs."

Frowning, Jack challenged, "Come on, this is too simple for a money laundering scam. In fact, it's stone-age stuff that no one would use."

"It's so simple it's brilliant," said Compton with an I-got-one-on-you smile.

"How so?"

"Most money laundering schemes involve putting dirty money back into a legitimate business and then taking it back out. All kinds of schemes exist. The Japanese mafia will build a golf course and charge their members millions for a membership. Then they incorporate the golf club and build a project in the US. Maybe another golf course. They sell it at a reasonable profit and the members get back their money, only the money is now clean."

"But that kind of scheme is traceable."

"It isn't, Jack. That's the beauty of the way Forbes' does it. With the police department's helicopter they don't have to worry about getting it out of the country. Buno just has to fly it down to Ensenada."

"Then what?"

"It's probably laundered down there."

"How?"

"Don't know, but I'll bet a million it's sent off to a secret bank account. Probably Switzerland or the Caymans."

"But why is someone trying to kill me? I didn't go to the IRS. If Buno knew I went to the DEA, which isn't interested in this kind of stuff, then so what?"

Compton slowed down his Volvo at a traffic signal. When the light changed he accelerated slowly and said, "That I don't know. Maybe he figures the DEA would pass your complaint on to the IRS. Who knows what they think. Buno has to be real careful. Hell, he's got to be paranoid. Hear me out and maybe you can come up with the answer." Jack said nothing, waiting for the PI to explain his theory as the car picked up speed.

"In the old days, casino operators just resorted to skimming money off the top. Of course the IRS has just about plugged every loophole, but there is still one way. Actually it's pretty easy."

"What's that?" asked Jack. Now his interest was piqued.

"If you can get the money out of the country without get-ting caught and laundered somehow, then you can stash it in either a Swiss or Cayman bank account. My guess is it is going to a Cayman Island bank because it's closer to Mexico. You told me the briefcase we saw Buno carrying in the club was the same one that they always take to Ensenada."

"Well," said Jack in a resistive manner, "It looks like the same one. One of those heavy-duty aluminum ones."

Compton fired up, irritated with Jack. "Quit acting like a defense lawyer and help me out. Forbes' card club is a legit money-making machine. But these mob guys are never satisfied with legitimate money. It's in their bloodlines to do otherwise. It's clear he's already doing business with Buno. We know they are in this together. Your girlfriend is the financial wizard who sets up the out-of-country secret bank account. Forbes also needs her to decide how much they can skim so the IRS won't close them down. She's a gaming expert and a CPA. Makes sense doesn't it?"

With regret Jack had to agree.

"Paint me your picture. Maybe I'm missing something," encouraged Compton.

"Forbes' problem is getting the money out of the country. He needs a failsafe way so he simply buys a helicopter for Buno's police department. Buno puts together that phony police department exchange program," he paused.

"Border Cities Police Program?" asked Compton.

"Yes. That gives him a perfect way to mule the skimmed money out of the country. Now, the range of a helicopter is not that far, so he's got to find a point where large aircraft can fly in and out."

"Ensenada," offered Compton. "It's got an airfield that will handle medium aircraft is my guess."

"Right. And it's also where Buno has guaranteed police protection once the skimmed money has been transported to Mexico."

"And you're the guy flying the aircraft carrying the dirty money."

"Exactly. I almost had it figured out, but I thought it was dope. Dope or dirty money, the problem for me is the same. Buno and Forbes must think I know too much. They're behind the attempts to kill me. Buno or Forbes sent someone after me. But whoever it was screwed up twice. Make any sense so far?"

Thinking for a bit as he drove, Compton said, "I can buy all of that."

"Why not just fire me?"

"You went to the DEA and Forbes and Buno found out somehow. Who knows how, but they did. The Feds could have checked your complaint out with someone at the police department and it got back to Buno. Doesn't matter. Buno and Forbes figure it's only a matter of time before you either go back to the DEA or some other agency."

"Go back?"

"Yeah. Because they know this will keep bothering you and eventually you'll go back. They know it just like I know it. That's why they've got to take you out of the picture, permanently."

Compton pulled his car up in front of Jack's condo. "Has Velda ever talked to you about what you do?"

"Yes, but in a pretty casual manner."

"What do you mean 'casual?'"

"She just wanted to know what I do for a living. Same kind of questions I asked her about what she does. Come on in, I'll buy you a beer."

He pushed the door open, followed by Compton. Harry started his squawking, *"Beer! Beer!"*

"Want a beer? Harry does."

"Thanks."

Jack went to the refrigerator and lifted out a half empty beer bottle. He took the cap off of it and poured some in the brass thimble. Then Jack removed two bottles and placed them on the kitchen counter. As soon as he set the full thimble on the kitchen table, Harry jumped up in a half fly and pecked away at the beer in the thimble. The message light on Jack's answering machine blinked. He flicked the switch on and a woman's voice said, "Jack, you know who this is." There was a pause. You could hear a woman breathing. Then, in a low throaty voice, she pleaded, "Please don't fly to Ensenada tomorrow. Your life is in danger."

Then she instructed, "Don't call me. My phone may be bugged. I'm calling you from a pay phone. Goodbye."

The answering machine stopped and then beeped. Both men were silent for a few seconds.

"Your girlfriend?"

"Yes. Looks like I'm getting set up."

"What do you mean?"

"Ray, Buno and Forbes are having her set me up. If I don't fly down to Ensenada tomorrow I'll be a hitter's target."

"Maybe she's telling the truth."

"Jesus Christ! I date some woman a couple of times who is working for the Mafia, and you believe she is suddenly getting a conscience? What kind of goofy thinking is that? It's a set up. My guess is they plan on taking me out tomorrow. That's why they don't want you flying down to Mexico with them. That's why they had Velda call me."

Conceding that Jack was probably right, Compton asked, "Got any ideas?"

The next morning, Jack arrived at the airfield an hour ahead of the scheduled takeoff time. Boomer was already there, dressed in his dirty flight coveralls. He looked like he had been on the end of a hog knuckle sandwich. With him in the maintenance shed was a balding, middle aged man whom Boomer introduced to Jack as a check-ride inspector for the FAA. Jack shook hands with the inspector and then went about his pre-flight inspection of the helicopter. The inspector looked through Jack's log book.

You've flown a bit. Lots of places in lots of machines."

"It's my living."

"Pretty impressive. You should hook up with an airline. They're hiring older guys now."

Jack ignored the cutting comment that was meant to be funny and helpful.

A few minutes before takeoff time a big Lincoln Town Car pulled up and Chief Buno got out with the aluminum brief case in hand. Buno walked over to the aircraft and said, "Ready?"

"Yes," said Jack. "Is Chief Hart flying with us today?"

"Hart's dead," said Buno flatly.

"Dead? Heart attack?"

"Yeah, dead. No heart attack. An accident. Let's get going," instructed Buno.

"We have an FAA inspector going along with us."

"What!" exclaimed Buno. "Get rid of him!"

"Can't. You never know when we get a check-riding inspector. My number just came up today. He either goes along with us or the aircraft stays tied down and he checks everything that was going on it, including your briefcase. Simple as that."

The FAA inspector walked over and introduced himself to Chief Buno. "I'm Charley Pitts from the regional FAA. I've been assigned this check-ride down with you fellows, but I won't be coming back with you." Buno glared at him as Jack said, "Why not?"

"I've been asked to do a couple of inspections on US aircraft based at the Ensenada Airport. One of them is going to be sold and the other is scheduled to come back later this afternoon, so I'll be flying back on a check-ride with them. Sorry I can't go both ways with you boys."

"A free ride," was Buno's contribution to the conversation.

"The Chief is pissed about this," muttered Boomer to Jack as they readied the aircraft.

Ten minutes later, they were flying across the border, directly for Ensenada.

CHAPTER TWENTY-NINE

She sat parked in front of Jack's condo with a nervous stomach, the decision had not been easy. As ruthless and cold blooded as she had conducted her life, her feelings for Jack were confusing. After a steamy relationship with a married casino boss when she was younger, she committed herself to making money and dating men only when she had the need for a physical relationship. Her good looks, a sense of class and a forthright attitude gave her these opportunities at will. Her elegant charisma could charm almost any man she wanted.

Jack turned off the motor of the Mercedes, trying to make sense of Velda being here. The return flight from Ensenada was uneventful despite the tension he felt in the aircraft. He was wary and puzzled with what was going on. She couldn't know that he had discovered her relationship with Forbes and Buno. How would she? If she did, she wouldn't be here. There was no reason for her to have warned him with the call last night unless he was being set up. He approached her car with caution, worried that a shooter might be trailing her. She opened the door and slowly got out of her car.

"Thank God you're still alive!" she exclaimed, her eyes moist and provocative. Jack looked at her almost contemptuously. Out of his flight bag he pulled the Smith & Wesson. Carrying it in his right hand, the weapon was concealed by the flight bag as he approached.

"Can I come in? I need to talk to you." she pleaded in a modulated voice. Nodding affirmatively, he turned his back and unlocked the front door. Velda followed him in, her perfume filling the room. Harry met him with his usual demand for beer.

"Beer! Beer!" Jack ignored the bird.

"Make yourself at home, I have to take care of Harry," he said guardedly. When he completed that chore, he entered the living room where Velda sat quietly and challenged, "How's the card club business?"

"Please, let me talk to you," she said with begging eyes, as surprise registered on her face.

Jack stared at her, his gaze measuring her, trying to repress his anger. Then he said in a hard tone, "You're a plant. You're involved with the NevadaLine Casino owners and you've been trying to set me up. So far it's been a pretty impressive performance."

Looking as if someone had just slapped her, she said hurriedly, "I don't know how you put that all together but it's true. I am involved with the owners. They wanted information about you. You were just another job I had to do when I first met you. But I didn't want to believe they would actually kill you. Now it's all different. I called you last night to warn you. Jack, I'm trying to save your life!" she pleaded. "I just put my life on the line for you! Don't you understand? You have to get out of Forbes' reach. He'll kill you!" Tears welled in her eyes.

"Warn me!" his whispering voice jacked up some octaves. "You spent weeks gaining my confidence. You were just trying to set me up, weren't you?"

"No! Why would I be here now? Why would I have called you last night? Jack, you've got to trust me," she exclaimed. "It's your only chance."

"I'm just a low stakes player in your game. You and your boys want me out of the picture because I went to the DEA. And that's a fucking laugh. The DEA treated me like a leper, but you guys decided to chop me off. Get out of my life." He waved the pistol toward the door.

She reached out and squeezed his bicep hard. "You've got to understand what happened." He turned away from her. She reached for him again and grasped his elbow, turning him toward her.

"Okay, what the hell did happen? I know at least I'm not hauling drugs. It's money you're moving to Mexico to be laundered. Right?" he demanded as his anger seemed to dissipate.

"Yes. I got in over my head. I needed the money. I enjoyed the good life," she admitted.

"You're a CPA. How much money do you need, for Christ's sake?"

"More, I always thought."

"That's not even an excuse," he fired back.

"I know. Now I have to live with it. I'm not begging for your forgiveness. I just don't want you killed. Can't you understand that? If Buno or Forbes finds out about this, I'll die a slow and painful death."

"No, I can't understand. There have been two attempts on my life by your people."

Velda released his arm. "That had to be someone else. Forbes and Buno didn't decide to kill you until last night. I was there. That's why I called you. I tried to warn you. They were going to kill you in Mexico. If they find out I warned you, they'll kill me. They had Hart killed, so there are fewer people in the loop."

Jack's adrenaline was pushing the red line. None of this made sense. He and Compton had figured out Velda's role. At least they thought they did. Now she was telling him that the two attempts on his life were not sanctioned by Buno and Forbes. What the hell was going on?

"Okay, you've warned me, now get out of my life."

"Listen to me," she begged. "I need to get out of this. It's no longer a money-making game. They are killing people. I'm not part of that. I never have been." Big tears rolled down her cheeks.

Softening slightly, Jack held his ground. "There is no way you can convince me you want out. For all I know this is just another trick."

"I swear I don't know what happened today but I know they were planning on killing you."

"No. If you're telling the truth, what happened was that I lucked out. Believe that?" he challenged.

"I had someone else fly down with me." He was referring to Ray Compton who had disguised himself as an FAA check-ride inspector.

"I can prove I'm not on their side anymore. I've crossed the line by being here, telling you this," she said with passion. Pulling a Mont Blanc pen from her purse she wrote a series of numbers and letters on the back of a magazine she picked up off the table.

"What's that?"

"The identification number and password that unlocks Forbe's secret bank account in Grand Cayman Island. There is close to three million untraceable dollars in the bank. It's stash money that Forbes keeps in case he has to go underground. "You will find the same identification information in the top left drawer of Forbes' desk."

"Oh, sure, I'm going to waltz into the NevadaLine Casino and pick my way through his desk."

Shaking her head Velda said, "There is another way." He listened quietly, pacing the floor, as she told him. When she was finished talking, he laughed incredulously and challenged, "Now you want me to break the law so I can prove you're not working with someone who I know is breaking the law."

"Yes," she said. "But I intend to help you."

"Now why on earth would you do that?"

"To get you enough evidence so you can go to the authorities so they will arrest Forbes and Buno."

He laughed, "I've already tried going to the Feds."

"But you didn't go in with any evidence. This time you will. And that changes everything," she said with enthusiasm.

"What about you?" he asked. "You can clear yourself from being an accessory to murder. Maybe the Feds will let you turn state's evidence, but the IRS will send you to prison."

"I'm the only one who can get the money out of the account. It's my signature on the paperwork. With the money I can buy us a new life," she said softly.

"There is no us. Who says I want anything to do with this kind of deal? Besides, Forbes will get the money out of the secret account before you have a chance."

"He can't."

"Why not?"

"His name and signature aren't on the bank documents that open the account and control the withdrawals."

"I don't believe you. Why would Forbes pack away all that money so that only you can withdraw it."

"Simple. He can't even afford to have his signature on a secret bank account. If someone finds out, the Feds will get him on RICO charges and he will lose the card club - his money skimming machine. So, he is trusting that I would never take it and run. He made me sit through a private viewing of a snuff movie. Forbes was sure that was enough to keep me loyal."

"A *what* movie?"

Velda drew a deep breath. "A snuff movie. It's a movie where they actually kill someone. They lure the actress into believing it is going to be a staged death but they actually kill her. It's a long and painful death because they torture the victim. It's awful, especially if you know beforehand that you are really watching a murder. People like Forbes are involved in this kind of deep porno S&M stuff. If you're working for them you get dragged into it. You know that if you don't do what they want, and stay loyal, you'll be tortured and murdered. It's the price you pay if you work for them. But you don't know it until it's too late."

"So, now it's too late?"

"If I don't get out, it's only a matter of time before Forbes shuts down the operation, has me withdraw the money and then kills me. I need your help."

"Why my help?"

"I know the layout. His house is huge and sometimes guarded, but I know where he keeps his records. You couldn't do it without me and it's just as important to me as it is you. Please," she pleaded, "just listen to me before you say no."

Jack laughed so hard he ended up with a painful stitch in his gut. Ray Compton was telling him about his bus ride back on a smoke-puking wreck jammed with locals from Ensenada. When he got to Tijuana late Tuesday, Compton called him and they met on the US side of the border. Then Ray got serious.

"It's a real simple deal. You fly them down with a load of dirty money. Hart, or as it was yesterday, Chief Buno, delivers it to the local police commander."

"Hart's dead."

"He is? What happened?"

"According to the papers it was a Mob hit. Velda told me Forbes and Buno decided to take him out. Guess that's the same as the Mafia, so the papers are half right."

"A Commandante Gomez is the guy who makes it work for Buno and Forbes in Ensenada," said Compton.

"How?"

"It's easy. Gomez just launders the money that Forbes ships him by running the cash through all of the pricey tourist shops in downtown Ensenada. He gives the shop owners a small fee and they do what ever it takes to make it look like they are receiving the money from tourists. With all the cruise ships stopping in the Port of Ensenada, it's a no brainer. Tax and duty free; European stuff, French knock-offs, it's shopaholic heaven. All they have to do is dummy up some paperwork. Christ, the Mexican government's equivalent to the IRS doesn't see it, or doesn't want too. It will be years before they figure it out. The dirty money is laundered through the tourists, and Gomez has a bagman, one of his police, who goes out and picks it up once a week."

"How'd you find this out?"

"Well, I followed a guy dressed in a uniform leaving Gomez' office with an aluminum brief case. I also bribed a shop keeper to tell me how the system worked."

"That easy?"

"Yeah. These people are only part of the puzzle. They don't see the big picture so, getting some woman who is tending a leather shop to tell you what you need to know is only a hundred dollar bill away. *Your* hundred dollar bill I might add."

After listening to Compton laugh at his little joke Jack asked, "How do they get it out of Ensenada?"

"Commandante Gomez handles it himself."

"How do you know?"

"Even though I'm getting too old for this gumshoe shit, I followed him. Gomez' bagman collects the laundered money and brings it back to the boss. Gomez himself takes it to the airfield and puts it on a plane. I think it was a Convair. One of those big prop jobs that can fly over water, but low enough to slip past the radar. I got the tail number, so I think we can figure out where the money is going once it leaves Ensenada."

"If they are putting this money in a secret bank account, why launder it? Why don't they just transfer it electronically?"

"By laundering it they end up with clean, untraceable money. Sooner or later they will want to use it. When the time comes, it won't be a problem. That's why they are going through the effort of filtering it through the tourists who hit the shops in Ensenada. The money that ends up in the secret bank account can never be traced back to the NevadaLine Casino or Forbes."

"You did a hell of a job, gumshoe."

"You paid for it."

"But none of this ties to the two attempts on my life."

"I know, but we have to assume that it's because you went to the DEA. Your guys are definitely into illegal shit, so they've got to be nervous. I mean, having you fly their helicopter is like having Benedict Arnold captain your ship."

"Velda was here."

Compton looked at him like he was crazy, drew his conclusion and said, "As long as she doesn't have any idea we have connected her to Forbes and Buno, then I guess we're okay."

"She knows about it."

"She's feeding you a line of crap. You shouldn't be talking to her."

"Maybe, but I don't think so. She confirms everything you have put together and doesn't deny her partnership with Forbes."

"Nice lady," said Compton sarcastically.

"Ray, she wants out because the game has escalated to murder."

"Just wait a minute," jumped in Compton with an edge to his voice, "aren't you forgetting that there were two attempts on your life before Velda suddenly claims Forbes and Buno have decided to do you in? That's before she got so righteous."

"They didn't tell her."

"I find that extremely hard to believe," said Compton reproachfully. "Man, you are really boxed in on this one. No matter where you run off and hide, Forbes and Buno will track you down. Forbes could probably do it alone, but with all of Buno's police assets it's only a matter of time."

"I don't want to be looking over my shoulder the rest of my life," admitted Jack.

"You will be, unless you can produce some evidence that the Feds can use to arrest, indict and convict both of our boys. Right now all you've got is a theory."

"Ray, I've got a plan and I need your help. Hear me out." He laid out Velda's plan to break into Forbes' house. Jack spoke without interruption for close to ten minutes before Compton said, "Stop right there. I'm a PI with a license that can be taken away from me with very little effort. I'm no break-in artist. But aside from all that, I still think the woman is setting you up. If you try to break in Forbes' house, you'll be killed once you're inside and it will be justifiable homicide. It's a number one fuckin' setup. Case closed. You need a professional if you are stupid enough to go through with this silly idea. Your next book will be written in the lock-up."

"Know of anybody who might help me?"

Compton shook his head and said, "If I did, I wouldn't tell you because I don't want to be a party to this. Jack, this is crazy. My advice is that you vanish in the middle of the night with your parrot and manuscript and let the dust settle. Go back to flying somewhere else in the world. Change your name and sell another book. You just drew a short straw by ending up flying for these guys, but at least you know how to get out of the country alive. And forget that woman for God's sake."

"I can't live with that."

"Well, said Compton, "I don't see that you have any other choice." Pausing a moment, he changed the subject saying, "I forgot to tell you that I checked in with the forensics lab. They were able to pull a thumb print off of the inside of the glove your bird picked up. What's really interesting is that it matches with one of the prints found on that extraction tool you brought back from Mexico."

"Damn, that's the connection. That's great news. It means the same person who was inside my condo was also down in Mexico."

"It is and it isn't," cautioned Compton. "Just because the fingerprints match, doesn't mean we can find who they belong to. I've already pulled in a major chit with a fingerprint analyst at the SDPD and had them run against the CAL-ID system which is a computer stocked with unidentified fingerprints taken from crime scenes. He also ran them through the National Crime Scene Index and the Immigration & Naturalization Service."

"What does that mean?"

"It could mean the search didn't make the match. Remember, we're working with computers, electronic equipment, input by other agencies, a whole bunch of unconnected information. Or it could mean the person had never been printed in the criminal justice system."

"Not being printed seems almost impossible."

Compton nodded and answered. "Yeah. I've thought a lot about the fingerprint angle. The cops wrote off the break-in and Mariana's death as the work of a random drug thief. Sounds okay until you tie up that break-in with the guy who jumped you in La Misión. I'm a hundred percent sure they're connected. Now, if we want to give your new girlfriend's story any credibility then it does point to somebody being hired by Forbes and Buno."

"But guys who do that kind of work usually have arrest records."

"Usually," responded Compton. "But like I said, they could have slipped through the fingerprint identification system or maybe they've never been arrested. Maybe they were recruited from below the border. Hell, it could have been a suckered immigrant who owed Forbes a gambling debt."

"Finding who those fingerprints belong to would solve this case."

"Good deduction, Sherlock," agreed Compton but you probably won't be able to tie it back to Forbes or Buno. They're pros at covering tracks and trails. They will have insulated themselves so well you won't even be able to make the slightest connection. My advice still stands."

"What's that?"

"Pay my bill and get the hell out of the country."

"How much do I owe you?"

Compton held up the invoice.

Jack wrote the private investigator a check for his services. Handing it to him he said, "Thanks much. You've been a big help."

"By the way, the lab produced a written report. It won't tell you anything other than what I have, but it's yours if you want it."

"Yes. I'd like to have it. Put it in the mail."

"I'll drop it off at your house this afternoon. I'm going that way, so it will save me a stamp. Let me give that your extraction tool back. It's in my trunk."

Boomer watched from his porch as Jack opened the car door and stepped out. He was vaguely surprised to see him. Usually they didn't see each other in between flights.

"Ever see one of these?" Jack said as he handed the wicked looking extraction tool to Boomer. Before Boomer could respond, Jack said, "It's an extraction tool. Cops carry them in their squad cars. You use it to get people out of wrecked cars. The point can shatter a window and the blade will cut a seatbelt like butter."

"Where'd you find it?"

"In my courtyard, in Mexico."

"When?" exclaimed Boomer as his eyes flickered.

"Last week. Someone jumped me at my house."

"Who? Mexican bandito or a jealous husband?"

"The same person who killed Mariana."

Sweat beads pushed out from under Boomer's gimme cap. "Jesus, how do you know that?"

"I hired a private investigator. He found a piece of a rubber glove in Harry's cage. Harry must have picked it up the night of the break-in, so the cops missed the evidence. The prints off the finger of the glove matched up with the prints on this little baby," said Jack as he hefted the extraction tool.

Boomer coughed like he was embarrassed and said, "Before you jump on this like a duck on a June bug, you gotta be sure. Any idea who the degenerate fucker is who would do this kind of shitwork?"

"It's got to be Buno and Forbes."

"Why do you say that?"

"Who else?" then he proceeded to explain his theory to Boomer. When he finished, Boomer nodded in agreement.

"I need your help."

"Sure," responded Boomer.

"You ready to do a little 'breaking and entering' work?"

"For you?"

"Yes. Who else?"

"There's a time to cook and a time to chill. Now you want to do some cookin'?"

"You in?"

"Yeah. A man needs to stay in shape."

"I just need a backup man."

"Do you have anything bigger than a .38?"

"Rifle or handgun?"

"Pistol?"

"Well, I've got that Army .45 I always carried but most people can't hit shit with one."

It's better than that lightweight .38 of mine."

Nodding, Boomer went inside. When he returned he handed Jack the .45 and said, "It's a good one and loaded to ream out the asshole of a garden snake at 25 yards."

Jack smiled at Boomer's description, took the heavy gun, and hefted it from one hand to another. Boomer went on as he picked up the ax and shaved a few reddish hairs off his thick forearms, "I wouldn't be sleeping easy if I knew some fuckin' weirdo was creeping around my house with an ax that could chop me up like ground meat."

Jack grinned as he shook his head. Then he told Boomer about his plan.

CHAPTER THIRTY

Laz Forbes built his mansion on the soft peak of a small, rocky outcropping southeast of San Ysidro. From this somewhat isolated bluff he could see the U.S. Mexican border to the south and Brown Airfield to the north. He had easy freeway access to his La Jolla country club, the Del Mar racetrack and the dog track in Caliente. It was less than five minutes from the NevadaLine Casino. The house was done in a grotesque Italianate style with sweeping marble floors and columns crudely decorated with faux gold trim. A chain link fence topped with razor sharp concertina wire surrounded the two acre parcel of land, allowing access through a remote control security gate.

Jack approached the fence at the rear of the property. The smell of fresh-cut grass mingled with a faint salt-sea odor. A foot short of the heavy chain link barrier, he stopped, searching for vibration sensors that would trigger an alarm. If the sensors were activated, all he had to do was grab the fence and a computer monitor would warn whoever was posted inside the mansion. Velda had assured him that the place would be empty tonight.

The night was hot, not a breath of cool air. He felt his body heat up, a trickle of sweat tracked his spine. In the dark sky, a fast moving military plane of some type gently banked, its navigation lights flickering. A flash of ground level light caused a spray of bile to burn his throat. Two teenagers on bouncing dirt bikes, the ring-ding-ding of their two-stroke engines announced their approach, headlights strafed the landscape. Fighting off the desperate urge to run, he rubbed the sweat out of his eyes as his heartbeat slowed.

Nothing. At least nothing he could see. No small metal boxes or electrical insulators. He shifted the large backpack off his shoulders and stared at the dogs.

Neither Doberman growled. Velda had told him they were trained to patrol the property silently. The dogs paced back and forth with saliva dripping from their eager jowls. From his backpack he pulled a large package wrapped in pink butcher's paper. Peeling it open he ripped off a glob of rich red hamburger that was laced with the contents of powerful sleeping pills. He tossed two chunks over the fence. The dogs pounced on them, devouring them in an instant. He heaved two more chunks of meat over the fence. One of the dogs, waiting in anticipation caught his meat in mid air.

He sat down and waited. Within ten minutes one of the dogs sat down on his hindquarters. Minutes later the other one lay down. He waited another five minutes and then threw a small piece of meat over the fence. The sleeping dogs didn't move. Standing up, he pulled the heavy bolt-cutters from the backpack and went to work.

He cut through the first link, stood back and waited. His eyes narrowed as he watched the mansion through the heavy veil of darkness, expecting at any second to be discovered. Lights on, gunfire, instant death.

The fence jumped and rattled. His pulse skipped and pounded at the sound of the bird that had flown against it. More sweat rolled down his spine as he cut a slit in the chain link big enough to squeeze through. Sliding inside the cut, with the .45 Boomer had supplied him, he approached the dogs. Neither moved as he dragged them by their collars over to the fence. He slipped a flexible bike lock through their collars and the fence link. If the sleeping pills wore off at least they wouldn't be able to get to him. Sensing that the new moon rise would soon expose him as he crept forward quickly, carefully avoiding silhouetting himself at the skyline.

The plan was simple. Break into Forbes' house. Snatch the pen set off his desk, the one with the Cayman Island bank account number taped to the bottom. Grab any other important papers in the desk and get the hell out. Piece of cake, in the morning he would take the stuff to the DEA. That, plus the information

Compton had collected regarding Buno's visits to the NevadaLine Casino, would surely be enough to cause their arrests. He smiled at the thought of the smart ass DEA agent and shoving information up that arrogant cocksucker's nose.

Stepping off a hundred yards, he ducked behind a bright red cabana next to a kidney-shaped pool. A Mercedes 500SL and a Rolls Corniche were parked in the driveway. The house was a two story pile of pink stone with elaborate windows, surrounded by a thick stand of fan palms. The solitude was alarming. It was deadly quiet, just as Velda had predicted. Forbes and his people would be at the casino this time of the night.

As he started to move the air roared in his ear as the bullets stitched into the canvas cabana a few feet to his left. Cordite spiced the air, memories of war, the smells of blood and excrement assaulted his senses as he spun hard and dove for cover. A fast glance left and right revealed nothing in the grainy black and grey of the night. Heart pounding, he scanned the night, expecting a wad of mashed lead to rip into his sternum. Velda must have set him up. Forbes' people knew he was coming. Compton was right.

Silence. Then a door clicked shut. Another guard, thought Jack, as fear-produced adrenaline pumped in his blood. In the night heat he waited for the men with guns to come.

It came in a gun-butt blow to his jaw that snapped him straight back. His boots slid on the gravel as sparks and minute fireworks illuminated his brain. A thin sweat of fear jumped out of his pores while he recovered from the shock of the blow. He swung back with cruel energy at the nearest body. A bone snapped as the bolt cutter found a target. He smelled blood and through his blurred vision he saw the shape of a crawling man. A second assailant hammered away at his rib cage, a ring raked his face. Blood streamed from the cut. The assailant clung to him in a bear hug as Jack grappled for the gun.

He twisted his gun hand around and pulled the trigger. The .45 caliber bullets tore through the man's rib cage. Shock grabbed him in vise grips. He stood there momentarily, heaving and gasping for oxygen. He jammed the gun into his belt, trying to remember the way out. Smoke and the smell of powder filled the air. Not the time to faint. The muscles in his neck bunched into thickened cords, he turned and ran faster and harder than he could ever remember. Zigzagging, he dove and rolled to the left. He twisted his body back to his feet, waiting for the bullets to rip through his torso. There was no muzzle flash. No ripping sound of bullets. No raising of an alarm, just the quiet night closing around him. As he dove through a slit in the chain link fence he was perversely satisfied. The muscles in his legs were on fire. He split the fence with an ungraceful shoulder roll, tearing his shirt and ripping another gash in his face.

He stood and checked to see if he was being followed. Gravel crunched like popcorn under the tires of a heavy car. The vehicle scrunched against the low driveway curb, then gained speed. Its headlights stabbed at the sky. The distinct ripping sound of an automatic weapon, probably an Uzi, joined with the roaring car engine. Jack heard the distinctive *thwaap* of a projectile that missed his face by inches, and felt the air as it went past him. Turning, he fired a close pattern of bullets at the car. Glass shattered, steel scraped and rubber burned. Lucky shots. The car hit the curb, bounced and jolted, and then rammed across the concrete. This was no fucking jog on the beach front, he was running for his life.

Jack breathlessly rasped into his radio handset, Alpha... ...this... is...Bravo."

"Go ahead Bravo," was the cryptic response from Boomer.

"Get gone," wheezed Jack, his throat tightening. He sucked air. "Some of Forbes' guys jumped me...Got away...Monitor me." Running down the slight grade from the mansion, he sprinted toward the center of San Ysidro.

"Will do. Stay low. Out." Boomer turned on the ignition and slowly drove his van away from the curb where he had parked. He was tempted to try to pick him up, but he knew Jack's chances of escape were better on foot. None of Forbes' goons would catch him with the lead he had. Crossing a paved street Jack dropped the gun in a storm drain opening. He didn't want some rookie cop to jump him running through a nice neighborhood with a hot gun in his hand.

The nighttime traffic was building. Exhaust fumes scorched his nostrils as he sucked new air into his hammering lungs. He darted across a street and sprinted down a broken section of sidewalk. The streets got meaner and more crowded. At a busy intersection he saw a chance window in the unforgiving stream of southern California traffic and blew through it. He leaped on the sidewalk on the other side of the street and ran hard toward the welcome jangle of the Tijuana Trolley.

The electric train rattled and shook on the narrow gauge track. Every twenty minutes one departed from San Diego and Chula Vista, bound for the border where it emptied its passengers where they could walk across the freeway overpass. The Tijuana Trolley system was modeled after a similar system in Germany. Passengers bought a ticket from a machine before boarding. A ticket checking conductor may or may not be on the car you boarded but you had to have a ticket. Big fine. He quickly pulled one from the machine and climbed aboard the trolley departing from the San Ysidro station. After leaping up the steel steps he tried to control his heavy breathing lest he draw attention. In spite of his sweat soaked clothes, cuts and blood stains, no one paid him any notice. He stirred restlessly as the trolley moved toward the border.

Minutes later at the end of the line, the trolley's passengers swarmed off and shuffled across the overpass into Mexico. With the crowd, he passed the Mexican Customs Station. He melted into the electrified stream of honking cars, smoking trucks and wallowing buses leaving the U.S. side of the border. He joined the throng in a filthy bus marked "Buena Vista, Central." The bus lurched past the ancient Tres Estrellas de Oro sign which identified the ancient bus station at the edge of the city. He was painfully aware of the damage inflicted to his ribs by the shooter, and he was sick to his stomach. He pressed his aching head against the window. He could see the globe on the Centro Cultural Fonapas. It looked like a gigantic discarded nuclear reactor out of place in the city center. A flash of modern architecture here and there in neighborhoods of cracked plaster, graffiti and fetid gutters which rose up to hills.

The bus turned onto Avenida Revolucion like a creaking box-car on wheels. Upgraded on the main drag, Avenida Revolucion was a contrast to the colonias in the hills where dirt roads were cluttered with abandoned cars, reeking garbage and emaciated children. On the dark side streets, in the seedy and dangerous bars, garish hookers, drug peddlers, con artists rivaled for co-exis-tence.

The bus came to a shuddering stop across from the Chicago Bar, the port of entry to Tijuana's Zona Norte, the red light dis-trict. The aging machine convulsively dumped out its passengers before it left in a cloud of diesel smoke and complaining engine. Now on foot, Jack passed store front marriage chapels, and divorce lawyers. He separated himself from the noisy crowd. Crossing a broken sidewalk strewn with fruit rinds and tattered plastic bags, dog shit and rusting cans, he searched for some privacy. Slipping down an empty alleyway and praying that the radio was still in range, he activated the push-to-talk button.

"Alpha, this is Bravo. Over."

Static burst in his ear as he listened intently. He waited thirty seconds before he pushed the button and spoke again. He was met with only rippling static. No response.

When Jack's first breathless call interrupted the silence in the van, Boomer instinctively knew something went terribly wrong. The original plan had been simple. After dropping him off in hidden view from the mansion, Boomer moved the van in case a cruising patrol car or one of Forbes' bodyguards spotted it and became suspicious. When he frantically ordered him to "Get gone," Boomer drove slowly away, losing his van in the busy bor-der area traffic. He kept the receiver turned on and waited for a call. When Jack's voice finally came out of the small speaker, some two hours later, it startled him. Reaching for the black plastic box, he knocked it on the floor of the van.

"Damn," he muttered picking the radio off the floor of the moving van, nearly sideswiping an on-coming El Camino truck with flaming decals pasted on its sun-faded hood.

"...is Bravo," squawked the radio in his hand.

"This is Alpha. What the fuck happened? You OK?" said Boomer excitedly.

"Affirmative. I'm OK. What's your status?"

"Waiting for orders."

Jack punched the talk button and gave Boomer instructions.

Velda was to meet him the next day at the Club Campestre if something went wrong at Forbes' mansion. That was the plan. It was out by the bull ring on the Rosarito side of Tijuana, at the Playas. Jack knew if she doubled-crossed him she wouldn't show up. Club Campestre was located a short distance from the Plaza Monumental.

He crossed Seventh Avenue where the old Jai Alai Palace took up the entire east side of the block between Seventh and Eighth Avenues. The smell of Basque food and paella, cooked on hot mesquite firewood, made him feel faintly nauseous as he went inside the dark, cool Chiki Jai restaurant building that was decorated with dirty stained glass windows and tired mariner motif. Dusty oil paintings of Marley and Elvis hung behind the bar exploring a historical time line long past.

He found his way into the dirty men's room where he flushed the grime and brown blood stains from his face. It mixed with the rusty water that gurgled down the leaking drain of the cracked porcelain sink. He couldn't do anything about the body odor that crept through his shirt. He was pleased to find his cuts were superficial.

Returning to the wildly busy street he blinked back the gritty air that assaulted his eyes. He flagged down an approaching cab. The driver pulled away expertly and twenty minutes later, after a screeching ride in a machine that bounced and wobbled on broken springs, Jack entered the parking lot of Club Campestre and the comfort of a dark night.

The crescendo of oohs and aahs rippled across the heat-spanked, waffle-textured tile roof that surrounded the expansive pool area. Jack jerked awake inside a dark womb-like enclosure. His mind clawed for explanation. He felt like he was on the edge of one of his dreams, either going under or coming out of the mist that often left him cold and confused. Then it came to him. Bone-weary exhaustion and the numbing experience of his escape from Forbes' gunners had put him out like a wind struck candle when he crawled exhausted into the cabana last night.

Two bundles of muscle with thick hair and incredible white teeth walked past the opening in the cabana wall in tandem. Their veined and hairless bodies with even tans, were thick with sharply defined muscle. Jack squinted as he looked toward the early sun at a male in electric-blue posing briefs. The man snorted and groaned as he did a series of squats under a heavy bar that was held by two rippling masses of female body-sculptors. By the pool, a gargantuan black man, quadriceps flushed with blood, went through a posing routine. A backdrop of bantering voices, faint sweat on skin surfaces, aviator sunglasses, bowls of orange slices and ice cubes and veins the size of shoelaces highlighted the black man's efforts.

Stupefied, he had wandered into a tribe of competitors and their entourages for the Baja Beautiful Contest. He checked his watch. A few minutes after nine. Damn, he thought. Velda was to pick him up at ten. He needed to check if she was being followed. He crawled out of the cabana and stood up. Walking past a woman doing a double biceps back pace, and a wizened little man who looked like a retired jockey with consumption, he left the hot pool area. The smell of sweating bodies and posing oil hit his nose as he entered the cool lobby of the club. Crossing to the other side, the front entry, he pushed through the door to the outside where the sun's glare shimmied on a string of automobiles. Squinting his eyes against the mirror flashes, he searched for the black Mercedes. Next to a spindly telephone pole topped off with a row of green glass insulators his car idled like a faithful dog waiting for its master to return. Velda stood next to it, her blonde hair shining in the sun. His chest tightened with the relief she hadn't set him up. She was here. He watched her for close to thirty minutes. Long enough to be comfortable that none of Forbes' people were in the picture. He had to be sure.

As soon as she saw him, she flashed an anxious smile and waved. As he approached, she let out a small gasp and said, "What happened? Are you okay?"

"Yes. I'm all right. I just look like shit because I slept in a cabana last night like a bum. That was after I had a shoot out with Forbes' goombas and a five mile run." In the car, Velda placed a cool hand on his neck, turned his face and planted a hard kiss on his lips.

"You're stinky," she said.

A minute later they were heading south through the dusty Mexican landscape.

CHAPTER THIRTY-ONE

"I didn't think you'd come."

"Kiss my ass," Velda laughed nervously from the strain of trying to find him and the fear of being followed by Forbes' men.

"Half the men in Baja would cut off at least one of their lips if they could kiss your ass," said Jack with a smile.

She grabbed the shoulder of his shirt. He flinched. Her fingers were dampish when he reached up to touch them. Scowling into the rear view mirror, he could see her eyes mist over, her face serious.

"We can't ever go back. You know that, don't you?" she told him.

"Not without some airtight evidence that we can take whatever authorities will listen."

"The police? Give me a break. Jack, listen to me, even if we can get some evidence it won't do us any good. Forbes will have us killed before they can lock him up. We can't go back."

The lumpish white scar tissue on his throat jumped as Jack answered in a flat way with his rasping voice. "I didn't even get inside the house. His shooters stopped me outside. That was probably luck. If they had waited until I got in the house I wouldn't have been able to get out." Jack jerked the car back from the imaginary center line of the pitted macadam road as an old Ford wagon chased by him. A taxi full of school kids. Houses made from garage doors and scrap metal dotted the hillside; the main road snaked up to the dump identified by a flock of wheeling seagulls.

The panoramic view of the ocean mesmerized Jack until he almost ran up the tailpipe of a smoking Buick Skylark, its muffler sparking at every bump in the road. The car he nearly tailgated was loaded down with a half dozen Mexican males with red hand-kerchiefs sticking out from under their blue hardhats.

"Where are we going? La Misión?"

"We can stay there until I can figure out what to do. We'll stop in Rosarito and get some food. Clothes, too if you need anything."

"Did they see you last night at Forbes' house?" she asked.

"Someone shot at me and I shot back."

"Can they identify you?"

"No. There is no way they would know it was me." He paused, then said, "Unless you told them."

She let the verbal sting hang for a couple of seconds. "Would I be here if I did that?" Not waiting for an answer, she went on." Forbes and Buno will be going crazy looking for you. They'll put it together and start a search for you. Jack, they'll throw every-thing they have into it. Between Buno's dirty cops and Laz' killers they can't miss. By now they'll know I'm involved with you."

"Why?"

"They suspect I'm involved with you and they won't be able to find me this morning."

"Are you? Involved with me?"

"Would I be here if I wasn't? I could have taken Forbes' money out of his secret bank account and run." Changing the subject, she asked, "Are you sure no one knows you have a house in La Misión?"

"Nobody except Boomer. And he's only seen the house from the air. Down here I'm just another asshole gringo and nobody gives you a second glance."

Thirty minutes later, Jack pushed the car through a drifting curve about a mile from Rosarito. "Watch for the cars behind us," he instructed Velda as he pushed the accelerator down. The big 450 cubic inch German-made engine responded and the car surged forward at close to 100 miles per hour. Keeping an eye on the rear view mirror Jack watched for a speeding car to separate itself from the smoking convoy that had built up in a pack behind a red and white tour bus. None did.

"Do you think we're being followed?"

"Not really, but there's always a chance that your employers had my house staked out and followed you when you picked up my car."

Behind them, dust billowed up like a rooster's tail. Jack let up on the accelerator and the aging luxury car dropped back, buffeted by the dusty winds. He slowed considerably when he reached the city limits of Rosarito and drove with caution. Curio shops, restaurants, farmacias, markets and outdoor vendors lined the narrow two-way main street through the tourist town. He turned on a side street and parked the dust covered car between a produce truck and a station wagon packed to the gills with blankets.

"Hurry. I'm still not sure we aren't being followed." He pulled her along as they walked back to the main drag where he pushed her into a corner curio shop that sold leather goods and blankets.

"Somtheeen' for the lady?" lisped a young Mexican woman in a tight leather mini-skirt.

"Look around. I'll watch the street," ordered Jack as he positioned himself by the fly-specked window. From the back of the store *banda* music thumped and tooted. He watched the caravan of cars and trucks pass by the store. Only one car could have qualified as a tail team sent by Buno. Jack relaxed as soon as he saw one of the male passengers petting a small white poodle with a pink ribbon in its hair.

"See anything you want?" he said to Velda who was engaged in a hand waving discussion with the sales girl.

Outside she challenged, "I thought you were so damn sure no one would be looking for us in Mexico."

"Can't be too careful. I don't know how many of those nine lives I've got left."

After stocking up with provisions they left Rosarito driving south on the old road. The brilliant sun cast a thin polish over the squalor, interrupted here and there with new beachfront resorts. As they drove by the white Moroccan-styled resort, Jack thought of the incongruity of the lavish hotels next to a used restaurant supply lot. Velda relaxed against the warm leather seats of the comfortable old car and tried to enjoy the ride. The car rolled past the lobster village of Puerto Nuevo that jutted out of the steep Pacific cliffs. Minutes later the road dipped toward the ocean slightly, and Jack braked as he drove down the slight cobblestone incline. A mile down the service road Jack swung the car into the garage.

"This really is a beautiful place. The surf is so relaxing, and that long, lonely grey beach is so peaceful."

"That's the problem. I come down here to write, but I end up walking the beach or sitting on the patio watching the sun set."

"Take me for a walk on the beach. We can pretend this isn't happening for a few minutes."

For once, Jack wished he had a better view of the road for the sake of spotting potential unwelcome guests.

As usual, pedestrian activity on the mile-long beach was pretty much limited to those who lived in the residences. At both ends of the beach, rocky cliffs rose sharply out of the sea. Unless one was willing to undergo a dangerous climb down from the shoulder of the toll way, some hundred feet above, the only access was through one of the fortress-like houses. Homeowners were heavily secured with barred windows and noisy alarms that went off with great regularity. The walk along the hard sand had stretched their tired muscles. When they returned to the house, Jack fixed a dinner of steak and corn on the cob, cooked over local mesquite wood on the patio grill. In a tired, almost melancholy state, they sat together on the patio, not saying much. Both knew their lives had changed radically. The sun hung on the horizon like massive steel. Then it slipped into the ocean without fanfare. Empty wine glasses glimmered in the last reflected light off the ocean. Jack rose from his comfortable wicker chair and gently pulled Velda from the couch. "We need to get some sleep. We've got to get up early and drive down to Ensenada tomorrow."

As they lay together, their legs entwined, the smell of her light perfume, and her splendid body went to work on him. Their love-making was sweaty and sticky. They kissed deeply and clawed each other throughout the night, in desperate coupling. Each time he entered her, he felt immense relief from a world that menaced him. They entered a comfort zone and slept hard.

Chomping on a frayed toothpick, Chief Buno read the Personnel Complaint Form. The Nature of Complaint section contained a brief summary of the allegations made by a white female, Tracy Ann Combs. Buno looked at the two officers standing in front of his desk and read aloud, "Complainant alleges that Officers Rick Tremble and Gilbert Snider forced her to participate in group sex on the pool table at the Police Officer's Association Hall." Stilled by Buno's presence, Officers Tremble and Snider glanced sideways at each other. Off duty, they dressed in the fashion popular with the rest of the Border City cops: cowboy boots, huge rodeo buckles and Dirty Harry magnums in their belts. Tremble's eyes darted around the office revealing his rat-like nature; he wanted to creep under the rug.

"Tell me," rumbled Buno as he flicked the worn toothpick from one side of his mouth to the other, "was that pool table pussy worth your badges?" Neither man said anything. They could tell the chief was as touchy as an open wound. Snider eased his weight over to his right leg. They said nothing. Then Buno's face colored and he raised his voice. "Don't dance me around on this. Christ almighty, I've got enough fuckin' problems running this department without having to deal with a couple of cock hounds that like to double up on cop groupies." He paused to give his martini-thickened tongue a rest. Then he heated up again and Tremble almost saluted as he blurted out an appeal.

"Honest to God, Chief, the woman wanted us to have sex with her. Gil and I just went over to the association hall for a couple of beers after we got off duty. The bitch showed up like a dog in heat, and the next thing we knew she was givin' Gil a blowjob."

Buno shut off Tremble's outburst with a brusque shout. "Shut the fuck up! I pull the pin on you two jag-offs and you'll walk out of here with nothin' but the thin shits. Neither of you will even be able to get a security guard job like your girlfriend who you claim likes it two at a time."

Snider's cheeks burned. Rick Tremble's stomach churned at the thought of being busted out of his job. Both were straining to cover their tension as they watched the chief's face turn into dark fury. His composure crumbling, Snider was the first to overcome the queasy feeling in his gut. He started to beg. What came out of his throat sounded thin, a singsong falsetto voice, "Please, Chief. Give us another chance. We didn't know this was goin' to happen. The broad was a consenting adult and we was off duty."

Buno played it back to Snider and Tremble just for effect and his carefully manicured hand flicked out and thumped the file in front of him. "You boys are gettin' about five fathoms deeper each time you open your goddamn mouths. I'm too busy for any deep stuff today, and I may give you a break, but if I do then you boys are goin' to owe me one." He paused for effect and continued, "A big one." Both cops bobbed their heads as Buno continued. "Get my meaning? I own your ass if you want to stay employed as cops in Border City or any other place." Both men grunted in unison, indicating they understood. With a pair of burning spots of anger on his cheeks Buno told them what he wanted done.

Officers Tremble and Snider said nothing as they walked down the long hall of the police building to the parking lot where the police cruisers were parked. There was nothing to say. The chief had made it clear what they had to do. Outside they paused against the glare of the sun as it bounced back from windshields, bumpers and chrome from the parked cars.

"Is this the best piece of shit they got for us?" said Snider vehemently as he opened the driver's door to a white Plymouth sedan. Stale heat, mixed with the smell of fast food leftovers, whomped him in the face. He continued to grouse, "A couple of fucking pigs must have used this wreck on a stake out. I'll bet the AC doesn't work worth a shit either."

"Where to first?" questioned Tremble as he deferred leadership to the black cop who was driving.

"Buno said we should take a look-see at the airfield, for what good that's going to do us. I'd just as soon find the mechanic as soon as we can so we can get him off our ass. That's, of course, assuming the mechanic will tell us where the pilot is."

"He will," said Tremble. "If we can't get it out of him Buno will."

"I don't want to think about it."

"What do you make out of this deal? What the fuck do you think is going on?"

"You know better than to think through this shit. We just need to pay Buno back. You know, get our chit cashed out."

Snider chewed on his lower lip, exposing bluish-red gums, and said, "Okay with me. Let's get it done."

Chuckling, Tremble said in a low voice, "Apparently the mechanic has no idea who he's fuckin' with. I don't know what he did, but once Buno gets his hands on him nobody will ever hear from him again." Both men laughed as they pulled out of the police department impound area.

Snider drove the ailing Plymouth past the office complex and small tower, at Brown Field. Passing the tower he turned the car toward a long row of tin-roofed hangers. It took them less than a minute to locate the Border City Police Department office and maintenance shed. It took Tremble a few minutes longer to open the lock because Buno had supplied them with a key ring full of keys. On the twelfth try the lock snapped open and Tremble pushed the door back. There was nothing in the dirty, oil-specked office that would distinguish it from any other mechanic's shed. Tremble pawed through the drawers of the stained desk that had once served a loftier position at city hall and said in a disgusted voice, "Ain't nothin' here. We're wasting our time."

"Need some oil?" inquired Snider as he tapped the side of the upside down 55 gallon drum labeled CALMEX PETROLEUM PRODUCTS.

Tremble looked at the white barrel with a green stripe around it and groused, "No. What in the hell do I need fifty- some gallons of oil for? Come on. We need to find the mechanic if we're gonna get Buno off our backs."

Snider bent his head down so he could read the lettering on the side of the barrel and said, "Why would they be using Mexican oil?"

Shaking his head, Tremble said, "Damned if I know and I sure don't care." He tapped the bottom and said, "But this is a shitty weld," as he rubbed his index finger on the rough rib of the weld that ringed the bottom of the lid.

"You a welder?" jibed Snider.

"My daddy was. This is a fat weld over a cut. See how wide the bead is?" he said as he picked up a mechanic's ballpeen hammer and tapped the welded seam. A bunch of paint flakes chipped off. Tremble tapped the flat part of the tin bottom near the edge. Then he tapped it closer to the center. The noise was different. He tapped it again. This time harder.

"There's something in here," said Tremble.

"Yeah Einstein, oil," grunted Snider, rolling his eyes.

Ignoring the black man, Tremble dug through the litter of tools and dirty rags until he found what he was looking for. "Stand back," he said as he began to beat on a short pry bar with a ball-peen hammer next to the weld. After a quick series of blows he punctured the thin bottom plate of the barrel. No oil leaked out. Tremble inserted the blade of a set of tin snips in the hole he had gouged out and began to cut away at the barrel bottom.

That night Boomer drove his van out to Brown Field comfort-able in the cover of darkness. He needed some time to think about the report he found at Jack's condo when he had gone there to feed the bird. Somebody named Ray Compton had pushed a police report through the mail slot. Compton's note on the out-side of the envelope read, "Here's the fingerprint report. The prints on the ax match the prints from the rubber glove. I'm still working on some leads." When Boomer read the note he had to take a deep breath to control his anxiety. No question in his mind. Jack knew who killed Mariana. He must have hired an investigator. Now things were gettin' down to the tight-ass level.

Except for a few light planes being worked on in their tiny hangers the area near his maintenance shed was quiet. He backed the van up to the door, shut off the engine and dropped down from the front seat. He opened the rear doors and wrestled a dolly out of the back. Funny, he thought, someone left the door open. As he stepped into the darkness of the shed his eyes were met by the strong beam of a flashlight and the universal order of, "POH-leese, don't fuckin' move." He didn't.

Buno turned the cheap handgun over on its side. He tapped on it with a thick stubby finger and said, "Walk this one by me again. You guys just happened to cut open a barrel and found these Saturday night specials in our flight shack?"

Snider spoke first. "Rick knows welding and noticed the barrel in the flight office had a bad seam."

Tremble nodded reflexively and said, "The guns were sealed in an aluminum tube. If the barrel wasn't upside down in the first place we probably never would have discovered the guns. It was the bad weld that made me suspicious."

"Any other barrels?"

"One," said both men at the same time.

"What's in it?" commanded Buno, looking directly at the thickset man dressed in coveralls. He was sitting on a steel chair with handcuffs clamped around his thick wrists.

"Same thing. More guns," responded Boomer in a heavy voice.

Lighting an oversized cigar, Buno turned his back on the two officers in order to let his thoughts rummage around in his head. What the fuck was going on? Dalton goes to the DEA alleging he was flying drugs while his crew chief was using the chopper for some kind of gun running scheme. Didn't make sense. Why would Dalton draw heat on his own partner?

Needing some time to think this through, Buno turned to Snider and Tremble saying, "You boys did good. Real good as a matter a fact. I need to do a little talking with Mr. Goodwrench here to see if I can piece this little puzzle together." Then he said in a much stronger voice, one which conveyed a clear message, "This is between us for now. I don't want to hear about this through the rumor mill. Get my drift?"

Both men nodded as they rose to leave the stifling atmosphere of Buno's office. Outside, Tremble was the first to speak. "Think we made our payback to Buno?"

"Fuck no," exclaimed Snider. "He ain't going to let us off the hook that easy, my man. No fuckin' way."

After Snider and Tremble left, Buno rolled his cigar around with his tongue and lectured Boomer, "Gun running is a federal offense, *mijo*. They bury good ol' boys like you deep. Real ass-reamin' deep!" Boomer said nothing. He just looked at the Chief. Neither man blinked. Buno got out of his chair and continued, "Okay. You wanna play some hardball? I'll have the boys from Alcohol, Tobacco and Firearms here pronto and you'll be in a federal lockup in about thirty goddam minutes."

As he reached for the phone, Boomer suddenly said, "I'll deal."

Buno laughed hard, lifted his hand off the telephone and said, "What the fuck do you have to deal with?"

Boomer cleared his throat and began to talk.

CHAPTER THIRTY-TWO

They rose early in the morning. He was tired, even though the night was dreamless. Velda wanted to sleep in. She was slightly irritated when she found out what he intended to do. Dressing quickly they left for Ensenada. Both were quiet as the car hummed along in the bright morning air. They were tense as they held hands, middle-aged romantics who had made the critical decision to run away. On the car radio a local station played a sad Mexican *corrido*. Clusters of shacks, usually grouped around *bodegas*, housed the working poor. Because of the fortunes of weather Baja escaped the debilitating diseases of Central Mexico. The greatest threats to these neighborhoods came from visitors.

The stopped at a suspect restaurant north of Ensenada. While they ate *albondigas* soup from dented tin bowls, hard fried eggs and *frijole* mush he told her his plans.

She responded icily, "Stealing the helicopter when it lands in Ensenada and flying it back to Border City is a dumb idea. You'll end up doing prison time or worse. This is insane Jack, and I want no part of it." Then in a pleading voice she said, "please don't do this. You don't stand one chance in a million of pulling off this kind of trick."

Jack thought if anyone could pull off this trick, it would be him. His life depended on it.

"What other choice do I have? The best shot we have at proving Buno is a crooked police chief is to drop their chopper at the front door of the U.S. Customs Headquarters loaded with the skimmed off money and a handcuffed Buno. They make the ferry run to Ensenada every Monday. I can grab the bird and fly it back. That's why we're driving down to Ensenada for a looksee.

I want to develop a plan for snatching the chopper and Buno next Monday."

Thirty minutes later Jack had parked the dust-covered Mercedes near the harbor of Bahia de los Todos Santos.

"Let's walk over to the police landing pad."

"Jack, you know what will happen if there isn't enough evidence on that helicopter when you steal it. This is crazy." Stealing Buno's helicopter the next time it was flown to Ensenada and flying it back was evidence of his insanity.

The harshness of the question caused a shudder in his chest. He knew what the consequences were. Velda was right. A prison term. Violent death. Simple as that. He would be staking everything on his belief that the helicopter would be loaded with dirty money when he hijacked it. He had been wrong about the drugs. It was the money that was being laundered. He should have thought of that. Big time drug deals had much more sophisticated transportation systems. If the bird was empty he would be charged with kidnapping and international hijacking. That's if he wasn't killed trying to take control of the helicopter in the middle of the Ensenada police compound.

They walked through the harbor area and over to the police helicopter pad. Finally, after studying the site Jack said, "Let's go. I think I've figured something out that will work." She was tired of waiting in the hot Mexican sun and emotionally drained. Waiting for more than three hours while he worked out exactly how he intended to hijack the helicopter made her angry and depressed. She fought the urge to jump on one of the passing buses and disappear.

Jack looked at Velda as they climbed back in the hot car. She was wearing one of his shirts tucked into her jeans. Her thick blonde hair was pulled back. Beauty and a clean smell radiated from her, even after hours in the muggy environment of the Ensenada harbor. Leaving him to his thoughts, she turned inward as she contemplated her future, iffy at the best.

They escaped the stench of the harbor and fisheries behind them. Jack powered the big car up the steep grade of the cliff road. An hour later they were sitting under a thatched umbrella on the outdoor balcony of one of the resort cantinas that dotted the road from Ensenada. Below, the surf broke and foamed like soapy water on the rocks. Viney plants that needed tending, pineapples of unknown age and broken pottery hung from the wrought iron railing surrounding the balcony. A green and white street sign that read LAKE HOLLYWOOD DRIVE had been nailed to the wall. Velda twisted the rose stem sticking out of the neck of a Carta Blanca bottle that served as a vase. She folded the brown cloth napkin in front of her in concentration. Sipping her banana daiquiri, she spoke. "What are we going to do? Hide out in Mexico for the rest of our lives?"

Jack twisted the fresh beer bottle in his hands, drawing wet circles on the tabletop. He responded. "We'll give it a few days. I think we are safe here. Maybe you can convince me there is another way out of this mess. Buno has to make his weekly ferry run down to Ensenada next Monday. We've got time to consider some other options."

Relieved that Jack was willing to think his plan through, Velda said in a cajoling manner, "There is another way. We can take the money and run. I can get it out of the bank in Grand Cayman. You know your way around parts of the world where Forbes and Buno will never find us. We can run, hide, and then live a pretty darn good life." Pausing, she continued to plead with him. "Jack, your plan can't work. Even if you can grab the helicopter with Buno in it, there's always the chance for the unexpected. Buno and Forbes won't be rushed off to jail by any federal authority. Buno's a police chief and Forbes will have the best criminal lawyers on hand in less than an hour. You'll be the one trying to make bail, and I'll be sitting down here like a damn fool."

"Keep tempting me," he whispered with a smile breaking across his craggy face. "Taking their money and living on an island doesn't sound all bad. But getting it out of the Cayman bank is another story."

"I know, but I've thought it out. I'll wire the money to another bank in whatever country we are going to. We leave Grand Cayman by air and fly to wherever we've wired the money."

"I need to think about it."

"You'll be a rich man. There's close to three million in the bank. Half is yours."

"I'll be a rich fugitive."

"How about being a rich fugitive with an adoring woman? Someone who will make you happy everyday?"

The next few days passed with warm ocean winds mingling with the cool evening breeze. They fell into an easy routine. They woke early and started their day with a walk along the deserted beach. After their early morning exercise, Jack would prepare a breakfast while she sat on the terrace patio and stared across the deep expanse of the blue-grey ocean. Almost always, in the far distance of the horizon, a ship of some sort migrated north or south. Seagulls and brown pelicans flew low over the breaking waters, and sometimes dolphins jumped from the surface. They were lulled into a false sense of well-being, despite the fact that they were hiding out in Mexico, vicious thugs on their tail and no protection. Each day she tried to talk him out of hijacking the helicopter when Buno was to bring it to Ensenada. It bothered her he wasn't tempted with the half of Forbes' money that she could get out of the offshore bank.

The sleepy border guard waved them on through with hardly any motion of his hand. "That was the easy part," grumbled Snider as Tremble drove into Tijuana. "I don't like this deal one damn bit," he complained. Adjusting his balls, he tilted his head back against the headrest and closed his eyes.

"What choice do we have, amigo? You knew damn well Buno was going to call in his marker. It as just a matter of time. He just did it a whole lot quicker than I would have guessed. Remember the last time? The time he caught us keeping that bundle of hash from those old hippies trying to mule it out of Mexico? It was over a year before we had to pay up."

"Yeah, but this is a hell of a price to pay for some head. It was you that got to dip your wick in that horny security guard," countered Snider in aggravation. They drove in silence until they reached the first tollgate. "Take a look at the map. That fuckin' mechanic. He had better have drawn us an accurate one or when we get back I'll kill the sombitch."

"Don't worry about the map. And don't worry about the mechanic. Buno'll take care of him. Just take care of the driving," lectured Tremble. He studied the hand-sketched map that they had been given. This ain't goin' to be that hard. All we got to do is to find the right house."

"What if we end up in the wrong one?"

Tremble looked at Snider with a quizzical look on his face and said with some irritation, "Then we keep on looking. We fuck this up and Buno will toss our asses in a hole we won't ever get out of."

Jack woke in the heavy darkness. The contour of Velda's body under the white cotton sheet was next to him. Her eyes opened and she murmured softly. Sliding deeper into the bed, his mouth found hers. His heartbeat shot up as their kissing became more insistent. He ran the heel of his hand up her legs, across her stomach and then cupped her breast. His hardness increased as he buried his head under the sheets and kissed her nipple. The scent of her hair and sweet smell of her body excited him.

"Now. Please," she whispered.

Suddenly, he tensed, hearing a sound, a muffled cough or scuffing of a shoe. Straining to listen, he placed the palm of his hand over Velda's mouth. "Be quiet," he ordered in a low whisper. Velda's eyes opened fully as fright swam into them. Her body stiffened but she nodded that she understood. He strained his ears from the sitting position he was in. The rumbling noise of the surf below made it difficult to hear anything. Velda started to move, but a touch of his hand on her thigh stilled her. She lay in the bed trying to control her breathing. A scraping noise caused him the jerk his head toward the door that led to the living room.

Someone outside? A neighbor having a late night smoke? A dog on the patio?

Any doubts he had vanished when he heard the second subtle scrape of a moving foot. Inside the house or out on the terrace patio? Goddamn surf noise, he thought. It was impossible to tell where the sound had come from or what caused it. Adrenaline dumped into his blood, he rolled over quickly. Reaching under the bed he picked up the loaded pistol Boomer had given him.

"Don't move until I get back."

Warily, he silently swung his legs to the side of the bed and stood. The light from the moon beamed through the linen shades, silhouetting him. His stomach burned as his nervous system went into high gear. He fought back the reflexive demand to breathe rapidly. Taking two long steps across the bedroom floor he dove into a painful shoulder roll. His body went through the doorway, into the expansive living area of the house. Springing to his feet, he held himself in a crouch with both hands aiming the heavy pistol from fully extended arms. Nothing happened. His heart hammered as he approached the kitchen. He found the light switch, sucked in his breath, and flicked it on.

An explosion of sharp white light blinded him. Instinct dropped him to the hard clay tile. He tried to blink the brightness from his eyes as he waited to be shot. He waited for the hammer of bullets against his body and the rattling shock that always trails the impact. He held back the panic that comes when you know something frightful will happen. Moisture dripped from his forehead and a thin lather of fear-sweat covered his skin. Then everything went dark. Trembling hard, he realized what had happened. The light bulb burned out and exploded into minute pieces of glass when he turned the switch on. Recovering, he searched the bedroom at the opposite end of the house. Nothing. But he still did not feel at ease. He sensed something wrong. Apprehension tugged at his gut. He walked across the cool tile floor and returned to the bedroom.

"Velda?" he whispered. No response. The noise of the surf was louder. The sliding glass door to the patio was open and the Pacific breeze whirled the light curtains. She was gone.

Angered that Velda would leave the safety of the bedroom, he stepped through the wide doorway onto the terrace patio. In a louder rasp he said, "Velda!"

Tremble's heavy gun barrel pierced Jack's rib cage, freezing him. A voice full of authority ordered, "Don't fuckin' move."

Jack's mind groped for an answer and control.

"Lay the gun on the floor, man, or your rib cage will be nothin' but splinters," demanded Snider in his best cop-got-the-drop-on-you voice.

Jack hesitated.

"Do it, please!" pleaded Velda. She was standing in front of another man. He had wrapped his arm under her armpit and across her naked chest. The other hand held a gun with the barrel buried in the thick tangle of her hair.

Bending his knees slowly, Jack laid his pistol on the flagstone floor of the patio. He tried to regain his composure as he watched Velda choke back the fear clawing at her throat.

"Inside," ordered the man with the gun jammed in his side. He turned slowly and entered the bedroom. Velda's captor continued to hold her as they shuffle-walked behind him and the man with the gun. These are American cops, his scrambled brain told him. How did they find him so quickly?

Inside the bedroom the man holding Velda released her with the order to, "Get dressed." Relieved to be free of his grasp, she quickly pulled on a cotton sweater and slipped into a pair of jeans.

"You too," growled the black man who had the gun stuck in Jack's rib cage. Jack stepped into a pair of beltless chino pants. The man guarding Velda snapped a handcuff on her right wrist. She flinched with pain as the cold steel device ratcheted shut, nipping flesh.

Pulling her body toward Jack the man said, "Give me your hand." Jack raised his right hand slowly and the man snapped the other handcuff around his extended wrist.

It was fearfully quiet for a few seconds. Then Snider said, "Through the door." He tossed his head at the open door separating the master bedroom from the rest of the house. Velda moved first. Jack responded more slowly. "Other room, asshole." Clumsy because of the handcuffs, Velda and Jack stumbled through the doorway. Snider followed close up, his gun cocked for effect.

"Stop." Snider reached to his left and tested the strength of the wrought iron spiral staircase that led to a small loft above the living area. The thick black support cylinder that ran from the floor to the loft was anchored in concrete below the tile floor. Snider tried to shake it. The steel column would not budge.

"Give me you hands," he said to Jack as he snapped his set of cuffs on his left wrist and threaded the empty cuff through the iron works. Snider pulled roughly at Jack's arm. Jack could smell pizza and stale beer on his breath. Then Snider clamped the empty handcuff around Velda's narrow wrist.

"Go back to the car and get the radio and the torch. I'll watch these two," Snider directed Tremble. Snider vanished through the front door where they gained their entry to the house.

Chained to the support pillar, Jack complained, "For Christ sake, you got us. Why in the hell do you have to chain us to these stairs. We aren't going anywhere."

Jack started to say something else but then pursed his lips. He looked at Velda. She had a soft fierceness in her face. Tremble walked across the tile floor and opened the door. Wind off the water pushed through the opening, making the curtains dance in the moonlight. Snider came back, breathing hard, carrying a hand held radio transmitter/receiver and a heavy battery operated lamp.

"Everything okay?" Snider asked as he tried to control his heavy breathing.

"Yeah. They ain't goin' anywhere. We need to get our butts down to the beach."

Both men left through the patio door. Jack and Velda could hear the shoes of the two cops crunch and scrape as they worked their way down the steep narrow stairway leading to the beach. When the sounds of the steps merged with the roar of the surf, Velda broke the silence.

"What are they going to do?"

"I think they are landing a chopper on the beach. Hear the blades?" After years of flying, Jack could instantly pick up the whup-whup-whup of a helicopter. Usually he could tell what kind it was before making visual contact.

"Whose helicopter? Why?" asked Velda, anxiety back dropping her voice.

"It's the LongRanger. BCPD's."

"Why?"

"My guess is someone is picking us up."

"To take us where?" choked Velda.

"They're going to kill me and after you get Forbes his money out of the bank, they'll kill you."

Outside the whup-whup of the LongRanger could be heard. Suddenly a bright beam stabbed up from the beach through the dark, its shaft of light probing the sky.

"How did they find us here?" whispered Velda. Her expression changed: disappointment replaced marginal hope. "They must have followed you across the border when you picked me up. Forbes has people who do this kind of thing. They're pros. I just didn't spot them."

"Could Boomer have told them? He knows where your house in Mexico is, doesn't he?"

Jack felt his back going up at the tone of her voice. "No. Boomer was going to lay low and wait for me to call if the break-in at Forbes' place was busted. He was going to my place, stock up Harry with food and water, and then hole up in a motel in Long Beach until he heard from me. He would have been long gone before Forbes or Buno would have sent their goons after him. Nobody can get to him." Then, in a sharp tone he said, "Be quiet!" Straining to hear against the whoosh and slap of the surf, Jack's trained ear picked up the whine of the engine as the bird hovered above the beach.

The contract pilot flicked the Bell LongRanger's landing lights and dropped the machine slowly toward the beach. He was uncertain of the dark landing site. The front seat passenger who navigated him to this spot on the beach gave him landing instructions. The pilot needed all the help he could get. This was a crazy deal, he thought. A back-up pilot for a helicopter sight-seeing service in San Diego, he was offered two large in cold cash to fly the machine to a location identified on the map as La Misión. He figured the deal had to be hinky but the price was right. When he was flying the BCPD chopper his concerns faded. Maybe this could turn into a real job, he thought. Settling the machine down on the sand just above the tide line, he flicked the fuel switch and shut down the engine.

From the rear seat the man ordered, "Stay here and watch the chopper. Don't let anyone near it. Come on."

The pilot, a tight skinny man, dropped down from the cockpit, stretched the kinks out of his legs and lit up a Camel. The stubby cigarette protruded from his mouth like a glowworm when he started to do a walk-around inspection. The helicopter didn't need one after such a short flight, but he wanted to make a favorable impression on his client. The two men who were on the ground when he landed the aircraft didn't speak. Guards maybe. His nerves were raw for some unexplainable reason. The moisture from the damp breeze off the ocean spread across his face.

Something hard touched the pilot's head. He jerked forward instinctively. The .22 caliber hollow-point blew a fist size cavity in his brain. He twisted as he fell, the lit cigarette still in his mouth. Small flecks of burning ash followed the body to the sand.

"Dead?" asked the shaken Tremble.

"Dead as dirt." Snider paused for a few seconds, looking up and down the deserted beach. The noise of the surf was enough to hide the muffled sound of the pistol discharge.

"Check his pulse."

Tremble bent down over the crumpled body of the pilot and surrounded his wrist with his fingers.

"No pulse."

The pistol in Snider's hand made two thump, thump noises. Officer Rick Tremble's neck flopped over, head shattered. With a death rattle, and a look of amazement on his ruined face, he lay still on the beach. Snider holstered his gun and stared at the body of his former partner.

CHAPTER THIRTY-THREE

When the two men entered the house through the terrace patio door, shock and disbelief ripped across Jack's face. Expecting Snider and Tremble, he was stunned when the thick body of Laz Forbes pressed through the doorway with Chief Buno. Jack stared at Buno. His eyes went hard and distant. He tried to gather up his thoughts that were racing through his mind. Velda recoiled as Buno came closer. Forbes moved around the room on light feet for a man with such a heavy body. His speech was strangely soft, almost dry. Buno clasped his small hands together and said, "Dalton, you have caused us a shitload of grief and trouble. You should have stuck to flying windmills instead of snitching to the DEA. Trying to break into Mr. Forbes' house was about the dumbest thing you could do."

He crossed the room and squeezed Velda's cheek hard saying, "Bitch. We'll be back and discuss our business future tonight." She said nothing, blinking back tears. Forbes pulled a roll of duct tape out of his coat pocket and wrapped a long strip around Velda's head, covering her mouth. The brakes of an eighteen-wheeler squealed hard in the night air. "You pricks," uttered Jack, looking at both men. He bit off the words like a shark snapping a leg bone. Somewhere in his mind he was looking for an escape plan. It did not look promising.

"Okay, Dalton. Let's go for a ride in the helicopter," ordered Buno as he unlocked the handcuffs. Velda winced as he took the empty handcuff and snapped it roughly on her slim wrist. In his left hand he held a black plastic Glock 9mm pistol that glinted dully. Looking at Velda he said, "We'll be back in a while for you, *chiquita*." Dread flooded Velda as she focused on his meaning. Jack stepped back, free of the cuffs, and rubbed his wrists.

"Bet you're wondering what's going to happen?" Not waiting for a response, Buno continued, "You are going to fly me down to Ensenada for a little powwow with my man, Commandante. When we return, we just might let her live. That means that you've got to get us to Ensenada and back without any problems."

"Use the pilot who brought you down here."

"He's dead. We just needed him to fly us down to where you were hiding." Jack focused his eyes on Buno, trying to concentrate on what he had just heard. There was no way Buno could let him and Velda live.

"Let's go," commanded Buno. He jerked his automatic pistol from the direction of Jack to the door and then he aimed it back. "Down to the beach," instructed Buno. Jack walked across the room in his characteristic rolling gait and then said, "I need my boots. I can't fly without something on my feet."

"Get them on," said Laz Forbes. "I'm in a hurry." Jack walked into the bedroom with Buno right behind him. He pulled his weathered Wellingtons over his sockless feet, then walked back through the house with Buno trailing him. Leaving the house, Jack descended the narrow staircase. He could feel Buno despite the distance between them. Behind Buno lumbered Forbes. From the stairs he could make out the helicopter which sat on the sandy beach like some sort of prehistoric bird. As they came near the aircraft, Jack spotted what appeared to be some rolled up canvas. Getting closer he realized the mass was two bodies. One was one of the men who had forced his way into his home.

"Tremble was a good country boy, but what I don't need is another guy like you who can screw with me," said Buno with a malicious laugh. "Just takin' care of business, *amigo*."

Buno addressed the other cop, "Get up to the house and make sure the woman don't get away from us. We'll be back in an hour or so. Be listening for the chopper. We'll circle the house a couple of times before we land on the beach. Don't unlock the woman until we come up for her. You do and it's your ass. *Comprende*?" Snider nodded. Then Buno turned to Jack and said, "Get your ass in the cockpit."

He hesitated. The breeze off the ocean chilled his skin. Opening the door to the cockpit, he reached under the seat and pulled out the balled-up Nomex flight suit. The dirty, oil-stained set of fire resistant overalls would be warmer than flying without a shirt. He unzipped the front and thrust his feet into the legs.

"Come on," growled Buno as Jack zipped the suit shut and, from habit, tightened the velcro at the cuffs and sleeves. Then he climbed up into the cockpit of the familiar aircraft. In the darkness, he reached under the seat as he automatically went through the familiar pre-flight check.

Forbes jerked open the rear door and hoisted his bulk into the back seat. Buno climbed into the right side seat and warned him, "Don't get any funny ideas about making a run for it or some other dumb shit move. Your woman back at the house will be dead meat if we aren't back before dawn. Jack's blood chilled as his hands moved over the controls. The message from Buno was clear. For a moment he couldn't think straight. I'm running out of lives, he thought and taking Velda with me. More dead women. They're going to kill both of us once Buno gets whatever he needs from Ensenada, he thought.

Watching Buno strap himself in, Jack split the throttle to flight idle and pulled the starting trigger on the collective. His body tightened as the engine fired up with a wail. Flicking on the navigation lights and the dull red night-flying lights as the aircraft lifted off. He gently banked the vibrating machine and flew south along the coast. His earphones burst into life. "Don't make any transmissions on the radio. Don't answer any calls. Understand?"

"Roger," said Jack automatically with soft rasp.

"Now fly us to Ensenada. When we get over the city I'll tell you where to go." Flying in the dark silence, he listened to the ratcheting sound of the helicopter, trying to think of a way to escape without getting Velda killed. As it moved across the cloud-laden sky, he tried to concentrate on the bleak future. Until Buno got the helicopter to its destination, Jack was sure he would be safe. So long as Buno and Forbes had to keep the bird in the air, and he was the only available pilot, he still had a chance.

Heavy Air

Jack flew the helicopter over the dark Bahia de Los Todos Santos and across Puerto de Ensenada. In the distance, the flickering lights of Chapultepec hills guided him toward the Ensenada airfield. As he started to descend, Buno grabbed his right shoulder. "Steer it that way," as he pointed the Glock in a southerly direction. Jack stepped down hard on the rudder and moved the cyclic control over against the stop. The helicopter banked over on its side as he snapped the tail around and flew south across the city below.

"Go to the left," directed Buno. Jack had no idea where he was to put the bird down, so he just flew on at a slow steady speed. The dense housing of Chapultepec hills gave way to small patches of produce plots and scraps of farms no bigger than a couple of acres. Then the land opened up and he flew over some well tended open space that looked like a horse ranch. Seconds later, two thin beams of light flickered below in the hands of someone who was crossing the beams in the sky. Jack glanced at Buno who grunted affirmatively. Lining the descending machine up on the lights, he clamped his hands tight on the cyclic and collective control, dropping the chopper on what appeared to be a huge tarmac parking area. When the helicopter's skids hit the surface, Jack automatically reached over to kill the power to the engine. Buno's left hand shot out and stopped him. "Leave the engine running. We'll be leaving in a few minutes," said Buno over the intercom. "You just sit tight and if you try to leave, that mean-looking Mexican cop over there will be doing a little fancy shooting with that automatic weapon he's got around his neck. And if I don't show up back in La Misión in about an hour, my man will gut your girlfriend and hang her over your pretty floor."

Jack nodded. The rotor blades continued to spin overhead as the engine idled. The Mexican with the automatic weapon moved a few paces closer to the aircraft. Jack saw him flick off the safety and set the weapon on automatic fire. The man who had directed them in with the two landing flashlights led Buno and Forbes away from the helicopter toward a large ranch house. Jack flicked off the red illumination lights inside the cockpit. Squinting hard to adjust his eyes to the heavy Baja darkness that surrounded the helicopter, he looked at the guard. The guard watched him from a distance of about fifty feet, just outside of the circle made by the whirling prop. Jack could make out his weapon. It was an M-16 with a forty round banana clip wedged in its chamber. Enough firepower to make the fuselage of the Bell look like a lace doily in a matter of seconds.

He reached down under the seat. His hand felt the bulky metal heavy object. He pulled out the heavy pistol-like device from where it had been stashed during the flight from La Misión. The single-shot flare gun that had been stored under the front passenger seat had been wedged between the back and seat of the pilot's chair. Sliding the gun onto his lap, while at the same time watching the guard, Jack broke the short stubby barrel open. There was a signal projectile in the chamber and three or four in a small canvas pouch. He wondered if you could go up against a shooter armed with an M-16 capable of slinging forty high-velocity rounds in less that three seconds with a tool designed to lob an inaccurate phosphorus projectile into the air. Chances, when they are slim, are better than none, he thought.

Firmly attached by the handcuffs to the spiral staircase, Velda shifted the best she could to achieve some degree of comfort. Her guard, Gilbert Snider, said little as he roamed the house, poking and pawing. Finding a pile of magazines, he sat down and thumbed through the pages. None interested him, so he lit a cigarette and walked out on the terrace. Returning, he spoke in a low voice, "Lady, you know they are going to kill you when they come back." He watched her intently, studying her reaction.

Velda looked at him with hard hate in her eyes. She knew they wouldn't kill her until she withdrew Forbes' money for him. After that she would definitely die. The best she could hope for was a less painful death, one without the torture Forbes was famous for.

Snider walked into the kitchen where he opened the refrigerator and rummaged about for food. Closing the door, with an apple and a beer can in his hands, he shuffled back into the living room. "Hungry?" he asked. Velda ignored him. Smiling he raised the can of beer. Foam bubbled out of the can from the hole. "Drink?" offered Snider to Velda. There was no response. Snider sat down in a large bamboo chair and stared out of the window into the dark Pacific night. Killing Tremble was a bad deal but he didn't want to think about what Buno had in store for him.

CHAPTER THIRTY-FOUR

The house of Ramon Dionicio Gomez was large and opulently furnished; more house than any Mexican police commander could legitimately afford. Gomez raised fighting cocks and registered quarter horses on his ranch that was tucked into the high valley just south of Ensenada. The ranch served as a staging area and distribution center for drug shipments that came up in trucks from Sinaloa through the heat and dust of the Mexicali Valley. Powerful trucks, pulling vans with bales of marijuana or blocks of cocaine in clever compartments, pulled into the ranch on a regular basis.

During the day, the lands of Ramon Gomez teemed with activity as horse handlers and trainers worked with over fifty head of prize quarter horses. Two ancient Mexican handlers oversaw the training of nearly one hundred fighting cocks. The fowl were housed in a large fenced field. Each bird had its own small wooden shelter from the hot sun. Behind the big house where Gomez kept Yolanda, his free-spending mistress, were three large barns. The largest and most secure was used for weighing, processing and warehousing drugs before distribution in southern California. Heavily guarded 24 hours a day, the barn was off limits to the ranch hands.

Buno and Forbes followed the man through a stucco arch. He walked across the expansive pool area that was lit against the night and through the double doors of Gomez' large office. Gomez extended a phony welcome to the Americans with a toothy smile breaking on his swarthy face. Gomez said, "We are ready. Are we not, señor pilot?" Rising from the straight back chair positioned directly across from Gomez' desk, a handsome younger man dressed in a brown tailored flight suit looked at Buno and Forbes with inquisitive eyes. He nodded his head affirmatively. The pocked flesh on Buno's face mashed together as he first looked at the pilot.

"We need to be alone," instructed Buno.

"Wait outside," ordered Gomez in a low voice. Watching the pilot leave through the oak doors, Gomez picked up a large cigar from the humidor. He clipped off the end with a small pair of gold scissors and struck a match.

Buno spoke first. "Can your pilot be trusted?"

"Can you be trusted?" countered Gomez looking archly at them through steepled fingers.

"What the fuck kind of answer is that?" demanded Buno.

Gomez responded with a bite to his voice, "He is to be trusted. And very loyal. He is a young man whom I am grooming to help run the business as it gets more difficult to maintain control. Besides, he is my sister's eldest son. He is family." The office was silent for a moment as Gomez moved across the polished oak floor to the massive bar against the wall. "Something to drink?"

"No," answered Forbes, taking charge of the discussion. "We've got some business to take care of and I don't want to do any drinking until we take care of this mess. Then we can all do a little celebrating."

"Where is your pilot?" asked Gomez.

"Sitting on his ass in the chopper."

"Does he suspect what is going to happen to him?"

"Yes, he knows. He knows that as soon as we don't need a pilot he's good as gone. That's why I have him sitting in the helicopter with the engine running. He thinks he is flying us somewhere else. He doesn't know we are about to switch pilots."

"We need to kill him here then."

"I know. When we go back to the helicopter I'll tell him there is some fluid leaking out of the tail rotor. When he gets out of the cabin, have your man blow him away, but be damn sure he doesn't hit the fucking helicopter."

"Si, let us finish our business," said Gomez.

The tail rotors spun in a lazy circle. In the dark they were a blur. Jack sat in the Bell's cockpit waiting for Buno to return. Lifting off and trying to make a run for it would be suicidal. The guard's automatic weapon had too much fire power at that range. One round through the aircraft's thin skin into a fuel cell and he would be ballistic. Up in flames, maybe for the last time.

Four men emerged from the double wooden doors that Forbes and Buno had entered. One was wearing a pilot's Nomex flight suit. Jack's heartbeat red-lined. Son-of-a-bitch, a replacement.

He opened the side door of the helicopter slowly with his left hand. With his right hand he aimed the large round barrel of the flare gun at the guard with the automatic weapon. He pulled the trigger. Nothing happened; the safety was on. He fumbled with the safety switch as the guard started to bring his automatic weapon up to a firing position. The whooshing sound of the flare leaving the gun caused the clustered up men to dive for cover. A gasping scream left the guard's mouth as he spun to his left when the low velocity flare burned into his right shoulder. A bloody nub replaced his arm. The automatic weapon lay on the ground.

"Shoot him!" yelled Gomez at the mortally wounded guard who screamed in agony.

Heart pounding at the max, Jack pushed the cyclic forward and revved the throttle as he pulled back on the collective. The rotors exploded into an invisible spin. His mind locked in concentration; his one chance to escape. The chopper, submerged in a banging rotor racket, reached the point of transitional lift just as Buno was scrambling to his feet. Jack jumped the rattling machine into a climb before Buno opened fire with his Glock. Three rounds hit the aircraft but did no damage to the controls. Gomez fumbled with the guard's rifle. He raised the unfamiliar weapon toward the aircraft and pulled the trigger. The automatic weapon spit out more than thirty rounds that were high, missing the bird completely. In seconds, the helicopter had spun around as they watched the narrow profile of its tail dive over the crest of a hill east of the ranch house.

The exhilaration of escape was pushed aside by the chilling reality. He had gotten away. But Velda was still being held prisoner at the house. He opened the throttle and pushed the aircraft to its maximum speed. He flew over the north side of Ensenada in a direct route toward La Misión. He tried to calm himself so he could think in the vibrating machine. All he had was a flare gun and a canvas bandolier of five flares. Forbes' crew was sure to follow. Probably in a car. Maybe in a helicopter if they could find another. He could beat them to the house by maybe thirty minutes, forty at best. That was not a lot of time to land a chopper on the beach, overpower her keeper and somehow get Velda out of the house before Forbes and Buno arrived. Nervous sweat oozed from his body as he tried to think through a plan and guide the helicopter over the moon-swept terrain below.

Buno, Forbes, the pilot and Gomez scrambled to their feet screaming orders and obscenities. Gomez yelled at the dead guard, who had bled out and Buno emptied the Glock at the climbing helicopter. The aircraft had spun around so he was shooting at its tail.

"The car!" yelled Gomez, as he started to run toward the large garage that housed his cars. Buno and Forbes followed, running hard. Gomez jerked open the door of his unmarked LTD yelling *"Mueve! Va! Va!"* He backed it out of the garage with Buno and Forbes in it and the pilot half in and half out.

"La Misión," directed Buno. "Dalton will go to his beach house. How far?"

"About fifty miles. He'll beat us there flying the helicopter," said Gomez.

Composing himself, Buno said, "Yeah, but he's got to get his hands on Velda and I got a gun guarding her. Ain't no way Dalton can sneak up on him with the helicopter. We can get there in time if we hurry."

Gomez turned his attention to the road ahead and drove as fast as conditions would allow him. Within minutes the putrid smell of the fish processing plant on the north side of Ensenada was behind them as they bounced across the Highway 3 junction. Gomez ignored the guard at the San Miguel tollgate. He drove through the dangerous curves at El Mirador and the Salsipuedes lookout point. Trapped behind a smoking bus for a mile, Gomez was finally able to push his car past the oil belching beast at the exit leading to the Bajamar Golf Resort.

Jack banked the helicopter out over the Pacific and shut off his running lights. With the moon to his back, he dropped the machine down hard on the sand of the La Misión beach. The crumbled bodies still lay there in a mound. Instead of shutting down the chopper he eased the throttle back to idle. The blades turned slowly in the humid night air. Taking the signal gun and the remaining flares with him, he jumped down from the helicopter and moved away from his house in a southerly direction. He passed the last house on the beach, a tiny brick studio where a recluse artist lived. He moved slowly across the sand to the road that ran parallel with the beach between the string of houses and the toll road.

A small animal burst out from under a small pile of rocks and bricks. He stopped and took a deep breath to slow his runaway pulse. Buno and Forbes had to be racing up from Ensenada to the house. He had maybe twenty minutes to free Velda before they arrived. Dog-trotting up the service road incline, he slowed to a crouching walk at the wall surrounding his house. Somehow he had to take out the guard. It wouldn't be easy. Buno wouldn't have left an inexperienced man with Velda. He was a thug with a gun and he had to be on edge now with the chopper sitting on the beach with its rotors whirling. But the guy was expecting Buno to return. I need that advantage, thought Jack. Twenty minutes, max. That's all the time he had to work with before a carload of guns would come roaring up the road and trap them.

Snider stood at the patio door and stared out at the beach to the location of the helicopter. The distance and the darkness made it hard to see anything other than a dark shape. Against the growl of the surf he could hear the engine turning at low rpms. Buno and Forbes should have been here by now, he thought. What was going on? Paranoia from dealing with Buno started to set deep in his gut.

The house was almost impenetrable from the east side. The side that ran parallel with the service road. The eight-foot wall that guarded the courtyard was trimmed with broken glass embedded in the top.

Pulling himself up to the top of the wall, Jack had to think. Time was running out. Any minute he expected Buno's car to leave the toll road and come lurching down the narrow cobblestone road to the house. Dropping down to the other side of the wall, hands cut and scraped, he landed in the front courtyard of the house. He moved slowly to the end of the house, hearing no noise except that of the surf and the slow *whup-whup-whup* of the idling helicopter parked on the beach. He slipped around the corner of the house.

The noise, and then chips of brick and masonry splattered against his face as the rounds from Snider's gun narrowly missed him. He jerked back, cracking his neck. He dove, then crawled and scooted closer to the chest-high wall that separated the ocean side terrace from the front courtyard. With the roar still ringing in his ears, he rolled onto his back and fired the flare pistol straight up. Breaking the hot tube of the fat pistol open, he inserted another flare. Four flares left. Fear and nausea licked at his insides as he heard Snider move across the flagstone terrace. He couldn't see him because of the burning flare. Jack hunched behind the wall. Squeezing his eyes tight to retain his night vision, he jumped to his feet. Under the full light of the parachuting flare his body was completely exposed.

"What the fuck!" exclaimed Buno from the speeding car, as they watched the flare pop open and then drift down. It illuminated almost all of the south end of La Misión beach in an eerie green light. Gomez bounced the LTD off the toll way and jerked it around in a hard switch back turn into La Misión in a series of nerve-crunching jolts. Forbes was breathing heavily. The pilot hung on and said something in Spanish. He got no answer from Gomez. The bouncing car almost knocked the MAC-10 fully automatic machine pistol from its holder on the dashboard. Slamming the car to a stop on the service road behind the houses, Gomez reached behind the seat and grabbed a Street Sweeper shotgun and a bandoleer of shells.

"Where's the house at!" shouted Gomez. Buno was in a state of confusion. He could locate Dalton's house from the beach but up on the service road it looked different. He started running up the cobblestone road toward the south end of the houses, toward the green flare.

Jack aimed the flare pistol like he was firing a real gun. Using the classic two-handed stance, he waited until the last moment to open his eyes. Snider had made the mistake of trying to spot him against the backdrop of the lime green flare. He could see nothing. He corrected his aim slightly and pulled the trigger. The flare pistol *whooshed* out of the barrel a millisecond before Snider pulled the trigger. Jack felt the hot wind of a bullet passing his face as the burning projectile from the flare gun plunged into Snider's chest with a mushy hissing sound. Snider unleashed a gargled scream of pain, then stumbled backwards for a step or two. For a moment he tried to steady himself in the fuzzy, surrealistic green light. Jack leaped over the low wall and gave Snider a crushing stiff-armed shot to his head.

Snider fell back on has tailbone with his legs askew. As he died he croaked, "Aw shit." Inside, Velda could see the beach-scape turn green through the windows and glass doors of the house.

CHAPTER THIRTY-FIVE

Catching his flight suit on the door latch, Jack careened through the patio door. "You okay?" he asked Velda, as he pulled the tape off her mouth.

"Thank God you're alive! What happened to the guard?"

Jack stepped closer to her and grabbed the handcuff chains. "He's dead. I've got to get you out of here. Buno and Forbes are right behind us."

"Who's with the helicopter?" asked Velda anxiously.

"No one. I stole it. I left it running."

"Where's Buno?" asked Velda, her voice pinched with fear. She jerked reflexively at the cuffs, forgetting she was chained to the stairs. "Ouch," Velda said as she pulled her delicate wrists against the iron staircase.

Jack pulled at the handcuffs and searched the room for something to remove them with.

"Use the gun."

"What gun?"

"The one he had," cried Velda, pointing toward the patio with her head.

"Shit." exclaimed Jack. "I left it out there." He sprinted back outside to the patio. Snider lay in a crumbled, smoking pile.

"Hurry!" yelled Velda as the tension escalated a couple of more notches. Jack found the gun, twisted it out of the dead man's hand and stumbled on a clay flower pot as he returned to the house.

"Turn your head." Jack placed the end of the gun barrel against one of the links and pulled the trigger. The noise was deafening inside the house. A small piece of link blew off. The handcuffs held.

"You all right?"

"Do it again. Same way. Hurry!" encouraged Velda.

He stuck the heavy pistol against the chain link and fired another round. The bullet went through the center of the link without breaking it. He moved the barrel over slightly and pulled the trigger. This time the chain link split, scraps of metal bounced against the stair railing. A ragged piece nicked Velda, cutting her cheek slightly. She didn't notice it.

The sound of the .357 bounced and echoed among the tightly configured houses. Buno and Gomez froze. Forbes and the pilot banged into them in the dark. Following the sound of more gunshots in Jack's house, they tried to batter their way through the heavy wall door. Gomez kicked at the door twice and Buno slammed his shoulder into it. The door creaked but did not give.

"We have to get out of here." He grabbed Velda by the wrist and jerked her toward the door. The handcuffs hung on her wrists like thick bracelets. She slipped on the tile and fell. He pulled her roughly to her feet. They were through the door and out on the terrace. Then they stumbled to the bottom of the stairs and sprinted onto the beach, heading toward the sound of the helicopter.

The wall door to the courtyard blew open when Gomez fired two rounds from the Street Sweeper shotgun into the ancient brass lock. Energized wood splinters and scraps of metal jumped from the door. Gomez kicked the door open. The four men thundered across the courtyard and into the house through the front door.

Jack and Velda clambered away from the stairs. Fear pumped through their bodies in waves. Chunks of wood and splinters slapped their backs as Gomez pumped two shots in their direction. Instead of crossing the open beach for the helicopter, Jack veered to the right and dragged Velda down with him behind the corner of a small brick house on the beach level. He snapped an unaimed shot from the .357 toward the sound of their pursuers.

Panic thickened his throat as they crouched against the brick wall. "We can't get to the chopper," he whispered, we'll never make it. We're going to have to go this way," he pointed north, "and try to get out on the highway. Catching a car is our only chance."

Rounds from the MAC-10 tore into the brick wall of the house where they were hiding. Pieces of hard brick splinters stung their faces. Clutching the flare gun in one hand and Velda's hand in another, Jack jerked them in a hard, thrashing run.

Two hundred yards on the beach to the south, the Mexican pilot skirted the spinning tail rotor of the helicopter. He stopped for a second to catch his breath. Sucking the moist ocean air, his chest heaved and trembled. Beads of sweat popped out on his youthful face after his run down to the beach from the road. Climbing up into the seat of the LongRanger, he scanned the instrument panel. Pulse activated, he scanned the beach to the north where he last saw his uncle and the Americans running. Now he could see nothing. Then he saw the muzzle flash from the guns of the men racing down the stairs. His mind churned desperately. He caught the muzzle flash out of the corner of his eye. If he could fly the helicopter, he could pick up his people and pursue their prey from the air. He would be his uncle's hero.

Jack and Velda sprinted hard for a few yards and then ducked down behind the corner of another house. He saw his pursuers move. He jerked Velda's hand and they started to run again. Velda was gasping for air and sobbing. The men behind them moved cautiously. Jack and Velda put some distance between them but they were running to the north end of the La Misión beach boundaries. The only escape route was to scale the steep boulder pile at the end of the beach or go through a large storm drain that emptied out in the rocks. If they could get to the storm drain that ran under the highway, they had a chance to get to the other side. Maneuvering to the east side of the road, where they might be able to get a ride from a passing car, was their only chance to escape.

Gomez sensed their quarry was moving so the three of them ran to a small wall and crouched behind it waiting for a shot from Jack's weapon. Nothing happened. "He's out of ammo," said Buno to Gomez. "Lets go!"

Whup-whup-whup.

"The helicopter! They've got the chopper!" yelled Jack, jerking Velda's arm. He cut his eyes west to the mechanical bird on the beach. In the moonlight he could see the rotors spinning faster. Christ, he thought, they must have brought the pilot from Ensenada. Once they got in the helicopter there would be no way he and Velda could escape. The pilot would pick Buno's people off the beach, and the helicopter would be used as an overhead shooting platform.

The MAC-10 spit out a stream of bullets that cut into the sand off to the left. Stooped over, Jack pulled Velda behind him and ran harder, zigzagging as their feet slipped in the soft sand. The shotgun popped twice, echoing off the cliff wall. Confused with the source of the gunfire, he jerked Velda hard. They stumbled. Jack recovered first and wrenched Velda to her feet. White seagulls, the inhabitants of the rock pile, scattered, floated and dove around them in a lazy fashion that was strange in contrast to the devastating cannonade of fire behind them.

"Don't give up," he urged as his chest heaved. "If we can get to the storm pipe up there in the rocks, we can get to the other side. There's got to be a way to the top. Come on!" The moonlight reflected off the choppy waves. The shoreline was deserted. Lights from a southbound ocean tanker glimmered in the horizon. Overhead, the red landing lights of a jet blinked as it began its long descent into the Tijuana International Airport. The Pacific surf exploded and sighed over the rocks.

Jack looked down the beach. He could sense them more than see them, moving in the pale moonlight. Buno was a few paces ahead of Gomez who was screaming *"Cabron, pinche perro! Fucking dog!"* His chest hammering, Jack scanned the rocky terrain in front of them. They had reached the point on the beach where the shoreline was dominated by large rocks at the foot of the cliff. The sea crashed into them, causing streams to run inward on the grainy sand and then recede, leaving dead fish, seaweed and other flotsam.

"Hurry!" he urged Velda. She was running out of steam. His voice sounded foreign as he cautioned, "Watch where you step so you don't twist an ankle." Looking up, he tried to pick a route up the pile of rocks.

The Street Sweeper shotgun roared again with a meaty thump. In the feeble light from a slice of moon, he could see them getting closer.

The young pilot lifted the unfamiliar machine and moved it cautiously, across the beach on a cushion of air toward Gomez and the Americans. He turned the throttle of the growling engine, causing the rotor blades to whirl crazily overhead. When he pulled back on the collective control stick, the helicopter jumped. It dropped hard on the sand when he overreacted, pushed the collective forward and twisted the throttle the wrong way, feeding excessive fuel to the engine. He pushed the left pedal to the tail rotor and the tail of the steel bird jerked to the right. Strong mechanical tremors rattled through the body of the aircraft as he swung it into a mushy arc, trying to control it. The pedals slapped at the bottom of his feet with the cyclic tugging and the collective pushing. He over-controlled on the pedals, making the tail wag back and forth. Then everything seemed to fall in sync as he pushed the pedals, pumped the collective around and lurched up the beach in the bucking and twisting aircraft.

Jamming Velda down behind the outcropping of a smooth rock shaped like a crescent, Jack flung a shot from the flare gun down the beach. A stream of burning light trailed the fiery orb and lit up the beach. The shooters lunged behind a sand dune with a hard concrete-like texture for protection. The flare missed them by more than thirty feet.

"That won't stop them, but it should slow them down," he rasped. "Come on, Velda. Our only chance is to get to the top before they..." Before he finished, the ripping rattle of the MAC-10 erupted again. The flashy blur of sparks from one of the high powered bullets chipped pieces from the boulder they were climbing. Reaching down to pull Velda up, he slipped and tumbled forward. Shock and pain grabbed his face as the bridge of his nose collapsed from the blow. Blood started to flow from his nostril.

"Jack!" screamed Velda as she clawed frantically, to raise his head to her lap. Another shot from below on the beach. He felt the missile slam into his head. His face went slate grey and his eyelids fluttered like hummingbird wings. Splotched with veiny red meat and clumps of white flesh, his face was a matted mess. Velda dropped beside him in shock. She cradled his mangled looking head in her arms. Exhaustion had bled her of any reserve. She bent over him, weeping and babbling incoherently.

The chance flight of the gull had saved Jack's face from obliteration. One of the high velocity bullets sprayed from Buno's automatic weapon struck a floating seagull. Its body exploded, showering his face with a red mist and thin strips of bird wings. Velda was crying as she wrapped his bird covered face. The noise of the whirling rotors and the air suction intake competed with the muffled thunder of the jet engine. It wobbled and bucked as the pilot frantically hovered the machine at a bizarre angle over Gomez. Gomez pushed his automatic weapon through the door and climbed aboard, almost falling when the ship bucked without warning. With Gomez in the cockpit, the pilot made a tight flaring turn and lined the see-sawing aircraft on the rock pile. The ship bobbled in the air as the pilot worked to synchronize the cyclic control stick and the tail rotor pedals.

Consciousness seeped back to Jack seconds after the blow to his face from the bird's body. Velda covered him as she sobbed. Pressed against the hard rock he winced with pain and struggled to get up. Pulling his hand away from his face with the bird gore and feathers on it, he realized what had happened. Velda didn't. "Come on! We've got to get to the storm drain! It's our only chance! They're almost on us," he pleaded. Stunned at his recovery, Velda scrambled to keep up with him. Bloody white feathers broke loose from his face and floated in the breeze.

"What the fuck is going on!" exclaimed Buno as he turned toward the sound of the hovering helicopter to see Gomez pulling himself through the door.

"Get them!" yelled Gomez in a screeching voice as the helicopter swung toward the boulders. The navigation lights on the helicopter were unlit but the rocking and wobbling bird was illuminated by the fading moonlight in the bleeding horizon. With a whup-whupping sound and a heavy *whoosh* the chopper dipped toward the surface of the beach and flew in a collision course toward the cliff. The pilot pulled it to the right, away from the rock pile that Jack and Velda were trying to climb. Startled at the erratic flying of the helicopter pilot, Jack thought, what the fuck was happening anyway. It must be the pilot's first time in a LongRanger, he thought as he watched him overcompensate the controls. Pulling her hard, Jack dragged Velda across a flat outcropping as he watched the helicopter bounce and jitterbug in the air.

Two more thumping rounds from the shotgun below them and the spray of shot against the side of the projecting rocks warned him his pursuers were closing the gap.

Velda sobbed and said, "I can't go any farther. Leave me, Jack, leave me."

Pulling her, he dragged Velda across a flat outcropping and pushed her over the hump of a camel-shaped rock.

"Don't fuckin' move!" came the hoarse command from Buno. He could hardly breathe, standing less than twenty yards away from them. Forbes, panting like an old dog that had run too far, climbed up beside Buno. The *clack-clack* of him chambering a round in his shotgun was loud, despite the distant noise of the wallowing helicopter. Jack froze like a cold statue, with gore and pieces of feathers sticking to his face. Instinctively, he knew both of them were going to die on the rocks.

CHAPTER THIRTY-SIX

Jack, flare gun at his side, watched the helicopter jerk toward the rock pile where he and Velda had surrendered. Above them on the highway, a heavily laden truck with grinding gears pulled its load toward the top of the La Misión mesa. Shadowy head-lights bounced over the beach and banging surf. For a moment the night was still. The sound of faint mariachi music from the Emporia carried along the rugged coastline. Expecting to feel the slamming shock waves of the high velocity slugs from Buno's automatic weapon tear through him, Jack turned and faced both men.

The LongRanger popped up like the cork out of a cheap champagne bottle. The machine lurched toward them in the dark moist air. He watched as an automatic weapon spit out some rounds on the rocks. The bullets landed below and behind them, causing Buno and Forbes to scramble for cover behind the jut-ting rocks. The helicopter roared overhead, missing them by less than a hundred feet. Jack watched the inexperienced pilot turn the bird clumsily in the air as it circled around. Buno and Forbes raised up, but ducked back down as the helicopter started to make another pass at Jack and Velda. He heard the bullets of the automatic weapon zinging off of the hard rock.

The helicopter came at them out of the thin moonlight, it reminded Jack of an assault ship hitting a hot landing zone with a load of jazzed up, scared-shitless grunts. Only this time, he was the one who was scared shitless. He stuffed a flare in the chamber of the gun, snapped the breach shut and stood up. His cramped legs, noodled for a second, then he regained his balance. The helicopter roared toward him with its passenger shooting wildly. *Wooosh!* Jack fired the hot red ball through the thin metal skin of the helicopter. The machine bucked, wobbled and then exploded as the superheated flare ignited a cell of avgas. Like a dying insect, it back slipped and plummeted, stabbing itself on a sharp rock outcropping where it lay dead and burning.

A wave of searing air smacked across Velda and Jack. Jerking his head up from his protection, he realized the downed aircraft was between them and Forbes and Buno. "Come on," he yelled as he pulled Velda out of their hiding place. Picking his way through the huge rocks, he glanced back. Both Forbes and Buno were up but the burning aircraft slowed them down as they cautiously circled the inferno. Dirty smoke from the burning pyre lofted skyward.

Pushing Velda, Jack yelled, "Climb to the top." Then he rolled over some rocks and lurched to where he fired a flare at the two men who moved cautiously up the rocks. He had one flare left. The mouth of the storm drain was less than a dozen yards away. Velda's face was red and she was breathing hard and fast.

They scrambled to the mouth of the storm drain and stumbled over chunks of broken concrete and other rubble. The pipe diameter was nearly eight feet. Clumps of cement hung from where sections of the pipe were connected every ten feet or so. Jack blinked, trying to adjust his eyes to the darkness of the drain tunnel. At the far end was a milky light, barely discernable. Forced to slide his hands along its sides, Jack could feel the vibrations of vehicles passing overhead.

An animal brushed against their ankles. Jack uttered "Jesus," and Velda whimpered and gripped the back of his shirt tighter. He moved as fast as he could through the pipe, splashing the seeping water that had collected on the tile's floor. Perspiring freely, he wiped the blood, sweat and feathers from his eyes and pushed on as fast as he could in a slightly bent over position. The shadowy light filtering in at the end was his target. He looked back at the entrance. Forbes and Buno still hadn't made it up the rock pile yet. But once they did, he and Velda would be easy targets. One spray from an automatic weapon and they would be dead. There was no other place to hide. Then Jack saw a whirl of movement at the rear and heard one of their pursuers yell, "Hurry, goddamn it!"

At the storm drain entrance, Silva Buno jammed a fresh clip into the MAC-10 and fired a full cycle burst down the cement tube. Sparks danced in the air as steel slugs bounced from wall to wall. Cordite smell and concrete dust assaulted Buno's nose as Forbes came up puffing up behind them.

"You hit anything?" asked Forbes.

Taking heavy breaths, Buno responded, "If they are in here they got hit." Then he reloaded and fired half a clip down the pipe. The noise was deafening. "They're either dead or on the other side." Buno, leading the way with Forbes struggling behind, said, "Let's go."

Lying on their backs, facing the opening they had entered, Jack and Velda's bodies were wedged together by the curvature of the pipe. A couple of inches of putrid water soaked through their clothes as they watched the outlines of two men come through the drain pipe entrance. Bullets whizzed by, some uninhibited by the concrete wall, others ricocheting back and forth. Sparks arched and danced like fireflies. Both of their bodies jumped like they were touched by an electrical charge. Velda strained to sit up but Jack's grip clamped her against the floor of the pipe. Trying to control his breathing, he whispered, "Lie still. It's our only chance."

Choking back the temptation to jump up and run, both of them worked to control their trembling. They could hear Buno and Forbes as they moved closer to them.

"Easy, goddamn it. I can't see anything."

"I can't either," retorted Buno.

"Ouch! Son-of-a-bitch," wailed Forbes scraping his scalp against the curved ceiling of the concrete pipe.

Jack squeezed Velda's hand and raised to sit up. Holding the flare gun in both hands, he concentrated on trying to aim it down the middle of the pipe at the murky figures coming at him. They didn't see him as he pulled the trigger.

The flare left the gun with a *whoosh* as it rifled through the heavy air in the drain pipe. It hit Buno with the pulpy thump of a ripe watermelon hit with a mallet. Green phosphorus smoke boiled up and the tunnel was filled with screams of agony. Rounds from an automatic weapon were fired wildly.

Jack rolled over to his stomach and scraped his knees as he rose to his feet. He jerked Velda up as the screams still echoed in the concrete chamber.

"Run," he ordered her.

Slipping and hitting his shoulder, a dull pain went through his arm. He pushed Velda toward the end of the tunnel. Jack turned and charged at the glob of flesh that was Buno in a screaming dance engulfed in the eerie glow of burning phosphorus.

Running the best he could in a semi-crouch, he hit the mass of Buno's torn, burning flesh and slid with it along the wet, slimy floor. Hit and spun around by the flare, Buno had reflexively pulled the trigger of the automatic weapon. Buno's body absorbed the impact. His muscle controls had shut down as Jack drove through him in sloshing steps. His target was Forbes who was still behind Buno. He knew he had incapacitated Buno with the flare, but Forbes was behind him with a weapon. The tangled bodies separated as he fought to get his hands on the fleshy body of Forbes. His hands grappled for Forbes' wrists. He found one and twisted hard. Wet and slippery, they had disappeared in the dark as Jack slipped forward, landing chest down on Forbes. He grabbed the fat man's neck and squeezed with all his strength. There was no resistance by Forbes. Exhausted, he lay in the gore and stink until he marshaled enough strength to push himself up on his knees.

"Velda!" he choked out.

No answer. Pushing himself away from the carnage he wiped his hands in disgust and spit some matter that hung from his lips. Carefully working his way to the other end of the drain pipe, he found Velda with her arms wrapped around her knees, sobbing uncontrollably. Jack bent over and pulled her head off her knees, gently.

"Come on. It's okay. They're dead. We've got to get out of here before the Mexican authorities show up. Come on!"

With Jack leading, they worked their way to the end of the storm drain. They were on the east side of the toll way. Their clothes were wet from lying on the floor of the drain. Velda's hair was splayed across her sweating face, her cheek still bleeding. A mush of human blood and gore covered Jack.

Velda squeezed his hand hard and asked, "What are we going to do?" The shock of escaping death was beginning to wear. Jack had shot down a police helicopter and killed two powerful men, including a police chief.

"Back to the house. We need to clean up and get out of here."

"The Mexican police will catch us there," she said.

"The police won't be able to put it together that fast. It's dark enough that nobody will pay any attention to us. It will be hours before they can figure out who was in the helicopter. Look." He pointed across the road, "It's still burning." Thinning black smoke, spiraled almost straight up in the windless night.

An hour later, Jack and Velda headed north on the tollway. They showered at the house before leaving. The only thing they took with them were the clothes they wore and Jack's unfinished manuscript.

CHAPTER THIRTY-SEVEN

After he had locked the doors and gate to the house, they climbed in his Mercedes. Velda sat in the passenger seat with worry marring her face. He turned the key. The engine boomed and the wide tires of the heavy machine yelped as he drove out on the service road toward the toll way.

He and Velda were struggling to comprehend what had happened. What the consequences would be. What they had to do to survive. Laz Forbes and Silva Buno were dead. The first priority was to get back across the border. If the Mexican police caught them, they'd be tossed in a hole with Baja dirt shoveled down on them.

Suddenly flashing lights filled his rear view mirror! A sob rose up in Velda's throat as the dancing lights reflected off of the car's interior. Jack's heart almost stopped dead cold. The car was gaining on them rapidly. The fight-flee syndrome cranked up in both of them. Then the car veered into the left lane and shot past them into the early bluish darkness. Three big, snorting rigs in a convoy blew past, rocking the Mercedes in their wake. A weariness crept through Jack's bones as the danger passed. Tired and cranky, his joints and body hurt from the trauma sustained in the running fight with Buno and Forbes. The occasional glimmer of house lights reminded him that they were still fleeing rural Mexico. Trying to rid herself of the sour taste of fear, Velda rolled her window down. The early morning smelled fresh and clean.

Velda broke the silence. "What are we going to do?"

"We can worry about that when we make it across the border," responded Jack testily.

"No!" she said emphatically. "I've got a right to know what you're thinking. Talk to me. Please!"

Jack's thought process kept shutting down. "Everything depends on how soon the Mexican authorities can put this together and connect it to us. I saw only a couple of local police when we left La Misión." He was referring to the scene they witnessed when they drove past the point where the drain pipe passed under the road. On the beach side of the road, wisps of greasy smoke from the destroyed helicopter wafted up through the clear dawn sky. Cars, including a police unit, jammed the narrow shoulder of the road. Jack couldn't see what was going on near the drain tile exit but there were no ambulances on the side of the road. That meant the authorities as usual were reacting slowly.

"As soon as the Mexican cops figure out the helicopter is operated by the Border City Police Department, things will get hot for us."

Velda interrupted him. "Maybe not. I mean, isn't there a chance that nobody other than Forbes and Buno knows about us?"

"Could be, but I don't have any idea. You know Forbes' operation a lot better than me. What do you think?"

"Jack, other than Buno and me, I don't think anyone else knew about the money laundering. There's a good chance Forbes and Buno kept the deal to themselves. Secrecy was a big deal with Forbes. If anybody else was involved, they'd be getting some of the action. That wasn't the case because I managed the skimmed money. All of it went into the Cayman Island account. It was all Forbes'."

"Everything depends on whether or not the police can connect us with the fight in the storm drain. If they do my guess is that we will be charged with murder."

"Murder?"

"Sure. What do you expect? Like it or not, I killed a bunch of people, one is still lying on my patio. "Once they tie this to us, the murder charge is a done deal."

"We need to get to the Cayman bank account. I can transfer to a bank in any country we want to live in."

Jack said, "Somebody will always be looking for us. Either the cops or Forbes' people."

"Forbes' people don't know where the money is. And if the cops can't make the connection, nobody will bother us. Jack, for God's sake. They're all dead!"

"We'll always be on somebody's list. The Mob, Interpol if we run, bounty hunters no matter what we do. Jesus, I don't want to live that kind of life."

"You're not listening! We will have close to three million dollars. You can buy lots of protection and hiding with that. We'll just disappear." She tugged slightly at his arm and said, "You'd be crazy to do anything else. Besides, one of the people killed was a helicopter pilot. There is a good chance you won't even be considered as a suspect. How would anyone know you were even down here. Only the dead people and I know you were in La Misión. They'll probably think that dead pilot was you. This is Mexico, not the U.S!"

"Boomer knows."

"That's not a problem, is it?" she asked.

"Shouldn't be. But I need to talk to him."

"Why?"

"So he doesn't say the wrong thing to anybody."

"We don't have time for that. We've got to get out of the country as soon as possible."

In less than an hour they would be in Border City if the Mexican police didn't catch them. If he was going to run he'd have to do it now. Driving toward the southern outskirts of Tijuana he struggled with his choices. Velda knew he was trying to decide. She said nothing until they passed through Customs without incident.

As the car accelerated away from the bored Customs agent's booth she said in desperation, "If you won't come with me will you at least take me to the airport? I am a criminal. I was cooking the books for Forbes before this happened. I don't have a choice."

"Yes, you do."

"Not unless I'm willing to serve some time in a federal prison. I've still got my parents to support. You don't really have a choice either. You'd have a terrible time proving to the cops that you killed those people in self defense. It will be impossible if the Mexican authorities get their hands on you. You'll die a shriveled-up old man in some damp cell in a Mexican prison. You have no choice!"

"I'll drop you off at your place and you can pack what you need."

"Let's just go to the airport now. What if the cops are there?"

"They won't be. There's no way they could have put it together this fast. But that doesn't mean we can jack around. We need to get out of San Diego as fast as possible. Besides, I've got to get my bird."

"Oh, shit," Velda moaned.

"He'll starve or die of thirst if I leave him locked in the house. We've got plenty of time. Quit worrying about it and start thinking how we can get out of the country without being traced."

Looking into the rear view mirror, he saw his face with eyes drawn tight into slits, lips tightly compressed. His thoughts racing. The specter of arrest and a jail sentence caused an unquenchable fear to permeate his consciousness. The flight syndrome won out. Velda broke the reverie as he neared her apartment. "Drive around back. I don't want the doorman to see me."

"This way?"

"Pull up over there." Velda pointed to a loading dock that was used to move furniture in and out of the building. He halted the heavy car gently.

"Are you coming back?"

He nodded. "I'll be back as soon as I pick up my things. Less than an hour. Don't bring more than two suitcases. You need to be sure you take all of your valuables and papers. It's doubtful we can ever come back, so take what's important. Deeds to property, passports, jewelry. You know what kind of stuff."

"Most of that kind of stuff is in my bank safety deposit."

"Where?"

"Downtown."

"We'll get it after I pick you up. Don't leave the apartment to get that stuff without me," he instructed. She opened the passenger door with one hand, and at the same time reached over and squeezed his arm. Pulling into the driveway of his condo, he opened the garage door and drove in. Inside the garage, he could hear Harry squawking and raising hell inside the house. He's going to be mad, flinched Jack as he opened the door into the house.

The blue-headed bird marched into the room like a pompous little majordomo. He bent down so the bird could climb on his wrist. He stroked his ruffled feathers with his left hand. Harry squawked, "Beer! Beer!" as he pranced up his arm and onto his shoulder. Stroking the bird, Jack walked through the foyer to the pile of mail that had been pushed through the mail drop in the door. A utility bill, an advertisement for a credit card, two catalogs and a large brown envelope that had been bent so it could be shoved through the mail slot lay in a pile. Kneeling so Harry could remain on his shoulder, Jack picked up the mail. He tossed all of it in a waste-paper basket except the large envelope. The envelope was from Ray Compton. Scribbled on the outside of the envelope was the message, "Here's the fingerprint report. The prints on the ax match the prints from the rubber gloves. I'm still working on some leads."

Pulling an Abercrombie & Fitch canvas briefcase from the bedroom closet, Jack stuffed the envelope from Ray Compton in one of its pouches. He opened his small personal safe that contained his personal papers, passport and battered flight log and transferred them to the canvas case. He removed the one hundred bills that he always kept for an emergency and put them in the leather money belt he used when he traveled. From the desk he grabbed the manuscript and packed it away. I'll finish my god-damn book on the run or in prison, he mused. In a large suitcase he stuffed as many clothes as possible.

After loading the suitcases in the Mercedes, Jack brought Harry out of the house on his forearm. Opening the driver side door, Jack pointed his arm toward the inside of the car and Harry hopped down on the seat and then fluttered up on the backrest.

Backing out of the driveway, Jack said to Harry, "You aren't going to like this but there's no other way. I can't travel as fast as I need to with you. You'll have to join me later." Harry twisted his head and gave him a blinking look of concern.

The door to the pet shop was locked. Jack knocked hard on it until the mincing little guy with frizzy reddish-orange hair unlocked the dead bolt. Recognizing him and seeing Harry, one of his good boarding clients, he said sweetly, "Oh my, what do we have here? A new hairstyle for the pretty boy?"

"I've got to make a trip out of the country. Can I board him with you?"

"Harry is always welcome here."

"I have to ask you for a favor."

"We're here to help," cooed the little guy.

"I need you to put Harry on a plane at the San Diego Airport in about a month or so. Can you do that? I'll pay you a hundred dollars to board him and two hundred to get him on the plane."

Two hundred dollars was too much to turn down for merely taking a bird out to the airport shipping terminal. The pet shop owner nodded *yes* as Jack was pulling the money out of his billfold.

"In thirty days or so you'll get a ticket with the destination where I need the bird sent and delivered alive. Once I get him, I'll send you another hundred dollars for your efforts. Okay?" Cooing and stroking Harry affectionately, the little man squinted a smile at him and told him not to worry. Jack scratched Harry on the head for a moment, then left. The pet shop owner blew kisses at Jack as he pulled away.

His bank had been open for less than ten minutes when he withdrew the eleven thousand dollars from his savings account. Requesting large bills because travelers checks could be traced, he wrote a check closing out his checking account. Leaving the bank, he used the pay phone outside to call Velda.

She was waiting on the loading ramp at the rear of her apartment with two large suitcases and a huge shoulder bag.

"Where's your bank?"

"Out by the airport."

"We're flying out of LAX."

"Why not from San Diego?"

"Two reasons. If someone is on our trail, the first place they'll send people is to the San Diego Airport."

"We need some time to figure out where we're going."

"Grand Cayman. That's where Forbes' money is."

"But where are we going from the Caymans?"

"You'll see. Where's your bird? I thought you were taking him with you."

"He's boarded at a pet store. I've made arrangements to have him shipped wherever we end up." Velda said nothing, her thoughts moving beyond the immediacy of the bird.

The Southern California sky consisted of the unusual heavy-blue stuff that warns precipitation is possible within minutes. They were less than an hour from LAX. Velda had withdrawn her savings and cleaned out her safe deposit box. By the time they had reached the Los Angeles basin, the sky had a look of stone washed denim. Their plan was to fly to New York. Then to Grand Cayman. They would pay cash and use false names for the tickets to New York and Grand Cayman. Jack's credit card would be used to purchase the tickets from Grand Cayman to Rio. It would leave a false trail if anybody was following them.

When they pulled up in front of the Bradley International Terminal in the Los Angeles Airport it was mid-morning. A sky cap approached them. "What airline?"

Jack gave the old black man with courtly dignity a ten dollar bill. "Need you to store these somewhere for a couple of hours. She needs to check out some flight schedules."

"Yes sir. No problem. I'll keep them for you right over here by our counter," referring to the small counter on rollers that contained baggage claims tickets and sundry items used by a team of sky caps. Velda headed off to purchase tickets for the flight to New York and Grand Cayman. Then she would have their baggage transferred to the United Airlines terminal where they could catch one of the hourly flights to New York.

Fifteen minutes after he parked the big Mercedes in front of the used car dealership near the airport, he had a deal. He sold the car for a third of its value to a salesman with a set of bad teeth and a you-are-a-sucker smile. While it was like giving a baby up for adoption, he needed the money and didn't want to leave the car to be discovered by airport security.

Velda stood inside the doors with her huge travel bag waving a handful of airline tickets.

"All set?"

"We board in fifteen minutes. I was afraid you wouldn't get back in time."

"You could have left me."

"Not hardly, come on, it's Gate 17. These are first-class tickets." He stopped and bought two tickets from Grand Cayman to Rio with his Visa card.

After the United wide-body rumbled toward the Pacific Ocean on the runway, it climbed hard and swung south and then northeast for New York. Jack, bone-tired, settled back in the thick first-class seat and dozed while Velda stared out of the tiny round window. Still, tension chewed at his gut like a painful ulcer. Rummaging around in his canvas briefcase, he pulled out the envelope from Ray Compton. Tearing it open he removed two sheets of paper. One was an analysis from the forensic laboratory. The other was a handwritten note from Ray. Jack read the note three times in disbelief before he examined the forensic report. After reading the report he studied the letter again. The words jumped out like neon beams. "I had my contact in the San Diego Police Department run the fingerprints we found on the rubber glove finger and the pickax through the military fingerprint identification system. With all the military people in southern California I figured it was worth the chance. The guy trying to kill you received a dishonorable discharge from the Army a few years ago. His name is Richard, aka Boomer Smythe."

CHAPTER THIRTY-EIGHT

Jack felt a jolt and was jerked to full consciousness. Velda's hand was on his arm as the wide-body DC-10 dropped into the steep landing approach in New York. Both of them were exhausted. They hardly said anything during the long flight. Out of his window he could see the commingling of the shipyards, the harbor and dozens of tall buildings that made up New York's skyline absent of the Twin Towers. Velda left her seat to use the toilet. She squeezed his leg with her hand as she slid past him.

He re-read the report from Ray Compton in disbelief. There really wasn't any question about the information. Boomer Symthe's fingerprint was found inside the rubber glove finger Compton found in his condo after Mariana was murdered. It was the type of rubber the pathologist found in her teeth. Everything pointed to Chief Buno as having everything to do with the attempts on his life. Even Velda was now convinced of that. The same fingerprint appeared on the extraction tool that was found at his La Misión house when he was attacked. But why, he asked himself. Why would Boomer Smythe try to kill him? It made no sense. No sense at all. He would call Compton when they landed in New York.

"You are where?"

New York."

"What on earth are you doing there?" asked the private investigator.

After listening to Jack's story of the shooting and escape out of Mexico, Ray Compton said, "Let me fill in some of the blanks for you. Forbes is not dead. There was an article in the paper about him being injured in an accident in Mexico. In fact, the article I read had a photo of Forbes getting out of a car with some bandages, but he didn't look that bad. Buno's dead, but nobody seems to be able to put all together. Lucky for you."

Jack's mind whirled as he tried to sort things out. It was good news and bad news. Velda was signaling that their plane was about to leave. "Listen," he instructed Compton, "I need you to help me with this. You need to go to the authorities about Boomer Smythe. I can hardly believe it, but if what you have discovered is true, Mariana's parents have a right to justice."

"I'll handle it. Don't worry. I'm also going to see if I can find out anything more about Velda."

Jack stopped him short, "Velda's proved herself to me. Don't waste my money on your theories. Got to go. I'll contact you when I can."

"Where can I reach you?"

"You can't. I'll get back to you when it's safe."

"Any news?" asked Velda.

"All bad. Forbes is alive."

Her face went pale. "Forbes is alive! That can't be!"

"They found Buno's body. No one seems to know what happened. Since it was in Mexico the U.S. authorities won't give it a second look."

The look of anguish on Velda's face did not escape Jack.

"What's the matter?" He gripped her hand as they walked to the gate and entered the loading ramp after giving the attendant their one-way tickets.

"Nothing," she responded. She didn't want to alarm him. With Forbes and Buno dead they had a chance. *If* Forbes was alive they could never relax. Plastic surgery wouldn't help them. Distance wouldn't either. She knew what kind of guy Forbes was. She had been managing his money. When he took something personally, he became obsessed with it. Especially his money. He'd hire legitimate investigators. He'd be on the phone every day calling his contacts. Every mob and police contact would be tapped. He'd use his government contacts to get information. Forbes would toss money around and lean on everybody until he had a scrap of information. Then he'd piece things together and send people, bad people, once he picked up the scent. There wasn't any place they'd be safe from Forbes.

Thirty minutes later, the plane loaded with tourists lifted off and set a course for the Cayman Islands. Jack and Velda had seats apart from each other in the economy section, so no one would remember them as a traveling pair. They focused their thoughts on what they would do once they landed and how they would survive.

The pickup truck with a camper drove at a steady 55 miles per hour on Interstate Highway 5 south. Twenty minutes later, the nondescript vehicle pulled up next to the Border City Police Department's flight shed. The driver, his long dirty hair covered with a Padres baseball cap, clinched the steering wheel so hard his knuckles drained of blood. The other man in the car spoke with a thick Russian accent. "The bolt cutters are in the back." The driver, squinting, looked through the truck window at the industrial lock hanging from the hasp on the metal shed. Then he abandoned the truck, found the long-handled cutters, and cracked through the lock. The man in the shotgun seat dropped from the right side of the truck. Heavy footsteps on the gravel. Both went to the rear of the truck where they wrestled a seven-foot-long, coffin-type box off the bed of the truck. They unloaded the unwieldy container and humped it into the messy maintenance shed. Sweat appeared on the foreheads of both men and moisture ran down their faces from the wrestling the heavy object. After clearing away a space inside the shed, they positioned the long box and moved the truck to an inconspicuous place. Both men blew pungent smoke from French cigarettes, leaned back against the hot tin shed and waited.

Earlier when he had received a call from the dispatch center saying he was needed at the flight shed, Boomer drove there without giving it a second thought. He entered into the dark room. Moving like a big cat, his face red and blotchy from tension and excitement, the big Russian took two steps and clamped a cloth over Boomer's mouth. In seconds, Boomer had succumbed to an ether-induced sleep.

When Boomer woke, the cloth gag tearing at the edges of his mouth served as a painful reminder that he couldn't talk. The more he twisted his hands, the tighter the thin nylon rope got. He was stark-ass naked. He heard the lid creak as it opened. Rough calloused hands surrounded his face and jerked the cloth gag from his mouth. He swallowed and gagged as he spit out, "What the fuck is going on?"

"You are about to be cooked," said someone in a thick Russian accent. What the hell were they doing to him? A fist exploded against his ear. An artery bounced against the muscle of his neck as his eyes lost focus. He moaned and melted on the clear plastic deck. The last words he heard were from a Russian voice that said, "Plug it in." The tanning bed lit up like Alaska's Northern Lights. He struggled silently with the ropes that bound his feet, and the gag on his mouth, desperately trying to loosen them. The click of the metal door told him that his captors had left him. He could feel the plastic warming up. A drop of sweat rolled down the bridge of his nose, then more. The heat was unbearable, and he could feel his blood coming to a boil. His body was being roasted to death in a tanning bed.

Peering out of the plastic porthole of the Cayman Airways jet, Jack and Velda watched a sea below that looked like a thick Oriental carpet of blues and greens. Under the calm waters, the seaweed, rocks and sand filtered colors up through the dominating azure. When the plane carrying Jack, Velda and 129 other passengers landed on Grand Cayman, they took a cab to the George Town bank where Forbes kept his secret account. Jack stayed outside the white brick building with the luggage. He sat under one of the table umbrellas in the bank's small courtyard and leafed through his manuscript. Velda had told him the transaction would take at least thirty minutes. The town was teeming with tourists, greedily searching for the duty-free bounty. Black coral and gold were the favorites.

Armed with the identification number, code word and matching signature, Velda was assisted in the transaction by an officious French born senior vice president. Forbes' account contained $3,122,000. After the bank official verified Velda's right to the funds, she withdrew $200,000 in cash, leaving the rest, slightly less than $3 million, in the account. The bank provided her with a plastic briefcase in which she stacked the cash. She then went into the bank's private wire transfer room and used the modern equipment. She left the bank with the briefcase full of money and found Jack sitting at the small courtyard table.

"Everything is taken care of. The money is in an affiliate bank in St. Thomas. A little bit more than three million. Forbes' won't be able to trace it. Think we can live off of that? I've also withdrawn a little more than $200,000 so we can live and have some emergency money in case we have to change where we are staying." Before Jack could respond, she instructed him, "Let's get a cab. The commuter flight to Cayman Brac leaves in just about an hour. We'll pay cash for the tickets. Once we get to Cayman Brac we'll be safe. Anyone who Forbes sends is going to follow our trail to Rio. Using a credit card to buy those tickets from Grand Cayman to Rio at LAX will draw anybody following us away from Cayman Brac. We can spend a few weeks on Cayman Brac deciding what to do. Besides, after what we've been through, we owe ourselves a vacation."

Jack couldn't help but be impressed with her power of organization.

"Forbes' sent me down here a couple of times to check on the account. Whenever I came, I stayed over on Cayman Brac. It's a much smaller island, about 90 miles from here. You'll like it. Maybe we can decide what to do with the rest of our lives. If we get followed to Grand Cayman no one will expect us to be on a

sister island. Whoever Forbes sends will follow our tickets to Rio."
She touched him on the face and kissed him softly.

He wished that he could be as sure of their future as she was.
Jack felt as if he was stepping off into an endless void where his
nightmares still lived.

CHAPTER THIRTY-NINE

Ray Compton, dressed in a pair of Dockers and a wild pink Polo shirt, looked over the cascading surf of Cayman Brac and commented, "Spectacular view." A deep mystical feeling developed in him as he looked out at the changing colors of the water breaking gently over the colored coral reef. He could get used to this life real easy. Jack read the written report Compton had carried with him from San Diego. Cayman Brac, the home of a couple thousand people known locally as Brackers, the Welsh, Jamaican, Scots and Irish who lived in small cottages surrounded by white picket fences, was a short flight in a prop-driven commuter plane from the main island of Grand Cayman. The easy going, laid-back life appealed to both Velda and Jack. The large cottage they rented on a month-to-month basis was nice, neat and unpretentious. Living in the village, a spread-out affair that managed to retain some of its original qualities despite the hustle and bustle of tourists, no one would suspect they were fugitives.

Harry hopped and fluttered on the cool tile floor trying to adjust to the new surroundings. Arriving with Compton, encased in a small wire prison, the bird was ecstatic to see Jack. The moment he laid eyes on him he was squawking, "Beer! Beer!"

"Thanks for coming and thanks for bringing Harry," said Jack. Compton could have easily refused to come to the Caymans. But it was the only way Jack and Velda could find out what had really happened since they fled California. Jack wasn't about to reveal where they were hiding in any long-winded conversation on the telephone.

Jack read the written report Compton had carried with him from San Diego on the flight to Cayman Brac. Almost three weeks had passed since they had fled southern California. Compton's fingerprint report, left at his house the day before they ran, had stunned Jack like a kick in the gut. No doubt about it, Boomer Smythe had tried to kill him at least twice. It was Boomer who killed Mariana and then made the attempt on his life when he was in La Misión with Velda the first time. It had to have been Boomer who directed Forbes and Buno to La Misión. But why? There was no reason that Jack could think of that would cause Boomer to try to kill him. Christ, he thought, Boomer was a guy he worked with and shared a common bond, not someone with a motive to kill him. It didn't make sense.

On the flight from New York to Grand Cayman, Jack had prepared a letter to Compton on his laptop. The letter described what had happened in La Misión. It also contained a detailed report of the flying activities that preceded the events in La Misión the night they escaped from Buno and Forbes. Jack sent the letter to Ray Compton with instructions to reveal to the authorities their discovery that Boomer's fingerprints were on the rubber glove thumb and the face of the ax blade.

A few days later, Compton wired him back with the news that he was no longer considered a murder suspect. The police were convinced that it was Boomer Smythe who had killed Mariana. Jack wanted a face-to-face meeting with Compton before he made any move off the island where he felt safe and protected. Buno may be dead but they still had to contend with the fact that Forbes was alive. He would be hot on their trail if he discovered their whereabouts.

After reading the report, Jack questioned Compton, "This is good news?"

"You're a lucky man," said Compton with an easy smile.

"How's that? What do you mean?"

"Two reasons. Your trip to the DEA and the fact that the Mexican police investigated the shooting in La Misión.

"Run it by me?"

"Before I took your letter to the FBI, I went to the DEA."

"Yeah, but what do they have to do with the laundering scam?"

Compton stood, took a drink of the strong Colombian coffee Velda had poured him. "Nothing really, but the fact that you went to them earlier was the original basis for establishing that you were not involved in the scam."

"They didn't believe me then."

"Fortunately, Agent Rixton not only remembered his conversation with you, but had recorded it in their files. But I can tell you he was a bit embarrassed that he hadn't done anything about it. He thought you were some kind of flake," said Compton.

"Funny, I had the same impression of him."

"So be it, but at least he remembered talking to you. Without that I have no doubt that you'd still be a suspect. That, and the fact that we were able to connect the fingerprints with this guy, Boomer Smythe, pretty much eliminated you as a bad guy. I know he flew with you, and you were friendly, but that's the way things shake out sometimes. I don't have to tell you that. Christ, you've been around the world a few times."

Velda stood. She had been listening to the conversation. Moving behind Jack, she placed her hands on his shoulders and said, "We are still fugitives. Forbes is alive. We can never go back."

Jack was silent for a moment and then said, "I'm still surprised somebody didn't charge me with murder. Christ, I shot down a helicopter crew and killed Buno in the drainpipe."

Velda interjected, "Also the guard."

"Yeah, the guard, too."

"Nobody saw you do it. There were no witnesses. That's what really saved you." Besides, once you reconstruct everything you come out of this okay. You were just protecting yourself. But you are damn lucky you don't have to go to the time and expense to prove it in a Mexican court."

"But they had to know it was my house where all of this started."

"That's the other reason you were lucky. The shootings took place in Mexico. Their cops don't have the sophistication or equipment necessary to handle a major crime out in the country. Hell, by the time the police got there I'm sure the crime scene was a mess. The locals were sure to have mobbed the scene and they must have run off with the guns and anything else they could steal, because the police didn't retrieve anything for fingerprinting." Then Compton changed the subject. "Are you safe here?"

"You mean the house or the island?"

"Both."

"The island's pretty safe. This isn't where the high rollers hang out. Mostly local folks. A few tourists. The real action is over on the big island. Besides, we bought tickets from here to Rio to establish a false trail." Jack ran his hands through his hair and squeezed the back of his neck with his fingers. Looking out at the blue-green waters he changed the subject, "Who was Boomer selling the guns to?"

"Here," said Compton, pulling an article from the San Diego newspaper, "I think this will help you figure out what was going on."

Jack took the small piece of paper and studied it. It told of an ex-Army sergeant who had been strapped inside a tanning bed in a maintenance shed at Brown Airfield. Two San Diego County sheriff's deputies stumbled upon the murder scene as they were patrolling the airfield. When the deputies pulled up to the shed with an open door, they were accosted by a Russian male identified later as Vasi Ivanov, alias Victor the Constrictor. Ivanov and another Russian gangster were wiping down the tanning bed to avoid a fingerprint trail.

Jack winced, picturing the terrible act in his mind like a scene from a cheap horror movie. Shaking his head in disbelief, he heard Ray Compton begin to speak in a slow voice.

"What the newspaper article doesn't tell you is that this guy Ivanov was the enforcer for a gun-running operation. The guns were," he paused, "hell, they still are, being assembled in Mexico out of Chinese parts. Somewhere in Ensenada. Your buddy Boomer was helping them bring the guns across the border."

"Impossible, I would have known if we were carrying guns back from Ensenada on my helicopter."

"Ever bring back oil drums?"

"Yeah. Almost every trip. Boomer had a small-time scam going. He'd buy the oil down in Ensenada for almost nothing and then sell it below the going rate at the airfield. He'd make forty or fifty bucks on each drum. I let him do it, because he needed the money. He worried constantly about having enough money to retire on."

"He hid the guns in the oil drums," said Compton flatly.

"What?"

Compton continued, "You were too close to it, Jack. And you had no reason to suspect Boomer was involved in transporting guns. Especially when he cooked up the story that he was bootlegging cheap oil across the border."

"He was trying to kill me because I went to the DEA," stated Jack.

"Sure. We'll never know if it was his idea or the people he was working for. It probably was the Russians. Their criminals are a mean bunch."

"When you went to the DEA, you told him, didn't you?"

"Yes."

"Did it bother him?"

"Now that you mention it, it seemed to, but I didn't pay any attention."

Compton rose and put his hand on Jack's shoulder. "Boomer knew that if you kept going to the DEA, or some other federal agency, that sooner or later he'd be caught. He was just protecting his investment and future earnings."

"How much was he making on each shipment?" asked Jack.

"He was bringing back about a hundred guns at a time. Based on that we estimate each trip was worth about a thousand bucks to Smythe."

"Jesus," expelled Jack from his pursed lips. "Now I can understand why he was trying to kill me. That's some pretty good money."

"No question about it. He was apparently obsessed with the fear of dying poor. It was his way of making up for the pension he lost from the Army," said Compton.

"What about Hart?" inquired Jack.

"The assistant police chief?"

"Yeah."

"The story gets pretty murky, but it's typical of what happens in the BCPD. Hart was strangled and shot execution style. The killer chopped his fingers off. Cops say it was the Mafia. That happened about the same time another Border City cop was killed. My guess is that its all somehow connected."

"Who?"

"A guy named Alvin Packer."

"Never heard of him."

"My sources tell me Packer did scut work for the chief. My guess is Buno had Packer kill off Hart. If Hart's left alive the Ensenada scam isn't safe. Then Buno had this dirtbag Packer killed. An official police report shows that our Mr. Packer died from a dog assault."

"Dog assault?" said Jack in disbelief.

"I don't buy it either. I was a cop too long to swallow that line. Dogs don't kill cops. Cops kill dogs."

"Damn!" exclaimed Jack. "All I wanted was a steady flying job so I could support my writing."

Compton nodded and smiled. "Yeah, you were flying with some bad 'perps'. The kind of folk who don't mind a little killing now and then."

"Heavy air," said Jack.

"What's that?" asked Compton.

Jack ignored Compton's question. Velda excused herself and went into the kitchen of the cottage. Compton looked at Jack and said, "Let's take a walk. I'd like to see the beach before I go back."

Minutes later, they walked on the thick white sand that shifted under their bare feet. A large game fish splashed the water hard. In the quiet small bay dappled fish swam near the shore in the 80 degree water. A couple of island children played on the beach. Across the bay they could see the colorful balloon of a parasail.

"You still comfortable with Velda?"

"Yes," said Jack emphatically. "Why do you ask?"

"Not sure. Just a feeling I have. Maybe I can't shake off the fact she worked for Forbes. Just be careful." Compton stopped walking and reflected, "I think you are making a mistake trusting her. This is a way of life for her."

Jack clinched his jaw and tried to be polite. He liked Compton, but trusted his own instincts. But if Velda hadn't trusted him she wouldn't have told him about the $200,000 in the briefcase. He had bought a small fireproof safe and buried it in a shallow hole next to a bush in the back yard.

"Thanks," was all he said.

CHAPTER FORTY

"Whattaya think? Bitchin', ain't it. What a fuuuuucking view," Crazy Ike drawled in a voice so dry you could almost hear it rattle and scrape. Clustered below the airliner, as the sun dropped, were the three sister islands of Grand Cayman, Little Cayman and Cayman Brac. He was dressed in his uniform for all occasions, pin-striped suit pants and a white, long sleeved dress shirt. The shirt was open at the collar, and both sleeves were turned back a couple of rolls, revealing thick wrists with salt-and-pepper hair covering the backs of his thick hands.

"Yeah, it's bitchin' alright," responded Laz Forbes, sitting in the first-class seat next to him. "Real bitchin'." His Sansabelt pants were too tight, and the thick of his middle hung over the wide band, straining against the buttons on his shirt. His big diamond and gold rings arrayed on swollen manicured fingers, were locked together in a tight clasp as in prayer. As the heavy jet rippled slightly against the light headwinds, he thought sullenly of the business decision he needed to make. If he zotzed her, he'd have to find another. A good one, one who understood the business. Well, those were hard to find. Muscle was easy to find, but brains were damn hard to come by. He knew he was fuckin' lucky he didn't die in the goddamn sewer pipe in Mexico. Buno bought the farm because he went charging in the hole first. The concussion from the flare knocked Forbes unconscious. When he came to and was able to rearrange the furniture in his mind, he left Buno's corpse cooking from the smoking flare sticking out of his gut and got the hell out of the tunnel. Getting out of Mexico was easy. He stopped a car on the tollway and made a greaser rich by paying him for a ride to the border with his gold Rolex. Crossing on foot was simple. He just acted like a cunt-simple drunk from the states who was returning from a get-your-ashes-hauled venture into Tijuana. *No problema.*

The wire he got from his Grand Cayman bank the next day was a real mind-fucker. He figured that she would have cleaned out the account, cut and ran to some place where he'd never find her. The broad liked the *good* fucking life. But he had to give her credit. A real ice-water broad. Letting her be the only signature on the Grand Cayman bank account was a mistake. But when he put the scam together he didn't see that he had any other choice. His name sure as hell couldn't be on it because sooner or later the feds would have his ass up on a RICO charge and seize all his assets. She instructed him to be at a George Town café one month from the day she sent the wire. Tomorrow was the meet. Strange fucking business he was in, he thought. She may be setting him up. That's why he brought Crazy Ike along with him. If he was gettin' set-up, Ike would know. He had a nose for this kind of stuff and wasn't afraid to start slinging lead if he smelled a hit. That's why he had been his bodyguard for all these years. You didn't have to tiptoe around with frozen balls when Ike was backing you up.

The two men exited the aircraft and walked down the aluminum steps into the heat of Grand Cayman. The hot tarmac burned through the soles of their shoes as they walked to the tiny terminal. At the rental car agency they rented the biggest car available. The attendant gave them directions to their hotel. Ike slid behind the wheel, and Forbes stuffed himself in the passenger seat.

"Okay, boss, how we gonna handle this one?" questioned the iron-throated Ike. His brows furrowed and his eyes focused on the road in front of them. He followed the signs leading from the airport to George Town as the evening started to drop around them.

"Let's talk about it at the hotel. I need to shower some of this sweat off my balls so I can think straight," grunted Forbes. They drove through the small, unpretentious city, past the monument to King George V, the Government Post Office, and the Square. The Cayman Island Royal Police Force drilled daily on the lush green square.

The six-story Radisson Resort Hotel located on Seven Mile Beach was a pile of soft pink stone with white trim. An over-abundance of plants had been placed throughout the lobby, and water gurgled in a large fountain. The island favorite, "Song and Dance of the Barefoot Man," was played by a small combo. Filled with tourists, its crowd was a comfort to both men. After checking in with fake names and paying cash, Ike ordered sandwiches and rum and coke doubles to be sent up to his room.

Walking to the elevator, Forbes told Ike, "Give me thirty minutes and then I'll come down to your room. We need to work out what we need to do in the morning. We don't want to be coming back here to finish off the job."

On the short morning commuter hop from Cayman Brac to Grand Cayman, she had rehearsed what she intended to tell Forbes. One chance to convince him that she hadn't run out on him. That she had no choice but to leave with Dalton. That's all she had. One chance. Once she withdrew the money from the secret bank account, Forbes had no reason not to kill her unless he believed her. Both of them knew that.

Her eyes looked at the large man sitting directly in front of her at the tiny outside table in one of the high dollar Relais El Toula Café. It was hard to get a fix on Forbes. It always had been. He was smiling, but his pit bull eyes were hidden by wraparound sunglasses. The small, outdoor patio setting with widely spaced tables afforded them the opportunity to talk privately. Alone at one of the tables next to the brick wall, Crazy Ike sat sipping tea. When she arrived and had been seated, he nodded once in recognition. He gave her the creeps. Now his hard eyes ignored her as he kept a watchful eye out for Forbes. They talked for less than thirty minutes. Forbes could feel the claws tickle his scrotum when he looked at her. She had always affected him that way. The white brilliance of her teeth flashed against the tangerine glow her skin took on from a month in the sun. She looked at her Patek

Phillippe watch and said, "It's time to go, Laz. Our appointment is in ten minutes."

The bank was a short walk from the café. Ike trailed them, a retinue of one. When Forbes and Velda entered the bank, Forbes waved Ike back, signaling for him to wait outside. Forbes was pretty sure that nothing would happen at the bank that would cause him to need Ike's help. Inside, Velda went through the steps of transferring the money and closing out the account. The money was electronically transferred to an account in Lucerne, Switzerland. This time only Forbes' name and signature appeared on the control documents that would be sent to the Swiss bank in the morning. Forbes was no longer at risk. The money had been laundered clean in Ensenada. Moving it to a secret account in another country would make it impossible to trace. It was no longer traceable. Even if it could be traced to the bank in Grand Cayman, there was no way anybody could find out it had been transferred to another bank in Lucerne. The Cayman bank with Forbes' money kept no wiring records once money was transferred out. The trail vanished into nowhere with a tap to the keyboard.

Outside in the clean warm Caribbean air, Crazy Ike's eyes searched the street for a problem as Forbes and Velda exited the bank. Ike watched as Forbes put his hand on Velda's shoulder, stopping her. The expression on her face told Ike she was listening intently to what Forbes was telling her. He watched her nod and leave Forbes, walking in the opposite direction. Forbes turned, looked up and down the street, then crossed over to where Ike had been stationed.

"Everything copacetic, Laz?" asked Ike.

"Yeah, so far."

"When do we leave? This place is too fuckin' small for me. Ain't nowhere to hide if you need to."

"Yeah." Forbes agreed with Ike's assessment. "On tonight's flight. She needs the rest of the day to get her shit together and do the job."

"Where was she hiding out?" asked Ike.

"Remember the other islands we flew over comin' in?"

"Yeah."

"She and Dalton have been living in a tourist cottage on Cayman Brac."

"Brick. That's a funny name for an island," said Ike.

"No. Brac. You know, like crack," laughed Forbes at his explanation.

"You trust the broad?" Crazy Ike squinted at Forbes.

"Don't know. She could have grabbed all the money a month ago and we would have had one hell of a time finding her. Probably never would have. She didn't, so that's got to say something for her." Forbes paused, and they walked a few yards before he continued. "You think I'm nuts not to off the bitch, don't you?"

"I think you need to be careful, boss."

"Yeah," said Forbes. "I will be. Listen, we got us a day to kill in the sun. Maybe we can find some broads. There's got to be some hookers somewhere on this piece of sand who would like to show us a good time. We got the afternoon to kill. After we get our tubes lubed we can try some turtle steak. Ever had it?"

"Fuck no, boss. But I've had me some good snapper." Forbes laughed at Ike's crude joke.

As they walked back toward the Radisson, Ike asked, "Same plan as last night?"

"Yeah. Even tho' I hate the fuckers, the sightseeing helicopter I rented will take us over to Velda's island at five o'clock so we got the rest of the day to fuck off. You need to get us a couple of clean guns from the locals. Some bar rat asshole with a habit will surely cough up a couple for the right price. We'll be out of here tonight on the midnight jet back to Miami."

By the time the commuter plane returned Velda to Cayman Brac she had a plan sketched in her mind. Riding home in the bouncing island cab, she tried to fit the jagged parts of the brutal task together. With Forbes, it was some kind of strange revenge she didn't understand. Honor should have nothing to do with this kind of deal. It was purely a money deal with her. She needed to get off the island as soon as possible. Hardness and a "me first" quality had always taken care of her before. She had to rely on her instincts. Forbes left her with no choice. He and Ike were coming to Cayman Brac just before dark. She took deep breaths, to harden her resolve. The vision of what Forbes would do to her if she failed, was horrifying. The only way out of the mess she was in to was to do what he told her.

Velda got to the cottage shortly after noon. Jack was gone. Even though she didn't expect him until late afternoon, she was relieved. He had left to go sailing before she departed for Grand Cayman that morning. The cottage came equipped with a small catamaran which Jack berthed in the marina. Trying to finish his book, she knew he would sail offshore, take in the sail and work on his book on the floating island. No distractions other than the seagulls and an occasional boat passing by. When he did this he wouldn't be home until dinner time.

She changed out of her cotton wraparound skirt and silk blouse into a two-piece swimming suit. Then she slid into one of his T-shirts. Taking a pitcher of lemonade from the refrigerator, and a tall glass, she walked through the small house to the screened-in back porch and sat down at the small wicker table. Hanging on the wall was the diving equipment Jack had bought shortly after they arrived. She smiled inwardly as she recalled the sales pitch made by the island boy that convinced Jack that he should purchase the Sea Hornet spear gun. The stainless steel gun fired a three-foot-long steel shaft, using a thick rubber sling for propulsion. At a short distance, the weapon had more killing power than a standard rifle, the salesman claimed. The salesman screwed the removable point on the shaft and used a freshly picked coconut to demonstrate the weapon's penetrating ability. At twenty feet, the spear gun's projectile ripped through the tough resistive skin of the coconut like a bullet.

She rose from the chair and lifted the wicked looking spear gun off its hook on the wall. Leaning against the porch railing, her hair combed by the warm afternoon breeze, she could hear the coconut palms rattle in the wind. The surface of the clear tropical waters danced lightly. A colorful catamaran with a wide yellow sail skipped across the surface, tilted over on one hull. She watched it disappear out of sight in the horizon. The white beach shimmered under the cloudless sky. A couple of tourists wandered up the beach and the babble of their voices came up to her. She raised the Sea Hornet spear gun to her shoulder and sighted the barrel on a small hurricane lamp that hung from the ceiling. Then she lowered the weapon so she could cock it. Straining hard with both hands, she was able to stretch the rubber sling to the trip lever. Inserting the arrow she made sure the steel shaft was locked into the firing mode. She flicked the safety lever and went through the process of aiming and squeezing the rigid trigger. Done. She stacked the loaded and cocked weapon against the wall and went out to the back yard where she dug up the safe that held her money.

The small four-passenger aircraft circled wide to the south of Cayman Brac and then landed with a soft yelp of its narrow tires. It taxied up to the open-air terminal. The passenger in the small aircraft peeled out two hundred dollar bills and handed them to the pilot who had just shut down the engine and electronic equipment.

"Any time you need to run over and back, just give me a holler," the pilot said. The lean man with a small white scar on his throat responded with a raspy-voiced, "Thanks. When does the regular commuter arrive?"

"In about an hour. It loads up right away and heads back to the big island. You need to be on time if you're going to fly back on it. It won't wait," said the pilot as he watched the man climb down from the aircraft. "Watch the prop," he cautioned.

Jack nodded and walked rapidly across the airfield to where his jeep was parked. He climbed in, turned on the engine and drove back to the small boat dock where the catamaran was secured. Tires squealing, he drove down the road. He had an hour to get his stuff off the boat and pick up Harry before the flight left.

Yesterday, when Velda announced she was going to take the commuter flight over to Grand Cayman, he offered to go with her. They had stayed away from the big island since first arriving, fearful that Forbes had sent someone to the bank to pick up their trail. Jack didn't like the idea of Velda going back. Too risky. But she insisted, claiming she needed to buy some things she couldn't get at the little store here on Cayman Brac. She told him she was getting stir crazy. That was understandable to him. Cooped up, isolated from the rest of the world, the stress between them was rising daily. Something had changed. Instead of bonding tighter, there was growing distance between them. He was sure that Velda was doing what he was doing: trying to sort out what to do with the rest of her life. Neither of them could go back to the United States. The chances of Forbes finding them was too great. He had lived all over the world, so he could manage to do it again. He couldn't fly helicopters all his life, but somehow he knew he could make things work out. Velda, on the other hand, had never done it before. He knew she was also trying to grapple with the reality of having to live in a foreign country for the rest of her life.

That morning, she insisted on flying to the big island alone. He conceded. Then, not really knowing why he did it, he followed her. He was getting stir crazy also. Fifteen minutes after she left in the island cab, he drove the jeep to the airfield. The commuter flight had left. Worry and doubt rumbled up in his gut as he watched the small plane ascend the deep purple sky. Ten minutes later he was in the air. For two hundred dollars, the pilot who flew tourists around the islands on sightseeing trips agreed to carry him over to Grand Cayman. With the throttle against the wall, the little four-passenger plane touched down at the Grand Cayman airfield just as Velda's commuter plane finished unloading. He debarked, hurrying to catch up with Velda. Before he could catch up to her, she got in a cab and drove away. From the queue at the terminal, he managed to catch a cab after the one behind Velda's was taken by tourists. While he followed Velda's cab into George Town, he tried to think of a way to explain why he was following her. What was he going to say when he caught up with her. He didn't really know, but had a gut feeling that something had gone wrong, very wrong.

Her cab stopped in front of the Relais El Toula Café. By the time he could get the cabbie to pull over in the busy traffic on the narrow street, they overshot the café by almost a block. He paid the cabbie, crossed to the other side of the street and fell into the flow of tourists. As he moved directly across from the café patio, he watched the maitre d' escort Velda to a table where a heavy fleshy man with large dark sunglasses sat. Jesus, it was Laz Forbes! Jack turned his head toward the shop windows and kept on walking. He knew Laz Forbes wasn't sitting there alone. He had some muscle with him. Why was she meeting with him? Suddenly a cold, harsh reality engulfed him. Forbes had found them. Ray Compton had been right about Velda. He believed that Velda would be accompanied on the commuter flight by Forbes and his muscle. They were coming to kill him! All he needed to leave the island was his manuscript, Harry and the money in the safe and his manuscript. The manuscript was in the catamaran. After he picked it up he'd go for Harry and the money. Once he had all three he'd wait in hiding at the airfield for the commuter plane to unload. Velda and Forbes would head for the cottage and he would escape on the commuter. At Grand Cayman he'd take the midnight flight to Miami.

Jack pulled up to the boat dock and left the Jeep's engine running as he put it in neutral and set the hand brake. After securing everything on the catamaran, he picked up the flotation vest he carried on the boat, slipped his arms through the openings, and zipped it up. Jack stuffed the sixty-odd pages of his manuscript under the vest to keep the wind from scattering the pages like confetti. He climbed back in the Jeep, released the brake and drove to the cottage. Velda must have cut a deal with Forbes, he thought. Since only she had access to the money Forbes couldn't harm her. But what would happen to him was academic, no wonder she had acted so distant in the last few days.

Velda selected a small carry-on suitcase from the closet and opened it on the bed. In it she placed all of her valuables, passport and other important documents retrieved from the buried safe in the same plain black briefcase the bank gave her a month ago. They had spent less than five thousand. The briefcase was stuffed with more than $200,000. She was ready to leave. They would take the early evening commuter flight back to Grand Cayman and then fly off the big island at midnight on the regular flight to Miami. Forbes had bought off on her story that she had to escape with Jack after Buno had been killed in the tunnel in Mexico. She was nervous when she met him at the George Town café earlier in the day. She was afraid he would see through her story. Counting on the fact she wired him the day she and Jack arrived in Grand Cayman a month ago, she was shit fearful of Forbes. There was no telling what his reaction would be.

Harry began squawking *"Beer! Beer!"* as Jack shut off the Jeep engine outside the cottage and gathered up his gear. The front door was shut. He looked at his watch. Less than forty minutes left but that was plenty of time to collect his gear and Harry and make it back to the airfield. He ran up the four steps that separated the front porch from the brick sidewalk. The cool sea air made the thin curtains tremble and dance. Unlocking the front door, he called out for the bird in his rasping voice. Only "Har-" came out of his mouth as he was hit in the chest with the tremendous force of a 3/8 inch diameter steel shaft nearly three feet long. There was a bone crunching *kawaaap* as the lethal arrow penetrated the thin SeaQuest 4 flotation vest he wore. The impact drove him back two steps. Clutching at the steel shaft that pierced the flotation vest, Jack's eyes fought to stay open as he tried to stand. Sparkling lights in the back of his eyes burnt out. The force of the steel arrow twisted him to the right and he fell in a crunching pile across a small wicker stool, face down. Thick red liquid oozed from his chest and covered the floor. Harry went crazy, fluttering his wings so hard he lost some feathers. Jack didn't move. A sucking sound came from his chest wound. Velda dropped the spear gun, calmly picked up her suitcase, walked out of the cottage to the Jeep. Harry ran up to Jack with short bird-steps, cocked his head, and chirped excitedly at the still body.

Ten minutes later, when she pulled the Jeep onto the tiny airfield tarmac, she spotted Forbes and Crazy Ike standing in the shade of the small helicopter they rented to fly them back to Grand Cayman.

"Dead?" demanded Forbes.

"Yes," said Velda somewhat harshly.

"How?"

"With a spear gun."

"You sure?"

"Yes."

Forbes looked at Ike with a mean grin and said nodding toward Velda, "We got us a creative little hit lady here. We can use her for other things than just cooking the casino's books."

Crazy Ike chuckled up the gravel in his throat. "Lets go, boss."

"Got the money?" asked Forbes looking at Velda with a new interest. Now he owned a lady hit artist.

Her faced paled and she brought her hands up to her face. "No! Jesus, Laz, I panicked, grabbed the suitcase and left the brief-case with the body."

"Get in," Forbes ordered Velda as he swung his heavy body up into the Jeep's passenger seat. Ike climbed in the driver's side as Velda, her mouth open in disbelief, said, "I put it in a briefcase to bring to you. I just forgot it. Jesus, I'm sorry." She was starting to panic.

"Honey, the flight back to the states don't leave until mid-night. We got lots of time but the money better fuckin' be there. I want *my* money and I want to be sure Dalton is dead. If he's alive we got problems. You especially got problems since it was your job to kill the cocksucker." He jerked around toward Ike and said, "Let's go. Show us the way, Velda."

Ten minutes later, they shut the Jeep engine off in front of the cottage. No noise except the surf and the sweeping sound of the coconut palm. Instinctively, Ike pulled his recently purchased gun from his shoulder holster and walked toward the back of the cottage. Forbes clutched Velda's arm just above the elbow and positioned her slightly in front of him. In his other hand was a 9mm automatic pistol. They walked cautiously up the porch steps in a curious type of lock-step.

Forbes released the hold on her elbow, and she opened the cottage's front door. She could see the briefcase where she left it.

"He's gone!" She exclaimed and instinctively stepped back.

"Fuck," uttered Forbes as he pushed her off to the side and aimed his gun inside the house with both hands, like cops do when they're clearing a room. There was a wide red smear across the tile floor. Forbes could tell the blood trail wasn't drippings from a minor wound. There was red stuff all over. The wide smear told him that Dalton had been gut shot and probably tried to drag himself to a telephone. She really shot the son-of-a-bitch, he thought. No doubt about it, with all that blood smeared all over the floor. If he ain't dead, Ike will finish the cocksucker off and then we can get the hell out of here, thought Forbes as a piece of lightening lit up his brain. A forged steel shaft entered just below his eye and crashed through the back of his cranium.

Forbes dropped like a poleaxed bull and screamed in rage as he reached up to pull at the thick steel tube skewered through his head. Blood gushed from his mouth, and his eyes remained open as he died. Velda shrieked in terror. Crazy Ike, running in from the back door, hurried his aim at Jack's back and emptied his weapon just as Jack tossed aside the spear gun and slipped. Falling across the wet floor in the direction of Forbes, Jack groped for the gun that had dropped from Forbes' hand. Four of the bullets from Crazy Ike's gun stitched across Velda's face, killing her instantly. Ike was frantically trying to reload when Jack shot him twice in the chest. Ike dropped his gun and crumbled as gunshot hammered against the inside walls of the small house.

Trembling from exhaustion, Jack inhaled the cordite in the air and observed the carnage around him. The arrow Velda shot him with was still sticking out of the flotation vest. He unbuttoned his shirt and pulled out the wet pages of his manuscript. The red dye in the flotation jacket, to mark location in the water for rescue aircraft, had soaked and smeared the pages. Luck had saved him. Velda had used a shaft without attaching the pointed arrow tip. When the dull shaft hit him, it penetrated the flotation vest, but the manuscript absorbed the blow. The impact cracked a rib and knocked him out, but didn't kill him.

CHAPTER FORTY-ONE

The puffy clouds threaded through the Baja sunset, pinks and lavenders, another beautiful Venetian sky. Jack worked a bit on his manuscript and shut his laptop. Yet another perfect 10 sunset. He stretched his back muscles and caught his reflection on the sliding glass doors. Harry, perched on Jack's old *sabino* ranch table with a butterscotch patina, sensed movement.

"*Beer! Beer!*" he demanded.

His worktable view allowed him to overlook the houses below and far out to the horizon. The blue Pacific offered endless fascination for him. The tile floor warmed his feet; the bright white gardenias in clay pots on the patio wall scented the light breeze, and his favorite palm swayed lightly, casting slender shadows on the bright white walls.

He added up the lives he left and counted himself very lucky. He was back in La Misión, safe in his house. The mind boggling events he had experienced during his work for the BCPD were the stuff writers dreamed up for their adventure novels. As his friend Compton said, his life was a book and a movie.

The authorities in Grand Cayman cleared him of wrong doing. Fortunately, Ray Compton dropped everything and flew to Grand Cayman with a forensic expert. The pathologist established the shooting sequence that led to the death of Velda, Crazy Ike and Laz Forbes. He developed evidence that eliminated Jack as a suspect. Ray Compton brought word that the deaths of Chief Buno and Commandante Gomez were written off as drug war casualties. There were no warrants out for his arrest in either Mexico or the U.S. There was no overwhelming reason for him to return to Border City.

Jack opened an account with a small bank on Grand Cayman and deposited the more than $200,000 left in Velda's briefcase. He left instructions that each month, differing amounts of less than ten thousand dollars, should be wire transferred to his accounts in San Diego, Rosarito and Ensenada banks. Jack packed his few belongings, bought first-class seats and flew back to San Diego with Ray and Harry. He mailed a copy of his new book to an agent in Los Angeles and gave him instructions on how to reach him in La Misión if he was at all interested in representing him. When Leon Longbill drove down to discuss the book it was a pleasant surprise.

The dapper agent arrived in full mufti for a Mexico safari-khaki suit, sturdy boots, and the Aussie sun hat favored by week-end warriors. He drove a rented HumVee painted bight yellow.

They met at the bar in the Emporia. "Beautiful, just beautiful," exclaimed the agent as he gazed out to the blue Pacific. "You're a lucky man, Jack."

"More than you know, Leon."

"Isn't this place the hideaway for stars and pols that I recently read about in the *Los Angeles Times?*"

"Don't know." Jack swiveled on his bar stool and pointed his beer to a wall of photos. Maybe you know some of those people. They're all friends of Alex. The beautiful selves."

"Alex?"

"The owner of the Emporia."

Casting a quizzical look at the events captured in the grainy photos framed by the brick wall Longbill thought that Alex should be a writer. No end to his stories.

"This new book has promise, Jack. Tell me more about the characters, they are real people aren't they?"

"Names changed to protect the guilty; the story is about my experiences during the last few months."

Longbill reflected on the taciturn author. "I think the ending is wrong, Jack. You let Boomer and Velda off as basically good people. They tried to kill you; Boomer tried twice."

"They weren't bad, they just got tangled up with the wrong people."

"And, Velda?"

I could have saved her, but I didn't. I have a problem with the women who hang around with me; they get killed."

"I daresay you're a bit hard on yourself," said Leon.

They watched the thin profile of an oil tanker glide north to Rosarito. Jack rubbed the keloid scar on his throat, his personal worry bead. He said," It was just heavy air, and I'm lucky to still be able to fly."

www.ingramcontent.com/pod-product-compliance
Lightning Source LLC
Chambersburg PA
CBHW062025170626
46813CB00001B/296